PRAISE FOR
THE SUN GOD'S HEIR:
RETURN

Elliott Baker pens an outstanding piece of literature in *The Sun God's Heir: Return*. It is a masterful composition, overflowing with eloquent literary devices. The writing style is articulate and packed full of visually detailed scenes and sensory descriptions... It is historical fiction blended with a touch of mythical fantasy... So many expressively powerful lines, I think my favorite is the description of a foreboding tempest: "The darkness of a storm was different from the dark of night. It was a cloying, clinging type of darkness, more an absence of sight than of light." *The Sun God's Heir: Return* is an epic story, taking you into a time where actions and words ripple from the past into the present and then invade the future. A truly remarkable story.

— Reader's Favorite

Alexandre Dumas meets Horatio Hornblower and The Mummy in this sweeping, swashbuckling tale.

— Kirkus Review

I heartily recommend this novel. Baker has skillfully crafted a tale with engaging characters, historically accurate details that pull you in, while artfully weaving in just the right amount of supernatural legend and myth.

— author K. M. Doherty – author of the Thomas Holland
series of magical fantasy books.

RETURN

THE SUN GOD'S HEIR
BOOK ONE

BY ELLIOTT BAKER

Published in United States of America

Issued by: Hypatia Press http://www.HypatiaPress.com

Paperback ISBN: 978-0-9978322-0-4
Library of Congress Control Number: 2016963777

Editor: Sloane Taylor
Cover Art & Book Design: KMD Web Designs

To my beloved wife Sally Ann.

CHAPTER ONE

1668, Bordeaux, France

THREE MEN bled out into the dirt.

René stared at the hand that held the bloody rapier. His hand. Tremors shuddered through his body and down his arm. Droplets of blood sprayed the air and joined the carmine puddles that seeped into the sun-baked earth. He closed his eyes and commanded the muscles that grasped the rapier to release their tension and allow the sword to drop.

Years of daily practice and pain refused his mind's order much as they had refused to spare the lives of three men. The heady exultation that filled him during the seconds of the fight drained away and left him empty, a vessel devoid of meaning. He staggered toward an old oak and leaned against its rough bark. Bent over, with one hand braced on the tree, he retched. And again. Still, the sword remained in his hand.

A cloud shuttered the sun. Distant thunder brushed his awareness and then faded. *Rain.* The mundane thought coasted through his mind. He wiped his mouth on his sleeve and glanced down hoping to see a different tableau. No, death remained death, the only movement that of flies attracted to a new ocean of sustenance.

The summer heat lifted the acrid blood-rust smell and forced him to turn his head away. Before him stretched a different world from the one in which he had awakened. No compass points. No maps. No tomorrow.

The Maestro.

The mere thought of his fencing master filled him with both reassurance and dread. René slid the rapier into the one place his training permitted, its scabbard. He walked over to where the huge black stallion stamped his impatience, and pulled himself into the saddle.

Some impulse caused him to turn his head one last time. The sunlight that surrounded the men flickered like a candle in the wind, and the air was filled with a loud buzzing sound. Although still posed in identical postures of death, three different men now stared sightless.

Their skin was darker than the leather tanned sailors. Each wore a short linen kilt of some kind that left their upper bodies naked. As strange as the men appeared, their weapons were what drew René's eye. The swords were archaic; sickle shaped and appeared to be forged of bronze. These men wore different faces and yet their eyes— somehow he knew they were the same sailors he had just killed. René blinked and there before him the original three men lay unmoved. Dead.

For an instant his mind balked, darkness encircled the edges of his vision.

Do not anticipate meaning. The Maestro's voice echoed in his head. *Meaning may be ignored, but it cannot be hurried.*

The darkness receded, and he reined the stallion's head toward home.

René approached the linden shaded lane to the château. The stately trees, their clasped hands steepled over the gravel drive, had always welcomed him. Now they were just a faded backdrop that moved past the corners of his eyes. Could it have been only hours ago that the anniversary of his sixteenth year had presented itself like a gaily wrapped gift waiting for his excited appreciation? The day had dawned as grand as any he had yet experienced, and he had awakened early, eager for the morning's light.

"Henri," he yelled, as he charged down the marble staircase and into the dining room. Breakfast was set and steaming on the polished mahogany table. Burnished silver platters and cream colored porcelain bowls held a variety of eggs, sausages, fruits, and breads. How Henri always seemed to anticipate his entry amazed René.

"*Oui,* Master René." Serene as always, the middle-aged major domo entered the dining room. Henri walked over to the table and poured a cup of tea for René. "*S'il vous plaît,* be seated, sir."

"I cannot. Maybe a roll and a link of sausage. Henri, do you know what today is?"

Henri paused as if deep in thought. "Thursday. *Oui,* I am quite sure 'tis Thursday."

René took a still sizzling sausage from a tray and did his best to fold it within a baguette. "*Non,* 'tis my birth date," he managed around a mouthful of sausage and roll.

"Which one is that, sir?"

"How do you not know? You were there."

"Well, I remember 'twas after the end of the war. Let me see. The war was over in..."

"Very droll, Henri. Your memory works fine, 'tis your humor that leaves room for improvement. Today is... so... I cannot explain, it feels like anything is possible today."

"Given that there is still plenty of day left, perhaps you might sit down and eat. I expect you will need all your strength for a day so filled with possibility."

"I cannot be late." René gulped his tea and shoved the rest of the roll and sausage into his mouth.

"Happy anniversary, Master René."

"*Merci* Henri." René checked his appearance in one of the grand foyer mirrors, and then strode toward the courtyard. The time had come to present himself to the Maestro.

René vibrated with excitement. He paused just inside the entrance to the training area. This was no way to face the Maestro. He sucked in a deep breath, exhaled, and reached for that quiet center. The torrent of chaotic thought stilled and that unique calm of intense focus settled around him. His friends Marc and Anatole sported their weapons in public. René had yet to earn that privilege. Disarming the Maestro was the only way, and since that possibility seemed as remote as the ability to fly, it generated a great deal of frustration.

Today, however, might be the day.

He approached the master and bowed, already deep within that inner awareness that catalogued and recorded the location of each element that made up the courtyard. He *saw* this space with every sense. He knew the groundskeeper had removed marigolds that had overgrown their bed, and that a chair had been added to the small table in its customary place against the lichen streaked courtyard wall. René focused on the Maestro's eyes. A slight man with pale hair, his face could have been struck from marble for all the information it conveyed. The Maestro bowed in return.

"Begin," said the master.

René walked to the stack of bricks in the northwest corner of the courtyard. The sound of birdsong faded, along with the warmth of the sun on his neck, the crunch of the dirt beneath his feet, and the breeze on his face. Paradoxically, while his attention narrowed to the bricks in front of him, it expanded to every movement within the courtyard.

The practice area was fifty paces by fifty paces, with one wall a scarred reminder of the Thirty Years War. Slicing the square into two triangular shapes was a well-worn path that measured a little over seventy feet and led from one corner to its opposite. René lifted the first two of two hundred and forty-one bricks, one in each hand, keeping his wrists straight with the palms down and his arms rigid in front of him. He walked across the courtyard and placed the bricks on the ground, then turned and walked back for two more bricks. Two hundred and forty-one bricks, always one left over like the condemned's reprise that never arrived.

The number of times he needed to move the bricks from one side of the courtyard to the other was never fixed, however, it rarely stopped at one. Three moves, sometimes four or five would constitute the day's beginning. At first, the torturous exercise had left five-year-old René in tears and incapable of lifting his arms, let alone a brick. This day, as René replaced the last brick in its original location, the Maestro spoke.

"Do you wish to spar with me?"

And René answered with the only answer, "*Oui*, Maestro."

"Choose your weapon."

René settled deeper into that trance-like state where he was able to respond to external conditions much faster than he could think. He selected a rapier from a table of various edged weapons, each one's deadly mirror bright angles reflected blue in the morning light.

"*En garde*," said the Maestro, as he flowed into position.

The sparring proceeded evenly, thrust and parry, until René exhibited weakness on his left side— just a touch, a whisper of indecision. The Maestro had a preternatural sense of the feint and was rarely fooled. Although René had long since become comfortable and deadly with either hand, this morning's strategy required the weapon be held in his left.

A deep breath here, a slight pause there. He must be subtle beyond the movement of a butterfly's wing, for he faced the Maestro.

Rasp.

The blades slid off each other. René moved to the left, opening his defense for a brief second. As the expected thrust came through, he circled his blade toward the hilt of the Maestro's and pulled down with all his strength.

Silence.

They both stared at the impossible, the Maestro's blade in the dirt. It was as if a deadly snake had sprouted there.

The Maestro favored René with a rare smile.

"You may now arm yourself." And with that, he leaned down, picked up his sword—checked to see that René remained *en garde*— smiled again, and walked from the courtyard.

René whooped and danced, exhilarated by the victory. To lift into the air like a bird no longer resided within the realm of the impossible.

He swaggered from the courtyard, rounded the corner, and ran into his father's study. Perched on the edge of his father's large mahogany desk, René adjusted his newly attached sword to be sure it was visible. "*Bon jour*, father."

Armand Gilbert looked up from his ledgers and his face came as close to a smile as it ever did. "*Bon jour,* to you, as well." René shifted a little, banging the sword against the desk. "What are your plans for today?" His father's gaze returned to the ledger.

Focused on the accounts before him, he failed to comment on his son's recent change in status. René stood and walked across the front of the desk. "No plans. Probably ride over to Martin's."

"Perhaps you might run an errand for me first. The *Belle Poulé* has finished her refit and is preparing to depart. Can you carry a payment to the victualer for me? This year's early grape harvest has left us a bit shorthanded."

"Happy to. And you no longer need be concerned for the safety of your money." René turned again and brandished the lethal addition to his attire.

"We live in dangerous times, but it adds little to be overly concerned." Armand glanced up, his expression once again approached a smile.

Unable to wait any longer, René placed his hand on the sword hilt. "Do I not look a little different today?"

"Today? Your birth date. I am sorry I have been so busy, what with the *Poulé*'s departure and all. I am sure Marie will make something festive for tonight's dinner and we will celebrate then."

"*Non*, not that, *this*." René struck a martial pose, his hand on the sword at his hip. "My sword. I am wearing my sword. I disarmed the Maestro."

"So I see. Well done."

For René, those two words spoke volumes from a man who was as spare with praise as the Maestro. "*Oui*, I am happy to carry the payment into town for you."

"*Merci.*" Armand reached into his desk drawer and withdrew a leather sack heavy with silver.

"Here. Make sure you get a receipt."

"I will." René grabbed the sack with an outward show of nonchalance, and headed for the door.

"René." He turned to face his father.

"Happy anniversary." A broad smile spread across Armand's face.

"Merci, Papa."

René decided to stop for a glass of beer at the Boar's Head to show off his new status. The tavern's location along the road from the port into Bordeaux caused it to be a favorite haunt for the young men of the town as well as sailors on leave. A few minutes more would make no difference to the *Poulé*'s scheduled departure. René strode in to the dimly lit tavern and exhaled the breath that had kept his chest expanded. The room was near empty, with three men seated around a lone table in the corner. No one he knew. He walked up to the counter and ordered a "small beer," more barley water than alcohol. The weight of his sword thumped against his hip. With this symbol, others would view him as an adult. He was sure that he had grown taller between yesterday and today.

The tavern keeper nodded in recognition "Where away, lad? You are excited about something."

"I am on a business errand for my father." He patted the money pouch. "As for being excited, 'tis my birth date today and a good day to be alive."

"*Oui*, 'tis. Well then, a happy day to you." The tavern keeper moved to one of the tables to retrieve empty tankards.

The three at the corner table rose and sauntered over to René. "Here is a likely specimen of a young man," the tallest of the three spit out through rotted teeth. A scar that ran from the corner of his right eye to the bottom of his jaw flexed an angry red with each word. He stopped, his face inches from René's. "How about you buy us a drink? A wealthy gentleman like yourself throwing a little charity our way."

The other two laughed. All three carried cutlasses. René studied the three men. Having spent eight months at sea when he was eleven, and another seven months at fourteen, he recognized sailors by the way they stood. Seaman just into port exercised care when moving about, for it was the land that challenged long accustomed sea legs. Although he was not concerned, the Maestro had taught him to use his head in any threatening situation.

Always take the line of least resistance. Never let useless emotions cloud your judgment.

"'Twould be my pleasure to buy three fine sailors a drink." René motioned to the tavern keeper and tossed coins on the counter. "Set these men up with whatever they choose.

"Gentlemen." René nodded to the ragged sailors, took a final swallow of his beer, and headed for the door.

The three men followed René into the street.

Again, the man with the scar spoke. "We will be taking the money you carry."

They drew their cutlasses and held them with the casual ease of long familiarity. Although the weapons were nicked, they were otherwise in reasonable repair. These men were veterans. A dead calm, much like the center of a storm settled over René. He radiated threat. The men took a step back.

"He is just a damn boy." The scarred man brandished his sword. "Stop wasting time and give us the coin, or you will be a head shorter before this day gets any longer."

"I cannot give you this money." René's voice was quiet, the words spoken without emotion.

"Then you are a stupid, dead child." The scarred man attacked, flanked by the other two.

René leaned back and allowed the first blade to sing past his chest. Almost faster than the eye could follow, he had drawn his sword. He stepped into the scar-faced man. With an elbow strike to the chin, he dropped the man to the ground like a rag doll released from a child's hand. He continued the turn, drew his blade across the second sailor's throat, and with a swift change of line he parried a thrust from the third. Frantic, the man tried a slashing overhand cut, which René pushed up and to the side. Then a quick thrust beneath the heart.

Three inches is all you need.

The scarred man rose and shook his head, his face a mask of blood-red rage. He lunged forward. René parried the thrust, and then riposted through his adversary's neck. The attacker's face wore a look of incredulity as a fountain of blood sprayed in rhythmic surges from his severed jugular vein. He dropped to the ground a second time, choking as he expired.

The fight had taken only seconds. Released from the eye of the battle's storm, René's every sense vibrated with the supreme joy of victory, of survival, of life. He had defeated three grown men. He was invincible. Then he looked down.

Three men were dead. He had killed three men.

The next morning dawned with no hint of change. The quality of light that shone through the mullioned glass windows was no different. The sounds and smells of the awakening château were familiar, but carried no comfort. The courtyard looked the same, but each sound, each smell, each stone's meaning had changed.

Although the incident was quietly taken care of, it could never be undone. Even if it had been grist for Bordeaux's gossip mill, no one would have blamed René for defending himself. No one but him. He could have disabled the three men and yet he had not. Within the fight's brief duration he had experienced an exhilaration facing real danger and a strange kind of joy in his power to defeat it. The Maestro never hesitated to wound him and had done so many times over the years, but in his heart, René was convinced he would never die at the hand of the master.

There was no pretending the three men's deaths were accidental, that perhaps he had reacted before the arrival of awareness.

To deny truth is to uninvite it. The more unwelcome, the less it appears, until you are left in perpetual darkness.

Some part of him had known the inevitable outcome of his actions. Against his level of skill, the fight was not self-defense, it was murder. He had murdered three men and that fact made him sick.

René had avoided the Maestro when he returned to the château. He needed time to gather the courage to face the master. His father had told him what he wanted to hear; that his actions were necessary. But the untruth only served to solidify his guilt.

He moved into that level of calm attention, which was the essence of the fencer's art, and walked into the courtyard. He approached the Maestro and, as usual, bowed before him never releasing his focus on the man's eyes.

"I think we will have a cup of tea this morning." The master gestured toward the small table set against the stone wall.

René stopped, confused. He had never been invited to join the Maestro for tea before and had never expected to be.

The unorthodox is the application of creative strategy and is usually necessary for victory.

There was irony in hearing the echo of one of the Maestro's previous lessons while facing him. René settled deeper into that level of trance that comprised battle calm and focus. If this was to be a chess match of will, so be it. He sat and then accepted the cup of tea from his teacher. He waited. The Maestro would move the first piece.

The Maestro smiled, an expression he rarely wore. "I am aware that you experienced some difficulties yesterday."

"I murdered three men."

"*Oui*, you did."

René had not expected the Maestro to coat the truth, but the three word confirmation shook him. The silence between them lengthened. René drew his sword from its scabbard and placed it on the table, hilt toward the Maestro. "I am grateful to you for teaching me, but I will never kill another man." René scraped his chair back.

"*S'il vous plaît*, keep me company a bit longer." The Maestro gestured at René's chair.

The Maestro had never used the word 'please,' and the command was of such proportions that René could not have stood had wild horses pulled him from the chair.

"Your skill is a weapon that should never be used with casual intent," said the Maestro. "Did you employ it with contempt?"

"*Non*, master."

"Did you employ it for personal gain?"

"*Non*, master."

"What emotions are you experiencing?"

"Disgust, sadness, anger."

"As I have taught you, all are cousins of fear and fear is useful only as the perception of danger, useful in the moment only. Useless in the past or the future. Is perception by its nature limited?"

"*Oui.*"

"Then you do not, cannot, have the entire picture. Destiny and free will are the paradox that confronts our every step. I have taught you to forgo judgment on yourself, for it is often inaccurate."

"I cannot change the way I feel. My desire is to bind wounds, not create them. With a sword in my hand, the outcome can only be death and more death. I will never pick up a sword again."

"René, the universe smiles when it hears the word never. Like all of us, you have a destiny for this lifetime. Although, with our limited awareness, it is difficult to understand, destiny is never involuntary. You have chosen this path, and it will bring to you what you need. There are many roads to awareness. Some are rougher and more painful than others, but all lead to our chosen destinations. I wish you well." The Maestro stood, bowed, and walked from the courtyard.

CHAPTER TWO

THREE YEARS LATER
1671, Bordeaux, France

"HENRI, WHERE is my red coat? I am riding today with Martin and Clarisse. I need the red coat. Are my boots polished?" René pulled open the drawers of his dresser. "Henri!" he yelled again.

"Here, sir, and not as young as I used to be," Henri wheezed out after running up the long staircase with a pair of knee length black boots that shone like polished mirrors. He coughed and leaned against the bed post. "Your red coat is in the armoire, sir."

René flung open the carved cedar cabinet. "*Mais oui*, 'twas here all along. Sorry for the urgency, but I cannot wait to get out there."

"I quite understand, sir, 'tis a beautiful day. I instructed the groom to saddle Orion."

"*Merci*. Now, if I can just get these boots on. Why do they make them so difficult? Is father around?"

Henri brushed a piece of lint from the shoulder of the coat and held it for René to put on. "I believe he is in the sitting room enjoying breakfast. Shall I tell Marie to set a place for you?"

"Not this morning. I just have time for a sip of tea. But I wanted to speak with him before I leave."

"Enjoy your ride, sir."

René raced from the room, jumped onto the polished mahogany banister, and rode it down the grand marble staircase to the main floor.

He ran through the mirrored foyer with its pillars and paintings until he came to a stop in the sitting room.

His father sat at a small table, his breakfast half eaten. Rene smiled. He was proud of the tall slender man who appeared younger than his forty-seven years. His close trimmed beard held no gray, like his thick brown hair tied back in a queue. With his somber, well-tailored dark clothing, Armand Gilbert looked the man he was, a prosperous merchant.

"Father, I heard the *Belle Poulé* berthed yesterday. What does she carry? Is there something for me? How is Captain Coudray? Still the toughest master on the seven seas? How about..."

"Slow down, son. Sit and have breakfast with me. There is plenty of time to hear all the news. The *Belle Poulé* will remain in port for quite a while. She needs to be scraped, tarred, and refitted before she sees the open ocean again. And *oui*, Jacques made it back. I am sure he will be happy to see his star pupil. After your last trip as quartermaster, he told me you will be a hell of a pilot one day. *S'il vous plaît*, sit."

"I am sorry, father, but I am already late. Promised to meet Martin for a ride. Perhaps we can have tea this afternoon."

A once outgoing and gregarious man, Armand Gilbert's serious expression had rarely softened since his wife's death. Looking at René, it did so now. "*S'il vous plaît*, hand me that ledger."

René circled the table and brought the gray leather bound book to his father.

"*Merci*. Is that how you are going out?"

"*Oui*. I look dashing, do I not?" René straightened his coat.

Armand swallowed a sip of tea. "*Oui*, you do look dashing, but you also look unarmed. The world has become more dangerous."

René's smile drained away. "Father, we have had this conversation too many times. I refuse to carry a sword. I am sorry that it causes you concern, but I will not do it."

"René, it was self-defense."

"I will never kill another man."

Armand fingered his empty sleeve and his expression changed to a rueful smile. "So many things on which I placed the word never that happened anyway. Just saying the word will not make it so. You are a grown man now. Be careful out there. We shall have tea later."

René leaned over and kissed his father on the cheek. "No need to worry about me; I am very good at getting out of trouble. I will see you upon my return."

René brought the giant black horse up hard. There over the crest of the hill his best friend Martin and Clarisse du Bourg waited.

"Orion, what say we make an entrance?" He patted the coal black stallion's neck. A seasoned five-year-old, at seventeen and a half hands, Orion was the essence of power. René leaned forward and released the horse. For one brief instant, horse and rider were motionless. Then Orion exploded into a gallop, giant strides eating the distance between René, and Martin and Clarisse. His abrupt arrival surrounded them with dust.

Clarisse's horse reared, forehooves striking out.

"Keep him back!" she yelled. Tall, statuesque, with one leg hooked over the *pommeau* of her sidesaddle, Clarisse controlled her horse, backing him away from René and Orion. In a quiet cadenced voice she calmed the skittish mount. René moved Orion to the other side of Martin, whose placid gelding stood motionless, refusing to acknowledge the angry stallions now on either side.

"Perhaps you need a gentler horse?" René said.

"A gentler horse!" Clarisse snapped. "Perhaps you need better manners. If I were a man, I would have already challenged you."

"My good fortune, I guess." René smiled.

Before she could continue, Martin interrupted. "Let it rest. No need to bicker. 'Tis a beautiful day, and we have food and wine. Let us be off."

"Except most of the day is already gone," murmured Clarisse, her bright blue eyes now dark with anger.

"What was that?" René asked.

Clarisse bolted. The men were left in a cloud of dust. "I guess she was ready to ride."

Martin grinned. "I have ten francs that says we cannot catch her before she gets to the river."

"A fool's wager. Orion can beat anything on four legs."

"Ten francs," said Martin.

"I will take that bet."

"'Tis not always the horse," Martin yelled as they took off after Clarisse.

In a burst of speed, René left Martin behind. The air was crisp and warm. René leaned forward and spoke into Orion's ear. "Come on, boy, will you let that insult go unanswered?" Almost as if he understood, Orion stretched out even more, and thundered after Clarisse's horse.

The thought that chasing an angry stallion might be a mistake passed through René's mind, but it was lost in the excitement of the moment. The river Garonne shimmered in the distance. They were not gaining on her. *This is absurd. There is no way that horse is faster than Orion. One thing is for sure, that girl can ride.*

René pulled Orion up and slowed him to a canter. He hoped Martin would have the presence of mind not to mention the bet. A long lock of hair fell over his eye. He tucked it back behind his ear, and projected a casual air.

When René cantered up, Clarisse was walking her horse along the river, allowing him to cool down before she let him drink. Without warning, her horse whipped his head around and reared, forehooves striking out. Taken by surprise, she fought to keep her seat. Orion screamed and rose on his hind legs, iron tipped hooves striking back. The horses moved in close now, each trying to bite the other.

René's awareness had altered with such swiftness that time itself appeared to pause. He projected an implacable calm, its intensity almost radiant. With his left hand, he pulled Orion's head around, then twisted right and slapped the other horse on the nose.

"Hold!" The world seemed to obey him. For an instant both horses froze. Nothing in that space moved, not even Clarisse.

"Clarisse, move him away." René kept his voice quiet and measured.

The world started again. Clarisse regained control of her mount and turned him as René moved Orion back, increasing the distance between the two horses.

René's mask returned—the feckless nineteen-year-old whose sole intent was to enjoy the day.

Clarisse's eyes were wide, her face flushed.

"Are you all right?" he asked.

Clarisse averted her face to cover the blush that betrayed her. "Of all the stupid...what did you think you were doing, sneaking up on us like that? They could have killed each other."

"If you were paying attention—"

"Attention? Why, you idiot. If you had—"

Martin rode into the space between them. "What happened?" René and Clarisse began to speak at once. "Hold on, hold on." Martin held up his hand palm out. "Anyone hurt?" Both shook their heads. "I have never seen either of you like this. Why ruin the whole day?"

René returned Clarisse's angry gaze. A year had passed since he last saw her. They were at some obligatory social function or other that Bordeaux's upper class crowded into their calendars. Something had changed. Perhaps the way the sunlight shimmered from her long curly black hair whenever she turned her head, or caused sparks of light to reflect from her deep blue eyes. Even her voice sounded different, softer in its stridency. A sheepish smile crept onto René's face.

"I apologize," he said. "I should have known better."

She returned the smile. "Sorry I yelled at you. No one can predict what horses will do." Clarisse tightened her grip on the reins to hold her horse well back. "Is there any chance you brought some of that wine your vineyards are famous for?"

"I may have done just that. I see a good spot over there. Shall we tie up the horses and spread a blanket out?" René dismounted and led Orion in the opposite direction from the other stallion. "Whoa, Orion, calm down. No more fighting today," René said, his voice even and quiet, as he rubbed the big horse's neck. "That girl has spirit. Have to admit, not many could have controlled that horse."

Orion snorted and bobbed his head up and down. René laughed as he tied Orion's reins to a tree. "You agree, huh?" He removed the satchel that contained the wine and walked over to where Clarisse shook a blanket out. "How can I help?"

"I brought some baguettes and cheese. Would you mind getting them?"

"Not at all."

René spoke in a low, calm voice as he approached Clarisse's horse from the front and patted him on the neck. "Whoa, boy, I just want to retrieve this satchel." He studied the lines of the stallion. He was not so certain Orion could have outrun this horse from a dead start. This was a powerful animal and his estimation of her horsemanship rose.

Clarisse spread out the blanket on a grassy clearing beneath the shade of a copse of old river birch. Gnarled limbs reached out over the water and granted them shade. René carried the satchel to her, while Martin released a long, slim leather box from behind his saddle. "What have you got there?" René called over to him.

Resplendent in gold brocade and ribbons, Martin was the picture of a stylish well to do young Frenchman. He kneeled, set the box on the ground, and then opened it. Nestled within a dark red velvet lining lay a slim, lethal shape. "A new rapier. Came all the way from Toledo." Martin freed the sword from its velvet embrace as if it were alive. He stood and slashed the weapon down and to the side. The blade shimmered in the sunlight as it sliced through the air with a hissing sound.

"Beautiful, right? I thought I would practice a bit. Here, you want to feel the balance?" Martin extended the sword's hilt toward René.

René jumped back as if Martin held a cobra. "Ah, *non, merci*. You go ahead."

"Oh, sorry. I forgot, you have no affection for swords. Come to think of it, I do not remember ever seeing you hold a sword. There are many good reasons to go armed these days."

"Well, 'tis just that..." Clarisse stopped laying out the napkins and cutlery and listened. "Y-you can get hurt with those things."

"Kind of the point, is it not?" Martin slashed the blade through the air again as if to emphasize his statement.

René backed farther away. "I guess I am not that good around sharp objects. I like my fingers right where they are, *merci*," he said, becoming very interested in what Clarisse was doing. "Clarisse, 'tis been a whole hour since I ate. What do you have in that satchel?"

Clarisse took out cheese and baguettes and then dug deeper into the pack, finding a few small pastries. "Will you open the wine?"

Martin moved away a few paces and began basic fencing exercises. René uncorked the bottle and poured a glass for Clarisse and one for himself. Unable to ignore the weapon, he watched Martin out of the corner of his eye.

"You seem distracted," Clarisse said. "If swords make you nervous, you could ask him to put it away. I am certain he would be happy to practice some other time."

"Martin sees that sword as a shiny new toy to wave around. I do not view swords that way." Martin came to the *en garde* position. René called out. "Higher and to the right or you will get skewered."

Martin paused. "Directions from the sword master himself."

"Uh, you know," René stammered. "I must have read it in a book somewhere." In that moment the wind whistled through the trees, opening a pathway for the sun to shine into his eyes, and in the glare, he was back in the courtyard, memories like a wall of water rushed toward him.

The sound of metal rasping against metal was ugly, frightful. Fear washed through ten-year-old René. The Maestro had, for the first time, picked up steel instead of bamboo for their sparring practice. René, on the other hand, had been practicing with a rapier from the time he was eight. He expected it to be worse, paralyzing. Relief that it was not almost cost him an ear, for the Maestro was delivering a vicious cut to the head. At the last moment, René brought his rapier over his head, the knuckle bow pointed in the direction of the thrust. There was a loud grating noise as the steel connected.

The wind stopped. The branch swung back to block the sun, and Clarisse was offering him an almond macaron on a silk napkin.

"René. René," she said louder, poking him in the arm.

"Sorry."

Clarisse studied the young man seated opposite her. Tall and slim with sun bleached hair, his green eyes seemed to change shade with each moment. "Where did you go?" She placed the delicate confection in front of him.

"I, ah...was caught up in the beauty of this place." He looked at her. "Amazing how beauty can be all around us, and how blind to it we can be." There was a pause as if neither of them could think of anything to say. The moment was uncomfortable and exhilarating at the same time.

Both began to speak—and then laughed.

"After you," René said.

"I was wondering if you might join Martin and me tonight. Antoinette is giving a masked ball, and 'twill be, well, excessive. 'Tis last minute, but they always are."

"I would be pleased to attend." René smiled.

Clarisse straightened and took a sip of wine. She watched him closely from the corner of her eye. "Would there be someone special you might bring?"

"Not at the moment. I think I would rather be surprised and meet my destiny as it plays out."

"Martin, are you an expert yet? Come over here and sit with us. I have invited René to come with us to Antoinette's."

Martin replaced the sword in its velvet case and, still breathing in short deep gasps, found a seat next to Clarisse on the blanket. "What? Is there no glass for me?"

"Given the skill with which you waved that sword around," René said, "I fear intoxicating spirits will lead to your doom. Even in its case, you may find a way to stab yourself with your new amusement, and I would be at fault for your demise. But worry not, I will step up and drink your share." He reached for the wine bottle, but Clarisse got to it first.

She poured a glass for Martin. "I think you are downright valiant—a knight. Here, *monsieur*, you deserve the finest wine available. 'Tis unfortunate this was the best we could find." She laughed.

"Is that a slight on our vineyards?" René postured. "I must challenge you to a duel. But, alas, you are a weak femme and I cannot challenge you."

"Weak femme, am I? Why you..."

Martin jumped up and assumed a martial posture. "You,

monsieur, are a... a... Gorgonzola!"

"A what?" René jumped up, laughing. "Are you calling me a cheese?"

"I am."

"Have at you, *monsieur*." René tackled Martin, and they wrestled, rolling down the hill toward the river.

"Watch out, you are too close to the water," yelled Clarisse as she leapt to her feet.

They regained their footing, and each struggled to take the other down when René slipped on a spot of wet grass. *Splash.* They tumbled into the cold water.

"Enough," yelled René. "*Touché*, you have me. I hit the water first. I should have known better than to duel with the deadly Roquefort, being nothing more than a common Gorgonzola."

René emerged from the water, shaking his head. He knelt before Clarisse. "I am forced by the stronger man to offer you my most humble apology."

"Still, I would see you thrashed for your insult. Gentle femme, indeed," she said. "Etiquette, however, demands that I accept your apology, the proper forms having been observed."

Martin walked over and struck what he apparently believed to be a martial posture. Clarisse bit back a laugh. His gold lamé clothing had not fared well, its ribbons lay limp against the soaked fabric. The ruffled collar had come loose and now hung over his left shoulder. With both stockings around his ankles, he could not have looked less fearsome.

"I hope, for your sake, that you have learned your lesson, *monsieur*." He placed his hat on his head. The large gold feather, now drenched, lost its struggle to remain upright, and then, as if to punctuate his statement, fell across his face with a wet slap.

All three fell to the blanket laughing.

"So what do you think, my brave young men? Shall we retreat to our domiciles after lunch, repair our wardrobes, and reconvene tonight at Antoinette's?"

"What will you go as?" René asked Clarisse. "You must join us to see."

CHAPTER THREE

AN ARMY of tall young men costumed as Orpheus returned René's glance as he passed through the mosaic of mirrors in the château's entryway. He smiled at his personal collage of mirrored reflections. The multicolored troubadour's blouse, over black pantaloons with a midnight black cape, fit in well with the riot of color visible on the moving crowd. René attached his mask, tying it in the back. Turning toward the mirrors, he was jarred by the mask's reflection. Like most masks that depicted Orpheus, it portrayed a caricature of a face with a large nose and downturned mouth meant to express sorrow. This particular mask, however, was a Venetian work of art. Despair radiated from its features, transcending the human condition and evoking the artist's intended response.

Straightening the mask, René entered the atrium and continued along a light filled hallway. Crystal chandeliers suspended from the high ceiling along its length caused the light of innumerable small flames to shimmer their reflection from the intricate patterns of gold filigree along the walls and the polished Italian marble floor.

Once through the hallway, René encountered the first of a series of open spaces, each promising to be more elaborate than the previous. He paused in the entryway of a courtyard whose columns were floor to ceiling cages filled with hundreds of singing birds. René had been in his share of Bordeaux's palaces and châteaus, but this one surpassed them all in its attempt to outdo its neighbors. The parade of historical and mythical beings flowed around him.

A voluptuous woman, barely clad in a Cleopatra costume, staggered forward and fell into his arms. She glanced up and giggled. René blinked as he breathed in her stale alcohol breath. He turned his head to find more acceptable air.

"Your pardon, *monsieur*." She made no attempt to stand. "My, what a muscular young man you are. Are you available?"

René disengaged himself, yet continued to hold her upright, his hands firm beneath her arms.

"*Madame*, may I escort you to a seat?"

"You may escor... excor... take me to a nice dark corner." She hiccupped, and then clamped a hand over her mouth to contain another round of giggles.

René scanned the room. "Are you here with someone?"

"You will do fine."

René signaled to one of the servants to assist him, but before the servant could arrive, an overweight, elderly gentleman accosted him.

"You, *monsieur*, unhand my wife. How dare you? Do you not know who I am?" The man barked "I demand satisfaction. Who are your seconds?"

René turned his head to his right to meet the man's glare. If he released Cleopatra, she would fall to the floor. Keeping her at arm's length, René lifted the lady until her feet no longer touched the floor and then gently deposited her in her husband's arms. "Would you mind holding her for a bit? I am afraid she has had more to drink than her constitution will allow. Forgive me, as I intended no offense. Your wife tripped. I merely prevented her from injuring herself. She did ask for you, sir— numerous times. You are most fortunate to have such a doting wife. I wish you both a merry evening." René nodded and then moved off through the crowd.

René breathed in a deep breath and exhaled, grateful he had avoided being 'called out.' Dueling was illegal, but that fact had not dented its popularity. Duels rarely ended in death. More often, they stopped at first blood, or 'touché.' This would satisfy the honor of the offended. Tradition called for the insulted party to choose the weapons and the degree of danger the duel involved. Although hiring an alternate was permissible, René had found avoiding offense the wiser choice.

So far, by trading on his youth, he had escaped difficult situations. This had given him a reputation as unusual, perhaps, but he hoped, not cowardly.

René approached a lovely young woman who happened to be wearing a Eurydice costume. By her height, he knew she wasn't Clarisse. Even though she was masked, René had a good idea who the mystery woman was. Still, there remained some doubt, which only added to the spice of the moment.

"I am so glad to have found you." He bent low sweeping his arm before him as he performed an elaborate court bow. "Though I would have gone to Hades for you, 'tis much more convenient to find you here. Will you join me in this next dance?"

"'Tis a good thing I was not in Hades, where you would certainly have encountered greater difficulty rescuing me," she said. "I would be honored to dance with you."

The young woman introduced herself as Aimee de Montrochez, and she proved to be a vibrantly intelligent Eurydice to his Orpheus.

As the party progressed, some of the revelers had dispensed with their masks. René spotted Martin, who had removed his. Dressed as Apollo, he had his arm around Aphrodite who had to be Clarisse even though she had yet to unmask.

"I see some friends," René said to Aimee. "Will you accompany me to greet them?"

"I may be willing to share you for a minute or two." She broke into a smile.

"We should keep our masks on and see how long it takes them to recognize us." René wrapped his arm around her waist and led her through the milling crowd.

"I have never seen a lovelier Aphrodite, although I must say your Apollo leaves something to be desired," René said in his best imitation of a stentorian boatswain he knew.

"*Bonsoir*, René." Clarisse nodded at Aimee. "And who is this lovely creature on your arm?"

"How did you recognize me?"

"I have an excellent sense of pitch. Once I hear a voice, I recognize it, especially if 'tis poorly disguised." Clarisse released her mask and smiled. "Sorry to have spoiled your illusion."

"Well, you fooled me," said Martin. "I was about to challenge you for being so insulting."

"Given your overwhelming skill with the sword, you had best keep the challenges to a minimum." René smiled down at Aimee before he glanced at Clarisse. "May I present *Mademoiselle* Aimee de Montrochez? My friends, Martin Devereaux and Clarisse du Bourg."

"Both your costumes are quite marvelous," Aimee said.

Martin wagged his eyebrows as he flared open his gold cloak, exposing the shin length white and gold chiton that hung over his lean frame. Clarisse turned to René. A revealing bit of white gauze defined her as Aphrodite.

René swallowed hard, unable to take his eyes off Clarisse. She glanced at Aimee. A long moment passed as the two women considered each other and then exchanged artificial smiles.

"René told me all about this afternoon's ride. Must have left quite the impression." Aimee sniffed into her kerchief.

"Martin redeemed my honor." Clarisse's painted smile widened.

"I will always redeem your honor, my lady." Martin bowed low. All three turned toward René.

"I, ah, thought the macarons were terrific." The stilted silence grew more uncomfortable until the music began.

"Ah, a cotillion," René said with gratitude. "Shall we?" The dancers took their places on the crowded floor. The cotillion required each dancer to change partners throughout, bringing René to stand before Clarisse.

"You have never looked so beautiful," René commented when they faced each other.

"You saw me this afternoon." She twirled under his hand. "*Oui,* but you had on riding clothes—or maybe I never looked closely before."

"'Tis necessary to look that closely in order to see my beauty?"

"Ah, no, of course not." He missed a step and stumbled back into the correct footwork. "What I meant was...well, what I mean is..."

"*Oui*?"

"There is no way out of this for me, is there?"

"Not that I can see."

"What I mean is that you are lovely. Today, tonight, and all the days to come." He stole a glance to see if he had talked himself from the hole he had dug. "And that I am an ignorant buffoon without any sense at all. Will that work, do you think?"

"'Tis not Molière, but 'twill do for tonight." She laughed as he spun her again.

As the dancers prepared to move to their next partners, René surprised himself when he blurted out, "I hate to let you go."

"I hate to be let go." Clarisse batted her eyelashes as she gracefully moved in front of the next man in line.

The round changed again and René found himself in front of Aimee, who wasted no time in asking, "Are you serious about her?"

René missed another step. "Serious? Although I have known of her for a few years, I did not meet her until this afternoon. What makes you ask?"

"Oh, nothing much. The field is open then."

"Sounds like a hunt of some kind." René stepped around her. "Should I be concerned? Are there weapons involved?"

"Depends on your definition of weapons." Aimee glanced down her nose as she curtsied low.

"W-what?" René stammered. Aimee's costume slipped a bit showing more décolleté than was polite. "I mean, what were we talking about?"

"Exactly. Do you think you could escort me home tonight?" She curtsied to him once more.

"Well, I...why, of course. 'Twould be my pleasure."

"It might, it just might." She winked as she moved on in the line.

What had just happened? The next few minutes went by in something of a blur, René moved through the dance steps and partners by habit until he heard a loud slap and a curse. Clarisse stood in front of Victor Gaspard. Apparently the fool had once again done something inappropriate, and Clarisse had rewarded him for his trouble.

René pushed his way through the dancers toward Clarisse. Gaspard was a couple of years older than René. A natural bully, rumor had it that he hurt people for pleasure. As a child Victor had been heavy. Now an adult, his height had caught up with his girth, and he was just big. If the rumors were true, Victor had already killed two men in duels, perhaps more.

Clarisse held her gown together across her bosom. Martin scowled and stormed toward Victor.

"Not good." René reached Clarisse and Victor seconds before Martin.

"What have you done now, you—" Martin started to yell.

"Clarisse, are you all right? Martin, see to her." René caught Clarisse's eye, and she nodded.

"Martin, I am feeling faint and need some air. Will you help me outside?" She draped herself over his arm and steered him away from Victor.

René turned to find himself face to face with the flushed Gaspard. The air snapped with Victor's rage. He required a target, and fate or fortune had selected René.

"Who do we have here? Why, 'tis our local coward, the sniveling pacifist. With all the heroes available, she must not be very good if you are the best she could find," Victor snorted.

"Well, weakling, what do you have to say?" echoed Maurice, Victor's habitual shadow. He edged nearer to Victor's elbow, parroting the words of his god in a whiny voice.

The crowd, their eyes glittering like jackals awaiting a kill, pushed and elbowed their way closer to René and Victor.

Aimee watched with a focused expression.

"Gilbert, get on your knees and apologize for the woman's actions. I have been grievously assaulted. Do you not agree, Maurice?" Victor folded his arms across his chest.

Maurice glowed with anticipation, a runt hyena posturing with the pack behind him. "Oh, I concur. Definitely on his knees."

"Embarrassing, but there is no pain. You would gain more

satisfaction by injuring me, especially in front of all these people."

"Given your cowardice, you refuse to duel. What do you suggest? Fight like the lower classes, bare fisted?" asked Victor.

"*Non.* I was thinking more along the lines of a game. I hold my hands together out in front of me, and you smack my hands. For each time you connect with my hands, you may punch me in the face. You get five tries." Victor considered himself a master swordsman, with lightning hands, an arrogance René counted on.

"Sounds like good sport, but what do you get?"

"If by some small chance you should miss all five times, I get to leave this soirée in one piece, with no offense taken on either side."

"Done. Your smile will look different when this is finished." Victor smirked. "Will you need someone to hold you up?"

"I think I can manage." René breathed deeply and allowed that calm, centered focus to settle within. When he looked into Victor's eyes, in that timeless interval between one instant and the next, a heavily muscled ancient Egyptian general stood in Victor's place, armed and armored in bronze. René blinked and Victor's habitual sneer once again faced him.

René's iron focus remained firm. He would consider the vision later. This moment had no room for its examination. He stood easily, balanced, aware, his hands held out, palms touching. As he anticipated, Victor made the first attempt as soon as he extended his hands. René moved them out of the way, and Victor's right hand passed through the space where his hands had been. So violent was Victor's swing that he almost fell. René reached out to steady him. Victor knocked his arm away.

"That one did not count," said Victor.

"Why is that?" René asked.

"Because you were not ready."

"I am ready now." He held his hands out again.

Victor tried once more to catch René before he was set. But as the Maestro had taught him, one must always be set. *Circumstance rarely waits for us to be ready.* Once again, Victor's hand smashed through empty air.

"One," the revelers called. René nodded to the onlookers,

grateful they were involved. He had little confidence in Victor's motivation to count to five.

This time Victor wound up with his right hand and swung his left. But again René's hands were absent, and Victor's angry swing met no resistance.

"Two," the glittering audience shouted. More people joined the throng around them, vying for a choice location to see the action.

René had pulled his hands up every time so far. On the next attempt, he moved them down out of the way. Victor's swipe missed by a league.

"Three," the chant increased in volume. Victor's face was a deep blood red growing darker by the minute, partly from the exertion but more from the embarrassment of not having connected.

There would be no good ending to this confrontation, but René hoped he could avoid Victor long enough to let the incident fade. He considered allowing Victor to punch him once, thinking that perhaps that would satisfy him. Again, he heard the Maestro's words. *Evil will never be satisfied. There is no bargain with the devil. Do not ever pretend that there is."*

Another attempt, this one turned Victor full circle like the dancing bear in the circus that stopped in Bordeaux the previous year.

"Four." The crowd jeered louder. For his last shot, Victor tried to secure René's arm with his left hand while striking his outstretched hands with his right. Even thus encumbered, René easily lifted his hands out of the way. Victor only managed to slap himself.

"Five," the throng roared, as hands grabbed René and carried him away from the contest. It was good they did, for René had seen only the promise of death in Victor's bloodshot stare. René caught Aimee's arm as the crowd hustled him along. "If you want to ride with me, now would be a good time to leave," he shouted.

"Timing is everything," she yelled back. They raced to where his driver had brought the carriage around.

"The young lady said you would be needin' immediate transportation." Marc gripped the reins tight.

Smart girl, that Clarisse.

CHAPTER FOUR

"WHEN I find that coward, he will regret this day," Victor muttered as he shoved a young couple out of his way. The man spun around. His expression flashed from anger to fear as recognition set in.

Maurice laughed and pushed him again, harder, knocking him completely off-balance. The young man tried to remain afoot, but the uneven cobblestones defeated him, causing him to stumble and fall to his knees. He scrambled to his feet, grabbed his lady's arm and hurried her away.

The day after the ill-fated soirée, Victor and Maurice scoured Bordeaux searching for René. As each hour passed with no sign of him, Victor's anger increased. "The coward must be hiding in his room."

"He cannot stay there forever," Maurice said. "'Tis hot and all this walking has made me thirsty."

"I know what I thirst for, and 'tis not wine." Victor grasped his sword's hilt. "I intend to disfigure this one. The fool is far too pretty and will surely thank me for giving him the look of a man."

Victor barged into a couple returning to their carriage from the day's shopping expedition. Overburdened, the man's packages spilled from his arms onto the unforgiving street. *Crash*, the familiar sound of breaking glass. Heads turned. A blood-red liquid seeped into the gravel between the stones.

"You clumsy oaf! Look what you have done. You will pay for that wine and everything else you have damaged."

"Do you dare to insult me?" Victor stepped closer, his smirk inches from the luckless individual's face.

Eyes widened as the man recognized Victor. He stammered, "Uh, I meant that..."

"What did you mean by 'clumsy oaf'?" Victor smiled with brutal anticipation as his hand again moved to rest on the hilt of his sword. Sweat beaded on the man's now pale forehead, his breath came faster in gulps. "Why, *monsieur*, I was swearing at myself for being such a clumsy fellow. I often get in my own way."

Victor joyfully glared down at the now shaking man. "I notice that you carry a sword, sir. Are you prepared to use it?"

"I am sure that will not be necessary. No harm has been done here." The man stepped to his left.

Victor moved to block him. "Oh, I beg to differ. You have accosted my sense of propriety. Even were you not speaking to me, my sensitive nature has suffered from the roughness of your tone. I demand satisfaction, *monsieur*. If you will send your seconds to meet with Maurice here, we can arrange to settle this debt."

"Surely no duel is warranted. I beg your pardon if I have offended you, *monsieur*. *S'il vous plaît*, accept my apology, and let us be on our way."

"If only I could. But I have been sorely unsettled, and all of these fine people witnessed that offense." Victor glanced at the crowd that had gathered for some afternoon entertainment and nodded. "I doubt if even first blood will satisfy the empty feeling I am experiencing. But..." Victor let the word hang there.

"But what, *monsieur*? I am most disposed to agree to any compensation you might require."

I will have your sword."

"My sword?"

"*Oui*, your sword. Clearly you have no use for it, and I want to make certain that you do not injure yourself with it."

The man withdrew his sword and handed it to Victor, hilt first. Victor pretended to study it. "Not a bad weapon, but I am certain 'tis made of inferior steel. Much like its owner. I must test it." He touched the tip of the sword to the ground and smashed his boot into the blade. The blade bent into an L shape. "*Non*, I must have been mistaken in my appraisal. An inferior blade would have broken. This one did not, so I am more confident you will not harm yourself with it." Victor handed the bent sword back to the man. "See that you are more careful when you are out walking, or you may find the next man less gracious and forgiving than I." Victor smiled. "Come, Maurice. Now I am thirsty."

CHAPTER FIVE

RENÉ ENTERED the Moor, one of the new chocolate houses appearing throughout Bordeaux. Dark mahogany tables crowded the floor and private alcoves, while Turkish hand-woven carpets created a garish spectacle of color on the walls. René paused as he caught sight of Clarisse. Seated opposite Martin, she laughed as she waved her arms to emphasize the story she told. With each gesture, her long black hair reflected shimmering cascades of light. René struggled to reclaim his attention and then walked over to the table. He bowed before Clarisse.

"You are quite beautiful today."

"Is that an attempt to make up for your *faux pas* the other night? If so, keep trying." Her full lips tipped into a heart stopping smile.

His heart raced. For someone who had spent most of his life conquering the mundane rhythms of life, that involuntary response almost undid him. Unexpected, this new emotion struck him like a hammer against a church bell. A soundless note that shook him to the core, knocked him completely off balance, and yet filled him with excitement. He took a deep breath counting on his training to see him through the next minute without embarrassment. With utmost concentration, he turned toward Martin. "And you, sir. How do you fare this fine afternoon?"

"Breathing in and out quite well, *merci*. And yourself?"

"Excellent." René broke into a grin.

The serving girl set two cups of steaming chocolate before

Martin and Clarisse. She glanced at René. "May I get you something, *monsieur*?"

"*Oui*, a cup of sweet hot chocolate, *s'il vous plaît.*"

"I am not unaware of what you did the other night," Martin said with a grimace. "I did not require your assistance. I can take care of myself, and that ass needs to be disciplined."

"He needs something, but not from you or me. Even though we are capable of killing a snake, it seems ill advised to go around looking for one to step on."

The serving girl placed René's drink in front of him with a thunk. He blew on the steamy dark liquid and then took a sip.

"How did your evening with Aimee end?" Clarisse cocked her eyebrow.

He choked on the sip of chocolate. He swallowed and cleared his throat.

"Are you all right, René?"

"That hot chocolate is hot. By the way, *merci* for alerting my driver. I needed to make a precipitous exit, and I was glad to see him out front. 'Tis probably a good idea to stay out of Victor's way for a few weeks. Do you not agree, Martin?"

"It still irks me," Martin said. "Where is the justice when someone like Gaspard forces you to hide in your own town? What is the point in accumulating wealth and power if you cannot use them to protect yourself and those you love? I am done looking over my shoulder."

"I suppose we could have him assassinated." René winked at Clarisse.

Martin laughed. "'Twould go poorly for you if your assassin missed."

"Leave it be, Martin. I have," said Clarisse. "Victor will soon find offense with someone else, and our lives will go on."

"I notice you are armed." René nodded at the sword buckled at Martin's waist.

"I have never been that martial, but I am taking lessons so that I will not embarrass myself. I command more respect when I wear the sword. 'Tis a good feeling." Martin stirred his chocolate. "'Tis all about respect."

The words of the Maestro echoed in René's memory.

Respect is another name for fear. No more, no less. A healthy respect for your sword will serve to protect you from those who continually need to test it in order to shore up their own self-confidence or, more precisely, their lack thereof. Know who you are, along with the limits of your capabilities, and other men's regard will flow to you naturally, for you will know the way, where they will not. Most will want to follow you, but some, in their blindness, will strike out at you, even though you be their only salvation. Their fear is too great. Of these men you must be most watchful. They will strike at you as a snake will strike at its own reflection, continuing to strike even when it has battered itself near to death against the mirror. These men you must kill, for there is no other way to be rid of their threat."

"René... René..." Clarisse reached over and touched his shoulder.

"Sorry."

"Where do you go? 'Tis not flattering that your attention wanders off in mid-sentence. Were you thinking of Aimee?" Clarisse asked.

René smiled, for it was impossible for thoughts of the Maestro and Aimee to exist side by side. "*Non,* a teacher I once had. Stray thoughts come up from time to time. But tell me," he said, changing the subject, "what entertainments do we have to look forward to? I heard Molière's *Le Misanthrope* will be presented at the new opera house this week. 'Tis supposed to be outrageous."

"Then we must attend. One of our servants will reserve seats for us," said Martin.

"Excellent. It opens Saturday. Aimee and I will meet you there." René drained his cup.

"I do not suppose anyone needs to ask me if I should care to go." Clarisse's blue eyes darkened.

"Forgive me. My dear Clarisse, would you consider joining me this Saturday in seeing Molière's new play?" Martin asked.

"What do you think, René? Should I attend with this dull, boorish fellow?"

"'Twould help him so much. He does the best he can, but worry not; I will be there to help you stay awake if his company gets too droll."

"With friends as good as this, I may as well shuffle off this mortal coil, for I am undone already." Martin uttered a long sigh. "Still, you are both amusing at times."

"Amusing, am I?" Clarisse took a swipe at Martin that he deftly avoided. "I am so amused that I think 'tis time I made my way home."

Martin stood and offered a hand to Clarisse. She pushed his hand away. "'Twas a pleasure to see *you*, René." She leaned over and kissed him on the lips.

The unexpected shock of her lips on his froze René in bewilderment. From the corner of his eye he saw Martin react in similar fashion.

"Now *that* was amusing," Clarisse said as she strolled from the shop.

René watched her until she exited the tavern. As she closed the door behind her, the small bell atop it sounded a tinkling note as if to punctuate her departure. He turned and looked at Martin who just shook his head. Both fell back into their seats.

"What was that all about?" asked Martin.

"I am sure I have no idea." René focused on his cup of chocolate.

"That girl has got a mind of her own, and that is the truth. 'Tis all I can do to keep up with her most days."

"Are you serious about her?" René met Martin's gaze.

"For the moment I am. If you are asking whether I am planning on matrimony any time soon, then my answer would have to be no. As fascinating as Clarisse is—and I must admit I have met no one who comes close—there are too many daisies in the field to settle on one just yet."

René sat back, quiet, thinking about the feel of her lips. "She is certainly different."

"She is that." Martin stared in the direction of Clarisse's exit.

CHAPTER SIX

THE NEARLY completed Galois Theatre was a gargantuan imitation of Roman arrogance, a marble monstrosity intended to surpass the Paris theatres. René and Aimee struggled to gain entry beneath the giant pillars; the opera crowd that surged around them was but one step from violent skirmish.

This night was special, even for the jaded Bordelais. Tonight's performance was the first premiere of Molière's *Le Misanthrope* outside of Paris. The play satirized the hypocrisies of French aristocratic society. Peopled with familiar characters, it was perfect for the local well-to-do, many of whom considered themselves only slightly lower on the ladder of humanity than the mythological gods.

Everyone was in attendance tonight. More than a few fights erupted over which seats belonged to whom. Martin and Clarisse arrived early with servants in tow to protect the two additional seats.

René and Aimee finally managed to reach them. "All we need are the barricades and we will have a revolution." René helped Aimee into her seat. "I wager we have more realistic warfare going on up here than there is likely to be down there on stage."

"Attending one of these is not for the fainthearted," Aimee said. "'Tis riotous out front. I have never seen so many carriages. I hope the building is sturdy."

René smiled. "Plenty of good Italian marble in this building. The opera house will be here long after we are gone."

"We brought wine." Clarisse pulled glasses and a bottle from her basket.

"You, *mademoiselle*, are not only beautiful, but brilliant as well," said René.

"Shhh, quiet, the opera is starting," Aimee said.

"Quiet?" Martin laughed. "I see little chance of that happening."

The play began, and the audience responded to every word, every gesture from the actors, often with more heat than those on stage. As the final act ended, the crowd erupted into barely restrained chaos. People argued while hawkers yelled out their goods, selling everything from wine to meat pies.

"Oh look, Paulette is down there. I must go and say hello." Clarisse stood and glanced toward the stairs.

"Would you like an escort?" Martin stood.

"I am not helpless, you know. 'Tis just downstairs and you can see me once I reach the floor. I will be fine. Have another glass of wine."

Clarisse pushed her way through the crowd to the hallway behind the gallery and then down the marble staircase. A group, arguing over the stupidity of the hero, blocked the closer of two doors that allowed entry to the main floor of the theatre. She elbowed her way beneath the giant crystal chandeliers that lit the marble lobby toward the door on its opposite side. This side of the theatre held private suites, where the very wealthy retired between acts. As Clarisse was about to open the door to the ground floor seating, she was grabbed from behind and pulled into one of the suites. The door slammed behind her and the noise of the crowd diminished to a dull murmur. She struggled to speak or turn around, but strong arms imprisoned her, and a calloused hand clamped her mouth.

"You can take your hand from her mouth, Maurice," Victor said as he walked around in front of her. "You may scream all you like. The amount and thickness of the marble that makes up these suites was intended to minimize the amorous sounds from within. No one will hear you."

"You are a pig, Victor. Let me go!" Clarisse struggled against Maurice's iron grip.

"I have been unable to flush out your friend René, but when he hears of this, he will come find me, and then I will finish the business we started." Victor reached forward and ripped open her bodice.

Clarisse kicked out. Victor deftly stepped aside. Maurice jerked her arms behind her tighter. She screamed.

"Take her into the other room." Victor pointed toward a closed door. "I believe there is a divan in there. After all, this should be civilized."

Maurice dragged the still struggling Clarisse into the other room. He forced her down onto the long cushioned seat. One of her arms escaped his hold. She twisted and jammed her fingers into his eyes. Maurice screamed and stumbled back. Clarisse sprang from the divan and cast about for an avenue of escape. Victor swaggered toward her, his thick lips curved in a nasty smile. Forced to retreat, she bumped into a table and grabbed the first thing to hand, a gilded alabaster statue. She flung the statue with all her strength. Victor raised his arms and covered his face. The heavy marble figurine struck him between the legs with every bit of her loathing behind it. He collapsed to the floor writhing in pain. Clarisse ran from the suite.

If either René or Martin learned of this attack, it would mean their death, for they would challenge Victor. Just as he intended. She retraced her steps back to the stairs, now grateful to be surrounded by the raucous throng of theatregoers. She took in a deep calming breath and then straightened her gown. The bodice was ripped, but her shawl remained, snagged on a jeweled pin. She arranged and tied it across her chest and climbed the stairs, composing her features and gaining control of her pounding heart.

"Where did you go?" asked Martin. "I was about to come looking for you. You never did get to Paulette."

"Oh, I saw someone else I knew." Clarisse sat and arranged her skirt. "You know me, always stopping to talk to someone. I could use a glass of wine if you have left me any. What were you talking about?"

René paused in pouring. His eyes met hers. "Clarisse, is something wrong?"

"Wrong?" She glanced away. "*Non*, of course not. I just cannot figure out what Alceste could possibly see in Célimène." Clarisse laughed, but it was hollow. "The wine, René. Are you pouring it or practicing the art of being a statue?"

René topped off the glass and then handed it to Clarisse. She turned to Martin and whispered something in his ear, causing him to laugh. René kept his gaze on Clarisse, but she avoided him.

René was fourteen when the Maestro took away his sword. "You are becoming barely proficient with the sword, so we will now explore the most powerful weapon of all. You will not always have a sword. You might not find a sharp instrument of any kind, and what will you do then?"

Having so often felt the bamboo rod for failure to respect the master, René straightened to answer the Maestro. "As you have taught me, I will improvise using whatever is at hand to defend myself."

"What would you use in this case?" The Maestro swung his arm to encompass the now-empty courtyard.

"I would use the bamboo rod you are holding."

Whack!

The rod came down against René's wrist. "Do you think that is possible in this case?"

"Probably not." René rubbed his arm.

Whack!

The rod came down again.

"No, Maestro. I think there would be a low probability of my gaining control of the bamboo rod in this case."

"Think precisely, boy. And think quickly. You may not always have the luxury of time."

"I would use my hands and feet and head. I would use the dirt beneath my feet and the sun above my head. I would use all you have taught me, and I would find a way."

"There is one thing you have not mentioned, and that is your

awareness. You have within yourself the ability to connect to a larger universe than the meager one you can see, hear, and feel. Within this universe are all the thoughts and emotions of those around you. With practice, you may be able to access some of those thoughts and emotions, as well as predict with useable accuracy what the next few minutes will hold—and sometimes even beyond that. With much practice, this awareness will reliably alert you to danger."

"Do you mean I will be able to read a person's thoughts?"

"I have taught you to recognize the thought that precedes movement, to be aware of the emotional currents that swirl around every life form. Why does it seem impossible to attach meaning to the movement of energy, for thoughts are but encrypted bursts of energy? I would not, however, waste time trying to parse meaning within a combat situation." The Maestro again attacked with the bamboo rod.

Returning to the present moment, René centered himself, allowing the mental and emotional currents swirling about him to register fully against his consciousness. He had learned to separate the individual strands of awareness, and he began to isolate Clarisse's thoughts and emotions from those of the crowd. Fear and Victor were predominant against a background of confusion, but it was impossible to decipher meaning while immersed in the emotional cacophony of the theatre.

Although the final curtain had come down, on the main floor there was disagreement over the ending of the opera, which devolved into a melee.

"Come, René, we must leave now if we expect to remain in one piece," Martin said.

René returned to physical awareness unsettled, his sense of threat still active. A part of him had been paying attention, because he remembered the end of the opera. Yet his inner self was still attempting to make sense of the impressions he had gleaned from Clarisse. Something about Victor, something important.

Martin and Clarisse were standing, as was Aimee.

"Come, let us leave," said Aimee. "I, for one, did not think Alceste deserved exile. René, you were so focused. Have you not seen a play before? René?"

"Me? Oh *oui*, I enjoyed it," he answered, still deep within the awareness of threat.

"Well, no need to brood over it." She laughed. "'Tis just theatre." René rose and took Aimee's arm.

For a brief second, his gaze caught Clarisse's, before she turned away. Was that fear he saw? They managed to get clear of the crowd and reach the carriages without incident. He wanted to protect Clarisse— no, he *needed* to protect her. The power of the thought startled him, and he was quiet throughout the rest of the evening, dropping Aimee off with the weak, if honest, excuse of having to work early with his father the following day.

CHAPTER SEVEN

RENÉ AND his father rode toward the port along the verdant banks of the Garonne River. Armand Gilbert sat astride his mount easily, the reins in his left hand, his right an empty sleeve tucked into his waistcoat.

The river road snaked through a valley of rolling farmland and forests. Long before they saw the tall ships' masts silhouetted against the cloud-filled horizon, René caught the smell. The unique combination of dead fish, tar, and the rancid fat ships used as a lubricant. About fifty yards ahead, two men walked toward them.

Hard to imagine a more disreputable pair.

As they came abreast of the men, the shorter of the two called to Armand. "Our ship made port, and we wondered if you could give us a bit of direction."

When the horses had come to a stop, the man came around to Armand's side. He took hold of the horse's bridle while pulling a pistol from the sash around his waist. "Get down. I am tired of walking."

"What did you do to get thrown off your ship?" asked René. "Shut up, boy," yelled the man as he redirected the pistol toward René. "Get off the damn horses, and throw down your swords."

René and his father dismounted. Armand dropped his sword to the ground. The shorter man snapped up the sword and then tucked the pistol in his belt.

"No load in the pistol, huh?" said René.

"I said shut up, boy."

Both thieves turned to Armand. "Hand over the coin you carry. Man dressed as you must have a pretty penny on him."

René's father had shared his love of maps with his son and always carried the valuable parchments protected within a tough burgundy leather case some three feet long. Half hidden by his father's horse, René loosened the straps holding the case and then pulled it from behind the saddle. He hid the case behind his leg as he walked toward the shorter robber who was clearly the leader.

"I do not think we will be loaning you our horses today," said René.

"And how exactly do you plan to do that and not become crow's meat?" The man flourished the filched sword.

Whack.

The man's sword lay in the dirt. René stepped forward.

Whack.

A strike behind the ear, and the man joined the sword. The leather map case had moved so fast as to be almost invisible. René radiated a deadly calm as he turned and walked toward the larger man.

"If you drop the sword, I will not be forced to hurt you." René's voice was quiet, lacking emotion.

"In a pig's eye," yelled the man as he charged.

René turned and backhanded a cut to the man's throat. He then tapped him behind the ear. The man joined his partner in the dirt. Both were unconscious.

René stared at the two men lying there, and in that instant he was outside the Boar's Head tavern again, staring down at the three men he had killed. The memory was startling in its clarity.

"Are you injured?" His father grasped his arm, returning him to the present.

"I am all right, Father."

"So fast." His father's voice was filled with awe. "I knew you were skilled, but I had no idea. The Maestro told me when you were much younger that you would be one of the greatest to ever wield a sword and that it was his privilege to teach you."

René laughed as he picked up his father's sword and handed it to him. "He never told me anything even remotely like that."

"I know he was harsh, and whether you believe me or not, there were many times I almost put a stop to your training. But I refused to let you end up like me." His father glanced at his empty sleeve, and then he remounted his horse. "I would not have you experience the living death that results from being unable to defend the ones you love. At least you have set a father's concerns to rest. I will speak with Jacques this very day, and we will begin planning your further education aboard the *Poulé*. We must inform the dockmaster of these two so that they do not ask directions of anyone else."

René looked out at the *Belle Poulé* where she rested on her side within a shallow channel. Shipworm was the bane of sailing ships and her seamen worked hard scraping and careening the hull, replacing the planks that were too far gone.

"Our unwelcome interruption has made me late for a meeting with the port commander." René's father scanned the ship in quick evaluation of her progress. "*S'il vous plaît*, René, give my regrets to Captain Coudray and let him know I will try to get back later this afternoon."

"I will. Have a good meeting," René said. His gaze never wavered from the ship in which he had spent so much time.

"René... René."

Reluctantly, he turned his attention back to his father. "*Oui, Papa?*"

"I expect a report from you on the ship's readiness. It will give me an idea of how prepared you are to accept an officer's billet."

"*Oui, Papa.*"

Armand Gilbert looked on his son with an understanding smile as he reigned his horse toward the port offices.

René turned and jumped into the longboat provided for transfers out into the channel. The men had already scrubbed the *Poulé* down with lye, killing the small vermin that collected on an extended voyage. At low tide, the crew had used ropes to pull the ship over to inspect her keel. The main work of the next few days would be to caulk the hull. The tide gently lapped against the boats snugged alongside the *Poulé* as the men painted the hull with tar from the bubbling pitch cauldrons.

"Ahoy, the master," René called from the longboat as it approached the *Belle Poulé*. He loved this ship and knew every line. Those wonderful days he had served aboard her flitted through his mind. During his first time at sea he had served as a cabin boy, young and inexperienced. Eight months of hard labor, excitement, and the occasional mind numbing repetitive boredom of the sea had passed by the time the *Poulé* once again entered the port of Bordeaux. On his second voyage, three years later, he was trained for the quartermaster's position. The captain had instructed him in the fine points of trigonometry and navigation aboard this ship. The wash of memories became a flood.

Captain Jacques Coudray turned from his inspection of the new planking and searched the horizon for the owner of that voice. His face split into a wide grin as he saw René approach in the longboat.

"Well, if 'tis not a shipworm returning to my hull. Break out the cannon, or we are doomed," Jacques called out.

René's boat smacked against the longboat in which Jacques stood. "Permission to come aboard, sir?" René asked, for he could no more ignore the formalities than stop breathing.

"Permission granted, Worm, and welcome," boomed Jacques.

René grinned at the nickname he had earned as a cabin boy for his willingness and skill climbing within the cargo hold's narrow spaces.

He crossed to the boat where the huge shipmaster grabbed him in a bear hug, easily lifting him off his feet. Jacques Coudray was a full four inches over six feet tall with muscle covering every inch.

"If you crack my ribs, sir, I will be of little use to you," wheezed René, barely able to breathe, let alone speak.

"Such presumption, Worm! Expecting you will be of any use! Still, 'tis good to see you, son." Jacques released René.

René took a moment to assess the changes time and the sea had wrought on his captain. With his long hair tied in the back and a flowing black beard, Jacques Coudray was the portrait of a young girl's fantasy pirate.

"You are still the same, not changed a bit," said René, secretly relieved. The sea aged a man faster than most other occupations.

"Cannae say the same for you, Worm. Looks like you grew a foot since I last laid eyes on you. Still practicing with that poxy sword master?"

"Not for some time now, sir. Do you think you can use an extra hand? Inexperienced though it may be."

"Oh, I expect we might find something for you to do. William, hand the man a brush. Do ya think he remembers what real work is? Perhaps we might remind him." The crew joined in Jacques's hearty laugh. "Start over there, boy."

Beginning to swab the hot tar on the hull, René grinned. "'Tis good to be back, sir."

The hot summer sun beat down upon the sea. René stripped to his breeches. The work was repetitive, but the hard exercise felt good after so long. Muscles rippled across his shoulders and arms. He still remembered the uneasy looks he had received on his first voyage after standing out on the yardarm during a gale. Twelve years old and twenty feet from the crow's nest, he had challenged the power of the storm as if the ship were not pitching from starboard to port with sails snapping like musket fire.

For a short time after the storm, the men made hand signs to avert the devil whenever he walked by, for sailors are a superstitious lot. The *Poulé*'s crew had never come across anyone who could root himself so strongly to a spot that it became nearly impossible to move him. The Maestro had taught him to connect to the energetic center of the earth. Once aligned with that force, it mattered little whether he was on the ground or sixty feet in the air perched on a yardarm. After a time, the crew's uneasiness passed. René had worked hard to gain their respect and was grateful when they welcomed him into the ship's fold.

The day spent applying pitch to the *Poulé*'s hull passed as days will when employed in honest labor. As the sun's light waned, Jacques called a halt to the work, and the men prepared to return to the dock.

"What do you say, Worm? Will you stay with us tonight and try something stronger than the watered wine you enjoy at home?"

"I hoped you would ask. I am loathe to leave work undone." René smiled.

"Oh, 'tis the work is it?" Jacques got out through his laughter. "Your father's offices are along the way. We will stop and let him know."

CHAPTER EIGHT

BORDEAUX'S SOCIAL calendar included a never-ending list of soirées and concerts hosted in the salons of the wealthy. Martin and Clarisse joined the small group of people invited to hear the latest quartet on the circuit. Clarisse glanced around at the guests. The audience, which numbered close to thirty, sported enough gold and silver trim that the gilded chandeliers looked dingy by comparison.

Martin surveyed the glittering company and then turned to Clarisse.

"I am to accompany my father to Amsterdam. The king is sending the Marquis de Pomponne as his ambassador, and he in turn requested my father join him as his secretary."

"And your father has asked you to assist him?"

"It appears I am finally ready to be given some larger responsibility. The thought of being part of discussions that will affect so many is quite exhilarating."

Clarisse smiled. "A small part."

"Well, of course a small part. They have yet to discover how brilliant I am!"

"What will your duties be?"

"Most likely keep my ears open and my mouth closed." Martin laughed. "Still, one must begin somewhere, and I am eager to watch the negotiations. 'Tis a chess match with huge sums at stake."

"As long as they postpone the next war."

"Do you think we will soon be at war again?" asked the man who was eavesdropping on their conversation. It was apparent, he hoped to hear the father's opinion through the son.

"I think it closer to the mark to ask will we ever not be at war with someone," replied Martin. "Still, war has its uses, I suppose."

Clarisse's eyes narrowed. "And what exactly does that mean?"

"As much as I am against war, and you know that I am, it does seem to have a salubrious effect on business. Through that, it supports as many people as it destroys. At least in theory."

"Some theory. Explain that to the mothers, sisters, and daughters. Somehow, I do not think your logic will be much appreciated."

"Logic does not care. Remember, I am not in favor, just trying to look at it dispassionately."

"I think we should change the subject, as you are sinking deeper into the mire with every dispassionate statement."

Martin laughed. "René failed to find my logic convincing as well."

"Where is René?" Clarisse bit her bottom lip. She had asked the question a bit too quickly. Martin squinted as he studied her. He paused for what seemed an eon. The silence finally drove her to speech. "I was curious, since he is usually around."

"Do I detect a hint of more than casual interest in René? Should I be jealous?"

"We are not exclusive. What right do you have to be jealous?" Clarisse turned away to cover the flush spreading across her cheeks. Composing herself, she again faced Martin.

"I am sorry, Clarisse. You know me, I am not territorial." Martin made a poor attempt at a laugh.

"Forgive me, dear friend. It must have been something left over from your previous discussion of the merits of war." She pulled him into an embrace. "I merely wondered where he has kept himself, 'tis all."

"Working on one of his father's ships down at the port." The silence lengthened, but just before it became uncomfortable, it was interrupted by the sound of a bell.

Martin took Clarisse's hand. "They are calling the quartet

together. Let us find our seats."

At the conclusion of the performance, Martin and Clarisse made their way to their host and hostess to thank them and take their leave.

Clarisse gave Martin a gentle push as they waited in the line to make their exit. "Find a way to speed this up. If I do not laugh soon, something is sure to burst."

"I feel the same way." Martin struggled to keep his face fixed in a smile. "When old Gustave let out that fart right at the end of the music crescendo, I thought I would fall off of my seat. But father would murder me for a faux pas like that."

They reached the front of the receiving line, tendered gracious goodbyes, and all but ran for the door. Once outside, they both collapsed against the side of the building laughing.

"It was so musical." Clarisse wiped her eyes. "You could tell he was a real lover of good music."

"And sausage," added Martin laughing. "Definitely sausage."

"My, oh my, something must be funny," Victor said, as he and Maurice walked up. "We were passing by and heard the mirth. Since I am sorely lacking any humor this night, perhaps you might share the joke with us?"

An icy feeling grew in the pit of Clarisse's stomach. "Come, Martin, I need to get home." She pulled Martin in the direction of the carriage.

Maurice moved to block their path.

"Let it go, Victor," Martin said. "I am satisfied concerning what happened at the costume soirée."

"Either you are more of a coward than I thought, or she failed to tell you."

Clarisse yanked on Martin's arm. "Come on Martin, let us leave. *Now*. Maurice, get out of my way."

"*Non*. Clarisse, what did you not tell me?"

"Nothing." Her heart threatened to burst from her chest. "Just a stupid prank from stupid boys. Come on, I need to get home." Clarisse pulled Martin's arm again.

Martin remained where he stood and faced Victor. "What are you talking about?"

Victor's flabby lips curved into a sneer. "Why, our little tryst during the intermission at the opera. You were so uncooperative, my dear. Poor Maurice has a black eye."

Martin turned to her. "Clarisse, what tryst? What did he do?"

Clarisse stood frozen. Though a warm summer evening, her skin had grown cold. She tried to speak, but no words came out.

"Did he hurt you?" Martin asked, his voice harsh with rage.

She forced herself to be calm, even though death's face leered at them on this sidewalk. "It was nothing. Just a harmless prank. I managed to give them both something to remember me by."

"That she did," Victor said, rubbing his groin. "You were lucky this time. But not next time, whore."

Martin slapped him. "You will give me satisfaction, *monsieur*. Though you have no honor, I am certain you will meet me. May I assume Maurice will act as your second?"

Victor smiled as he reached up to touch his face. "You may, and I accept with gratitude. I have longed for this moment ever since the night of the masque. Did you think that you and Gilbert would get away with your insults? Oh, *oui*, I will catch up with that coward as well. He cannot hide forever. 'Tis unnecessary to have your second contact Maurice. Tomorrow in the usual field, at dawn, and swords will do fine. I will be there. Will you?"

"Tomorrow at dawn," said Martin.

"*Mademoiselle* du Bourg." Victor's smile grew wider as he tipped his hat. "Come Maurice, they need to spend some time worrying about tomorrow."

Victor and Maurice sauntered away down the street. Their laughter echoed off the building's granite walls.

Clarisse turned to Martin. "You *cannot* meet him tomorrow."

"What would you have me do? Where would I live with the level of humiliation he would be certain to heap upon me?"

"It matters not where. Your life is more important. *S'il vous plait*, call this off, Martin. You know you are not an accomplished swordsman."

Her entire body trembled. Martin put his arm around her. "I

will send Louis to speak with Maurice. Perhaps we can limit the duel to first blood. There are many things I have yet to experience in this life. I have no wish to die, but I do not see a way out. Come, let us get you home. *Merci, ma chère,* for trying to protect me. I understand why you failed to tell me. Unfortunately, fate does not always ask our permission for its offerings."

He helped her into the carriage and then took his place beside her. The ride to her home was somber. Clarisse spent the time holding onto Martin while her mind raced. When they reached the du Bourg château, they waited for the servants to open the wrought iron gates. The Devereaux's chauffer drove the carriage beneath the arch and into the cobblestone courtyard. Martin got out and held out his hand to Clarisse. After he helped her down, she hugged and kissed him.

"We will find some way out of this."

Martin held her by both arms, forcing her to look him in the eye. "I want your promise you will not come to the field tomorrow morning."

"But, I..." she sputtered.

"Your promise, Clarisse. Having you there would hurt more than the sword."

She sagged in his arms, and he pulled her close against him. "I promise," she whispered through her tears.

"*Bonsoir,* Clarisse." He hugged her once more then turned and climbed into the carriage. "Louis, home *s'il vous plait.*"

CHAPTER NINE

Château du Bourg, Bordeaux, France

CLARISSE RACED up the staircase and into the château. "Father," she called out as she ran through the entryway, narrowly avoiding a collision with the footman. "Where's my father?"

"In the study, *mademoiselle*." The servant jumped out of her way.

She flung open the study doors and came to an abrupt halt. Her father dropped the book he had been reading onto the side table and stood at her precipitous entrance. His whole demeanor was one of censure. Edmund du Bourg refused to accept less than appropriate behavior in his daughter. Without propriety and manners, civilization—as he defined it—would fall. And though he and his wife had done their best to instill a gracious demeanor in Clarisse, her behavior had often left the qualities of quiet and demur to be desired. "Clarisse?" His voice was filled with disapproval for the most unladylike way she had barged into the room. Thick, dark eyebrows lowered as he regarded her.

Realizing her mistake, as well as the wall he erected when he was disappointed in her comportment, Clarisse stood still and collected her thoughts. Her father demanded thoughtful behavior and speech.

She spoke quietly, "Father, Martin has been forced to challenge Victor to a duel."

In the space of a heartbeat it was clear he understood the situation and his expression filled with compassion. "Be seated,

Clarisse." His voice echoed his concern. He gestured toward the chair facing him.

"Father," she said, louder than she intended. She paused, forcing down the molten fear that threatened to erupt within her. Collected, she continued, her voice quieter, measured. "Father, there is no time. We must do something before dawn tomorrow."

"Sit *down*, Clarisse," her father commanded. She dropped onto the edge of the chair. "Have you asked Martin to forgo the duel?"

"*Oui*, and like some idiot primate he explained that he could not live here with the embarrassment of being called a coward."

"And you responded with something like...'so move somewhere else.'"

"You already know his answer to that. We have to *do* something. He does not stand a chance. Victor wants to kill him. As the challenged, he has the choice of what will satisfy him, and he will never accept first blood." Her voice broke as a sob escaped.

"Like all young men, Martin is unable to see beyond appearances." Her father paused. "He could hire an alternate. But if he did, Victor's response would be the same as if he had declined the duel." He leaned forward and took her hands in his. "Clarisse, 'tis the times we live in. Duty requires I inform Martin's father, but I know Adam, and he knows his son. Nothing short of keeping Martin in prison will stop this duel from happening. The law will not let us stop something illegal before it has occurred."

"Then act illegally. Hire someone. If Victor is still alive by tomorrow morning, Martin will die."

"Would you have me do that?"

"In a heartbeat," she replied hotly. "One Martin is worth a thousand Victors, a million. I would do it myself if I could."

"I cannot." He stood. "I will, however, contact Arnaud Cloutier. A court physician, Dr. Cloutier is in town to speak at a medical conference. He is an old friend, and I am certain he will be willing to accompany me tomorrow."

"You would attend the duel?" She jumped up and hugged her father. "Oh, *merci, Papa*."

"Clarisse, if there is any way I can protect Martin, I will, but he is above the age of consent now, and I cannot go against his wishes."

Sadness and truth shone in his dark eyes. In that moment, her hope died and instead became a black abyss sucking her in. *Non! I refuse to give in to hopelessness. I will contact René. He will think of something.*

She started toward the door, stopped, and then turned back to her father. "*Papa*, may I take a carriage to Château Gilbert? I need to tell René what is happening."

"Change into something more appropriate, and I will alert Alfred to bring the carriage around," he said. "Have faith, Clarisse."

"I would rather know how to use a sword," she muttered as she dashed to her room to change.

Clarisse ignored modesty and jumped out of the carriage as soon as it stopped in front of the château. She ran toward the entrance. "René!" she called, banging on the door. "Propriety be damned. René, hurry."

Henri opened the door, She barged right by him and into the foyer. "René!" she called again.

"He is not here, *Mademoiselle* du Bourg."

"Where is he?" she demanded.

"He was working on the *Belle Poulé* and probably decided to stay over at the port. I could send someone to fetch him in the morning, if 'tis important."

"Henri, 'tis urgent. I need to see him tonight. *S'il vous plait*, saddle me a fast horse. I can be at the port in two hours, and he can be back here in another two. 'Tis almost midnight. We have barely enough time."

"*Mademoiselle, Monsieur* Gilbert is also absent. I cannot authorize your riding alone to the port."

"Henri, would you let me ride if I might save René's life?"

"Is there truly a life in jeopardy?" His gaze bored into her.

"*Oui*," she said. "Martin and René may both die."

"John will saddle a horse for you. Orion's the fastest, but he nicked a foreleg. Marc will go with you. He is a good rider. Probably not as good as you, from what René tells me, but he will keep up and he knows the port. *S'il vous plait*, wait in the sitting room while I arrange for the horses."

Henri left and returned a short time later. "Come along, *mademoiselle*. We are ready." He guided her outside to the stables where Marc held the reins to the horses.

"*Merci*, Henri," she said, as he helped her mount. "Where will I find him?"

"The *Belle Poulé's* crew usually stays at the Gull. He will be with Jacques Coudray, and everyone at the port knows Jacques."

"Do not worry, *mademoiselle*, we will find him," Marc added. "I know the port like the back of my hand. Lord knows I have delivered enough supplies there."

The ride was endless. Although there was a full moon, the road soon blended into a gray sameness. The Gilbert mount had neither the stamina nor the speed of her horse, and she had to force herself to manage its pace in order to coax the most out of the animal. Finally, lights from the port came into view as they cleared the last rise and started downhill. Marc pointed toward the longest quay. "The Gull is to the right and down a ways."

The weathered name on the tavern was unreadable, but the carved seagull perched on the sign was enough to identify the inn. Both horses stood blowing, completely lathered. "*Mademoiselle*, we need to find someone to walk them and rub them down."

"We need to find René first and then we can tend the horses." They entered the Gull, still busy despite the hour. René and the *Poulé's* crew were not in the tavern.

"Can you tell me where the *Belle Poulé's* crew is drinking tonight?" she asked the portly proprietor.

"Jacques and the boys went to a party, but I will be daft if I can remember where," he said, scratching his bald head.

Clarisse prompted him, forcing herself to maintain an even tone, "Think, *monsieur*. 'Tis important."

"I am certain they mentioned a tavern. Name of a bird I think."

"Do you know how many taverns in this port are named after birds?" Marc asked.

The innkeeper started to laugh. Clarisse glared at him. "*Pardon, mademoiselle.* There are many, and I am sorry I failed to pay attention. Since they were not drinkin' here, where they took their money was their business." He raised his voice to carry across the tavern. "Any of you know where the *Belle Poulé*'s crew is drinkin' tonight?"

There was a lot of head shaking, but no one answered.

"Come, Marc. 'Tis almost two thirty. René does not have Orion to get him back when we do find him." She grabbed his arm and tugged him out the door. "All right. You take that side of the street, and I will take this one. We will meet at the other end of the port." She started up the street.

"*Mademoiselle*, I cannot let you go off by yourself in a port! You will be robbed— or worse."

Clarisse faced him. His gaze faltered and then retreated from hers. "I will take this side, you take the other." He nodded and then darted across the street.

An hour of trawling taverns passed before they found the *Poulé*'s crew, singing in the Raven. Explaining to René took thirty seconds, but since both of their horses were blown, getting him a serviceable mount wasted another half hour. She kissed him before she let him go and watched as he urged the horse to a full gallop, disappearing from view as he topped the first rise.

"Come, Marc. We need to see our horses cared for, find fresh mounts, and return to Château Gilbert." She took a step toward the stable and then paused. She glanced back at the road and the dust sent into the moonlight by René's horse.

Mon Dieu, let him be in time.

CHAPTER TEN

RENÉ HAD never been fond of drink. Previous unsuccessful experiences with excesses of brandy had kept him from joining the crew in their cups. He was nearly sober when he mounted, and riding full-out finished the job. He more than once wished he had Orion under him and was painfully aware that before the night was over, he would probably kill this horse.

René's time on the *Poulé* had taught him to read the stars, and as they moved across the sky, time slipped away. If only the horse moved faster or the sun slower. At least thirty minutes from the field when the pink colors of false dawn lit the horizon, he prayed they had spent some time talking, and hoped against hope they would enact all of the formalities of the duel slowly and to the letter. Leaning over the horse's neck, he urged the mount faster. He raced the sun, and he was losing.

René left the road following a well-worn path through scraggly brush and weeds. Enough horses had trampled the path that he was able to hold his mount to a gallop. From the edge of the scrub, the land was a series of hills punctuated by quadrangles of flatland. As the horse struggled to ascend the final rise, a group of men came into view. Only one of them wore the customary white shirt. Duelists wore white so that first blood would be easily identified and the contest ended. According to Clarisse, it was doubtful Victor would have let Martin off that easily.

The horse was blown, finished off by the last rise. It stumbled and then went down. René kicked free and jumped before he was trapped beneath it. He rolled to his feet and ran, leaving the quivering horse to die where it foundered. As he approached the group, Martin was lying on the ground, attended by a physician. Edmund du Bourg stood nearby. Victor spoke to Maurice, his face a mask of boredom and contempt.

Ignoring Victor and Maurice, René ran to Martin's side and knelt. "Will he live?" he asked the physician, who had stopped ministering to Martin. The doctor turned to René and shook his head.

Blood covered Martin's shirt, seeping from a dozen wounds, while only a few spattered drops of his blood marred the pristine white of Victor's shirt. Martin was still conscious. "Protect Clarisse. He means to hurt her." Martin's voice was a rasp, blood bubbling out of his mouth with every labored breath.

"With my life. I swear. But you will protect her yourself."

"I do not think so."

"Do not talk like that. Stay with us. Clarisse needs you." René looked frantically to the doctor whose expression brought the moment into hard, cold focus.

Martin gripped René's arm, pulling him nearer. René leaned down, his ear close to Martin's mouth.

"Clarisse is awful at hiding her emotions. I saw in her eyes at the Moor. She has chosen you," he whispered.

"She loves you," René insisted. "Martin, Clarisse loves you."

"Take care of her, *mon ami*. She is worth everything. *S'il vous...*"

Unable to speak, Martin offered a weak smile. With a last breath, his hand released René and fell limp to his chest. Blood continued to seep into the hard-packed clay.

René fell back to sit beside Martin. His eyes burned with years of unshed tears. Martin had been his best friend for as long as he could remember. They had shared everything but René's training with the Maestro, which had been a sworn secret. If only he had not been singing at the Raven, or if Orion had been healthy, or...

The Maestro's voice sounded in his ear.

Do not spend a moment's time or energy on what could have been. You will need that time and energy for what is.

Maurice leaned over, his face close to René's. "Coward's tears are cheap, Gilbert. At least your friend held a sword. If only briefly."

René took one last look at Martin and then stood, entering that state of quiet potential where power resided. Even the elements around him accorded him courtesy as the movement of the air stilled. His focus narrowed and, for him, time slowed. Ignoring Maurice as though he did not exist, he turned to Victor. Like a lion gazing on a wounded buffalo calf, René's focus was total. For a brief second, Victor's bored expression changed to one of apprehension. Then his sneer returned with all its customary disdain.

"Do you even know why you needed to kill him?" René asked, his voice dead quiet.

Victor shrugged, a simple movement that displayed the depths of his evil.

"Gaspard, you are an ass," René said. "A small, frightened boy who needs to hurt others to shore up the constant fear that he will be found out. You are a stain upon the fabric of life, a cretin, a breeding mistake, and you have reached the end of your timeline. I find I cannot allow you to continue hurting others. Is this a sufficient insult, or are you so stupid you need me to slap you with a glove?"

Victor was stunned into speechlessness. "Is this some kind of joke, Gilbert? I will not be accused of murdering an unarmed man."

René leaned down and picked up Martin's sword with a hand meant to hold a sword of its caliber. "I believe this one will do fine."

Monsieur du Bourg, stepped in and grasped René's arm. He looked gray. "There has been enough bloodshed this day. *S'il vous plaît*, do not add to it. Clarisse will be stricken as it is, and she will need you."

"*Merci, monsieur*, for your concern, but there are times that we cannot let pass if we are to call ourselves men. I do not refer to the ridiculous notions of honor, but to the fact that we have in our midst a poisonous serpent. You do not leave such a dangerous thing within your house to endanger those you love. You crush the life from it. You must trust me that this will not go as everyone expects."

"As you wish, *monsieur*. You are above the age of consent, and I may do nothing but watch." *Monsieur* du Bourg's expression mirrored the sorrow and futility in his voice.

René turned to Victor. "You are the challenged party and as such may choose the weapons and the level of the duel." He loosened his cloak and allowed it to fall to the ground. He removed his cravat and opened the first two buttons on his shirt to expose his chest.

Victor smiled. "I choose swords. We fight until one is dead or unable to continue."

"Are you certain that those are the rules you choose to abide by?"

"Where do you find such spleen, Gilbert? Are you stupid? Let me reaffirm my choice. The contest will continue until one of us is either dead or completely incapacitated. Do you need me to define each word? Your lack of respect for your betters irritates me. You may run crying from the fight now." He laughed, and Maurice quickly joined in.

"*Monsieur* du Bourg, will you act as my second?"

"I will, *monsieur*," he replied formally.

"And have you gentlemen heard and understood the rules Victor has chosen to be bound by?" asked René.

Both *Monsieur* du Bourg and Dr. Cloutier responded, "I have."

"Maurice, will you show me the boundaries that have been marked out?" asked René.

"What boundaries? There are no boundaries, little boy. It would not matter if there were. You will not last long enough to reach one."

René turned to Victor. "Will you allow me to loosen up? I have had a long ride."

"Get as loose as you want. 'Twill make no difference."

Every sword is different, as every person is different. Take a moment to acquaint yourself with a new weapon and it with you.

René lunged forward, stretching out the long muscles in his left leg, and felt the balanced weight of a fine sword in his hand. Coming back to *en garde*, he moved the sword quickly through its paces until he felt confident in its balance. He had chosen to fight using his right hand. Even though Victor did not warrant it, Martin's sword did. René walked over to stand in front of Victor.

"*En garde, monsieur.*" René's awareness expanded to

encompass everyone and everything on that field. He knew the hard packed clay, the direction of the sun's rays and the slight wind that blew from the north, and he knew precisely where Maurice stood.

Victor let the moment lengthen and then languorously stretched, coming to the *en garde* position in a desultory way. "I am nice and warmed up after my duel with Martin— and I use the term loosely. He..." Victor lunged forward in an attempt to surprise René with a thrust.

René had not been surprised by a dueling move for many years, but Victor was unaware of that fact. René parried the thrust easily. As he circled Victor's blade there was a rasping sound and then the blade was on the ground.

Victor stood there perplexed, a look of disbelief on his face. René leaned over, picked up the blade, and tossed it to him. "You need to hang on to this if we are to duel."

Victor exploded in anger. A cut, a thrust, and again that rasping sound—and his sword lay there in the dirt.

René leaned down once more to pick up the sword, never letting his eyes leave Victor. Again, he tossed the sword to Victor, smiled, and shook his head. The other men stood rigid as if frozen in disbelief.

Victor paused, his expression no longer feigning boredom. He began to fence seriously with René, attempting to use his superior weight and height to wear down his opponent. The impossibility of the situation washed across Victor's face as if something dark had slithered across his soul.

René easily blocked a tip cut aimed at his wrist and in return flicked the sword into Victor's left shoulder. Blood trickled down his arm.

Gaspard disengaged with obvious relief. A good swordsman would first try to disable his opponent's sword arm. To attack the other was evidence of inexperience—unless of course your intent was to lengthen the contest.

Victor tried a feint to bring René's sword out of line. Refusing the feint, René sliced off a piece of his right ear. Blood flowed copiously from the wound, but it was still not debilitating. Victor disengaged again. There was absolute silence. Every man there—except Victor—saw that René had purposely chosen a lesser strike than the one offered by Victor's feint.

"What is the matter, coward? Can you not bring yourself to take a better thrust?" Victor sneered.

René ignored the verbal taunt. He reached through Victor's defenses and cut a piece from the other ear, quickly followed by a stripe down the left cheek.

Gaspard glanced over at Maurice. As Maurice took a step, *Monsieur* du Bourg drew a flintlock pistol from his sash. "If you take another step, I will blow your head off."

Fear and bewilderment flashed in Victor's eyes. His face was a ruin. Like a wounded bull, his world had narrowed to René's sword.

The ugly rasp of steel on steel rang out as Victor's sword again fell into the dirt. René leaned down, wiped the blood off the hilt, and tossed it back to him. Again and again, his blade a gray blur, he speared through Victor's defenses to cut him. And still he refused to touch Victor over the eyes so that dripping blood did not block his sight and force a stop to the duel.

Gaspard disengaged again and stood there panting. His left arm, its tendon severed, swung useless.

Victor's actions had required his death. That René had prolonged the duel, slicing away the very humanity of another soul, filled him with a grasping darkness that threatened everything he believed in.

Raising his gaze to meet Victor's, René once again saw the implacable visage of an ancient Egyptian general. Recognition that echoed down thousands of years exploded within his mind and then faded along with the visible form leaving in its place only a weary futility.

"Let us finish this, Victor."

Victor's sword slowly came to *en garde*. René feinted, a high thrust to the face. As Victor sluggishly attempted to block, René slid his sword three inches into Victor's stomach. Victor dropped his weapon, but René heard no inner shout of victory. Some almost-memory deep within his soul had demanded one last cruelty. A stomach wound was always fatal, but it allowed hope to bloom, and then only pain, while the wounded prayed for death.

Victor crumbled to the earth as Dr. Cloutier hurried over to him. René lowered his sword and stood quietly. No one spoke. The physician did his best to staunch the bleeding and bind up Victor's wounds, but every man there knew that he was dead.

Maurice took a step toward René, his face a red mask of rage and fear. "You bastard. You killed him. You are still a coward and I challenge you."

"Calm yourself, Maurice," René said, his voice quiet. "I will not duel with you, no matter what you say. I have no wish to kill two men this day. One is more than enough."

"Coward. You are afraid to face me. Dung eating peasant. All of Bordeaux will know you to be a coward."

René ignored Maurice and turned to *Monsieur* du Bourg. "Am I finished here, sir? I would like return to the château. Clarisse is waiting."

"There is nothing more to be done here. The duel is over, and we will see Victor returned to his home. René, you know there will be repercussions from this duel. Even though it met the requirements of tradition, the Gaspards are too powerful for this outcome to remain unanswered."

"It will be what it will be. As the universe has cast my vows in my face, I will make do with what fate offers me." René was unable to keep the weariness from his voice.

As René turned to leave, Maurice pulled his sword and thrust it toward René's back. Faster than the eye could follow, René turned enough to allow the sword to plunge past his chest. A swift scrape of metal, and Maurice's sword was in the dirt.

"I can see there is another serpent here," René said. "One who will stab a man in the back. All right Maurice, you may have your duel." He tossed the sword back to Maurice. "*Monsieur* du Bourg, may I have the honor of your seconding me again?"

"Maurice, this is madness. You have seen the skill of this man. You cannot hope to defeat him." Ordinarily a man of great energy, *Monsieur* du Bourg stood smaller, tired, empty.

"Never. It was only luck. Victor was tired from his first duel. I am not tired, and luck does not last forever," Maurice yelled, the vein in his neck pulsing with malice.

"Will you fight to first blood, then?" asked *Monsieur* du Bourg.

"*Non*. I will fight the same duel Victor fought."

"And you will die the same way," *Monsieur* du Bourg muttered under his breath before he announced that the match would last until one party was either incapacitated or dead.

"One last chance, Maurice," René said. "I will not play with you, nor will I stand here a minute longer than I have to."

"*En garde*," screamed Maurice, as he lunged forward.

René nudged Maurice's sword out of line and slid Martin's blade through his heart, killing him instantly. Maurice fell to the ground, his face, a rictus of disbelief. René turned to *Monsieur* du Bourg. "I will be at home if I am needed," he said, each word filled with regret. "And I will see Clarisse home safely."

"*Merci, monsieur.*"

"I must borrow Martin's mount and will see it returned to his stable." With that, René swung atop Martin's horse, recognizing the saddle Martin had used on their recent ride—a ride impossibly distant now.

CHAPTER ELEVEN

THE WEIGHT of death sat heavy upon René's shoulders. Along the tree-lined drive of Château Gilbert, a few leaves had begun to redden, but in this world, at this moment, there was no room left for color or beauty.

Clarisse waited within, and he dreaded telling her what had happened. How he had failed. As he approached the manor, a pressure in the pit of his stomach built, and the feeling of dread expanded. With it came a surprising nostalgia for his early years with the Maestro. Dread was not a welcome emotion, but it was familiar, just one of the many faces of fear. The Maestro had taught René how to manage fear and right now he needed that strength. He rode into the yard, heading for the stables. "John?" he called.

"In here." John answered as he walked out to greet René.

"Would you prepare a carriage for someone to take *Mademoiselle* du Bourg home? I will need a mount saddled as well."

"*Oui*, Master René." John reached to take the horse's bridle.

René dismounted and handed the reins to John. The walk to the manor seemed endless, every step heavier than the last.

"Henri?" he called, then forced himself to continue through the entryway.

Henri appeared before the sound of René's voice faded. Although the man's posture was as correct as always, tension was evident in every muscle.

"May I take your cloak, sir?"

"Where is she?" René removed his cloak and handed it to Henri.

"*Mademoiselle* du Bourg is in the sitting room. There is a brandy decanter on the table," Henri seemed to take great care to fold the cloak, never taking his gaze from René.

René walked into the sitting room. Clarisse was seated, staring into the fire. He was still for a moment, unable to share the pain of Martin's death with anyone, especially her.

Some sound caused her to glance up. She stood and took a faltering step toward him.

In an instant, René was at her side. He held her up and gently eased her into the chair. He knelt beside her.

"I was too late." Guilt ripped the words from his throat. Hot tears filled his eyes. Before today, the last time he had cried he was six, and all he got for the tears was a smack from a bamboo rod. Coming now, they were unexpected. He fought to hold himself together.

Clarisse held his head in her arms and laid her head atop his. "'Twas not your fault. The responsibility lies with Victor. He should be punished."

"Victor is dead, or will be shortly." He stood and walked over to the brandy decanter.

"Dead? Did Martin..."

"*Non*. I killed him. And Maurice—and even the horse. I was the Grim Reaper's right hand today."

There was silence while he poured them both a snifter of brandy. He handed her the glass and then sat in the chair opposite her. They drank in silence as if each was trying to envision the future. "You must leave Bordeaux, René. The father is much the same as the son."

"My intention was to ship out on the *Belle Poulé*. Perhaps six months or a year will allow things to settle. She will be ready to sail in about six weeks. Until then, I will do my best to avoid trouble, but I refuse to hide like a frightened child." René rose and then paced in front of the fire.

There was silence again as if neither one was willing to broach the pain of their loss.

Clarisse stood, crossed to René, and laid her hand on his shoulder. As he turned, they hugged. The feel of her body against his and the smell of her hair released an avalanche of emotion he had long fought.

He leaned back and gazed into her eyes. A moment later his mouth was pressed against her pliable lips. She returned his kiss with a passion that surprised him. They clung to each other, stretching the moment. René took a step back and regretted the action, but he had to or lose all sense of reason. "Forgive me. I cannot handle any more guilt."

"What have you done that deserves guilt?"

"I let my best friend die, I desire the woman he cared for, and I killed two men, all in one morning. Can you think of anything else? I might as well get it all in."

"Were you not challenged? A duel requires consent on both sides."

"Oh, they both had the trappings of a duel, but it was murder. I trained with a sword from the age of five, Clarisse. Fighting Victor and Maurice was like fighting children. Neither stood a ghost of a chance against me, and I knew it. I vowed never to kill again and I failed. Seeing Martin lying there and knowing Victor might hurt you, my vow crumbled like the hubris of a child's sandcastle before the afternoon tide. I had to pick up the sword, and once it was in my hand, the rest was inevitable."

"He *would* have hurt me, René. That was why Martin fought the duel. I am sorry you were forced to kill, but you have protected me." She reached for his arm. "As for your desire, you only echo my own."

Unable to hold Clarisse's gaze, René turned away. "I never found the courage to tell my best friend how I felt about you. And now I never will.

"'Tis strange, almost as if my emotions have been turned off. Like when I fence, but then 'tis a calm sort of quiet. This is more like a mountain of water held back by a precarious dam made of ice." He turned and wrapped her in his arms for a brief moment. "I will not run from my emotions, but I need some time to sort this out. I told your father I would see you home safely, and John will take you. I must return Martin's horse and sword to his family and tell them what has happened."

"But not alone, René. I will go with you and then home from there. We will get through this together."

René paused, the need to shoulder the burden himself, perhaps as penance or punishment, lessened as he gazed at her. He nodded. She took his arm as he escorted her to the door.

Henri was there with their cloaks. "Your father should be home later this evening. May I tell him when to expect you, sir?"

"*Oui*, Henri. I need to tell Martin's parents..." René paused as grief overwhelmed him. Regaining control, he continued. "I will not be gone long."

They walked out to where John waited with the carriage and horses. "*Merci*, John, but I will drive the carriage. *S'il vous plait*, tie Martin's horse to the back, and we will be off."

René helped Clarisse into her seat. He took his place and snapped the reins gently against the matched grays. The carriage wheels clattered along beneath the changing linden trees.

When René and Clarisse approached the Devereaux manor, he was relieved her father's carriage was already out front. They sat quietly for a moment as servants came down the stone steps to assist them. René stepped to the cobblestones and handed Clarisse down. He turned to a young servant dressed in the Devereaux livery. "Would you see that Martin's horse is rubbed down and fed?"

"*Oui, monsieur*." The servant hurried to the back of the carriage to untie the horse.

René offered Clarisse his arm. "Shall we? This will not get any easier."

They entered the house, allowing the servant inside to take their cloaks. "May I take the sword, *monsieur*?" asked the man.

"*Merci, mais non*. I will need it a little longer."

The majordomo bowed and then ushered them into the study. *Monsieur* Devereaux stood behind his wife's chair. He placed his hands on her shoulders as much to comfort her as to keep them from trembling. Defeat haunted his eyes. She moved her hand, briefly touching his before she dropped it back into her lap.

Adam Devereux was a slight man who looked as though he was fighting to support an infinite weight and losing. Martin had been their only child. *Madame* Devereux wept softly. A small woman, and yet, in that moment, she was the stronger of the two, radiating a quiet strength, a woman's strength, from beneath her grief.

Monsieur du Bourg and Doctor Cloutier spoke quietly in front of the fireplace mantle. When her father saw Clarisse, he came over and took her in his arms, an unusual show of emotion for the man. This left René standing alone, and he looked up, meeting the eyes of Martin's father, who walked over to him.

Not allowing himself to look away, René spoke, his voice quiet, broken. "I am sorry, *Monsieur* Devereaux."

"*Monsieur* du Bourg has told me of your actions this day," Martin's father said.

René could not maintain eye contact, and his gaze dropped to the floor as if magnetized.

"I want to thank you, René. If there ever was a pestilence that needed destroying, it was Victor Gaspard. In your actions, you have perhaps saved the lives of dozens of our young men."

"I was too late to save Martin," René said, still unable to look the elder Devereaux in the eye.

"Look at me, son," *Monsieur* Devereaux commanded. René looked up through eyes filled with tears.

Martin's father placed his hands on René's shoulders. "Your timing was God's timing, and not your own. You stood in for Martin once before at the masque and I know you would have done so again here. Were you there earlier, it would have helped nothing, for Martin would not have allowed it. God rest his soul. You have rid the world of an evil young man who debased the life God gave him. There is no guilt here, only regret. And regret is something we mortals live with."

"I would like to return Martin's sword to you, sir." René raised his hand to remove the sword from his belt.

"*S'il vous plaît*, stop." The older man laid his hand on René's.

"The sword now belongs to you. Consider it a gift from Martin. I know he would want you to have it. I expect you to continue to use it to protect those never meant to hold a sword. Those of us who pick up the sword are always burned by it, but we do so anyway to protect those we love. That pain is one of the costs of love, and I can see you are a man able to make a great payment on its behalf."

"I do not know what to say."

"Your deeds have spoken. Your words are not necessary. If there is any way I can help you in this life, you have but to ask. We are in your debt, sir, and it is a life debt." *Monsieur* Devereaux glanced toward his wife.

"Come here, René."

René walked to her and then knelt before her chair.

She put her hand on his head. "*Mon petit* René, how you have grown. I remember you two ragamuffins getting into everything. Stealing pies. Oh *oui*, I knew it was you boys. Whom do you think I made the pies for anyway? Beloved other son, we are proud you were Martin's friend. Do you think you could visit me from time to time?"

"I will soon sail on the *Belle Poulé*, but I will visit you often before she leaves, and when I return you will have to throw me out."

"We will pray for your safe return." Her eyes shimmered with tears that would be shed in the days and weeks to come.

"I believe the Devereaux need time to rest." *Monsieur* du Bourg motioned to René and Clarisse to follow him. "Adam, Elizabeth, I will return this evening. Is there anything more I can do for you now?"

"*Merci*, Edmund, for all you have done. We will be fine. *Merci*, Doctor. My wife and I are grateful for your efforts," *Monsieur* Devereaux replied.

"I am only sorry I could not do more, *monsieur*."

Clarisse hugged Martin's mother. Then she spoke quietly to *Monsieur* Devereaux, after which she gave him a hug. René offered her his arm, and they followed her father and the doctor out of the study.

"I will take Clarisse home with me," said *Monsieur* du Bourg.

"René, I can see your actions today still confuse and pain you, as they would any honest man. I advise, however, that you do not remain in this state of mind for long. I assure you *Monsieur* Gaspard will not. If I may put a blunt point on it, I expect him to send an assassin to challenge you immediately, or worse, attack you from behind. I have seen you fight and know you to be a master swordsman. No matter how you kept that fact hidden all these years, René, you must take up that persona now and protect yourself, for you have made a powerful enemy."

"I will take care, *Monsieur* du Burg, and *merci*."

"*Papa*, may I have a word with René? I will only be a moment."

"Of course, *ma cheri*." The two men continued toward the front entry.

René clasped her hands in his. "I will call upon you later. We still have many things to discuss."

"*Oui*, we do." She gazed into his eyes, her need and grief were almost insurmountable. "We will get through this, René."

CHAPTER TWELVE

Château Gaspard, Bordeaux, France

THE SERVANTS carried Victor into the sitting room, where his parents and the Gaspard family physician awaited him. Victor was conscious and in great pain. A single mote of light caught the pupil of his eye, the one not completely swollen shut, and forced him to wince. Even that slight movement created excruciating pain. The doctor had selected the sitting room to treat Victor because of the meager additional light the bolt holes in its southern battlements permitted. He glanced toward Victor's parents, but his expression held little hope for their comfort.

"Is it absolutely necessary to attend him here?" his mother whined.

"Be quiet, woman." François Gaspard turned toward the doctor, his expression a study in disgust. "What is your prognosis?"

The doctor's primary skill was the ability to reassure his wealthy noble patients and to convince them of their immortality. But as he stared down at Victor's lacerated form that skill seemed to fail him. He cleared his throat. "As you know, *Monsieur le comte*, these types of wounds do not usually respond to treatment, but I am well experienced and will do my utmost to—"

"I asked if he will live,"

"*S'ils vous plaît, monsieur*, your son is conscious. Perhaps we can discuss his condition elsewhere?"

"He was stupid enough to have failed at the one thing he was good at. I see no reason for pretense over his condition. I ask again, doctor, will he live?"

The doctor coughed and went to take the father's arm. François Gaspard glared. The doctor jerked his hand back and redirected it to smooth his neatly-trimmed beard.

"I do not believe so," he admitted. "My experience with this type of wound is that contagion inevitably sets in. While I have found the application of honey and boiling water to be most efficacious on other wounds, I do not have any great confidence in their application here."

"Is that a *oui* or a *non?*" asked François, his lips twisted in a sneer.

"*Non, monsieur.*"

"Do what you must," Victor rasped in a voice rent by his screams. "I will not die."

"Of course not, *mon cher,*" said his mother, as she pursed overly rouged lips, her gaze resolutely avoiding the horror in front of her. "You are to be married to a niece of the finance minister himself. How else will we—"

"Silence, woman." François faced the doctor, his gaze a fiery sword. "The servants will see you paid." With that he stormed from the room.

A sick quiet filled the space, as if all pretense at humanity had somehow been leeched from the air. Even Antoinette, always deep in her own mental cocoon, appeared at a loss.

"I, ah, well." The doctor looked to Antoinette for some guidance.

She drew in a deep breath and from the vapid expression on her face, it was clear she had reentered her usual version of reality.

"You heard the man. Heal him." A simpering smile returned to her face as she took on the wheedling tone of a spoiled child asking for another sweet. "But must you work in here? You see, I am hosting a tea this afternoon, and it simply must be in this room."

"*Madame*, if I am to irrigate his wounds, I must be able to see them. The best light is right here. We may be able to move him this afternoon, but I make no promises." The doctor gestured to a servant. "You there, help me move him closer to the windows."

"Mother." Victor's voice scratched through the word, pain in each syllable.

"*Oui, mon cher.*" she said, from her spot ten paces from the deathbed.

"Closer."

She edged nearer, her gaze upon the ceiling, the floor, the doctor, anywhere but her son.

"Look at me," he said in a voice that sounded like a log being dragged through gravel.

She glanced at him desperate to find somewhere to rest her eyes that would not cause her to retch. She stared at his shoes.

"Look at *me*," he demanded.

Speechless, she at last forced her gaze to rest on his. "There must be vengeance."

"I am certain that your father..."

"Promise me," he said, fiercely insistent.

Here at last was something she could understand and savor. "I promise."

"*Madame*, I must attend to my patient." The doctor moved to Victor's side.

"No laudanum," said Victor, through clenched jaws.

"This will be painful, and we have the power to deaden that pain."

"I want to remember this day, each moment, so that I may—" He stopped as a wave of pain made him convulse. "—properly repay this debt. Bring me a piece of leather to bite down on."

One of the servants raced from the room.

Antoinette took a deep breath and wrinkled her face at the acrid smell. "I have things to do." She left the room, calling to the servants to attend her as she went.

The doctor shook his head and rounded on the last servant. "Bring me plenty of boiling water and as large a quantity of honey as you can find."

CHAPTER THIRTEEN

RENÉ DROVE up to the stables. The waning afternoon light had leached all color from the buildings, leaving only sepia shapes in the approaching darkness. John came out and took hold of one of the grays' bridles.

"How is Orion's leg?" René asked.

"He will be fine. That beast is made of iron. You can ride him in a day or so."

"A day or so," René said, with a bitter laugh. With Orion under him, he would have reached the dueling field in time. "Has my father returned yet?"

"He has. I just finished putting his tack away."

"*Merci*, John."

René listened to the crunch of the gravel under his boots as he walked to the château, and the creaks and sighs of the building as he made his way through the house. At the door to his father's study, he paused, as if remaining outside might forestall the day's reality. He mustered himself and gently knocked.

"Enter." Armand Gilbert sat at the table, his ledgers open before him. He held a glass of brandy and stared into the fire. As René entered, he stood, rushed over to René, and then embraced him.

René was stunned. "Father, are you well?"

"Now that you are here, I am. Let me look at you." He stepped back to survey René. "Are you wounded?"

"*Non, Papa*, I am uninjured."

"Sit down. Would you like a brandy?" His father settled himself in one of two deep green leather chairs placed before the fireplace.

"*Merci*, but I have had enough brandy for one day. It just clouds the pain, and fails to remove it." René sank into the soft leather chair opposite his father. Both were quiet for a moment. The only sound in the study was the reassuring crackle of the fire. The reflected light from the leather bindings of the books that lined the polished wooden shelves created a warm and protective space. For perhaps the first time that day, René allowed himself to relax.

"Go through the events, leave nothing out, and we will decide where to go from there," his father said.

René relived the day. With his father, and in this space, he allowed himself to share his emotions as well as his actions. The Maestro had taught him the need to let out the poison within a wound to prevent its rot from spreading. By the time he finished, the fire had burned down and the room was darker, but in some inexplicable way, the space was brighter, the objects within it in greater focus. There came again a quiet moment, but this time, without the despair. Somehow, relating the story to his father had cleansed René of the self-loathing he had entertained earlier. He saw the day's logical progression and fate or not, there was no choice along the way that he could have made differently. He accepted this now, making room for the grief and regret.

"You cannot stay here." His father stared into the flames as if he hoped to find the answers within. "I simply do not have the power to protect you. If Victor was a thoughtless bully, his parents are truly evil, and you have never heard me accuse anyone of that. François and Antoinette Gaspard are both ruthless in the pursuit of their whims. They will crave vengeance. Their wealth provides connections to the royalists and the King which make this vengeance a certainty and not a possibility. If they do not have you killed outright, the crown will charge you with an offense punishable by death—treason, most likely. Our house has an unpleasant history with the Gaspards." He absently rubbed the stump of his right arm.

"I will not stay hidden in my room."

René's father barked a bitter laugh. "Indeed not. You will have to leave here for a time. I can see no other way."

"Where would you have me go?"

"*I* would have you stay here, where I can enjoy watching you go through your life, but that is not to be. You must have allies. No matter how skilled you may be—and I am quite content in your skill—one man cannot withstand an army alone." Armand Gilbert sat straighter, as if he had come to a decision. "We stay with our original plan. You will ship out on the *Belle Poulé*. She cannot be ready to sail in less than a month, and 'twill probably be more like six weeks, which leaves you open to the Gaspards' machinations. The only logical place to wait out that period is aboard the *Poulé*, surrounded by Jacques and his men."

"I realize I have to leave, but we need some basic understanding. My convictions about killing are unchanged. I care nothing for the ridiculous idea of honor and refuse to kill on its behalf."

"That may be easier said than done. If you are challenged, you must fight to establish the fact that you are dangerous. At first, people will have doubts about the duel, given the persona you have affected these last few years. If they perceive you as being dangerous, that will cause some delay. Any delay is of advantage to us. We need time for the *Belle Poulé* to finish provisioning and loading her cargo. I want you to join Jacques tomorrow and assist him in preparing the ship for departure. I will expedite the loading of her cargo. You will sign on as a junior officer, and I expect you to learn everything you can. Hopefully in a year's time you may return."

"'Tis all I have ever wanted to do. I am ready, but what about you? Unable to harm me, *Monsieur* Gaspard will attack you, will he not?"

"Oh, most assuredly he will, but it will come in the form of a mercantile attack, and I have fended those off for almost twenty years. Gaspard will not harm me personally. To do so would be to admit defeat after failing all these years to stop my business. Still, I will pay more attention and increase my security. Perhaps I may even begin to exercise my sword arm again. At one time I was more than capable of using my left arm." He stood and walked over to the fireplace and then held his hand toward its warmth.

"Your position as my son entitles you to all of my worldly possessions when I am gone, and that is on record. I will execute a letter of credit you may access through any of the major trading companies, depending, of course, with whom we happen to be at war. Jacques will also have monies aboard you may use for trading purposes should you see a good opportunity. We have five ships in our fleet, and they will all be notified of your position if for some reason you are unable to contact me."

René stood next to his father before the fireplace. "The logic of your plan makes sense and yet leaving you still seems like running away." René paused in thought. "I will join Jacques aboard the *Belle Poulé* by tomorrow afternoon, but I need to speak with Clarisse before I leave."

Both men stared into the fire, hoping perhaps to see the future within its flames.

René's demons had receded. He was sad, but the sadness could now be borne and turned into something other than melancholy. As the Maestro would say, *Nothing ever ends; it always becomes the beginning of something else.*

Facing Clarisse tomorrow would be one of the hardest things he had done, but he would think of that when it came. "*Bonsoir*, Father. I will see you in the morning." René turned toward the oak door.

"*Bonsoir*, son. You did well today, and I am proud of you." René climbed the stairs as if his feet were encased in cement, his thoughts empty, focusing only on his bed. Henri had laid out his nightclothes, drawing hot water and filling a porcelain basin for him to wash. Afterwards he climbed into the feather bed with a bone weariness he had not experienced since his days with the Maestro.

Exhausted, he fell asleep and found himself floating. Disoriented, he glanced down from a spot near the ceiling. He was still in his room. The dying fire gave the room a reddened flickering aspect. There was a figure lying in the bed. He focused his attention on the figure and saw himself, asleep.

When the unexpected happens, the usual human response is to allow the mind to become fragmented, desperately searching for answers instead of focusing the consciousness and allowing the answers to manifest in their own time, the Maestro's voice whispered.

He sought to take a deep breath, allowing his body to enter that state of calm, but there was no breath, and no body to breathe it, only the calm born of his intent. Another glance at the motionless form below showed a silver cord connected to the center of the body, his body. René followed the cord's shimmering length. He had the sense that his consciousness was in some way tethered to it and unless severed, it must return him to his physical form.

An awareness of movement filled his perception. He rose through the ceiling, and floated above the château, the silver cord trailing behind him. The barns and vineyards visible below were lit by silvery moonlight. There was no moon this night. The world shrank and the light about him diminished until all was unrelieved stygian darkness. Still, he sensed movement, and after a time perceived a faint distant spec of light that inched closer. Contrary to his expectation that the inexplicable nature of this experience should make him afraid, he felt buoyant, confident, as if he was returning home after the successful completion of some difficult task.

Before him, a circular threshold of light grew rapidly until it surrounded him. And then he was hurtling through it, its walls a blur of brilliant pearl. After a moment of kaleidoscopic confusion, René found himself floating near the ceiling of a small whitewashed room. A young man wearing a gold belted linen kilt, bordered in green, with a golden medallion resting on his bare chest, stuffed clothing and bronze instruments into a leather bag. They were medical instruments. And somehow, René understood the exact use for each. An overwhelming sensation of familiarity washed over him. He forced himself to relax and allow the meaning of the scene below to come to him. Booted footsteps marched up the stairs followed by a forceful knock on the door.

The young man ceased packing and turned to face the door. "Enter."

The door opened revealing three men in full battle armor.

Although their dress was archaic, René recognized them as soldiers from ancient Egypt. The obvious leader was a head taller than the other two and heavily muscled. Swarthy with black hair and eyes, everything about the man shouted death. "Wait outside," he told the others as he entered the room and closed the door.

"Horemheb, if you have come to kill me, you did not need to bring assistance." The young man smiled.

The soldier laughed. "You speak the truth. The martial arts have never been one of your strengths."

"But you *have* been sent to kill me."

The smile died on the soldier's face. "The head priest has instructed me to remove all resistance to the return of the glorious Amun-Re."

Their eyes met, and a lifetime's worth of memories crossed between them. They had been brothers and disciples of the young Pharaoh Akhenaten since their selection at the age of twelve.

"It appears you are preparing to take a trip." Horemheb fingered the leather bag. "Perhaps I can facilitate your departure. It would be...unwise to delay."

"Is there any way I can persuade you to accompany me?"

"Pharaoh has charged me to remain and protect his family."

Both men had been initiated in the mysteries of Maat and knew the larger truth, the words unsaid, for Pharaoh had taught them to perceive the energies that surrounded a man, energies that never lied. Unable to maintain eye contact, Horemheb looked away.

"Gather your things. There are men waiting below to see you to your ship." Horemheb started toward the door. He stopped and turned back to face the young doctor.

For an instant, Yochanan's brother and closest friend looked back at him and then the moment passed.

"Do not return, Yochanan. The next time we meet, I must kill you." The soldier left, closing the door behind him.

"Go in peace," the young man said to the empty room. He continued packing.

CHAPTER FOURTEEN

RENÉ AWOKE disoriented, his mind filled with fragments of what seemed more like memory than dream. A sense of calm purpose surrounded him. He dressed and went downstairs to find that his father had already left the château. The dining room table had been set for one, with white china dishes covered in silver warmers and a steaming mug of hot chocolate. The smell of hot porridge, sausages, warm rolls with butter and strawberry confit comforted the air. Famished, he filled a plate with healthy portions from each dish and then pulled a chair up to the table. When he finished, he sat back sipping his hot chocolate and considered what to say to Clarisse.

Henri entered the room. "Will that be all, sir?"

"*S'il vous plait,* will you ask John to saddle a horse for me?"

"I was told by *Monsieur* Gilbert that you would wait for him and that you would ride to the port together."

"*Oui,* but I must do something before I leave Bordeaux. If he returns before me, tell him that I have gone to the du Bourg's to speak with Clarisse. I will not be long, and I will come straight home."

"Your sword, sir," Henri said offering the sword to René.

"*Merci,* Henri." René took the sword belt and buckled it across his hips. "I have only worn this outside the château once. I hope this day goes better."

"As long as you are going armed now, are you fully armed?"

"*Non,* I suppose not. I will go by the armory and complete the job."

"Be careful, sir."

"I will. No need to worry."

Henri nodded and walked from the room.

René looked down at the sword hanging beside him and the memories attached to it rose unbidden.

"What is the killing range of your sword?" asked the Maestro.

"Three to four feet," responded fifteen-year-old René.

"What if your enemy is five feet away?" asked the Maestro as he backed away from the boy.

"I would move toward him."

"What if he's twenty-five feet away and has a pistol aimed at your heart?" The Maestro moved quickly across the courtyard, pulling a flintlock pistol from his waistcoat. He turned and aimed the pistol at René.

René was by now accustomed to the Maestro's deadly surprises. Even so, this one startled him and he was at a loss for the proper response. Given the Maestro's respect for weapons, the pistol was real and it was loaded with a real projectile. He had to act. He threw his sword at the Maestro, and dropped to the ground. There was an immediate report and a piece of the wall behind René exploded. He glanced up. The Maestro nodded, the pistol in one hand, and the rapier in the other.

"Bon." The Maestro showed a half-smile. "Right choice, wrong weapon. To throw your sword is a choice of last resort. If there is anything else at hand, throw it first, but do not bother throwing something that will not serve to distract or delay your enemy."

He then selected two knives and handed them to René. He reloaded the pistol and picked up a one-foot square wooden shield. "I am not using a full load, but if it strikes you, you will find it extremely unpleasant. Your goal is to hit me with at least one knife before I can level and aim the pistol." The Maestro drew the pistol as he finished speaking.

René had long since lost his surprise at the quickness and fluidity of the Maestro, and there were no excuses. René had only pleaded "I was not ready" once. The bruises received over *that particular sentence did not allow its use again.*

Thunk. Thunk.

Both knives thudded into the wooden shield the Maestro held over his heart. The pistol had not quite cleared his sash.

"I see you understand the concept. Now, let us make your reaction automatic." He tossed the knives back to René.

In all of their practicing, the shot from that pistol never once touched René.

The bridge of stone stood sentry over the Garonne river a mile or so ahead. René allowed the horse to proceed at a slow walk. He was in no hurry to face Clarisse. He had thought of a dozen ways to say what he needed to say, and each was flawed. How would she respond to his decision to run, to leave on the *Belle Poulé.* Most likely, a year would pass before they could be together again. He could almost hear the disappointment and anger in her voice.

Two men on horseback charged out from one of the orchards that lined the road. Facing René, they stopped, blocking the roadway. Both had the hard look of mercenaries. Their weapons were well-kept serviceable tools. He continued until he was twenty feet from them and then stopped.

"'Tis a nice day?" The larger man leaned forward on his pommel.

"'Tis, but I have an appointment and would appreciate your allowing me to continue."

"Are you René Gilbert?" asked the shorter man whose face bore gifts from previous fights.

"*Excusez-moi*, did I miss hearing you introduce yourself?"

"There is no need for you to know who we are."

"Then I might as well remain anonymous too, since we seem to be playing some kind of game."

"Oh, we know who you are. We passed Armand Gilbert earlier in the day. You look a lot like him, you know," said the first man.

René entered that space of quiet and death. "Have you harmed my father?" he asked, his voice a quiet monotone.

The men's horses shied back. "*Non*, we have no business with *Monsieur* Gilbert, just you. Heard a tale of your skill with a sword. Hard to believe a boy your age could be that good. Perhaps you might show us." The larger one pulled his rapier from its sheath.

"Are we going to do this on horseback? I would hate for these blameless animals to be injured."

"How considerate," the man said as he dismounted. The scarred man stayed on horseback until René dismounted and then slid from his saddle, all the while keeping his attention on René.

"Will you consider ending this at first blood?" René untied his cloak and tossed it over his saddle.

"Sorry, boy, but that is not what we get paid for. Nothing personal, you know."

"Well, I would like to avoid killing either of you if possible. How about doing this one at a time? There is less chance of your being seriously injured if you fight me one at a time."

Both men attacked, their deadly blades thrust toward his heart. "*Non*, I did not think so." René withdrew a throwing knife from his waistband, and used it to block the shorter man's sword thrust while he engaged the first. They were both veteran swordsmen which eliminated René's compunctions when confronted by the untrained. Still, the Maestro had taught him to accomplish a task with the least amount of risk and effort.

René circled between the two horses, putting a horse between himself and the larger man. He bent low, reached between the legs of the horse, and severed the man's Achilles tendon. The overconfident mercenary screamed and dropped to the ground. René smacked the agitated horse on the rump to keep it from trampling the man to death and then walked over to where his attacker struggled to pull a pistol from his sash. René kicked it out of his hand and then faced the shorter man.

"*En garde, monsieur.*" René moved toward him.

Although a veteran in his middle thirties, the man froze, his expression one of shock at the speed with which René had disabled his partner. He managed to back up a couple of steps, giving himself time to regain control. He faced René with a determined glint in his dark eyes.

"You are quite good, *monsieur*. You would have made a fine

mercenary. Lots of money for a man good with a blade. You know—
" He thrust his sword toward René's heart.

René forced his opponent's rapier up and to the right, using the opening to tip-cut a slash across his chest. He then disengaged, giving the man a moment to feel the strike.

Fear is your greatest enemy as well as your greatest ally. Allow your adversary to sample fully its bouquet.

"You stupid boy, you have cut me," the man yelled as the bottom half of his shirt changed from white to blood red.

René smiled, which only increased the man's fury. The mercenary charged René, attacking with a wild series of cuts and thrusts that were easily parried, visibly sapping his strength. The moment he began to withdraw and regroup, René attacked, slicing his foe on his chest and shoulders and then above his eyes. Each strike meant to reduce the man's ability to fight rather than kill him.

The man bled from a growing number of wounds, and with each drop of precious life force lost, he grew weaker. He attempted to gather himself for one last attack and failed.

The mercenary drew back, breathing heavily. "You will kill me now, *oui*? Done in by a stupid boy. Well, I will not die running."

"If you yield, no one need die today." The mercenary lunged forward with a high attack. René turned just enough to allow the blade to slide past him and then he tip-cut the tendons in the man's wrist. The mercenary's hand, no longer functional, dropped the blade. He stood there, swaying, waiting for the final cut. René backed up a step and sheathed his sword. "You are no longer a threat to me, and I have no need to kill you. Do those who follow you a favor, and do not pretend there were others here besides me. While I have not killed this day, I will not be so merciful if I am truly threatened."

René mounted his horse. "Oh, and one other thing. I do not like pistols or muskets pointed at me, and the moment I find one raised in my direction, I will kill the man attached to it. It would be a fatal error to be that man."

René turned his horse and took the road back to his château. If Victor's father learned of René's connection with Clarisse, he would kill her or worse. To keep her safe, René could have no personal contact with her. There would be no discussion of their future.

"*Dieu merci* you are unhurt," said Armand Gilbert as René rode up. "We were preparing to come after you. I got word Gaspard had sent men to kill you."

"Two men," said René.

"Are they both dead?"

"*Non,* and they are no further threat. I apologize for leaving without asking you first, but you had already left. I wanted to see Clarisse one last time, to explain why I have to go away. It was fortuitous they attacked me on the road into Bordeaux. Even a dolt like me should have seen that any contact with Clarisse would alert François Gaspard and expose her to his machinations."

"I am just glad you are safe." His father dismounted. He turned to the grooms "*S'il vous plaît,* take our horses to the stables. And, Marc, organize a rotating watch around the château until we leave."

Marc took the reins from René's father. "I will see to it, *Monsieur* Gilbert. No one will disturb you. It is good to see you, Master René," he said with a smile.

"You mean in one piece." René laughed. "*Merci,* Marc. I seem to have become very popular lately."

"Come, René, let us walk. We have things to discuss."

The crunch of the gravel beneath their feet was the only sound for some minutes until finally, René spoke. "I am sorry, Father. I can only guess how much this troubles you. Martin's last words to me were to protect Clarisse from Victor. If François Gaspard gets even a hint I am involved with Clarisse, he will not hesitate to hurt her. I have killed one snake only to have enraged a nest of vipers. It feels like I am running away, and yet I cannot think of a better course of action."

"Occasionally, time is the only tool we have to apply to a problem," René's father said as they walked into the entryway of the château.

Henri rushed in, his arms thrust forward to grab René. Visibly realizing the impropriety of his actions, he came to an abrupt stop, his arms falling to his sides. "Are you hurt?" he asked, flushed.

"I am fine, Henri. I believe this is the first time I have ever seen you agitated," René said.

Henri pulled his dignity back around him. "'Tis only your imagination, sir. I was checking your garments for tears. You are always so hard on your clothing."

"Ah, concern for my wardrobe. Well, that explains it," René said. "Henri, do you think we could have something special for dinner tonight? I will be living at the port until the *Belle Poulé* sails, and while the port is known for a lot of things, fine cuisine is not one of them."

"*Certainement*, sir," Henri turned and nodded to *Monsieur* Gilbert. "Will you be needing something, sir?"

"*Non*, Henri, I expect we will be talking late, so a fine dinner will hold both of us in good stead."

"I will see to it, sir. And if I may take your coat and your cloak, I will be about it." Henri gathered the garments and left the room.

CHAPTER FIFTEEN

Château du Bourg, Bordeaux, France

CLARISSE PACED, then sat and picked up a book, only to put it back down. Standing again, she went to the fireplace and lifted the iron poker. She pushed at the logs, causing sparks to fly from the hearth. Replacing the poker, she resumed pacing. *Madame du Bourg* sat knitting, occasionally pulling on the skein of purple wool that filled the wicker basket at her feet.

"If he can, he will, *ma cherie*." Her mother counted stitches under her breath.

"I need to know he is all right." Clarisse's voice rang with frustration.

"Your father heard from Dr. Cloutier. Two mercenaries limped into town this morning, both bloodied and helpless. From what I have heard, I am sure he is fine."

"*Maman*, can Alfred drive me to Château Gilbert?"

"*Non, ma petite*. 'Tis not safe for you to go there today."

"Alfred will be with me."

"Alfred is no man-at-arms, Clarisse, he is an aging chauffeur. I am sorry. When your father returns, perhaps he will take you."

"*Zut alors!*"

"Clarisse!"

"*Pardon, Maman*. I will wait for René out front." Clarisse attempted a smile and managed to keep from running as she left the room. She went out the servant's entrance, her thoughts in a muddle. A delivery boy stood beside his cart. She walked over and looked into the cart. It was a sturdy one-horse carriage, filled with cabbages, sides of bacon, and sacks of flour and sugar.

The boy was tall and wiry. Clarisse judged him to be about thirteen. "What is your name?"

"My name is Brice, *Mademoiselle* du Bourg," he said. "Is there something I can do for you?"

Clarisse tapped her index finger on her chin while she studied him. "Actually, Brice, there is. I need help moving something from the tool shed around back. Can you spare the time?"

"*Oui, mademoiselle*. Yours is my last delivery today. What would you like moved?"

"Go on back there and wait for me. I will just be a second."

Clarisse ran back into the château, slowing as she approached the sitting room. "*Maman*, I am going to Marie's."

"I thought you were going to wait for René here?"

"You are probably right. I do not think he will risk a visit. Send for me if he does. I may stay at Marie's for dinner." Clarisse turned to leave and then called over her shoulder. "*Je t'aime, Maman*."

"I love you too, dear. Have a nice afternoon."

Clarisse raced through the house and across the yard to the garden shed, a red brick building at the rear of the property that held tools and seeds. She pulled open the door. Brice waved from his perch on the seed sacks. Unless she needed seed, there was nothing much to move, and his worldly thirteen-year-old smile told her as much.

"Take your clothes off," she ordered, as she unbuttoned her dress.

The boy was attired in brown wool breeches and hose with a white shirt and vest. Soon he was down to nothing but his sardonic smile. He sat back down and watched her. She had pulled her dress over her head and was unfastening the farthingale from around her hips. Then all she had left was her chemise. She sometimes wore linen drawers, but unfortunately not today.

"Turn around," she commanded.

Pulling the chemise over her head, she grabbed his clothes and slipped them on. Thankfully his clothes were reasonably clean.

Unable to completely button the tight shirt, the larger vest, probably from an older brother, helped retain her modesty. Her hair was coiffed in a braid, so she tucked it into his cap. "All right, you can turn around now."

The boy's eyes widened in surprise. He had delivered to the du Bourgs for some time, and while undoubtedly accustomed to the peccadilloes and sexual appetites of the French upper class, this was obviously new.

"I do not understand," he said.

"I need to borrow your cart for the afternoon." Clarisse neatly folded her things and placed them on an adjacent seed sack. "I will make sure you are paid enough to get you out of any trouble you may receive." She turned toward the door.

"Wait. I cannot sit out here naked. What if someone needs a rake? They might shoot me!"

Clarisse looked around for something to give the boy and then gathered her things in her arms. "I cannot go into the house to get something of my father's. Here, wear my dress until I get back."

"They'll shoot me for sure."

Clarisse pulled up in front of the Gilbert stables. In late summer, the heat and rhythm of the day allowed for a lengthy lunch break. Though the stable appeared deserted, John Calb would have left one groom to watch over the horses. She smiled when a young boy appeared as the rig came to a stop.

"I have a note for *Monsieur* René." Clarisse kept her head down and lowered her voice.

The boy walked over. "I will take it to 'im, but I have to wait for the rest to come back from lunch."

"The note is from *Mademoiselle* du Bourg. She expressly told me I was to put it into his hands." Clarisse coughed. "'Tis of a personal nature, and time is of the essence. You need to call René, er, *Monsieur* Gilbert, *tout de suite*."

"*Monsieur* Calb will skin me alive if I leave this stable."

"'Tis very important, and I will watch the stable for you. If *Monsieur* René fails to receive this note, *Monsieur* Calb will be the least of your problems. Now go!"

The boy's eyes grew wide. In a flash he turned and sprinted for the manor. Within minutes, he was heading back with René.

As he approached the cart, René visibly became more cautious. He slowed, studying the young driver. Clarisse looked up and their eyes met. René stopped dumbstruck, his expression that of a man struggling to accept reality's gift. She allowed a wicked smile to tweak the corners of her mouth.

René glanced at the young boy. "Alban, they tell me you are a fast runner. Take a message to Marc. I believe he is working in the vineyards. Tell him I will need him in an hour. Have him find something for you to do, and return with him at that time."

Alban sprinted toward the vineyards as René took the horse's bridle and led the rig into the deserted stable.

"I have never been very style conscious, but I must say, you look fetching," René said as he helped Clarisse down from the cart.

Clarisse grasped his arms, her face ashen. "Two bloodied mercenaries came into town. I was so afraid you had been hurt. I could not wait." She traced a finger along the curve of his jaw. "Are you..."

"*Non*, I am fine. When the mercenaries attacked, I realized if François Gaspard suspected you meant something to me, he would use you to get to me." His words poured out along with his fear. "I could not live with the possibility you might be hurt. I had to return home."

"I mean something to you, then?" A coquettish smile brightened her face.

René reached out to touch her. The need greater than any he had known. He drew her into his arms and gazed deep into her eyes as he lowered his head. His heart stuttered when she stretched upward to meet his lips. He kissed her with all the desire he had managed to keep under control—until today, when the fire of her presence released its bonds. They clung to each other as if life demanded it.

Flushed and breathless, Clarisse glanced around. "René, is

there somewhere..." Her voice came out a throaty whisper.

René wrapped her hand in his. He led her toward a small room at the back of the stable, a room John Calb kept against those nights one of his horses might need his attention. The bed stood in the corner with its stitched quilt pulled tight. Sun streamed through the window and cast a golden glow across the minute space.

Clarisse had removed her vest before they reached the room. She dropped it on the floor and then kicked the door closed with her heel. Blood pounded through René's veins. To finally be alone with her, like this, was more than he had ever imagined. René gathered her in his arms, not sure if this was the right thing to do, but knowing he had to touch her, had to hold her.

She opened her eyes and smiled. "*Oui*, René.

Unable to control the emotions that tore through him, he crushed her to his chest and kissed her. Her full breasts burned through his silk shirt and all thought but her disappeared. He whisked the remaining buttons from her shirt.

CHAPTER SIXTEEN

Château Gaspard, Bordeaux, France

VICTOR WRITHED. The all-encompassing pain overwhelmed the light of the single oil lamp. Crimson shadows danced in the corners of the room. He faded in and out of consciousness, determined to withstand the pain as some kind of atonement for his weakness. He made no sound, save for occasional grunts or labored gulps of air. His only thought was of René. Hatred so colored his internal vision that René's image appeared to him tinged with red. Within that hatred a sound reverberated—a discordant droning, deep and without resolution.

Then, from within that sound, a voice came. "You will die without vengeance."

Victor forced his eyes open, first one, then the other. There was no-one in the room. *Must I go mad as well?*

"You are not mad," said the voice. "But you will die, and René will live."

Victor struggled to sit up, but the reward for his effort was agony. A punctured bubble of pain from the infection eating his gut rose in a maleficent caress. He tried to scream, but his damaged vocal cords refused him even that release. Gulping short breaths, he managed to regain control. "You are only the pain."

"I am the pain, but I am not *only* the pain. There is a way."

"What are you?" Victor forced out the words through clenched teeth.

"An older part of you that once lived long ago."

"I have never lived before. Go away."

The pain increased until a wish for death formed in Victor's mind.

"Perhaps some small proof," the voice echoed in his throbbing head. Between one instant and the next, the pain disappeared like a candle's flame blown out by a quick breath. Then, like a tidal wave of boiling oil, agony once again submerged Victor's consciousness.

"Take the pain away," Victor screamed, but the agony only increased.

"I am afraid the pain is necessary, if our bargain is to be struck. You will need more focus than you are capable of, and pain, supported by your hatred, is the only way."

"Will he die in agony?" Victor forced the words out past each searing breath.

"With everyone he has ever loved preceding him."

"I must be there."

"I assure you that you will be in attendance."

"Do it!" Victor screamed within his mind. No sound escaped his lips. The pain's crescendo had robbed him of breath and in that instant, his soul disconnected from the body it wore.

Victor floated in a gray featureless limbo. He could think, but felt no sensations at all. The voice spoke again. Heard within his mind the words were thoughts and not of sound.

"Do not be afraid. You are not dead, nor have you finished the life you chose this body for. You are merely loaning it to me for a time."

"Who are you?" Victor strove to see, to see anything, but gray sameness swallowed him. Was this real, or had he created some kind of reference to hold his sanity within? Cold terror snaked through him.

"I am an ancient persona of the soul you are today. My physical incarnation took place three thousand years ago in ancient Egypt where I was a general and then Pharaoh. In that incarnation I learned the way of Maat, the way of power, and I was able to forestall the complete disintegration of the persona which occurs shortly after the physical body dies. My name then, and now is Horemheb. I have waited."

"How are you able to do this?" Victor collected himself, hoping to launch some kind of attack on the origin of the voice.

"Here, let me help you."

Suddenly there appeared around Victor the golden sand of a dry desert floor. Boulders cast long shadows from a waning sun. He could smell the desert. He looked down at himself and saw his form dressed and unharmed. He knew it to be an illusion. Walking toward him was a large swarthy man, dressed and armed as an ancient warrior.

Victor tried to summon anything he could use to strike at the figure but he was unable to move.

Horemheb laughed. "You have no power. You never did. Your only choice was to relinquish your pain, which any child will do. Once made, that choice is irrevocable. If I ever return this body to you, it will be because I have found a better one. You have lived a short life of stupid choices, but they were your choices." Horemheb continued past Victor and walked toward the setting sun.

"Wait. You promised that I will be present to see Gilbert suffer."

Horemheb paused and turned. "And I will honor that promise. Until that time, then."

"Wait." The persona that had been Victor receded into the matrices of potential, and another soul, an ancient soul, reveled in his place.

I am.

Horemheb commanded the body—now his body—to forestall death for a time. There would be continuous pain, but the dark arts allowed him to keep the body alive temporarily, and later, perhaps, for eternity.

Fully in control of Victor's body, Horemheb watched with pleasure as the terrified mercenary stood before François Gaspard and visibly fought to control his breathing. A muscle in his cheek twitched, its rhythm, no doubt, paired with his rapidly beating heart.

Horemheb relished every moment of the man's fear, remembering countless others who had trembled in his presence three thousand years ago.

"*Monsieur*, I hired two experienced mercenaries. I would not have welcomed a fight against either, yet Gilbert disabled both, and from the looks of them, easily."

"I am not interested in why your plan failed. They must have been drunk. How could a boy without experience defeat men such as this?" François Gaspard glared from behind the broad pecan desk in his book-lined study. A fire blazed in the hearth, but the room remained chilled. "My son was a powerful swordsman, trained by the best. Yet he was defeated, humiliated, apparently by a master swordsman. There is more to the boy than we were aware of."

"Just so." The mercenary breathed deeply, his body involuntarily shaking at his unexpected reprieve.

Deep in thought, the elder Gaspard gazed straight ahead, through the mercenary, as if the trembling man before him had disappeared. The only value Victor's father placed on life was in its use to him. A pig, a horse, a man, they were all the same.

After a short time, his gaze once again focused on the mercenary who had managed to control his breathing, but not the twitch.

"I will allow this first failure, for we have labored under incomplete information. I charge you again with killing this boy in a fashion that will ease my frustration. Use what resources you require. Do *not* fail a second time." Victor's father paused. The chill in the room deepened. "If I have to plan and execute this task myself, then I will have no use for you."

Those who were no longer useful to François Gaspard served his occasional need for amusement, his primary entertainment that of pain and its creative application. Horemheb well knew the father's loving punishments. Victor had experienced them all his life.

"I will not fail to accomplish your wishes, *monsieur*."

CHAPTER SEVENTEEN

RENÉ NEEDED some air. Ten hours of loading cargo had taken its toll. He had been aboard the *Belle Poulé* for a fortnight, and under Jacques's direction, the men shadowed his every movement. After he had inventoried each crate of wine in the hold, he asked the boatswain, Emile Lamert, for permission to go ashore.

Emile always seemed to be present whenever René went ashore. There he was, all six feet of him, standing beside the longboat as they prepared to lower it into the water. Word was Lamert could lift one of the culverins by himself and had once done so to reset the cannon's blocks in an engagement. The story was probably more legend than fact since the average cannon weighed a ton or more. Still, no one challenged the tale.

Being guarded twenty-four hours a day had grown tiresome. In a moment of nineteen-year-old rebellion, René considered losing his two-man shadow.

"Going in to wet your whistle, are ya, Worm?" The boatswain's stare would have melted varnish.

René remained calm and returned the boatswain's gaze, grateful for his years facing the Maestro. "Working in the hold is dry work."

"That it is, son, but there are worse things than being in need of a drink." The boatswain stepped closer. "Jacques has made a pledge to your father to keep you in your skin, and since he is the captain, 'tis my responsibility when his eyeballs ain't on ya. I hope you are not thinkin' of causin' mischief? Cause if you are, I promise to be standin' at the end of that road along with a world of trouble."

"I thought to have a small beer at the Gull." René hated lying, but he was going to explode if he failed to get a moment to himself.

"Have you got more work for me?"

Emile hesitated. "Nah, you stood your watch. You ain't a prisoner. The dockmaster wants to see our revised loading schedule, so I will join you at the Gull soon." He turned to the two large sailors who were to guard René and spoke, his voice a low growl. When the boatswain spoke quietly, the crew had learned it was a damn good time to listen. "Horsehair glue will not stick to him like you will. Is that completely understood?"

"*Oui, Monsieur* Lamert," they answered in unison.

They secured the boat, and Emile jumped onto the dock. René and his guards walked toward the Gull, which was about halfway down the main street. Along with the ever present smell of stale beer, the sounds of loud voices and smashing furniture rose and fell as they passed tavern doors.

The two men were so close to René they bumped into him when he stopped short. "I think I left my cloak here. I will just be a second." He turned into the nearest tavern.

René knew this was the height of stupidity, but once he had made the decision, he completed the task. He sprinted through the back door, then down different alleyways, and continued until he was sure he had lost his warders. Coming to a stop, he leaned against the wall of a building to catch his breath. A quick drink and then back to the ship. Oh, he would catch hell, but it would be worth it, or so he thought.

He chose the Trident because the crew never frequented it. The tavern was darker than the ones he had been in before, with a subdued undercurrent of dissatisfaction. René almost wavered in his decision until two men rose from a nearby table and bumped their way through the tavern to the door. He strode over and sat down. An older woman who had seen her share of life came over.

"Whatta ye have, young sir?" she asked, scratching her backside.

"Dinnae bother asking for wine cause we ain't got none." She laughed. "Not worth the drinkin' even if we did."

"A small beer," René said.

"Will you be wantin' somethin' to eat?"

"What do you have?"

Her face cracked into a grin. "Nothin' a bright young lad like you wants."

"Then why do you ask?"

"The longer I stand here, the less time I spend lugging trays around." She turned and walked back to the bar.

Always attuned to threat, René studied the room and its inhabitants. He listened with his ears and his intuition, the latter being the more reliable of the two. An undercurrent of threat eddied through the tavern, but he was armed. This small rebellion was stupid and childish and he regretted ordering a drink. He would pay, down the beer, and return to his ship.

"Here you go, love." The serving woman plunked the tankard down on the rickety table.

"*Merci.*" René laid coins on the table. Her face lit up, the payment being more than the cost of the drink.

"And *merci* to you, young squire." Her toothless smile broadened as she scooped up the coins, and sauntered away from the table.

Satisfaction over his successful escape vanished as he sipped the bitter watered down beer. After two sips, his vision distorted and his rock solid balance faltered. Was it possible there was something in the drink? He needed air. René stood and weaved drunkenly toward the door, but his vision had narrowed, and the door looked to be a thousand leagues away.

"Hey, watch out there, boy," a voice growled right before he crashed into a table. The seated men jumped up as pewter mugs splashed their contents across the scarred wood.

"Looks like the lad needs some assistance," a voice said from the doorway of the tavern.

Two men appeared, one on each side of him, and dragged René from the tavern. He struggled to fight back, but his body no longer answered his commands.

"Good thing we kept an eye on all the taverns," said one of the men to the other.

René's vision and hearing rapidly deteriorated. His last thought was of Clarisse as a dank blackness swallowed him.

At first, there was no sensation at all, unless a dissociated floating counted as an impression. Then René was moving. As he focused on the sensation of movement, his apparent speed increased. The walls of a tunnel materialized around him, its poorly-defined sides shot through with a collage of light and color. The tunnel ended and the light increased and his awareness of movement slowed, until he found himself floating, once again, a disembodied consciousness.

René allowed himself to sink deeper into that unique unity of focus the Maestro had taught him, and the details of the vision solidified. He sensed no threat. Somehow, he recognized where, and more importantly, when he was. He remembered.

The bright sun blazed its shimmering reflection from the Nile into the northern palace. The daily sounds of Akhetaten, the Egyptian capital city, filtered into the palace despite its position on a hill overlooking the river. The hubbub echoed against the giant rose-colored marble pillars adorning the immense Hall of Audience. The Pharaoh, Akhenaten, leaned against one of the pillars as if to enjoy its coolness as he looked out upon the late afternoon sun dancing on the Nile. He tilted his head upward; his eyes focused on René, and he smiled.

Welcome back. The warm voice of an old friend and teacher filled René's mind.

There was a knock on the huge doors of the chamber, and the robed vizier entered. "The esteemed general Horemheb, and the court physician Yochanan Ben Avram to see The Lord Akhenaten, may he live, prosper, and be healthy."

"Thank you, Ay," said Pharaoh, waving away his approaching assistance. Akhenaten slowly made his way toward the royal throne, pain evident in each movement. Once seated, he nodded to the vizier. "Show them in."

Two men entered the chamber. Both were young in years but old in experience. One wore hobnailed sandals, which made a rhythmic clicking noise on the marble floor tiles. The other, Yochanan ben Avram, was of medium height with curly brown hair and compassionate clear brown eyes. The large gold medallion on his chest indicated that he was Pharaoh's physician.

Akhenaten studied him as he approached. A rainbow of radiant colored light sprang into being around the physician. Somehow, Akhenaten shared a higher form of sight with René that allowed him to perceive the colored light. The doctor was surrounded by a brilliant golden aura tinged with purple about his head. The strong, prominent energy system revealed years of meditation and study. A small amount of deep browns, which René intuitively understood to indicate worry, hovered close to the young man's shoulders. There   was   something   about him that tugged at René's consciousness, some almost memory that struggled to return. As for being able to see the energies swirling around the physician, that skill felt normal, natural, even familiar.

The general marched toward the throne. Horemheb was a giant of a man, over six feet in height, hardened and muscled by military service. One of the youngest generals, his swift rise through the ranks came as a result of his decisive victories in Nubia five years prior. His role was to protect Egypt from her many external enemies.

That task is insignificant compared to the successful completion of the other.

Pharaoh's thoughts were clear in René's mind. Akhenaten studied Horemheb with his higher sight and René sensed Pharaoh's dismay at having chosen such a man to defend the light. Horemheb's   aura was shot through with red and black— understandable given his profession—but deeper within, he was filled with sickly reds and browns, the colors of greed and ego.

He is the one who will betray Egypt. Again, Pharaoh's thought came to René.

The two men had reached the dais. Pharaoh waited as they prostrated themselves on the marble floor before it.

"May the Lord Pharaoh be well, may he live, prosper, and be healthy," said Yochanan Ben Avram, his forehead touching the floor.

"May the Lord Pharaoh be strong, may he live, prosper, and be healthy," said Horemheb. Although he knelt before Pharaoh, his posture shouted his reluctance to kneel before any man.

"Rise, both of you, and follow me into my chambers. We have much to discuss and need not do so in this cavernous hall." Akhenaten attempted to rise from his throne.

Yochanan ben Avram rushed to his side and took his arm to assist him through the door at the edge of the royal dais. Walls were no impediment to René's etheric body. He flowed into the next room and then hovered near the ceiling. The room was still large, but more intimate. Wall hangings and rich carpets softened the black marble floor. The cedar couches upholstered in golden cloth sat facing each other in one corner. Servants placed silver platters laden with a variety of meats and fruits on an adjacent table. Yochanan poured Pharaoh a glass of water. The glass was a work of art, threaded with veins of gold and electrum.

"I will leave soon, and it will be up to you two to see Egypt through the times ahead," Akhenaten said. He sipped the water.

"No, exalted one, you will regain your strength and lead us yourself," protested Horemheb.

The physician remained silent.

"Not this time, general," Pharaoh replied. "I have given both of you all I know, and I confer the mantle of initiate upon you. You know the truth, and you must defend those who cannot defend themselves from the darkness that will surely come to cover the earth. This darkness is insidious. It will creep upon your thoughts like a lioness stalking a wildebeest. Only through continued vigilance and expanded awareness will you maintain communication with your Self and the larger whole. Horemheb, you will have the more difficult road to tread, for you must defend Egypt from her external enemies. Beloved friend, I know you will do your best, and I forgive you in advance for any errors in judgment you may make."

Horemheb's eyes flashed, then he lowered his head. "Thank you, Lord. My sword will be Egypt's defense."

Akhenaten sat back and looked at Yochanan, who met his gaze with such determination Pharaoh was forced to smile. "Beloved physician, whose understanding approaches my own, you see, do you not?"

Yochanan lowered his head. "I do, Pharaoh."

"Great darkness will cover the Earth for a period, and men of good intent will despair. The light must *not* be lost again. The fire must be banked against that time when the kindling of love will allow it to burst forth in all its splendor. I command you to create a structure that will allow the knowledge and skill to be passed down through the generations. It must have different levels, for each man and woman may only be given that which they can accept and use.

"Yochanan, I foresee your people will be a conduit for this fire down through the ages. Though it will burn them terribly, they will survive and succeed. They will be reviled and persecuted, for the darkness cannot abide the light. They will fall and forget, but there will always be a few who will carry the light."

Akhenaten sagged against the padded side of the couch. Yochanan reached for him. Waving his hand away, Pharaoh mustered the strength to continue. "Your people will soon be enslaved and forced into labor. The remaining priests of Amun-Re dread them, and rightfully so, for they stubbornly hold to the concept of the one, a truth I have tried to bring to my people. Once I am gone, the old priesthood will reclaim power, destroying the worship of Aten and all who worship the One in any form. The light will always dispel the darkness, and so the darkness is afraid."

"Will they ever be freed?" asked Yochanan.

"I have spent this lifetime trying to release us all from bondage. I have failed, but I am encouraged to believe the work done will not be in vain. When your people are ready, a leader will appear, and they will begin their trek along a hard road into the future. You will do your part to make it possible for such a man to exist."

"What of me, sire?" asked Horemheb.

"I charge you to protect my son and daughters, and my wife and mother. My brother, Smenkhakare, will rule along with my wife Nefertiti after I die. You, Horemheb, are to protect the succession for as long as you are able. When I am gone, the darkness will rush over Egypt like the waters of the Nile at inundation. The priests will re-establish the worship of Amun-Re, and take the people from the light of the sun back to the darkness of the temples.

"Rather than fighting against the inevitable, you must protect those I have loved. You have ever been at war within yourself, General. I fear it is not a war you can win yet. But I want you to know in the fullness of time, you will succeed." He paused. "I have grown tired and wish to rest. Know that you both have my blessing."

Horemheb and Yochanan stood and bowed to Pharaoh. "Yochanan, would you remain a moment, perhaps make me something to ease my sleep?"

"Certainly lord," replied Yochanan.

Horemheb backed out and then turned to exit through the door into the audience hall.

Akhenaten waited until the click of Horemheb's boots on the marble floor faded into silence before he spoke again. "You may not remain in Egypt. It is no longer safe for you here."

"From whom am I in danger?" asked Yochanan.

"The war within Horemheb will not last much longer, and it will not be won by the light. He will make a deal with the priests, for the lure of power is too strong for him to overcome. They will not abide your presence."

"Where would you have me go?"

Pharaoh paused to collect his breath. "To Greece. I have ar-ranged passage for you, as well as funds for the establishment of a school there. I expect you to maintain your connection with Egypt and to find a way to instruct those here who are receptive. But this you must do in secret. In the not-too-distant future, maybe fifteen or twenty lifetimes, a new city will rise on the coast, called Al Iskandariyah. It will become a center of learning, where scholars from all over the world come together. There will be a great library, a thing of wonder. That freedom and knowledge will not survive long, but it will last long enough for the seeds you will plant there to grow into a forest that can never be completely destroyed again. In this future lifetime, you will be called upon to guard the power of the ancients." Pharaoh took a deep, difficult breath and then another, his face wrinkled with the pain.

"May I give you something to ease you?"

"Thank you, but I would rather spend these last moments with a clear head. The pain will not last for long." Akhenaten gave Yochanan a wan smile before he tilted his head to stare up at René. "Dying is easy. Living within love is hard." He returned his gaze to Yochanan. "Do not hesitate to communicate with me when I am gone, for I will remain to help and advise you."

"If I did not know that to be true, I would quail before the enormity of the task you have set before me," said Yochanan. "Who am I to carry the weight of the truth?"

"A good man who knows enough to allow the truth to carry him." Pharaoh reached for his water.

Yochanan placed the glass into his hand. Akhenaten took a sip and then peacefully relinquished his physical incarnation. The glass slipped from his hand and shattered upon the unyielding marble floor. Yochanan sat back. The sadness on his face was laced through with fear and doubt. "Beloved Master, how can I do this?"

How can you not? It is who you are, and we cannot be apart, for we are always one. Akhenaten's voice echoed in Yochanan's head and René's as well.

Fear cleared from the young physician's face, replaced with a calm surety. He stood and walked from the room to advise the vizier that Pharaoh was dead.

CHAPTER EIGHTEEN

Off the coast of Bordeaux, France

RENÉ WOKE to a vicious headache. The world swayed, and a wave of foul seawater washed over him, smashing him into a bulkhead. He tried to stand and banged his head against the deck above. Dark as the inside of a tomb, a scant four feet separated the two decks. He rose again, careful to keep his head above the bilge waste that threatened to submerge him. A chain ran through a ring attached to an iron collar around his neck, its nether end securely bolted to the deck beneath the rancid water. His hands and feet were also manacled, each by two feet of heavy chain.

A ship under way. A slaver.

As the next wave crested below his chin, the rancid smell of sweat, bile, and human waste overwhelmed his senses, making him retch.

Focus on the breath. Come back to that rhythm.

His breaths were shallow because the awful stench was too much to bear. He extended his other senses. Without light, his eyes were useless, but the smallest sound gave voice to the space he was in, and the movement of the water told him something of the ship's speed and the weather and condition of the sea. He was the only one in the hold, if he failed to count the rats—and he chose not to count the rats.

Deal with the moment. Take stock of your weapons.

The Maestro's advice edged into his mind.

What weapons?

In his mind's eye, the fencing master's bamboo rod flashed. *Do not waste time considering what you do not have.*

René found his center and calmed himself. *I am alive, I am uninjured, and I have all you have taught me. Someone has made a bad mistake leaving me alive. The first rule of combat: Do not underestimate your opponent.*

He tensed a muscle in his left foot, held it for a count of ten, and then released it. Familiar with most of the muscles of his body, he had worked hard over the years to be able to control each one, both singly and in combinations. He would be ready when the opportunity came.

The strike of a wooden mallet reverberated as the hatch peg fell to the deck. The warped hatch opened a crack, illuminating the hold for the first time. René remained still. The hatch opened wider, and an intense beam of sunlight fell upon him. Even with his eyes closed, the brilliant sunlight blinded him.

"Do you speak English, Frenchie?" a man asked. René nodded. "You move a muscle, and I will take this food and water away and close the hatch. Don't know why you need to be fed, but the boatswain says you're to be conscious and in reasonably good health so you can enjoy meeting the sharks. You got a week or so." The man reached down into the hold and placed the bucket of slop and tin of water on a ledge within the reach of René's chain.

"What ship is this, and where is she bound?" René asked, not bothering to inquire about why or who.

"None of your business, boy. You will not be goin' far anyway."

"*Merci* for the food and water."

"Don't be thanking me. 'Twould be better for you to die down here. Sharks are a bad business." The man pulled himself out of the hold, banged the hatch shut, and knocked its wooden peg into place.

The pail held the garbage left over after a meal, but it was edible and he was hungry. He might not be fed again, and he would need every bit of his strength. He ate, drank, and slept as much as the rats let him. He killed one and threw it to the other side of the hold. Did rats eat rats? Possibly, because after that, they left him alone, at least for a while.

The days blended one into the next. Locked in the dark, the passage of time became unknown. The same crewman fed him once a day, but hunger was his continuous companion. He was never sure if he had eaten in the last twenty-four hours. At least they gave him enough water.

Crack.

A wooden mallet struck the hatch peg, its sharp retort rang through the hold followed by a high pitched screech as rusty hinges once again contested the hatch's opening. With his eyes no more than slits, René saw the shape of a man standing empty-handed in a shaft of brilliant sunlight. From the way he stood René knew him for the sailor who had brought him food each day. Short and stocky, and built of rock hard muscle, this was not a man to have as an enemy.

"Captain says for you to come up on deck for some air. If you try anything at all, 'twill be the last time you see the sun 'til you go swimming." He glared down at René. "Did you hear what I said, Frenchie?"

"I will not give you any trouble. You have my word."

The sailor laughed. "You are something, boy. I will say that for you. You always say thank you, even though you will soon be a dead man and you know it. Now you be giving me your word. And funny thing is, somehow, I know when you give someone your word, you keep it. Simple as that. Sorry you got yourself into this trouble. I guess powerful people didn't like their son sliced up, even if he had it coming." He unlocked the chain that ran through the collar around René's neck. His arms and ankles still had shackles and short chains, but he was able to stand for the first time.

"Do you need help ta get out?"

"*Merci*, but I think I can make it."

"There you go thanking me again. You're an odd one, you are," said the man.

"What is your name?" asked René.

"You surely don't need names where you're going, but if 'tis any comfort to ya, my name is James Bailey."

"*Merci, Monsieur* Bailey."

"Funny boy."

The bright sun defeated René's first attempt to open his eyes. The joy of the light on his face surprised him. Then emotion disappeared into iron held focus. Joy held no seat in this arena. He willed his eyes to adjust. He needed every minute on deck to memorize distances, numbers, combat readiness of the men, and their morale—anything and everything that he could learn. Doing his exercises had helped, and even though he could have stood unaided, he pretended to be suffering from his stay in the hold.

The boatswain, a large man with scars on his arms and face, walked over to stand in front of René. "Chain him to the mast."

Their gazes met.

"Don't look at me, boy." He backhanded René in the face. "Look down at the deck when I talk to you. You're some over-fed nobleman's kid thinkin' you make the rules. Surprised you ain't cryin' for your mama. You got a mama, boy?" he asked and laughed. When René didn't answer, he hit him again. "I asked you a question, boy. Don't try my patience, 'cause I ain't got none."

"My mother died when I was born." René studied the man's feet to see how he moved. All the while he cataloged everything in his peripheral vision.

"Well, not to worry, you will be seeing her soon." The boatswain turned to walk away then turned back and hit René again. His bitter laugh floated across the deck. "I just had to do that."

Though they had chained him in a way that forced him to stand, René had enough slack to turn and see most of the ship. He was aboard an English slave ship. She was an older carrack in design with the raised forecastle. She had seen better days, though. The fact that she was still on the seas suggested either a cutthroat reputation or an experienced captain. Under the wear, the ship was surprisingly clean, her ropes and sails newly repaired and in good order. Second rate though she might be, she was seaworthy. This was a veteran crew, competent in their tasks, and not likely to make mistakes that might allow him to escape. Escape. Even if he could, where would he go in the middle of the ocean?

Do not rush fate. One thing at a time. Do what you can do.

His master's voice echoed within his head.

He had to pick a fight and hope he survived long enough to create allies. The next time the big boatswain walked by, René laughed. "What are you findin' so funny, boy?" The man stuck his face within inches of René's.

The boatswain's right leg was shorter than his left and René doubted anyone brought that fact to his attention without regret.

"You walk funny." René called out loud and clear. There was no profit to him if he got beat up and no one knew why.

All work within the sound of René's voice stopped. Silence reigned. René had guessed right, and now he needed to survive his insight.

The boatswain froze, disbelief written on his face. The disbelief changed to rage. "What did you say?" Spittle flew from his mouth.

Even the captain had turned to watch. René counted on the fact that Gaspard's agent had given the captain a great deal of money along with explicit instructions that did not include throwing a dead boy overboard. What he could not know was how close to dead the agent considered acceptable.

"I said you walk funny," René said—louder this time, so there was no mistake in his words.

"Do you know what a cat is, boy?" The veins in the man's neck pulsed. His eyes were shot red with blood.

"A small animal?" René asked.

There was a laugh from the men standing around the mast. The boatswain's gaze turned like a snake seeking prey. The laugh died. Only the sea continued to speak. In the presence of death, the men remained silent.

"You, James, bring me the cat. I don't think this boy has ever seen a real one. Your education has been sadly incomplete, boy. You'll be thankin' me for this. I promise you." The man's voice was a rough whisper.

"Gob, there's no need to add harm to the kid. 'Twill find him soon enough," said James.

"Bring me the damn cat, Bailey."

James walked over and handed the boatswain the cat-o-nine-tails. He caught René's eye and shook his head. The cat had nine sinuous thongs of blood-encrusted leather dangling from a well-worn wooden handle.

"This here's a cat, boy. As you can see, it ain't no small animal. Now, there is a skill and a talent to usin' a cat, both of which I am proud to say I have. You see, you need to take care the thongs don't get all stuck together with blood and skin, which they're wont to do. If that happens, the cat'll take yer organs right out, and that's always a bad thing. So you need to run your fingers between the thongs every couple of strokes, to keep 'em separate. I gotta tell you—as much pride as I take in usin' the cat, sometimes I lose track. I try to keep count, but before I know it, I plumb forgot to clean the damn thing. I surely hope that don't happen today."

"I also have a skill and a talent, and I will kill you with it," René said in a low voice.

The man hesitated, confusion written across his face. He laughed a quick bark followed by an angry shake of his head.

"Pay attention, boy." He raised the whip before René's face, separated the thongs of the cat, and petted it in a sensual way. "Turn him around, and chain him up. You there, strip off his shirt."

A stroke cracked against René's back, sending blood and skin flying. "It usually takes me ten or twenty strokes to get warmed up, so don't get too excited yet."

You have my attention now.

René centered himself and forced down his awareness of the pain. He counted on his estimation of the captain and Gaspard's instructions. If he was wrong, he would be too hurt to try anything.

"Two."

The whip cracked and pain sang along the bloody stripe down his back. René refused to cry out. He needed the respect of these men if he was to survive.

"Three."

Crack.

Blood trickled down the back of his legs. Time wavered, and he faded in and out.

"Ten."

Crack.

The force of the cat drove him into the mast.

"Enough, Boatswain." The master of the vessel had a stern voice long accustomed to command.

"But Cap'n, I ain't nearly finished. I was just gettin' warmed up." The boatswain's voice was thick with frustration.

"Part of our bonus is to deliver this boy alive to his fate. I do not intend to lose money to satisfy your pleasure, sir." The captain was a tall, somber man with sharp eyes. He did not seem like the type of man to brook dissent. He called out to the crew, "Do any of you wish to donate your share to the boatswain's pride?"

A chorus of denials rang out, along with a few variations on "leave the boy be." As the men dispersed one of them muttered, "That is one tough kid. Never seen a man take ten without makin' a sound."

"Mister Bailey, unchain the boy and see to his wounds. He needs to be alive and aware in order for us to meet our commission." The captain turned back to his work.

The boatswain stood there seething. His hand twitched. Droplets of blood jumped from the sodden leather to land on the deck. He leaned close enough for René to smell his foul breath. "We have time yet, boy. You and I still have business before the sharks get ya."

René's eyes met those of the wielder of the cat. "I have made you a promise, sir, and I always keep my promises."

The man was mute in response.

"Come on, out of the way," James said. "Orders is orders." He unlocked the shackles that held René to the mast.

The boatswain cursed and then stalked away. He glanced back once. Hatred pulled his lips into a snarl.

"Come on son, let's get you somewhere I can wash you off and put some grease on those stripes." James helped René over to a keg where he could sit. "This is going to smart some, but 'twill do you good."

A bucketful of salt water crashed over René's back. He almost passed out from the shock. With teeth clenched, he forced the pain into that mental box where it would wait like an evil gift for a better moment to entertain it. He refused to cry out.

"I never seen a man take stripes like that," said James. "Do you not feel pain, boy?"

René laughed. A sob caught in his throat. "Oh, I feel pain all right. But I intend to survive, and screaming will not help me."

"I am sorry son, but there is nothin' gonna help you. The captain's a hard man, and he will do what he's contracted to do. You may count on it." James sponged blood off René's back then put some kind of grease on the wounds. "'Twill either heal or 'twon't. Not much else I can do."

The ship's master had walked over to check on René. "Mister Bailey, will he survive?"

"Not if I return 'im to the hold, Captain. That is the truth of it." The lookout atop the mainmast interrupted their conversation.

"Ship two points to the northeast."

"Where from," called the captain.

"Flag's English."

The fact that a ship was flying friendly colors was no guarantee she was harmless.

"Sound to quarters, Lieutenant," said the captain to an earnest young man standing beside him. "Don't open the gun ports yet, but ready the men."

"Aye, Captain."

"James, lock the boy in the small cabin, which is empty at present. Make certain there is nothing in there he can hurt himself with or use to get into trouble."

"Aye, Captain," James said as he turned to help René to his feet. "Come on son, let's get you below. Better quarters than you had before by a damn sight."

With his arm around René's shoulders, James helped him navigate the deck to the hatch and ladder that led below. Getting down the ladder was a bit of a trial, but once in the cabin, René stretched out on a bunk with only his arms and ankles shackled together.

"Get some sleep. I'll check on you later." James stopped at the door and turned. "Sorry, kid." James closed and locked the door.

René fought to remain conscious. Although his body demanded he shut down, now was not the time to sleep. He strained to listen to the comments from the men above deck.

"Did you hear what the boy said to 'im?" one sailor asked, with a coughed laugh.

"Yeah, I heard 'im. Ain't never heard anyone speak to the boatswain like that," said another.

"Not and live," said a third. "That is one tough kid there. Sorry to see him go. He'd a made a good un."

A scuffle was taking place right outside his cabin door.

"Gimme the keys," the boatswain demanded.

"No. Captain said to leave 'im be," said James.

"Give me that damn key, or you will be swimmin' with the kid," shouted the boatswain.

The ship lurched as splinters of wood exploded through the corridor six feet from where they stood.

"We're under attack," James yelled.

"We ain't finished yet, Jamie my lad. That was a bad mistake." The key turned in the lock, and James charged into the room.

"We're under attack," he shouted over the din. "I ain't got the key to the shackles. Only the boatswain has those. I will be catchin' hell from the captain, but no one should drown locked in a box." He turned and scrambled up the ladder.

René followed and stuck his head above the hatch cowling. Aft and to the starboard quarter, a smaller ship was rapidly gaining on the slaver. Moments later, it surged alongside, as grappling irons flew over the gunwales to pull the two ships into a deadly embrace.

The rigging of the new ship was Dutch. A privateer or pirate, depending on who was at war. The Dutchmen poured over the rail waving their cutlasses.

He spotted the boatswain positioned behind a group of sailors. René cast about for a weapon, then climbed above deck and pulled a belaying pin from the pin-rail. A wave of agony washed over him. He sucked in a few deep breaths to settle himself and pushed down his awareness of the pain. One of the deeper cuts had opened; blood trickled between his shoulder blades. He surveyed the deck and picked out the sides. At this point, there was no telling who would end up an enemy and who a friend. Fate had presented him with an opportunity, and he would make the best of it. First, the shackles.

The boatswain dove behind another group of sailors as a Dutch falconet swiveled toward the slaver's deck. A bloody mist of bone fragments and flesh exploded as the grapeshot decimated the sailors the boatswain had hidden behind. When the smoke cleared, René and the boatswain stood face to face, separated by nothing more than ten sword lengths of bloody deck.

"Thank you, Lord," the man yelled. He ran toward René, pulling his sword free and waving it over his head. "You're mine now, boy."

"Boatswain!" the captain shouted as the man ran from the fight toward René. "Hold. Leave the boy. You're needed here now."

The man ignored the captain and continued toward René. He came up short when he saw René had a belaying pin in his hands. Then he sidled up toward René, smiling.

"Found yourself a toothpick, did you boy? And what do ya think you can do with that?"

For René, time and space narrowed. There was no Dutch ship, no din of battle, no smoke or flying splinters, only an enemy who needed to be killed. René settled into as wide a stance as his shackled feet allowed and waited.

"Cat got yer tongue, boy? I would like to have more fun with you, but as you can see, I am needed elsewhere." The boatswain laughed and thrust his sword.

René turned, allowing the boatswain's forward momentum to carry him past. As he went by, René hit him in the face. There was a loud crunch.

The boatswain rose sputtering, yelling, and spraying blood. "You broke my damn nose. You're dead. Don't care about no bonus." He aimed a cut at René's head. René blocked with the belaying pin and then jabbed the boatswain in the gut with the tip.

He backed away out of reach again.

Doubled over, the boatswain glanced up. His eyes were glazed with blood lust. He cast about for reinforcements. There were none. "You're damn lucky, kid, but your luck's over. All you're holding is a piece of wood."

He lunged in with a high feint, his true intention a disemboweling stroke. René refused the feint and caught the blade on the chain between his shackled hands. He jerked it up, and then came down hard with the belaying pin on the pressure point at the juncture of the man's wrist. The sword came loose. René snatched it out of the air and pivoted, slicing through the man's throat. There was a great gush of blood and an instant of total disbelief in the boatswain's eyes as he died, crumpling to the deck.

"I do my best to honor my promises," René said to the corpse. He found the keys to his shackles and removed them. He reveled in his regained freedom no matter how short lived it might be. He lifted the cutlass. Shorter than the rapier and curved, a sailor's weapon of choice, it would serve.

René had not yet decided on which side to fight. Why he made his choice was forever a mystery, but he would remember the certainty that it was the right one.

The captain was engaged sword to sword with a Dutch sailor. An accomplished swordsman, the captain was never in any real danger from the Dutchman. As René's field of vision widened, another Dutch sailor appeared aiming a musket at the captain's back.

When all you have to throw is your primary weapon, be damned certain you have no other choice.

His life was not at stake, and yet his muscles were already moving. The cutlass sliced through the air, spinning, catching the glint of the flames. It sank into the sailor's chest with a distinct thunk. The captain had dispatched his opponent and turned in time to see René throw the sword. The musketeer collapsed to the deck, his musket going off as his fingers spasmed. The captain nodded to René and then waded into the fight again.

René stood there for a second, once again weaponless. He picked up his belaying pin and ran over to a Dutch sailor engaged with one of the English crew. Smashing him on the head, René relieved the man of his cutlass before he hit the deck.

"*Merci*," René said to the unconscious sailor. He smiled at the relieved Englishman and went to look for more of his new enemy.

Another Dutch sailor challenged René. The privateer's life was measured by a heartbeat. René disarmed and incapacitated his opponents when he could, killing when there was no other choice. He had picked up a second sword and wielded both. Walking death, he began to turn the tide of the fight almost single-handedly. This was his first melee, but he was within his element as never before. The English sailors followed him as he plowed through the privateers. The Dutchmen retreated and scrambled over the rail to drop down into their ship. The privateers had used poles with pegs along their length to help get aboard the higher Carrack, and René now grabbed one.

"To me!" he yelled. He leapt from the rail of the English ship, holding onto the pole as it sailed over to the center of the Dutch deck. The English crew followed him.

The privateers dropped their weapons when René turned to face them. The air stilled as he walked through the Dutch crew. Soon the sound of metal striking wood grew to a cacophony as they threw their weapons to the deck. The Englishmen stopped behind him, aware René needed no assistance. When the last Dutchman had dropped his weapon, the English crew roared their approval. They made certain of the disarmed sailors, pushing them into a seated mass in one corner of the deck.

René remained on the Dutch ship, awaiting the English captain's disposition. The captain descended to the deck. He was wounded, and one of his crew worked to bandage his arm as he walked.

"Enough. I will not die of this. Leave off." He walked over to stand before René who then lowered both of his swords to the deck.

"You knew what was planned for you, sir, and yet you saved my life and fought for my ship. Why?"

"I took you to be an honorable man, and I had no opportunity to make a judgment of the Dutchman's captain." René met the man's eye. "Do you think I made the correct choice?"

The captain smiled. The crew relaxed. A smile on the captain's face was unusual. Even injured, the man stood ramrod straight. That suggested a fighting background, and indeed he was dressed formally, in an old style British naval uniform with the epaulets of a captain of the lists. Probably, he had always worn that uniform. Intelligent eyes that missed nothing studied René. "You are an unusual young man. I am sorry, but I never learned your name. Would you honor me with it now?"

"I am René Gilbert, *monsieur*. I have trained for a position at sea—just not the one I was given aboard your ship."

"Edward Gordon, Captain of the *Albion*, at your service, sir." The captain clicked his heels and made a slight bow. "It is clear to me, as to all of us, that you have indeed been trained—something to do with a sword, perhaps?"

"I have had some training with a sword." René smiled.

"I have never heard the word 'some' used more inadequately." Laughter rang across the deck. "I expect you're hungry. Let us have dinner and talk about your future." Turning to his men, he said, "Secure this ship and lock her crew within their hold. An extra tot of rum for all hands." He then turned to the man who'd been trying to bandage him. "See that every man receives care, ours first, and then theirs. Come René, we're done here."

The captain pulled himself up a rope ladder thrown from the *Albion*. René followed him. Once aboard, the captain repeated orders to secure the ship and headed for his cabin. "James, tell Cook I have a guest for dinner and to allow the men an extra ration of rum tonight."

René made his way over to James and offered his hand. "You have saved my life, sir. I will find a way to repay you when I am able."

James returned the handshake. "Can't say why I did what I did, but I am glad things worked out. I will make certain the doctor gets a look at you when you're finished with the captain. Somehow, I do not think you will be using the hold as quarters again."

And that is a good thing.

Captain Gordon held the door for René and motioned him to a seat at a heavy oak table. Taking a bottle of brandy from the armoire, he poured two glasses and handed one to René. He then took the chair at the head of the table.

"It appears we have a few things to talk about," Gordon said, with a sardonic half smile.

"Captain, I mean no disrespect, but you are still bleeding. Would it not be better to wait until you have that shoulder attended?"

"Shortly you will meet my good friend Albert Hopkins, our physician. He has kept me on this earth even when I may have chosen to leave it. I cannot imagine it'll be long now. You see—"

The door banged open, and a corpulent red-faced man carrying a well-worn leather satchel barged in. Struggling to catch his breath he wheezed, "Edward, you idiot." Seeing that the man had company, his demeanor changed to one approximating proper respect. He cleared his throat while gasping for air. "Excuse me, but you are wounded. Would this be a good time to take care of that?" He paused and then added, "Sir."

"Albert, I would like you to meet a remarkable young man. I have the honor to present to you *Monsieur* René Gilbert. René, the honorable doctor Albert Hopkins, surgeon late of His Majesty's Navy."

René stood and offered his hand to the doctor. "I am pleased to meet you, sir. And while I look forward to trading pleasantries with you at a later time, I think we would both be happier if you attended the captain's wound."

"Nice to meet you, son, and I like the way you think already." The doctor moved to Gordon's side. He pulled off the remnants of the captain's shirt and inspected the wound. "Not deep. Didn't catch any tendons. All right, let's clean it out and sew it."

The doctor took the bottle of brandy from the captain and poured some of it into the wound, sluicing it out. The captain's face paled a little, but that was his only reaction.

René had always had a keen interest in medicine and watched Doctor Hopkins closely. Although a man given to food and drink, the doctor's hands belied his size. His movements were sure and swift. Using silk thread, he quickly closed the wound with small, neat stitches.

With only alcohol to deaden the pain, a surgeon's speed was a definite asset as long as skill accompanied it. René was pleased to see that in this case it did.

René waited until the doctor tied the run of stitches. "I had the opportunity to watch dissections at the medical school in Padua. My fencing master felt I should be thoroughly familiar with both the inside and the outside of the body."

"Would you be interested in apprenticing with me?" Hopkins asked.

"*Merci,* doctor. Under any other circumstances, I would leap at the opportunity. Unfortunately, I do not think I am destined to save lives. Most of my training has been in the other direction. I appreciate the honor of your offer, sir, but I must decline."

"There," the doctor said as he finished. He then took out a clean strip of linen and bound the captain's arm with it. "I will return to check on that, Edward.

"Now you, son. Off with what's left of that shirt."

René's lips tightened as he struggled to remove his shirt. Both Hopkins and Gordon had to help before it came loose.

"Here, sit on this keg. James did a good job with you, but a bit of brandy and a couple of stitches will not hurt."

As the brandy poured over René's wounds, he stiffened and remained silent. The captain met the doctor's glance and shook his head.

"Have you sewn up here in two shakes," the doctor muttered as he stitched René's back. "There. Now I want some of that brandy to drink."

"Thomas," the captain yelled at the door.

The door opened, and an elderly man appeared in the doorway. "Yes, Captain?"

"Tell Cook we will be three for dinner."

"Not for me," said Hopkins. "A brandy, however, will hold me in good stead. I still have work to do before I eat."

"Just the two of us then," said Captain Gordon. "And have Cook find something celebratory, the best he can. You might tell him time is of the essence."

"Right away, sir." Thomas backed out and then closed the door.

The captain poured the doctor a brandy and handed it to him.

"This young man saved our ship, and there is no denying it. I have never seen a sword handled with such speed and precision. Never. It was like the men facing him weren't even armed."

"I, ah..." René coughed.

"Don't even bother to say anything," Gordon said. "Too many saw you for you to pretend it didn't happen."

"I was trained with a sword from the age of five by a master swordsman." René sipped his brandy.

There was a pause as if the captain was weighing his words. The ship rocked gently. "I cannot deny my task was murder. The money from this commission released this ship from debt and freed me, and others, from certain ruin. I was once a moral man, but things happened that changed my life. I do not apologize for my deeds, but instead hope to make amends to you with my actions from this moment on. What would you have from me? You have given me my life and the lives of my men. If it be within my power to grant, you may rest assured you will have it."

"I must return to Bordeaux to protect my father and...others. I have only the clothes on my back. Have you searched the Dutch ship for plunder?"

"We haven't found her lock box yet, but we will. There's gold aboard that ship."

"What will you do with her once she is off-loaded?"

The captain paused. "I had planned to sink her after taking what we need. Now that I have cargo to trade, I cannot spare enough men to take her back as a prize.

"Would you consider taking off everything of value except basic supplies, guns, and powder, and giving me the ship?

Gordon shook his head. "It would be suicide to go over there alone. Even if I left you with enough Dutch crew to man the ship, I couldn't give you any men to stand at your back. It matters not how good a swordsman you are. You cannot take on the whole crew by yourself."

"You are correct, I need to sleep. But I only need one man. Given the circumstances, I think I can convince the Dutchmen to act in their own interest. If I can show you it is possible, will you consider it?" René asked.

"Let me think on it. We will talk again, after you look over their ship and sound out the men." A knock sounded on the door. "Come in, Thomas."

"Enjoy your dinner, Captain," said Doctor Hopkins, heading for the door.

"Albert, get me the casualty figures when you're able."

"Yes, sir." the doctor said as he left.

CHAPTER NINETEEN

RENÉ CLIMBED up to the forecastle. "Good morning, Captain."

"Ah, *Monsieur* Gilbert. Allow me to present Lieutenant Abbott. Lieutenant Richard Abbott, *Monsieur* René Gilbert," said the captain. Impeccably attired in navy wool and gold braid, the lieutenant was a tall stick-figure of a man with intelligent eyes and a large nose.

"Pleased to meet you, Lieutenant." René shook the offered hand. "You run a tight ship."

"We've a good, tough crew, but outmanned and surprised... well, the men wanted you to know you've got a lot of free drinks coming when we hit port."

"My motivation was to remain alive. Even now, as I think of my decision on who to fight, I cannot give you a clear reason for my choice. Perhaps it was the fact my English is better than my Dutch."

Both men laughed.

"A more probable reason is the care I received from Monsieur Bailey. I have to admit, I am glad of the decision I made."

"So are we all," said the captain. "It still leaves us, however, with a bit of a problem. We can probably disguise you or let you off somewhere before we dock, but keeping a ship's worth of men quiet is simply not possible."

"Have you given more thought to my request?" asked René.

"I had planned to take everything off the *Vrijheid* and scuttle her," replied Gordon, who turned to René and smiled his half smile. "Tell me what you're thinking, son."

"How many men would I need to sail the *Vrijheid*?" René asked.

"Well, ideally a brigantine would take a minimum of twenty-five, but I believe you could make do with eighteen." Captain Gordon pulled out his pipe and paced the forecastle. "With that few, you had better hope no trouble crosses your bow. Here's the way I see it.

"One, the crew needs to think you've died for us to get paid and you to get Gaspard off your back, even for a short time.

"Two, we need to make certain that thought does not become fact.

"Three, you've got to sleep.

"And four, I cannot spare you any trained men. I could send over a couple of troublemakers, but they'd be more harm than help. We need to address these points, or we're spittin' into the wind," said the captain.

"I need one man. One man I can trust. Will you give me James Bailey? I will not have you order anyone to go with me, but if he is willing to go, will you transfer him?" asked René.

"Aye, if he is willing."

"We have dealt with numbers three and four. For number two, no one can guarantee that, and I accept it as my responsibility, not yours. That leaves us with number one, a way for me to appear to die without actually doing it."

René looked out at the ocean's endless horizon. Of the many faces the sea presented, early morning was one of his favorites. Bright and filled with possibilities. "Can you stay here another day and let me spend the night aboard the *Vrijheid*? I need to talk with the men left aboard her. Then you can start by taking off the men you will need, leaving me the eighteen I choose. With James and myself, that makes twenty, and we can run with that. Will you leave us armed? Even though I do not plan to get into any scrapes until the crew has come together, 'twould be suicide for me to take out an unarmed ship. To put men at risk in a ship unable to defend itself would be the height of folly."

The captain turned to Lieutenant Abbott. "Have we taken off

their powder and shot?"

"No, sir. As we have enough of our own powder and shot, we thought it prudent to get their cargo first," Abbott replied. "So, it is possible."

"What if you cannot control the men and they turn those guns on the *Albion*?" asked Gordon.

"I can control the men." René's words came out ice-cold. From their expressions, neither man had the slightest doubt as to the truth of that statement. "The reality is—and I mean no offense, sir—when you cut the *Vrijheid* loose, there is no way the *Albion* could catch her with the wind or against it. If you will share your trading schedule with me, I will make certain we do not make the same ports."

"No offense taken, for I cannot argue with truth," said the captain. "I am in agreement if James chooses to accompany you. If not, we will have to think of something else. Without someone to watch your back, not even you will survive that ship. By the way, James is murder with a musket or a sword. He is the only man jack aboard who would gainsay the boatswain."

Lieutenant Abbott reached out to shake René's hand. "To the *Vrijheid* and her new captain."

"Give you joy, sir," said Captain Gordon.

"*Merci*, Captain."

René went topside to seek out James and found him up in the crow's nest overseeing repairs to the topgallants. A steady breeze rocked the ship on the swells. He scampered up the rigging to the cheers of the men on deck, and in short order, joined James.

"You there, tie it down right. We get a blow and it comes loose, 'tis you I'll be sendin' up here to retie it," yelled James at one of the men on the arm. He turned to René. "I had not expected to see you up here. Feeling dizzy?"

"I have spent many a long hour on the yard. A boring post most of the time unless you get weather. Then 'tis all the excitement a man ever wanted, and more."

"'Twill be that," James agreed. "Now that you're here, what can I do for you? I'm thinkin' you're not here to enjoy the sight."

"I need to get off this ship. Preferably alive. The captain has offered me the Dutch ship, along with eighteen of her crew. She will keep her powder, shot, muskets, and supplies aboard. I have experience as a navigator and can sail us where we choose. I have demonstrated my sword skills. What I require is a man I can trust to help me run the ship. I need a lieutenant."

"What are your intentions? Will you keep her a privateer?"

"*Non*. We do not need to steal to make a good living. I come from a trading family and know my way around alcohol and weapons. I have worked as quartermaster and have the knowledge and skill to make us money."

"Do you intend to sell slaves?"

"I do not, and I might take back what I said about privateering if I encounter a slave ship. I will not abide traffic in human misery or those who pursue it. I know what kind of ship this is, but my judgment of the captain is that he would not have chosen this vessel if his survival had not depended on it. Am I being naïve?" René asked as he surveyed the repairs to the yard.

"No, you've the right of it. Five years ago, one of the sailors we took on had the sickness. When we come into port, they took the captain's ship out into the harbor and burned her and everything the captain had with her. We had some hard times after that. Worked on other ships until the captain could buy the *Albion*. Best we could do. We could barely refit to make her seaworthy. She has never carried a slave under this captain, and no matter what, I don't think she ever would. Now the *Albion's* got a real cargo, 'twill not even be a thought. Soon as she makes port, he will rip out that hold."

James reached for the mast as a heavy swell canted the ship. "He didn't know why you had killed the boy. Still, he knew it had been a fairly fought duel. He's a good man, the captain, and he will be payin' for what he almost did for a while yet. Hey, turn it 'round!" he yelled at one of the men in the sheets. "As to your proposition...what share do I get? That is, if I decide to join you on this fool's venture."

"Half of what I get, you get. So if I get nothing, you get half."

René smiled.

"Smart-mouth boy. I expect I will have to be callin' you captain or some such?" James smiled back.

"I think that would be wise in front of the men. Ship's discipline and all."

"I am your man. Everyone dies; might as well have some fun beforehand. Now, you talk a lot. Let me see if you can do what you say. Get out there on the yardarm and help tie down those sails. Since I expect this will be the last time I give you an order, I may as well enjoy it."

René was already barefoot, so he jumped onto the yardarm and walked out to where the men labored All work ceased as every eye watched him. Eighty feet above the deck, he walked the yard as if strolling along a country lane on a windless summer's day.

When he reached the sailors working on the rigging, he said, "Mister Bailey seems to think I might be of assistance. Tell me what you need me to do."

After he spoke with the men aboard the *Vrijheid,* René was confident about seventeen. The eighteenth was the cook, and René had never met a surlier individual. A short man with long greasy hair and bad teeth, he responded to René's questions with bare civility. René had encountered grumpy, dissatisfied people before, but it was unfortunate the cook had a skill they needed.

When questioned about their work, the men were forthcoming, but when René mentioned their previous captain, they refused to meet his eye. The problem nagged at him. He and James separated the *Vrijheid's* crew into two groups, one to go to the *Albion* and the other to remain aboard the *Vrijheid.* Next came the ship's inspection. As they approached the mainmast, René stopped in disgust.

The mainmast was where corporal punishment took place. For larger offenses, flogging was typical, although more often with a single whip than the cat. The mast of this ship was stained solid red, from the edge of the deck right up to the height of a man. Undoubtedly, every man among this crew wore stripes on his back. The stain was ugly, and it would be the first thing cleaned when he took command. "'Tis a good thing their captain is already dead," said René, his jaw hardening.

"Aye, 'tis, for he wouldn't last long as crew," said James, his expression an echo of René's. "Leave the mast to me. We will finish unloading cargo sometime tomorrow afternoon. Since we never fired a shot at this ship, she is ready to sail. The remaining Dutch crew will be transferred before nightfall. Will you return to the *Albion* tonight?"

"*Non.* I will stay aboard the *Vrijheid* and get the feel of her. Captain Gordon copied what he needed from the *Vrijheid's* log and gave me the original. I have work to do and only this night to get it done. Gather your gear together with anything else you think we will need and bring it over early morning. My plan is to leave at dawn the following day." René clapped James on the shoulder. "And get some sleep. It may soon become a rare commodity."

"Aye, aye, Captain," James said, this time without the sarcastic overtones. "I will see you at sunrise tomorrow."

Enough for one day. René closed the *Vrijheid's* log. He rose and went out into the passageway. There were two other small cabins below deck and a hatchway down into the cargo holds, one of which held the eighteen men he hoped would see the advantages of sailing under him. He climbed down the ladder onto the deck and walked, surveying his new ship. With the exception of cleaning the mainmast, the ship was in reasonable repair. It was an older vessel, but René was certain she would move well. He completed his tour around the deck and headed back toward his cabin. He stopped, stretching out his senses. Something was off.

"You have a sense that is the combination of the other five, plus some indefinable awareness that has yet to be adequately understood," said the Maestro as he feinted and drove a

thrust toward René's head.

Parrying the thrust, René tried to tip-cut the Maestro's wrist, only to have his sword blocked and pressed down.

"How do you develop this sense if you cannot define or understand it?" asked René, parrying a thrust to the outside by circling the Maestro's blade and pushing it away from his body.

"Belief is the key. Faith is the door. Persistence will at last open it. I have not surprised you in a while. Do you think you can react quicker than I can act?" The Maestro thrust below René's left hand.

René swept his blade down and to the left, parrying the thrust. He followed through with a backhand cut to the Maestro's face that was easily blocked. "Non, I expect I am not that fast. Then how can I parry a thrust from you?"

"By using that sixth sense. We all have it; very few develop it. You have learned to watch the eyes of your opponent for the physical signal that an action is imminent. I have also taught you to hear the thought as it forms, even before your opponent's body recognizes it. The ancients believed in thought transference. One of the meanings of the ancient Egyptian 'Eye of Horus' signifies the ability to read other's thoughts. You will find that some experiences beggar explanation. You are at the beginning of a road that will go far beyond your current beliefs. Trust the evidence your reality brings you." Before the end of his statement, the Maestro had pulled a small dagger from behind him and stabbed René in the arm while forcing René's blade up and to the left with his rapier.

With blood seeping down his right arm, René stepped back and sucked in a deep breath. He transferred the sword to his left hand, and stepped forward again. "En garde."

René returned to his cabin, his sense of threat remained, unsatisfied. He would do what he could to prepare. Bordeaux and Clarisse waited and nothing in the universe would prevent his return.

CHAPTER TWENTY

CAPTAIN GORDON descended to the deck of the *Vrijheid*, followed by Lieutenant Abbott. "May I have a word with you, sir?" he called to René.

"*Oui*, Captain." René checked the last water barrel and then presented himself.

"Is there somewhere we may talk in private?"

"Of course. The captain's cabin. Follow me."

Located aft, mid-deck, Gordon inspected the Dutch captain's previous quarters. "He lived a damn sight fancier than I do. Still, being alive has its recommendations." Gordon tugged a heavy chair from the table and sat. "I don't suppose you have anything to drink?"

"Only a small amount of brandy that should best be kept for medicinal purposes."

"Oh, that will not do, will not do at all. Richard, have a couple of your men smuggle some kegs of rum back onto this ship. There are times when 'tis more valuable than gold." Gordon smiled.

Abbott nodded and left the cabin. "There's a storm coming," said Gordon.

"*Oui*, I sensed it, too."

"Will you be able to manage in a storm? You have to convince eighteen men to follow you. Oh, they'll get her out well enough, but after you're out of our guns' range—which we shall conveniently misjudge when we fire on you—will they follow you or toss you overboard?"

"They will not toss me overboard easily, but I am not invincible. I have given it some thought. This turn in the weather may even be fortuitous. If they want to survive, the storm will demand they work together under my direction. The sea, as you well know, is not forgiving. 'Tis a good plan, but I am open to a refinement if you have one."

"As to the loyalty or threat from your crew, that will be something you will have to figure out. As for keeping Gaspard's contract, we need to convince the *Albion's* crew of your death. We will smuggle over one of the *Vrijheid's* men who died yesterday. I have had Hopkins keep it quiet. The dead man is about your size. When you cut loose, have the men make a ruckus as if they're in a fight for their lives. Then have them toss the body overboard far enough away so that making an exact identification will be difficult, especially in a storm. Here, take this." The captain put a paper-wrapped package in René's hands.

"What is it?"

"'Tis a red shirt like the one the dead man will be wearing. We will bring him aboard in a barrel of rum. Make certain you pick the right barrel. Shame to waste good rum." Gordon laughed.

"No ruse lasts forever, but if we succeed, 'twill at least give you some time before Gaspard becomes aware you live. He is not a man to accept failure lightly. Well, I need to get back to the *Albion*. I expect this will be the last I see of you for a while." Gordon stood and extended his hand. "It has been a privilege knowing you, *Monsieur* Gilbert. I hope you manage to straighten out your affairs."

René clasped the captain's hand. "It has been an honor to know you, sir. Good fortune, Captain."

"And to you, son, as well."

Captain Gordon climbed back aboard the *Albion*. Lieutenant Abbott shouted orders to the ship above, and the Albion's men lowered a half dozen barrels to the deck of the *Vrijheid*.

"Secure that one to the aft rail and stow the rest in the hold," the lieutenant called out to the men. He walked over and shook René's hand. "Well, sir, I wish you the best."

"Thank you, lieutenant."

"Here is a present from the captain. He expected you might find a use for it."

Abbott handed over a carved wooden box. Inside was a small sword, longer than a cutlass but shorter than a rapier, with a silver hilt inlaid with precious stones. This was not a dandy's weapon; the blade was fine Spanish steel and had been used and cared for. There was a tooled leather sheath to go with it.

René was speechless. An heirloom such as this was priceless. "*S'il vous plaît*, tell Captain Gordon I will take care of his sword, and I will not dishonor it. It will be my pleasure to return it to him when next we meet."

"I'll be off then. Good luck." The lieutenant grabbed the ropes and pulled himself up to board the *Albion*.

The sky grew darker and more threatening by the minute. Then, as if the storm had taken a deep breath, the wind died. There was absolute calm, like the moment after a wave had returned to the sea in preparation for its next assault. It was time. In the confusion of separating the two ships, René hurried below decks. The next time the crew of the *Albion* saw him, he would be wearing a red shirt, and the ships would already be separated.

The deck of the *Vrijheid* appeared deserted. James waited with the crew below, ready to charge on deck and take control of the ship as soon as the *Albion* released her lines.

René's discussion earlier that morning with the crew of the *Vrijheid* flitted through his mind as he waited for the jolt that would signal his ship's release from the *Albion*.

He had entered the hold by himself, and after a short spirited discussion, James had obeyed his order to lock the door behind him. There would be no turning back from this point. Now was the time to establish himself as the *Vrijheid*'s new captain. He was armed, his sword held casually at rest by his side.

The lock made a loud click as James turned the key. René stood before them. Stunned, the men's expressions betrayed their disbelief that one man, one enemy, would come before eighteen men alone. René waited. The expressions changed as bewilderment became anger. A few of the crew started toward René.

"Anyone who comes within four feet of me will die. I have no time to explain or justify my actions aboard the *Albion*. I have killed a number of your shipmates. I regret that more than you know, but I intend to take over this ship. You have seen my skill with a sword. I will captain this ship, with you or without you. Are there any among you so foolish that you dare attack me now, unarmed? I hope not. On my honor, I will give each of you the opportunity to exact revenge with the weapon of your choice, once we are free of the *Albion*."

Not one man ventured another step. They looked at each other and then to a man, took a step back. Self-preservation had won the moment and the Dutchmen stood silent, focused on René. These were good men. They were not his men yet, but they could be reasoned with. René had chosen each one based on his sense of the man as well as his skills.

"I am a trained navigator, and I come from a family of traders. You do not have to accept my assertions, as I will prove them to you if you see fit to stay with this ship. A storm is coming, and the *Albion* will cut us loose. They may try to scuttle us, but we have a better than even chance to escape. Once loose, there is no way that ship can catch us.

"We are only twenty men, and that is a skeleton crew for a balmy day, let alone a storm. I have chosen each of you for a reason, and together, we can do better than just survive. If we defeat the storm, we will decide what is to become of this ship. I must warn you, I will not surrender this ship to you. Whilst I cannot take on eighteen of you, at least ten will die. You may not believe that statement, but 'tis important you know the truth as I see it." René paused for effect and then asked, "Who will sail with me until we have cleared the storm? If you will, take a step forward."

The cook stepped forward followed by the rest of the men. "*Bon*. If one of us prospers, we all will. James!" René called. "I am certain you will understand, however, if I do not unlock the door until we are free of the *Albion*. There is trust, and there is stupidity. If we survive, we will have the time to gain the one and reduce the other."

René rapped his sword hilt twice against the hold door. Again the click of the key and James held the door open. James locked the hold behind him and turned. "What do you think?"

"I think we have a crew. Most of these men were impressed from English or French sails. My hope is that there is no love lost for the Dutch ship that took them.

"Now we wait. A good swell is building and that alone will carry us away from the *Albion*," René said. "Return to the unloading. The storm will be on us before they can off-load everything, so drag your heels on the cases of muskets and the ax heads if you can. Every trade item they fail to remove is to our advantage."

As the wind rose, the sheets hummed and then shrieked. The men of the *Albion* rushed to cast off the lines connecting the two ships before the storm's fury turned them both into tinder.

The smaller *Vrijheid* struggled like a fish on a line, its hull banging against the *Albion*. James unlocked the hold, and the men poured out. René stopped them. "When we are fifty yards off, I will show myself on deck and yell to the *Albion* as if I have been left behind. 'Tis then I want every man jack of you to cheer and shout the devil at the *Albion's crew*. Convince them you have killed me while I retire below deck. 'Tis important the crew of the *Albion* thinks I am dead. Otherwise, they might decide to come looking for us. We brought over the body of one of your men who died in the fight. He will be thrown overboard to simulate my death."

Someone muttered, "No respect for the dead."

"I apologize for the indignity of tossing him, but I promise we will say a service for him once we are away. If we cannot convince them I am dead, you are all as good as."

The *Albion* released her last line. Without canvas, the *Vrijheid* slipped off the Albion's stern as the larger ship caught the wind. "All right, here we go."

The Dutchmen poured out of the hatchway and raced up the masts to raise enough sail to gain steerage. The ship fell away from the *Albion* faster and faster. Thunderous black clouds and driving rain blocked the sun. The noise of the rain battering the ship's deck almost drowned out the sound of the cannon as a shot burned through the air overhead. Although a part of the ruse, it was closer than René would have liked for the *Vrijheid* had moved away from the *Albion* faster than expected. René came up on deck wearing the red shirt and stood within a clump of men who waved their hands and yelled. He called out to the *Albion* and made certain they saw him before he slipped back out of sight. Hidden behind barrels lashed to the deck, James pushed a red shirted body over the side.

The *Vrijheid's* crew worked the storm. He had chosen well. Whether they accepted his leadership was another thing. Time would sort it out. Their ship was far enough away from the *Albion* for René to return to the deck. On the small chance the storm brought the two ships within sight of each other, he had changed shirts. Once above, he fought the wind across the heaving deck going from hand hold to hand hold until he reached the main mast. He cupped his hands around his mouth and shouted to the men in the rigging. "She can hold a little more top sail. Shake out the gallants."

The *Vrijheid* responded smartly to the additional sail. Pleased, René relieved James on the whipstaff and settled into guiding his ship through the storm. James and he had double-locked the arms locker and holds with new locks from the *Albion,* so there would be no weapons available to the crew. He had also put a new lock on the captain's quarters, and it had the sturdiest door on the ship.

The storm blew steady through a long afternoon and night. René stayed at the helm guiding his ship. He had James set up watches for the men resting them as possible throughout the night, making sure they were well fed.

Early the next morning, the storm blew itself out. Daylight increased as the rain slackened. The wind stayed high, as if wanting one more chance at the *Vrijheid*. James brought René a cup of hot tea. "Here, let me take the staff while you drink this. I wasn't certain there for a while, but it appears we've weathered this storm all right. There will soon be another one brewing, and 'twill not be from wind and wave. Are you ready?"

"As ready as I will ever be. 'Twould be nice if the wind died down a bit, however, if only to save me from yelling. Hard enough to communicate as it is. My Dutch is unused at best." René kept an eye on the topsails for a sign the wind was ready to ease off. "James, if the weather holds true, we will have a period of calm after the storm. One extra sword will make no difference. I want you to stay here, hold her on a west by southwest course. Make certain we avoid meeting the *Albion*."

The wind died as if someone had emptied the last gusts from Aeolus' bag. "Well that's it then. Wish me luck." René put down his tea, loosened his sword in its sheath, and strode toward the center of the deck, where the men were already congregating.

"Good luck," said James.

The men of the *Vrijheid* formed themselves into small groups, except for the cook, who stood by himself. On most ships, men took pains to be friends with the cook, no matter how grumpy he was, if only to get that little extra sometimes. That was not the case here. René allowed himself to settle into that quiet calm center where all would come together as it must.

"For now, my name is unimportant. What *is* important is I have taken command of this ship. I chose each of you for your skills. This ship will never again be a slave ship for either cargo or impressed seamen. Those of you who no longer wish to remain with this ship may leave at the first port we reach. Believe me, we will need every one of you to reach that port. I will not give up my ship voluntarily, so you will have to kill me to take it. Now will be the only time I will entertain your grievances. I can only guess how your previous captain ran his ship, but from the look of the main mast, 'twas with a heavy hand." The men glanced over at the cook, confirming a thought that had been building in René's mind. "James Bailey will be lieutenant and quartermaster. In the future you will speak to him, and he will relay your concerns to me."

The men shuffled their feet, uncomfortable with something, yet they remained silent.

"Is there a man among you who would challenge me for command?" René called out, his hand on the hilt of his sword.

More shuffling and then the cook walked over and pushed a huge man to the front.

"What's your name?" René asked the man.

"John Abel," The man stood well over six feet tall, every inch muscled and lean.

"Do you wish to challenge me, John?"

"I suppose so."

René paced back and forth, occasionally turning his back on the men. "I have never heard a more indecisive challenge in my life. What kind of captain could you have had? I expect he died hiding in a barrel somewhere. What kind of a coward trains a crew who think they might perhaps possibly want to challenge me?" The crew moved back from the cook. "On top of that, one look at the mast tells me this so called captain was a small, vindictive man more interested in seeing others hurt, always holding back in a fight. A coward, for certain. Hard to follow a man like that, one who always wants someone else to do his fighting for him. He must have been one of those small, frightened men who stab you in the back." René purposely turned his back on the cook offering him an easy target. If his suspicion was correct...

The cook lunged toward René, a dagger aimed at the center of his back. But René's preternatural awareness of the space around him had given warning of the attack, and the man lunged through empty space. With Gordon's sword at the ready, René faced the cook, whom he now knew to be the *Vrijheid's* captain.

"Just as I thought, your captain is a stab-you-in-the-back coward. One who will hide and pretend to be someone else to escape the responsibility of his actions."

"Don't stand there, get him," the Dutch captain had dropped his charade and screamed at the men. "He is only one man. He cannot kill all of you."

None of the men moved.

René took a step toward the man. "I don't want to kill any of you— except perhaps you, coward."

"You're holding a sword," whined the *Vrijheid's* captain. "Not a fair challenge against a dagger. You will kill me."

"Oh, I intend to kill you, but you're right, it needs to be a fair challenge." René tossed his sword to John Abel. "John, hold that for me until I finish cleansing the ship of this piece of garbage."

The *Vrijheid* captain's mouth twisted into an evil grin. "You've got a sword now, man. Kill him!"

John met René's eyes and nodded.

"Well, if you're not going to fight, at least give me the sword," pleaded the Dutch captain.

John shook his head.

René pulled a dagger from his belt and smiled. "Will you come over here, or do I have to chase you all over the ship, coward?"

"I will show you who's a coward." The cook held up his dagger and inched toward René. "Do you see this blade, boy? See the groove along its edge? 'Tis filled with poison. One touch and you're dead."

"I guess I will just have to avoid being touched." René said as he turned. Again the captain's blade struck nothing but air.

Furious, the man charged again, but this time their blades crashed together. The Dutch captain was well versed in the art of the knife, no matter that he preferred to attack from the rear. Thrust, parry, and then there was a line of blood running down his face from ear to jaw. He jumped back and looked around wildly, but there was nowhere to go. He charged René again. This time, when he withdrew, his left arm hung useless, its tendon sliced.

"I would prolong this, but we have a ship to run." René turned and blocked a thrust, and as the Dutchman went past him, he slid his blade through the man's throat. The *Vrijheid's* captain fell to the deck and convulsed as he bled out.

There was silence aboard the *Vrijheid*. No one moved.

"*S'il vous plait,* John, may I have my weapon back?"

"Yes, sir." John handed René his sword hilt first. René replaced the sword in its scabbard, and mentally thanked Captain Gordon for the weapon, relieved he had not been forced to use it. "Would you take a detail and dispose of that," René said, looking at the dead man on the deck. "Be careful of the blade. John, what was your rank?"

"I was the boatswain, sir." John answered.

"I would be pleased if you continued to fill that rank and those duties, sir," said René.

"Aye, aye, Captain." The big man cast a proud grin at his new captain.

"*Vrijheid* has been the name of a privateer and sometimes pirate vessel. I am changing the purpose of this ship and so will change the name. We will hold a proper de-naming ceremony after which this ship will be known as the *Seahawk*. There is one more task I want done immediately. Clean that mast and deck. I want to see the shine of wood, and only wood."

The men cheered.

"Do not mistake me. If you deserve flogging, you will feel the whip, but my intent is for the discipline to serve us and not the other way round. We will run this ship well, and we will get rich doing it. As of now, we are the LeClarisse Trading Company, and we will act honorably behind that name. Is that understood?" René said meeting the eyes of his crew.

"Aye, Captain." was the mixed response. These men had heard promises before, but René was confident they would give him a chance to prove his words.

"John, detail someone to relieve James at the whipstaff, as he and I will need to eat and then sleep. There is only a small chance of us running up on the *Albion*, but to make sure, we will change course to east by southeast. Oh, and we will need a cook. Is there any chance one of you has some experience? It would be a damn shame for us all to die of malnutrition after having survived this long."

The men turned to look at a small man who stood in the back. They pushed him forward.

"And you are?" asked René.

"I am Calvin Downs, sir," he answered, doing his best to control the tremor in his voice.

"Tell me you know something about cooking?"

"Well, sir, I am the cook. The captain made me say I was gun crew.

"The saints are smiling on us now. At least, I hope they are."

René stole a look at the crew. The men were grinning. René nodded. 'Twas a good sign when a crew cast their favor upon a cook, a very good sign.

James approached. "Have you a port in mind, Captain?" "Once we are certain to avoid the *Albion*, make for the Port of Bordeaux. I have unfinished business there."

CHAPTER TWENTY-ONE

THE SUN was in his eyes, and René blinked to clear his vision. He had fallen asleep in the captain's cabin aboard the *Vrijheid*—the *Seahawk*—after the storm, but he was no longer aboard ship. Instead, he appeared to be back at Château Gilbert, in the courtyard, waiting for his fencing master to appear and begin the day's practice.

This is a realistic dream. But is it a dream? Everything is so real. He walked to the training table and chose his favorite, the rapier.

"En garde," *said the Maestro from behind him.*

Knowing better than to speak or question the Maestro, even within a dream, René turned to meet the first strike speeding toward him. He raised his rapier in time, blocked a high strike and then disengaged. Taking a deep breath, he deepened his focus and balance as he centered himself. The Maestro would explain in his own time. René's responsibility was to remain uninjured long enough to hear the explanation. He settled into that cold, calm state of focus and faced the master. A feint, a thrust, as the Maestro's sword danced with incredible speed and precision. Disengage, block, and riposte. René bided his time for an opening. Somehow, this sparring match felt different. René was stronger and older, but more than that had changed. He had gained a quality of awareness that only the specter of death could provide.

The Maestro advanced. His sword, a singing blur, touched

René's left shoulder.

René winced. That answered the question as to whether I would feel pain or not.

René ignored the pain and turned into the next strike, blocking the Maestro's blade by forcing it down and to the left. As he moved forward, he continued the turn, stepped into the Maestro and transferred all the power of the turn from his legs through his torso and into the point of his elbow, striking the Maestro below his left ear. The man collapsed into the dirt like a wooden marionette whose strings had been cut.

René secured the Maestro's sword with his boot and then took it from his hand.

Never leave an opponent armed. Do not assume incapacitation. *Even within a dream, as he faced his fencing master, the lessons the Maestro had drummed into him every day except Sunday came back to him. The thought made him smile. The wise choice was to allow the Maestro to awaken on his own. René sat at the table and poured himself a cup of tea. He examined his arm. Although it was bleeding, the wound was only a scratch.*

The Maestro twitched and then sat up. René waited for the meaning of this experience to come to him. The man had a huge smile on his face as he stood and came over to the table. René pushed off his chair.

"Do not stand for me. Our relationship has changed." Maestro *rubbed his jaw, moved it gingerly. "That was an excellent strike. I could not have done better. May I sit?"*

"Of course. Would you like tea?"

"Oui."

René poured and waited patiently. Taught to be intensely aware of his surroundings, he noticed that the shadows on the courtyard wall had not changed position.

"This will perhaps go quicker if you ask," said the Maestro.

"Why am I here?"

"René, you are a member of an ancient brotherhood. We have all agreed to return lifetime after lifetime, to protect our younger siblings until we are no longer needed."

"Then this brotherhood has chosen poorly, for I have killed

many more than I have protected." René stood abruptly and walked over to the pile of bricks lifting one from the pile. Holding the brick he faced the Maestro. "I am death incarnate. I have protected no one, least of all those I love."

"We rarely know how well we are doing in any lifetime. I assure you that you have indeed saved hundreds and hundreds more unborn. Each act, like a pebble tossed into a pond, reverberates, each created wavelet adding to or canceling out others. Even the smallest act has effects much larger than recognized at its inception. Do you trust me?"

René studied the brick in his hand and then tossed it back on the pile. "My intuition confirms your identity, but this place is a construct. If this is but a dream, then you may represent a symbol I am unaware of."

"And if this is not a dream? Over the years, I have taught you to recognize the illusory nature of the world. There are an infinite number of realities played out at the same time, and this place is but one. I felt its familiarity would aid our exchange of information. I can easily change it if you wish."

"Non, I find a certain comfort in facing the unknown here," said René with a wry smile. "I trust the Maestro, and even if you are only symbolic, I do not think I could create a deceptive symbol in your form. What would you have me do?"

"What are your plans?"

"To return to Bordeaux and kill François Gaspard."

"Revenge?"

"Non. I have sampled revenge, and I like neither its taste nor its after-effects. The only way I can protect my father and Clarisse is to remove the threat he poses. Gaspard is high in the lists, with the king's ear. No matter how much wealth I acquire, I will never be able to protect those I love as long as he remains." Unable to stay seated, René rose and began to pace.

"François Gaspard is not your enemy, René."

"If not Monsieur Gaspard, then who?"

"You have an ancient enemy, once counted your dearest friend. He will do his best in this lifetime to remove you from the stage, but as I have taught you, you must patiently gather your

resources, choosing the ground and time of your conflict. Your final battle with him will occur in a place where the only limits are those you accept.

Until you reclaim the skills and awareness you have earned over hundreds of lifetimes, you will have no chance of victory."

"Can you tell me his name?"

"You will come to his name in due time. For now, know that your true enemy is not François Gaspard."

"What if I choose to ignore this dream and return to Bordeaux anyway?"

"You will fail, and mankind's misery will be prolonged for thousands of years. Time is a moving river, and one's vision of it has certain limitations based on the available light and the shape of any particular stretch. Make port at Marseilles. Your best destiny will be found there."

The courtyard began to fade.

"Wait, I must know of Clarisse's safety," called René.

The Maestro was already becoming transparent. He smiled sadly. "She will not be harmed by the Gaspards. Destiny is never arbitrary. It is an agreement forged in love between the souls who create it."

Then the sun was again in René's eyes, but coming from the portholes in his cabin, the captain's cabin aboard the *Seahawk*. He sat up. The ship gently swayed, accompanied by the reassuring sounds of a vessel making headway. From the angle of the sun, he had slept for almost twenty-four hours straight. As he swung his legs over the side of the bunk, his heel banged into wood with a hollow sound.

He inspected the bottom of the bed. It sat on a raised wooden foundation. There should have been drawers or moveable boards, but he found none. He walked to the end of the bed and inspected the baseboards. They were the same. Why build a bed without storage underneath? Space on an ocean-going ship was always at a premium. Often, trade goods filled the captain's cabin.

René pulled the down mattress off the bed. The bottom of the bed was wood, but it had an unusual pattern of slats and a space at one corner. René slid the board, creating a space at the other end. He then pulled the perpendicular board until it filled that space which created another space. He continued until a board in the middle of the bed popped up. He leaned over to pull up that piece of board and then stopped. An eerie sensation slithered along René's spine. Something was not right. He studied the configuration of slats and the space left beside the loose board. Grabbing a large pewter candleholder, he wedged it into the space. Then he pulled up the remaining board to reveal a storage space beneath the bed.

Bright sun beamed through the windows, illuminating the secret space. Within lay two padlocked oak chests. The larger was a rectangle two feet by one foot by one foot and the second, half the size of the first. There was also a flintlock pistol armed and aimed at the hole. The insertion of the candleholder had blocked the wire from increasing tension on its trigger mechanism.

Carefully, René released the wire from the trigger and lifted the weapon from its frame. The padlocks were old and rusted and offered only momentary resistance. The larger one was filled with silver. In the smaller, the brilliant gleam of gold reflected the sun's light. René sat back on the wooden slats and contemplated his luck. Without the storm, the *Albion*'s crew would have discovered the captain's secret stash. Now, the *Seahawk* would get a first class refit with enough left to fill her hold.

René rummaged through the clothing he found in the previous captain's sea chest. He located a shirt that looked about his size and pulled off his own. He stopped. There on his left shoulder was a newly formed scab. It was a wound left by the touch of a rapier, the Maestro's rapier.

Do not challenge meaning, for it will either blossom in its own time or not, and as you cannot force a flower to grow, neither can understanding's tempo be commanded.

He placed his finger on the scab. The wound looked clean, but he would douse it with brandy and cover it. Wounds had a way of festering on a ship, and he would need to attend to those on his back. He hadn't asked the crew if anyone had any medical experience. He would see to that as well. He glanced at the wound once more and then continued dressing. For now, he needed to read through the captain's rutter. Every piece of information he could learn of the *Seahawk* and her history would be crucial if he was to captain her successfully.

"Come in." René set aside the logbook. No response.

"Come in," he called again, louder. The door remained closed. René slid his sword from its scabbard and stepped toward the door. Standing to the side, he yanked it open. There before him was a thin tow-headed boy of about eleven, attired in tattered oversized clothing. The lad did his best to remain in a posture of rigid attention, but he could barely stand. His undernourished frame shook so hard, his teeth chattered. "Your p...pardon, sir, but Mister Bailey said I was to be your steward, sir."

The boy appeared terrified. His gaze fixed on the sword in René's hand then past his shoulder, then back to the sword, anywhere but René's eyes.

"Relax, I am not going to use this sword on you." René paused. "Unless you deserve it."

The boy turned whiter.

"That was a poor joke. What is your name?"

"Sir...my name..." He stuttered.

"You know, the one your mother gave you. People use it to get your attention."

"An-Andrew, sir," the boy answered. "Andrew Merchant, sir."

"Ah, *bon*. You are English, *oui*?"

"Yes, sir. I was aboard the *Regency*. But the *Regency* ain't no more." The boy grasped the sides of his legs as he struggled to get his trembling under control. "Mister Bailey said the first thing you'd be needing was something to eat, and I was to bring it soon as you were up and about." Andrew kept a watchful eye on René's sword.

"Andrew, let me make one thing clear. You do not need to fear me unless you make a large mistake in your allegiance. I will expect your best no matter what you're doing, but mistakes happen. As long as they do not happen through sloth or negligence, we will use them to learn from, you and I both.

"How long have you been aboard this ship?"

"Seven months now, sir."

"Turn around, Andrew. Let me see your back."

The boy turned and pulled up his shirt. His back was covered with countless lash-stripes. Angry welts ridged through them, some of them obviously of recent application. René's expression changed from disgust to anger. Apparently no one aboard this ship lacked such scarring.

"I am sorry you had to sail under so poor an excuse of a man as your previous captain. You will be expected to do your work, and you will be paid. It will be up to you whether you decide to sail with this ship or not when we reach port. Do you understand? If you decide to return home, we will arrange it. At the least, you will write and tell your parents you are safe and have found gainful employment."

Andrew's eyes glazed in disbelief. His shoulders slumped lower with each promise. "Yes, sir."

René nodded, understanding the boy's reaction. "Do you know why you were chosen for this crew?"

"No, sir."

"A ship is not run by muscle alone. There are times when cleverness is called for. There are places where a fully-grown man cannot reach. I have done all the jobs you will be called upon to do, and I am none the worse for it." René paused to think on the responsibility he now shouldered. "Well then, go and see if cook has something for me. Mister Bailey was correct, I am famished."

As Andrew turned to go, René said, "*S'il vous plaît,* ask Mister Bailey to attend me at his convenience."

"Yes, sir, Captain," said Andrew, racing up the gangway.

For an instant, he was that young boy. René smiled and then returned to the maps and rutter of the previous captain. He spread out the map and plotted a new course, one that would take them to Marseilles.

"You asked for me, Captain?" James Bailey knocked on the open cabin door.

"*Oui*, come in Mister Bailey, and close the door."

"Sir?" Attired in an older-style navy uniform minus its insignia, James Bailey stiffened to attention, his blue eyes alight with the humor of the situation as he stood before the table. "I felt it proper to begin duty in dress, sir."

René bit back a smile and addressed James with the seriousness the moment called for. "James, we will need to establish and maintain a proper formal relationship so we can get this ship on an even keel, but in private, I expect you to let me know when I am being a horse's ass. Otherwise, I am bound to enter the realm of stupidity more often than I would like. Do you think you can do that?" René gestured for James to take a seat.

With his usual half-smile, James said, "I expect I might be able to do that."

"*Bon*, let's get to work." René spread out a map on the table. "My long-range goal is to build a trading company to challenge the Gaspards—or at least one strong enough to protect itself. My father's company, Gilbert, Ltd., has five ships at sea, with a new one in the yards. At some point we will combine our strengths, but for now, remaining invisible is our best defense. We will make port at Marseilles.

"I thought you planned to return to Bordeaux."

"I have changed my mind. I now believe that it would be foolhardy to challenge Gaspard with little more than I had when I left."

"You have a ship."

"Which will need a good deal of work before it is a threat to anyone."

James appeared distracted, his gaze directed around the room. "I am sorry, have you eaten anything? I will have Andrew bring you something."

"I was looking for something potable. Prerogatives of rank and all that." James smiled.

"There's brandy in the cabinet."

James rose and walked over to a large mahogany armoire and took out a silver tray on which stood a decanter of brandy and two glasses. "Will you have one?"

"*Merci, non,*" said René still focused on the map. "I am not that sharp under the influence."

"Out here, I expect that'll change," James said.

"I expect it will, but not today." René turned the map so that James could read it. "Captain Gordon will go first to London to sell his cargo and get the *Albion* refitted and then on to Bordeaux to claim the balance of his fee. Unfortunately, 'twill be some time yet before I can risk contacting my family. As hard as it will be on them, I believe we need to let the waters settle over the news of my death first.

"I have not given my name to the men aboard this ship, and for now, I think it wise to use a *nom de guerre*. I shall be René Dalembert. 'Tis a poor way to begin, by lying, but I see no other way around it. I refuse to enslave these men further. If they want to get off at our first port, so be it. I can ask they keep secret my sword prowess, but secrets between two people rarely last. With twenty, well, we will not be in port for long. What I do not want is for young brawneys calling me out to prove themselves."

"'Tis certain I cannot nursemaid the bunch of 'em," said James. "We will need more men we can trust in on this. The boatswain seems to be reliable."

"I agree. Still, we will have to find at least one other to keep an eye on the men while we're in a French port. I mean to stop in Marseilles for refit." René paused, smiling. "And trade goods."

"When did we come by the currency to acquire a cargo?"

"When I found the previous captain's lockbox. We are in business now. We also have enough to pay the men, which may help a bit with their loyalty, given we have had little time to earn it."

There was a knock on the door. René called out, "Come in, Andrew."

Andrew entered, followed by the cook, carrying trays of steaming food, which they put on the table. Downs was not much taller than Andrew, but his clothing was clean, and his demeanor was fastidious, which boded well for the health of the crew. He was a slim man with red hair and a freckled sunburned face. He placed the food on the table with confidence. The aroma from the platters gave proof to the man's expertise, and his sunburned face meant the crew welcomed his presence above deck. That was not always the case for a less capable cook. René was grateful for this stroke of good fortune.

"By your leave, sir," Mister Downs asked, preparing to withdraw.

"Mister Downs, is there any chance you have some chocolate in the larder?" René feared he already knew the answer.

"No, sir, but I am certain we can pick some up at our first port. If you let me know your food preferences, I will take care of it."

"*Merci*. I am not a picky eater, and whatever you have will be fine. How long do we have before we must resupply food and water?"

"We've got two months, maybe three, 'til we need to make port. We were on our way in when we ran into the *Albion*. Will there be anything more, sir?"

"I can see there is plenty here for me and Mister Bailey, so that will be all for now. *Merci*, Mister Downs," René said. Andrew hesitated at the door, and René added, "Andrew, report to the boatswain, and see what he has for you to do."

"Help yourself, James," René said as he took one of the bowls of stew. "She has been out long enough that we will need to check the hull for shipworm."

"I have already sent one of the men over the side, and we're working the bilge pumps pretty hard." James picked up a journey cake from one of the platters. "We will need to put in to refit before long."

"Marseilles is large enough that we should remain unnoticed, and Gilbert Ltd. has a factor there. We will arrange for a cargo as well as obtain information." René stood and poured himself a small beer. James stood as well.

"What are your orders?"

"Gather the men together. I want to know where we stand if we are called to battle. Have you had an opportunity to inventory the ship?"

"I inventoried the shot and powder first and then the supplies. We'll inventory what cargo we have next. We have enough powder and shot to get through two engagements. After that, we will be throwing our socks at 'em."

René rolled up the maps and replaced them in their leather tubes. The well-worn leather in his hand brought back the memory of that day on the road to the port, but now was not the time to entertain memories. He cleared his throat. "I make us about five weeks northwest of Marseilles. Let us hope there are no engagements we cannot handle. I will be topside in ten minutes. Assemble the men."

"Aye, aye, Captain," James said as he left the cabin. René shortly followed him above deck.

The men were gathered before the aftcastle. James and John Abel stood on the raised deck facing the men. René joined them and surveyed his crew.

"I have decided we will make port in Marseilles in order to refit and take on cargo. Your previous captain has left behind a gift for you. I have found enough gold and silver for us to refit the *Seahawk*, purchase a cargo, and pay each of you for your trouble."

The men roared their approval. René waited until they quieted and then continued.

"Well, Mister Bailey, let us see what we have to work with. *S'il vous plait*, call the men to quarters."

"Clear for action!" bawled James.

The men raced to their previously assigned stations. "What do you think, Mister Bailey? Can we fight?"

"We can either fight or run, but not both. We haven't the men."

"My thought as well. We cannot hope to survive a cannon battle. Our best strategy is to run if we can or, failing that, come in close enough to grapple. Man to man, I believe I can reduce the odds a little."

"A little?" James cocked his eyebrow.

"Unfortunately, the odds still do not favor our survival. We will begin fencing lessons this evening."

"Yes, sir," James said while motioning to the boatswain.

A golden trail followed the ship, painting the ocean until it reached the setting sun in a blaze of red gold. René had commanded lanterns be lit so there would be enough light on the deck. Each man was armed with a three-foot length of oak, that being the most prevalent lumber aboard. Not as forgiving as bamboo, oak was still reasonably safe. René didn't want to accidentally lose or maim any of the men. Until he gauged their proficiency with a sword, they'd spar with oak.

"Any man who manages to take this length of oak from my hand will be richer by a gold sovereign before the day is out," René said, to an increasingly positive murmur from the men. "I intend to teach you how to fence. During these fencing lessons, I will not tolerate anything less than your complete attention, which you will soon find expeditious to give me. I can only teach as I was taught. So, come to *en garde*, if you know it, and if not, to whatever position you would take to defend yourself. If you learn nothing else but this balanced stance, your life expectancy will increase in a fight."

The men came to a variety of positions with only a handful having any real idea of the basic stance of fencing. René demonstrated *en garde*.

"*S'il vous plait,* copy this stance as well as you can, and hold it." René went from man to man, correcting his stance, his arm placement, or both. Then he watched his crew struggle to hold up their bits of oak.

After a short time, one man cursed and lowered his wooden sword. "I ain't standin' here holdin' up a bloody piece of wood."

Faster than a blink, René was in front of the man. *Smack*, the oak was out of the man's hand and on the deck. He then thrust his own wooden sword into the man's solar plexus. An eerie silence pervaded the deck, except for the man bent over wheezing, desperately trying to regain his breath. The men there knew full well of their captain's skills. René addressed them.

"If we are attacked, my life will be at stake. I want you to know I am deadly serious when threatened. You *will* learn to fence properly. It will hurt, but you will learn anyway. The only promise I make to you is that the more you pay attention, the less pain you will receive. Fencing is always painful for someone. Your only choice is who that someone is. Now, *s'il vous plait,* show me *en garde.*"

The men snapped into their best approximations of *en garde,* including the first man, who was still gasping to regain his breath.

"*Bon.* Now hold this position until your muscles are more than familiar with it." René walked among the men, widening a stance here and pushing an arm up there. After a number of minutes, the men began to sweat, no one wanting to be the first to lower that wooden sword. Arms began to shake, but no one gave up. René smiled. He had chosen a good group of men; they could and would learn.

"All right, swords at rest," he called.

The men lowered their swords with some quiet inadvertent groaning but they managed to remain standing, their focus on René.

"Mister Abel, would you please demonstrate *en garde*?"

While he was the largest man there, John Abel was also the most coordinated. He assumed a close approximation to the proper position for *en garde.* His balance and familiarity with the position argued for some previous training.

"Close, Mister Abel. Very close. Move your arm a bit higher. *Oui,* and widen your stance a bit." René turned to face the boatswain. Without warning he thrust toward the man's chest. Abel managed, barely, to parry the thrust. "*Bon!* Your enemy will not wait to see that you are ready, and neither will I. Because your first position was correct, you were able to block even a thrust from me. We will not be able to go over more than the basics on this voyage, but if you choose to stay with this ship, you will never meet your equal in a sword fight. Now, let us begin practice. Mister Abel, will you help me teach *en garde*?"

"Yes, sir, Captain." Facing the men, the boatswain bawled, "All right, you dolts, assume *en garde.*"

The men came to the *en garde* position again, but this time with much greater attention. René and the boatswain went from man to man, correcting both arm and stance until all the men were in correct position.

"And now hold that pose." René walked between the men. Though a few were shaking with muscle fatigue, not one allowed the wooden sword to drop until René permitted them to rest. When he called them to *en garde* again, the swords went to a much closer approximation of the position, along with an increase in their confidence level.

The lesson went on for three hours, and by its completion, the men were thoroughly exhausted.

"I have instructed the cook to increase rations, as we intend to be in port within a short time. I am pleased with this first practice session. You are men, not boys, and it will, perhaps, be harder to progress, given that you will have to unlearn such habits as you have already developed. But I assure you, you will get stronger as the lessons continue.

"Mister Bailey, a tot of rum for each man this night. They have shown me they deserve it. We have fought our first battle gentlemen, and while we may not have won, we did not lose either."

There was a moment of silence. Unsure how to respond, the men glanced at each other.

"Your proper response is, 'Thank you, Captain,'" said René.

"Thank you, Captain," the men roared.

"Mister Bailey, set the watch please. I will take my sightings and then will retire to my cabin."

CHAPTER TWENTY-TWO

Marseilles, France

RENÉ DALEMBERT had little trouble convincing the Gilbert Ltd. factor in Marseilles he was a trusted business associate of Armand Gilbert. After all, who knew the man better than his own son? After establishing his bonafides, René asked about the possibility of acquiring coffee to trade. The factor gave him a letter of introduction to certain Arab merchants who might be able to arrange the purchase of coffee. Although illegal to export, goods like coffee were always for sale at a price. In return, René agreed to negotiate a cargo for Gilbert Ltd. as well as for himself.

As he reined his horse into one of the seedier districts, René loosened his sword within its sheath. In this part of Marseilles one could be attacked for a loaf of bread. At last he approached a rundown warehouse beside a large camel-skin tent. Several robed Arabs sat in front of the tent smoking a strangely shaped communal pipe. The men grew quiet as René dismounted. He tied the reins to a post and walked toward them, stopping within a courteous distance. Several stood, their posture casual, but with their hands never far from their weapons. René nodded and said, *"Salaam alaikum."*

The reaction was immediate, almost as if he had uttered a magic spell. The men relaxed, and the eldest returned his greeting. "My Arabic is limited," said René. "I am, however, willing to learn."

"That, young man, is the most powerful thing you will ever say." The elder stood and crossed the packed earth to stand before René. His French was flawless. "Will you share refreshment with us?"

"*Merci*, my pleasure, sir."

The elder gentleman motioned for René to follow him. "Let us go inside where it is cooler."

The exterior of the tent was stained, and weather worn, but the inside was a riot of color and texture. Beautifully woven carpets were strewn across the floor. Each depicted a different scene from bloody conflicts to pastoral vistas. Colorful silks rippled along the tent walls while aromatic oil lamps created an inviting atmosphere.

His host, tall and powerfully built, was no stranger to the sword given his stance: balanced, aware. He wore a simple tunic and dark pants, with only the deep blue gem at the throat of his kaftan as evidence of his power and wealth. Swarthy of face with striking hawk-like eyes that missed nothing, he was a powerful individual, and yet René found great peace in his presence. Unusual, considering the man was a complete stranger. René's father had taught him the importance of trading relationships, including the host-guest relationship among Arabs, and he was content to remain silent until they completed the obligatory social observances.

The gentleman sat on several cushions and motioned for René to do the same. A young woman brought a tray of sweetmeats and finger cakes, and placed it on a carved cedar table between them. At least she appeared young. She was swathed from head to toe in a black burqa, which covered the lower part of her face. They sat quietly as she returned with a pot and two small cups before she bowed and left.

The man poured a coffee for René and for himself and then settled back. Keen eyes missed nothing.

"*Merci*." René sipped the beverage. The coffee was unlike any he had ever tasted. It was hot, sweet, and strong. Being from a winemaking family, René was accustomed to paying attention to the nuances of taste. This was redolent with many levels of flavor.

"I believe this is the best coffee I have ever had. My name is René Dalembert, and I have a letter of introduction from *Monsieur* Desseud at Gilbert Ltd." René handed the letter to his host. "At your convenience, I would be grateful to discuss possibilities of mutual interest."

"*Monsieur*, I thank you for your manners. I am Sheikh Ammar Faruq Ghassan, envoy and trade representative from the Sultan, Hamzah al-Rashid of Morocco. In due time, we will indeed speak of many possibilities, but for the moment, perhaps we shall enjoy the coffee and cakes and speak of small things. You appear to be much older than I sense you are. If it is not indelicate, may I ask your age?" The man took a date from a bowl full of exotic fruits.

"I am nineteen, *monsieur*, and although certain experiences have moved me through life a little faster than most, a little faster than I might have liked, I hope my youth will not cause you discomfort or hinder our discussions." René sipped the coffee. "Have you been gone long from your home?"

"Thank you for inquiring, sir. I have been a year and eight months on this particular trip and am preparing to return to Morocco. And you?"

"It seems like years, but it has only been shy of three months." René hesitated.

"You seem to be reticent to talk about your past."

"'Tis inconvenient, but there are certain people who will be safer if the knowledge of my existence is not made public. As you surmised, I am without a great deal of experience in the world, but I am confident of my ability to discern honest intent. 'Tis unusual for me to experience this level of trust after only a few moments meeting, but I do not sense danger in you—at least not toward me. *"S'il vous plait*, allow me to start again. I will not begin this relationship by lying to you. My name is René Gilbert. My father is Armand Gilbert, of Gilbert Ltd. There is a threat that hangs over my family should the fact that I live be discovered. Until I am able to protect those I love, I must keep my continued existence a secret." René surprised himself by divulging such private information to a complete stranger. Yet his senses, which he trusted implicitly, left him peaceful and at ease.

"You have gifted me with a large confidence, and I will not betray your faith. You may call me Ammar, for I am certain we will become the best of friends. You are not the only one who has studied the sword, and I too feel the connection."

René stared at him. "How did you know I studied the sword?"

"We are known by the thousand things that accompany each of us as we make our way through life. That you have trained with the sword is evident by the way you walk, the way your head moves, and how your eyes track each movement around you. You were taught by a master, and it will be a pleasure to learn from you, as well as to teach you what small knowledge I have acquired." The sheikh smiled. "We would be honored for you to stay and dine with us. We have much to discuss."

"Is it possible for me to send a message to my ship?"

"Certainly." The sheikh clapped his hands.

The young woman reentered carrying a small table with a tray of writing materials. How did she know he needed writing materials? She glided across the carpets, each step graceful and controlled. René's awareness expanded the way it did when there was danger, yet his inner voice told him he was safe. The girl never looked at him, but she seemed to see everything within the tent. She set the writing table before him and then placed the tray and paper on it. She arranged the quill, ink, a small bottle of sand, and a wax pot with a candle to heat the seal on the table. Then she bowed and backed out of the tent, each step flowing and silent.

René penned a note to James that he was meeting with Sheikh Ammar Faruq Ghassan and that he would return to the ship in the morning. He sprinkled sand over the ink, allowed it to blot, and then folded the paper, sealing it with a bit of wax.

René waved the paper to cool the wax. "I would be obliged for this to be delivered to James Bailey of the *Seahawk*. The ship is anchored on the south bank, but she is beached now, and you will find him and my crew at the Grog house. I have told him I will return in the morning if 'tis not an imposition for me to find someplace to sleep."

"Not at all. I expect you to spend many nights with us, as we have a lot to talk about. Akeefa!" The sheikh clapped his hands. The sound of the clap had not yet faded from the air before the girl bowed her way back into the tent. "Show *Monsieur* Dalembert to a tent where he can rest and refresh himself?"

"Yes, Father." She bowed again and motioned for René to follow her.

So, she can talk. René turned to the sheikh. "*Merci,* I look forward to speaking further."

He followed Akeefa into the fresh air. There were more tents arranged in a large circle behind the large one, and she led him through a maze of pathways to a smaller dwelling at its outer edge. René copied her as she ducked under the overhang. As the larger tent had been, this smaller version was also filled with colorful silks and carpets woven so intricately that from the corner of his eye the animals appeared to move. There was a divan, bowls and pitchers of water for washing, and the customary cakes and coffee. Akeefa stood beside the doorway.

"If there is anything you require, you need but ask." Her voice, like the rest of her, was under her complete control. "Someone will come to take you to my father when it is time to dine."

René nodded. "*Merci.*" Akeefa nodded and turned to leave. "Am I permitted to talk with you?"

She laughed. "When you have something interesting to say. Until then, make yourself at home."

René sank into the cushions and then poured himself a glass of water. He reviewed his meeting with the sheikh and his daughter. An exciting sense of anticipation signaled that something valuable was, or soon would be, within his reach. Almost like finding a key to a door you never knew existed, a purpose began to coalesce. He poured warm water from the pitcher into a bowl, lifted the soft cloth from the table, and began to wash himself. The sun was just starting to set as a lone voice called the Musselmen to prayer.

Torches blazed throughout the encampment when a young man requested entrance to René's tent. Dressed in a dark blue kaftan of rich brocade, he looked to be about René's age. His black hair and beard were neatly trimmed. "Come," he said.

Each took the measure of the other. The young Arab smiled, and though that sardonic smile spoke volumes about his perception of the world, René sensed a quiet center that spoke even louder of his martial skills. As he stood to follow, René paused and considered his sword lying on the cushions.

The young man followed René's gaze before he spoke, "Allow me to introduce myself. I am Khalid Rafiq Ghassan, youngest son of my beloved father, the sheikh."

"René Dalembert, and I am honored to meet you," René said with a slight bow.

"Forgive my intrusive suggestion, but I realize you are not yet familiar with our customs. Taking a weapon into a meal would be..." He paused. "...impolite."

"I agree and apologize for the thought. As of late, I have felt more comfortable with the sword than without it."

"It is the times we live in, but as my father says, balance in all things. Still, I must admit that I am as yet woefully inept at finding that balance, let alone maintaining it." Khalid put on an imitation of his father. "Eating is a joyful recreation of life, and the symbols of death are not welcome at this activity."

"I agree with your father and would be pleased to leave that symbol behind for longer than dinner."

"Come, he also believes in punctuality, and I am hungry," Khalid laughed as they walked toward dinner.

René returned to the large tent now bright with candles. The long table in the center was covered with white silk and laden with steaming dishes both Moroccan and French. He was ushered to a seat at the left hand of the sheikh, and he bowed as he approached the chair. Khalid went to take his seat to the right of the sheikh beside another young man who could only be his older brother. As much as he resembled Khalid, the brother was a younger version of the sheikh. He was a large man with the same nose and hawk-like piercing eyes, and he, too, radiated power.

"You are surprised to see the table, perhaps?" said the sheikh.

René nodded as he seated himself. "I am. You must forgive me. My education concerning the cultures of the world is sadly inadequate."

"Not at all." The sheikh sipped mint tea from a clear glass. "I have seen many peoples and many traditions. Some deserve to be preserved. Some, however, can be a bit tedious—like sitting on the floor. I find at my age that a comfortable chair is far superior to a pillow, no matter how soft the pillow is. Would you like tea?"

"*Merci*, I would." The quantity and variety of dishes, along with their pungent aromas, assailed his senses and his mouth watered. Tagines of chicken and lamb, bowls of couscous, and platters of flat bread filled every space. For a brief moment, he was back in Bordeaux at one of the elaborate holiday dinners Marie had prepared for them. The sheikh's daughter glided to his side and poured tea from a long-spouted teapot. "*Merci*."

"It is an honor to serve you, sir."

Only her eyes were visible behind the burqa, but her voice belied her words.

"I am certain it is," he said in the same vein. She shook her head and strode away.

Saucy was the only way to describe her. His awareness of her somehow reminded him of the Maestro. As if he were in the presence of barely restrained threat. Ridiculous. Another serving woman filled his plate while he waited politely to begin the meal.

The sheikh raised his tea glass. "I would like to welcome *Monsieur* Dalembert into our home. René Dalembert has come to us through some unfortunate circumstances, and who amongst us has not encountered unfortunate circumstances of their own? He is a merchant like ourselves, and perhaps we may find business that is to our mutual profit. " As he spoke René's last name, he turned to René, smiled, and winked. "René, I would like you to meet my sons. On my right is my eldest, Abdul Karim, whose expertise is animals, horses specifically. And next to him..." Before the sheikh could continue, there was a commotion at the front of the tent followed by the sound of metal on metal.

The sound was familiar to René who was in motion with the first clash of steel. On his feet, having already snatched up the silverware and serving utensils from around his plate, he darted in front of the table, and placed himself between the door of the tent and his host. Black-turbaned men waving scimitars charged into the space. The short, curved swords were perfect for a confined area such as this. René needed a better weapon. He threw the heaviest of the serving pieces, striking an attacker in the eye. The assassin shrieked and grabbed his face. René then struck him on the breastbone. In the man's moment of paralysis, René snatched his sword, ran him through with it, and then reclaimed his position in front of the sheikh. All of this took perhaps fifteen seconds—but for René, time was never a factor.

You will always have enough time to do what must be done.

The Maestro's words settled René, like a reassuring hand on his shoulder. A commotion in front of the tent drew René's attention. Although he sensed the tide change, there would soon be more men surrounding them. This was a well-planned assassination. The sheikh's sons, armed with daggers, held their own, and for now the stream of assassins entering the tent had ceased. Two of the killers had disengaged and charged René and the sheikh. Already moving, René touched both with the scimitar to redirect their attention away from the sheikh. Even though they were trained swordsmen, their faces registered shock at being pinked so easily. They turned to René, and then shifted their positions so that they now flanked him. The one on his right struck first with a thrust that René parried. As the man disengaged, René threw the eating knife from his left hand. The man fell back, clutching his throat.

The other assassin, who from his expression appeared confident that this distraction would be the right time to attack, stepped in with a slashing cut at René's head. His confidence was misplaced. He died with his heart split by René's counter-stroke. The sheikh had armed himself from one of the fallen men and waded into the fray.

So much for defending my host. René smiled to himself.

Khalid and Abdul Karim were outnumbered but clearly at home wielding their swords with control and skill. The expression on Abdul Karim's face was almost gleeful. By now the attackers had realized their imminent defeat. Half their number were dead, and with no reinforcements, they panicked. As one, they turned and fled the tent, followed by René, the sheikh, and his sons. Torches lit the space before the tent as bright as day. René never forgot the sight that met his eyes as he emerged.

At least fifteen men lay scattered dead or dying in the courtyard before him. Moving like a ghost in the middle of the remaining assassins was the girl who had served him. The burqa was gone, and long black hair cascaded down a white silk shirt to the waistband of her black pantaloons. She wielded a curved sword with a skill unmatched by any man he knew with the exception of the Maestro. René forced his amazement aside and joined the fight. He moved deliberately, killing the men that surrounded her, even as she cut them down from within the circle. Within moments, the remaining assailants threw down their swords and flung themselves to their knees. She stepped back and then turned to René. Her expression softened as the two kindred souls recognized each other. She smiled, gave a brief nod, and then was gone.

The sheikh tended Khalid, who had received a minor wound. But for that, the party had escaped unscathed. René stood alert as Abdul Karim walked toward him.

"You are a remarkable fighter, and it has been an honor to share a conflict with you. Are you wounded?" asked the elder brother.

"*Non*, I seem to be all in one piece. How is your brother?"

"Just a scratch. We inflicted greater than that on him when we were children. Come, let us clean up and then we can continue with dinner. A little late perhaps, but Father is strict when it comes to meals, especially when we have welcome guests." Abdul Karim took René's arm and led him to another tent.

"Who was that young woman? I have only seen one other who could handle a sword like that."

"Oh, that is Akeefa, my sister, a continuing embarrassment to us all. Yet you are right, for she can defeat any of us with a sword. I apologize to you for the indignity of her actions. I assure you she will be reprimanded, not that it will do much good." Abdul Karim held open a tent flap for René.

CHAPTER TWENTY-THREE

THE NEXT morning, René awoke to the awareness that someone was standing outside of the tent, but he sensed no danger.

"Do you wish to enter?" René asked.

"*S'il vous plait*," a young boy's voice answered.

"Give me a minute." René rose and pulled on his breeches. "Enter."

The tent flap opened, and a young boy of eleven or twelve entered and placed a tray on the short table next to him. On the tray was a pitcher with steam rising from it and a beautiful porcelain bowl whose glaze depicted the sun on an oasis. There was also a pristine white towel. The boy bowed to him and recited in flawless French, "The master inquires if you would join him for breakfast."

"I would be pleased to," said René. "Allow me a minute to wash and finish dressing."

"I will wait outside."

René walked over and dipped the towel into the warm water. The evening had stretched into the early hours of the morning, with course after course interspaced with that strong, sweet coffee. In the end, as tired as he should have been, he was doubtful sleep would come to him. With all that had transpired, he was filled with a new kind of excitement, certain that he was in the right place at the right time. He glanced in the small mirror as the Maestro's words filled his thoughts.

There will be times when you will be able to sense the flow of your destiny. Sometimes a choice will be required between one road and another, but more often, there will be only one path in front of you. Take strength and confidence from this awareness. We were never meant to wander aimlessly through life.

René had asked whether one could call forth the awareness at will.

And the Maestro's sardonic reply: *"Perhaps with a great deal more attention and practice than you are presently capable of. As you may use everything around you as a weapon, so may you employ every bit of information that you are able to glean from each moment."*

The "what" or the "how" of his life's purpose still eluded him, but for the first time he was confident of its direction. He tugged on his shirt and completed dressing, excited and ready to experience whatever awaited him. René joined the boy outside.

Breakfast was in the same tent as the previous night's dinner. As he entered, the sheikh's voice filled the space. "Come in, come in, *monsieur*. Come sit here by me. I trust you slept well."

"Quite well, sir." René took a seat to the right of the sheikh. "And you, sir, did you sleep well?"

"As well as an old man with numerous responsibilities will. I must say, I slept better knowing you were here." The sheikh passed a cup of coffee to René.

"You are surrounded by well-trained people, not the least of which is your daughter, Akeefa. Am I permitted to speak of her? If not, I apologize. My experience is not yet extensive enough to keep me from being rude."

"You are right that you lack experience, but you do not lack manners or perception. Not speaking about a problem will not persuade it to go away, not that I would wish my lovely daughter to go away." The sheikh paused in thought. "I remember when, as a child, she informed me she no longer wished to hear the word 'no.' I am quite certain she employs selective hearing even today. Do you wish to marry my daughter?"

The unexpected question left René speechless. The sheikh sipped his coffee and waited for a response.

"I..." René closed his mouth. This was an important answer.

He paused and centered himself as if going into battle. The sheikh smiled.

"I realize, sir, that yours is a serious question and will be a foundation of our future dealings. You honor me that you would even consider me a possibility, for despite my inexperience, I am aware of your love for your daughter. I have, however, a previous commitment to a young woman who I was forced to leave behind. And so, I must answer you no; I am not free to marry Akeefa." René fervently hoped he had not offered offense.

"Thank you for your clear and unequivocal answer. You are refreshingly without guile, a shortcoming I will have to correct if we are to join our fortunes. Still, it is pleasant to hear an unvarnished truth. I have trusted you with my life, and now I choose to trust you with that which I value more than my life. If you were not the man you are, I would send you out to sea immediately, for I believe Akeefa has chosen you."

René sat back, unable to speak.

The sheikh smiled. "I do not believe, however, there are enough seas on the globe to prevent Akeefa from fulfilling her desires. At least, there have not been up to now. I cannot fathom what kind of relationship you and my daughter will forge, but of one thing I am certain: it will prove interesting. I wish you success and survival. I do not wish you peace, for you will have none. Still, you are young, and peace is not such an important thing to the young. That brings me to the point. I must tell you that while it is our tradition to eat first and then discuss business afterward, I must forward my daughter's request, for I fear for our safety, let alone our peaceful dining, if I delay." The sheikh straightened up. "Akeefa asks if you are willing to spar with her after breakfast."

"What do you think?" asked René.

"Such wisdom in one so young," said the sheikh. "If you were any other man, I would advise against it so strongly I would be moved to tears if you should decide to accept. But you are not any other man, and while I promise you it will be educational, I do not fear for your physical safety."

"I notice you specified my physical safety." René tried to control his facial expression, but the smile slipped out. "And what of my mental, emotional, and spiritual safety?"

"Ah, my boy, there are no guarantees in life." The sheikh laughed. "I believe that there are things she can teach you and things you may teach her. There is risk in every moment. Surely, you have been taught that. There is also reward inherent within each moment of risk. I have asked, and now at least *I* can relax and enjoy my breakfast. I might advise that you do not eat a heavy meal this morning."

If René's sudden lack of appetite was any indication, a large meal was not a concern.

A servant escorted René to a fencing arena, its boundaries marked off by poles topped with white silk flags. The warehouse on one side and the tents on the other three served as walls. A rack filled with swords and edged weapons from many different cultures stood along one side. As he was the first to arrive, René walked over and inspected the swords to find one that suited his needs. There was a cutlass, shorter than a scimitar but heavier. It would be a good match to the curved scimitar Akeefa used the previous night. He stretched out, pleased with the sword's balance.

He went through a series of exercises and had just finished when she entered. Though he had his back to her, he knew the moment she stepped into the space. He turned and bowed to her, and she returned the gesture.

Akeefa was dressed like the night before in a long sleeved white silk shirt over black pantaloons. Her hair was an infinite black shimmer tied behind her. She was beautiful, with flashing dark eyes and a heart-shaped face, but not in a fragile, fashionable way—more like a wild panther, sleek and deadly. Her drop earrings, each set with a fiery ruby, sparkled in the sun as she turned. He backed away from the weapons so she might choose a blade for the session. Neither of them spoke, yet they seemed to have exchanged a staggering amount of information. Their fields of thought and emotion impinged upon each other, creating a line of resistance that almost crackled.

René cocked an eyebrow when Akeefa chose the cutlass, a twin to the one he held. His impulse was to question her choice of weapons.

Once again the Maestro's voice played in René's mind. *Do not waste time on what you do not know.*

He backed off to allow her space to loosen up, but it appeared she was ready to begin.

René cleared his throat. "What rules would you like to follow?"

"Whatever rules you feel constrained to follow or not will be fine."

"May I ask our objective?"

"Why, to know who we are of course." She swung the cutlass once through a short arc. "Are you ready to begin?"

René shifted his consciousness as he came to *en garde*. She did the same.

This match is going to be interesting.

The only other person he ever encountered that exhibited the same level of intense mental focusing was the Maestro. In between that thought and the next, she attacked—just like the Maestro.

René gracefully turned, allowing her thrust to go past his chest. More than just the knowledge of who they were was at stake here. Facing her, he breathed deeply and slowed the world even further. She shifted with him and attacked again. Their swords clashed with that unique music heard only from the hearts of fine steel. The cutlass was more of a brute force weapon than the rapier. He admired the effortless way she moved the heavy blade.

Patience is a necessary skill in life, for the impatient lion rarely eats so well as the one who waits.

René settled into himself and reached out to anticipate her movements. He was content to wait until she tired. The only problem was that she failed to tire. Because of the additional weight of the sword, cutlass contests were usually short. In all of his years of working with the Maestro, René had never seen him tire. Was there some skill this slip of a girl knew that he had never learned? Her speed and power reminded him of the master, and he had only beaten the Maestro once. His emotions signaled that he should be afraid, but the emotion of fear was as familiar to him as his own hand. He had befriended it long ago. The Maestro had made certain of that. So why did he feel this way?

Pay attention to that which is out of the ordinary. There are no accidents. Everything must have a cause. Many forces, not all within the physical realm, can threaten the self that burns within you. Fear is but an emotional response to disorder. Through the use of your will, you can ignore the incoming emotional signals, maintaining the integrity of your vital field which is crucial to your ability to focus.

She was mentally manipulating his personal vital field and through it, his emotions. Instead of the fear that would have been the natural response to such knowledge, René experienced a joyous surge of wonder and a fierce desire to know this skill. First, he had to disengage from the mental onslaught. Risking a slashed hip, he lifted one of her earrings into the air with a lightning flick of his sword. He deftly caught the earring and pocketed it.

She stopped and demanded, "Give me back my earring."

"Teach me how you are manipulating my emotions."

She attacked, and the mental assault doubled. René gave himself over completely to that quiet center, moving with speed and grace into each thrust and parry. He no longer felt the pressure of her thoughts. Feeling and perception had been replaced by knowing. This was where the Maestro had been leading him, and it had taken this girl—this master of the sword, he corrected himself—to help him cross into that state of emotionless motion. If he could have experienced an emotion in that moment, it would have been gratitude. With another flick, he released the other earring from its bondage, then pulled it from the air and pocketed it.

Again she stopped, her lips drawn tight. "You will regret that."

"Not as much as you will regret allowing anger into your space," he said, as he prepared for her attack.

Instead, Akeefa paused. The light of recognition blossomed within her dark eyes.

She is truly a master.

He brought his sword to a rest position only a tick off *en garde*.

"You were not influenced by my mental assault. How did you manage that?" she asked.

"How did you create the effect?" he countered.

Akeefa smiled, and it was as if there had never before been a sunrise. René quailed. He recognized a greater threat than any sword. He relaxed further into that unique sense of stillness and returned her smile. Every moment of their relationship would be fraught with danger for both of them, but the rewards would far outweigh the risk. "Let me put the swords away, and we will have tea with Father."

She released the *en garde* position and waited, a half smile on her face.

René reversed the sword and offered her its hilt. Complete and implicit trust was necessary if this relationship was to be anything but deadly.

She turned and replaced the weapons on the rack, but not before carefully wiping each one down with a cloth.

A master always takes care of his tools.

The voice echoed back to René as they walked from the practice arena.

CHAPTER TWENTY-FOUR

AKEEFA SAT before the mirror. When gazed upon from certain angles, the gold filigree dolphins frolicked around the glass, their delicate artistry a joyful metaphor of freedom. Her father received the mirror as a gift from Louis XIV. Citing his lack of appreciation for its unique beauty, she promptly appropriated the piece.

Her servant's sour expression added little to the finely crafted mirror. Sabah brushed Akeefa's hair with angry strokes as if the brush was at fault for her young charge's recent adventure, uncovered and unrepentant. Sabah could no more have left the tent without her veil than she could have voluntarily ceased breathing. Theirs was an old argument and they had agreed to disagree. Well, at least Akeefa had agreed.

Poor father. He had given in to her young demands for a sword, and the training to go with it, far too easily. He expected her to get bored rather than go on to outstrip every available teacher in Morocco by the age of thirteen. The Spanish swordmaster came afterward. At first he had been insulted by the request that he train a woman, but eventually, once he finally condescended to meet her, he had agreed to train Akeefa. He had left that first meeting visibly shaken. He was the one who showed Akeefa how dangerous her anger was, how any denial of her freedom would provoke it. René had identified that weakness in one session, and that was mortifying.

The thought of him was exciting. He was too strong to be

susceptible to pressure. He had attained the power of the calm center. She too had found that calm center, but was unable to remain there. He could help her. If only she could work out how to encourage him to do so. For the first time, she was unsure how to go about fulfilling a desire. The situation was unsettling and frustrating, but even that was somewhat exciting. She did love a challenge.

"He is beautiful, is he not?" Akeefa turned toward Sabah.

"How am I expected to brush your hair if you keep moving? Be still, child." Sabah continued brushing while her lips moved as she counted silently.

Akeefa dutifully faced forward. "But he *is*, you must agree?"

"He is a kafir and beneath your notice."

"Oh, stop being so old-fashioned, Sabah. We have traveled throughout Europe. Have you never even looked outside your own tent?"

"The only reason I would have to look outside my tent would be to empty the chamber pot, and I have never found anything of great interest at the end of that walk." Sabah placed the ivory handled brush onto an engraved silver tray.

"Well, I think he is beautiful. Such eyes, and the way he smiles. Father told me he is betrothed, but unable to return home. I have not persuaded Father to tell me why yet—honor and such— but I will. I will know everything about him." She stared into the mirror, not really seeing her reflection.

"Come dear, it has been a long day, and you will need your sleep." Sabah fluffed the mattress and turned down the coverlet. She continued tidying up, moving a pillow here, folding a blanket there.

"It has been a long and exciting day, and there is no way I can fall asleep. Sabah, go ahead and find your bed. Perhaps meditation will allow me to put this day to rest."

"But surely if you lie down..."

"Thank you for taking such good care of me. Good night, dear Sabah." Akeefa kissed her on the cheek before she gently pushed the woman out of the tent.

Akeefa chose her favorite pillow and sat upon it, back straight and legs crossed. With her hands comfortably in her lap, she moved through the levels of her mind, stilling each one until she was in that place of no place, that time of no time. Her breathing slowed, and while her awareness narrowed, paradoxically it expanded as well. In her mind's eye, she was aware of every spark of life within the camp as if looking on a velvet night sky filled with fireflies.

Tonight, however, the meditation refused to go easily. There was a light of great intensity within the camp, a fire that made even her father's vital field seem dim by comparison. Her intuition told her René would be aware of any attempt to make direct mental contact. To do so uninvited was unacceptable, a gross invasion of privacy, and besides, coercion would destroy what she hoped to build. She found herself abruptly back within her tent, the candles having hardly burned down at all. She crawled beneath the coverlet and resigned herself to a sleepless night.

René awoke at dawn when someone passed close by his tent. Last night was a late night with the sheikh and his sons as they discussed their proposed trading venture. The sultan, Moulay al-Rashid, needed weapons to consolidate his rule. While in Marseilles they would purchase flintlocks and then sail to Malaga to pick up a shipment of the finest Toledo swords. Making port in Larache, Morocco, the weapons would be sent overland to the sultan in Fez. The *Seahawk* would then continue on to Casablanca to sell her remaining cargo. René had spent enough time beside his father that his negotiating skills were better than his youth might have indicated. Still, he was in the presence of a master. The smile on the sheikh's face proved René had presented himself well. Their agreed upon plan was for him to increase his trading fleet under the auspices of the Sultan.

He had also received permission to use the fencing ground for his own practice. René rose and headed there. In the future, he would ask when the space would be available so as not to impose on

Akeefa's schedule, but for now, it was empty.

He approached the rack of gleaming weapons. He chose his favorite, the rapier, and removed it from its velvet niche. It was a beautiful piece made of Spanish steel with a gold-filigreed bell guard. He picked it up and tested it. As expected, its balance was perfect.

René warmed up in preparation for the exercise regimen the Maestro had created for him. Lunges to stretch the large muscles in his legs. Then a series of exercises that constricted one muscle group after another until his body told him it was ready. He paused to remove his shirt before it was drenched with sweat. He stood with the rapier down and to the side and focused his mind until he was secure within that unique mental perspective that allowed him to work through his exercises while viewing them through the Maestro's critical eye. His first thrust cut through the air.

After a short time, he sensed her watching, as if the quality of the light had changed, for her approach had been silent. He smiled to himself and continued deeper into his workout, his upper body glistening with sweat. There was no beginning nor ending to any movement he made, each one gliding into the next—perfectly controlled, completely at ease, and yet radiating power—as though he commanded the very air, the way the sun struck the blade. A glorious dance, each step was filled with the years of pain and effort demanded. Finally, it came to an end. There was no transition between action and rest. All movement simply ceased.

He turned to her and bowed. "I am sorry if I have taken up your time and space."

She remained still as if frozen. René stood close enough to her to experience the rush of anger and embarrassment filling her as she suppressed her weakness, fighting to regain control.

"I am sorry to have intruded, but I could not turn away," she finally said.

"You are welcome to watch. You have much to teach me. We will need to know each other much better, if we are to be of any value to each other as teachers or students." He walked over to the sword rack and wiped down the rapier.

She followed him. With her gaze fixed on the ground, she spoke. "I am not so certain I have anything to teach you, but I would formally ask to become your student."

"*S'il vous plait,* look at me, Akeefa."

She slowly raised her eyes to meet his. Her body was motionless, but René sensed the war taking place within her. A war fraught with violence barely restrained.

René settled into that focused calm that presaged battle. The threat his psyche had detected, however, was aimed not at him but at herself. "Akeefa, the master-student relationship is much easier than that of master-to-master. No one reaches our level without a fierce sense of self. I learned that one never completely tames the self, for it is at home, whereas we are merely visitors. The only way for us to learn from each other is to place our lives completely into the hands of the other. Trust is the one road we may walk together and live, for we are each death incarnate, and it will accompany us wherever we go. The moment one of us steps from that road, one of us will die."

Silence filled the space between them as they faced each other and began the process of disrobing the soul. A tear slid down her cheek. The tear was an expansion of awareness, not weakness. His overwhelming emotion was joy at the exchange of something so precious. Only a moment passed, yet it could have been a thousand years. The bond forged in that instant could not have been any stronger had it taken millennia to build. There was nothing more to say. Words were, after all, a poor medium of exchange. René finished wiping down the blade, put his shirt on, and together they walked from the fencing ground.

CHAPTER TWENTY-FIVE

RENÉ GLANCED around the *Seahawk*'s deck at the purposeful chaos. "Mister Abel, report," he said, while he kept a careful eye on the supplies coming aboard. James oversaw the loading of the gunpowder and lead shot. The job was a tricky business. More than one ship had sunk in port because of carelessness with gunpowder. A stray spark could be disastrous.

The *Seahawk*'s refit had taken four weeks to complete. René had wanted new swivel guns for the forecastle and aft, and the *Seahawk* now boasted two falconets, commonly referred to as 'murderers.' Able to sweep a deck with grape shot, they were a strong addition to the traditional broadside. In addition to the guns, René intended to train as lethal a group of fighters as there was on the seven seas. He now had an almost full complement of sailors, and with the men the sheikh was bringing, the *Seahawk* would be a dangerous ship to interfere with.

"All crew present or accounted for, sir," the boatswain said briskly.

"What is our current roster?"

"We are at eighty-one including you, sir."

"More than I expected. How deep did you have to dig to find that many?" René smiled.

"Seems there are rumors of plague, and most of 'em were more than happy to get out. I had the two cabins refitted as per your instructions, and we added another for the servant. Would you like to inspect them?"

"I will. Our guests are used to a bit more accommodation than is usual at sea, and I mean to make them comfortable." The sheikh, Akeefa, and Khalid were sailing with René aboard the *Seahawk* while Abdul Karim went overland to purchase swords. The *Seahawk* was to rendezvous with him in Malaga to collect him and the Sultan's weapons. "Have we loaded the alcohol?"

"Yes, sir, both the brandy and wine," John said. "They'll hold us in good stead once we reach Malaga."

"Where is the lad, Andrew?" René asked as he descended below.

"Mister Bailey's got him working in the hold, packing the tight spaces." He followed René.

As they approached the sailors working, René yelled to be heard over the noise of loading. "Mister Bailey, do you have a moment, sir?"

James Bailey completed his orders to the crew loading barrels of fresh water before walking to René. "Yes, Captain."

"I am glad Andrew has decided to remain with us. Has he communicated with his family?" René asked.

"Yes, sir. As per your orders, I helped him write to them. We have received no word from them yet, but I expect they will want to see some of those wages. He'll need some work on his letters, but we have time. He's a good lad and a hard worker. Don't worry, I will keep an eye on him."

"Excellent. Carry on Mister Bailey." René strode toward the hatch. "Mister Abel, I would like to inspect the cabins set aside for the sheikh and his daughter."

"Aye, aye, Captain." James turned back toward a load of supplies being winched below deck.

René followed the boatswain down the new stairs built to replace the ladders. The passageway was still quite narrow, but the two existing cabins had been enlarged and a third one added. Akeefa had insisted Sabah's cabin be next to hers. René inspected the cabin, satisfied his guests would be as comfortable as was possible aboard ship. The cabins were small but well-appointed with carpets and wall tapestries, along with sea bunks, desks, and chairs. Meals would be taken with René in the captain's cabin.

"That will be all, Mister Abel," René said.

"Thank you, sir. I will report to Mister Bailey when we're ready to sail." The boatswain backed out of the cabin.

There was a moment of quiet when the incessant hammering stopped. René paused for a second to consider the voyage ahead of them. A shrill whistle, the boatswain's signal that their guests had arrived, pulled him from his reverie. René took one last look around then went out, closing the door behind him. He made his way above deck. The loading had stopped and the men crowded the rail to get a look at the passengers.

René signaled to James. "The men will have plenty of opportunity to meet our guests. I would like to be away with the tide."

"Aye, Captain. I will see to it. Excuse me, sir." In the blink of an eye, James grabbed the closest man hanging over the gunwale and hoisted him over the side. "The next man I see whose hands are touching that railing will find himself swimming back to Marseilles after we leave port."

The men snatched their hands off the gunwale as if it was made of molten lead. As one, they quickly returned to their allotted tasks.

René watched the sheikh, Akeefa, and Khalid approach the dock. Sabah and a group of ten men accompanied them. The party dismounted.

"Permission to come aboard, sir?" the sheikh called.

"Permission granted, sir, and welcome." René nodded to Akeefa. Their eyes met. They had agreed she would act the role of the dutiful daughter and remain covered according to her traditions. René had promised to find a way for her to exercise, but it would have to wait until they were under way.

"This is the boatswain, John Abel. He will show you to your cabins. We expect to depart on the afternoon's tide." René passed the sheikh, Akeefa, and Sabah over to the boatswain and went to find James.

Khalid was in charge of the sheikh's men and would facilitate their integration. Although Khalid was no younger than René, he still sported a youthful aura of adventure and reckless confidence. Given his new mantle of responsibility, René felt—

and apparently, appeared—years older.

"Khalid, I would like you to meet Mister James Bailey. Mister Bailey is the lieutenant aboard the *Seahawk,* and as such is next below myself in authority. You and your men will be under his direct command," René said. "Is this acceptable?"

Khalid straightened and bowed, first to René then to James.

"I will be pleased to accept your authority, and that of Mister Bailey. Three of my men speak French, two speak Portuguese, and Mister Haddad, well, I have yet to find a language he does not understand. Due to my father's persistence, I speak French as well as English and a small amount of Dutch. We will work hard both to be of service to you and to learn the predominant language aboard so we can be useful should difficulties arise."

"*Merci,* Khalid." René turned to James. "I must see to the comfort of the sheikh and his daughter. *S'il vous plaît,* settle and assign Khalid and his men."

"Aye, aye, Captain."

There were bound to be problems at first, but René was confident they would come together as a crew.

Akeefa's unmistakable voice raged as René approached the hatch. Those 'difficulties' seemed to be showing up sooner than later. He hurried toward the ruckus.

"How can you expect me to remain day and night in this tiny cell?" Akeefa yelled.

The sheikh was calm, at least outwardly. "My dear, this is not so large a ship. If we are to have room for cargo, passengers must give up space."

"Let the crew give up space."

"Akeefa, you know the crew does not have cabins, and neither does your brother. I believe my cabin is larger than yours. If you wish to exchange with me then that will be fine." The sheikh led her into his quarters.

"This is not much better."

René spoke from the doorway. "Akeefa."

She turned to him and immediately quieted down.

The sheikh's eyes widened in amazement. He had been about to speak but instead remained silent and backed farther into the cabin giving the two more space.

"You may have the captain's cabin which is located mid deck aft, but you will have to abide me coming in and out, for I will need the chart table. I will be able to work topside, but not if the weather turns foul. When your father and my officers and I need to meet to discuss business, your presence will be too distracting, so you will need to use your father's cabin or the smaller cabin then, but I am certain we can work something out."

"May I see your cabin?"

"Of course. Follow me." René led the way up the stairs to the captain's cabin. He opened the door, and motioned for her to enter.

Akeefa stepped inside. René sensed the battle within her. Clearly she needed to retreat from an unwinnable position without losing whatever dignity she had left.

"In truth, 'tis not that much larger than my father's cabin."

"I am sorry, but there is no extra room on a ship this size."

"It becomes clear that the primary purpose of the ships I traveled on has been to transport my family in comfort." She inspected the furniture in the cabin. "What do you suggest?"

"That you trade cabins with your father, and he in turn will trade with me. As he and I are partners in this venture, I do not believe he will be inconvenienced having me use the chart table when necessary, and you will have your privacy and a somewhat larger space." René led her back down into the passageway.

"Thank you. I cannot promise anything, but I will do my best," Akeefa said as she followed him to her father. "Father, you must take the captain's cabin, since you are the elder here. I will make do with your cabin."

"Where will the captain sleep?" The sheikh frowned.

"Oh, he assures me he will be most comfortable in the cabin originally assigned to me. He will, however, have to use the table in your cabin for meetings and such, but I felt certain you would not mind," Akeefa said. "Sabah, where's Sabah? We have much to do to make this boat livable."

The sheikh glanced at René, who nodded. Resigned, the sheikh walked toward the stairs to go above decks. He was wise enough to move out of harm's way.

"Akeefa, we leave on the tide. Is there anything else you require? " René asked.

"Is it possible for me to exercise?"

"I have asked James to find space in the hold, but I will not know for sure until we are underway for a day or so. We are not at final trim yet. The hold must be balanced so we do not capsize in a strong wind. 'Tis also my intention to train the men to fence. Against a larger ship or a man-of-war, we are at a disadvantage in both the number of cannon and the weight of lead we can throw, so I must find advantages where I can. I would love to add your expertise to their training, but I do not think your father or brother will allow it." The moment the word 'allow' left his lips, his connection with Akeefa signaled his mistake. He had inadvertently dropped a grenade. He backed up a step and waited for it to explode.

"*Allow?*"

"You know what I meant," he interjected, before she gained headway on the thought. "There is a certain propriety that must be followed. You must understand the difficulties in having a single woman aboard."

"Sabah is not married."

"*Non*, but then she is not beautiful, either. I know you do not want to make this harder than it must be. We shall talk it over with your father and brother and see what will be possible and what will not." He moved toward the stairs, then turned and caught her eye. "I know what you want, and you may trust me to do my utmost to help you obtain it."

Akeefa uncovered her face and smiled.

"If you will excuse me, I have work topside that must be attended to." His heart rate increased and along with it, a strange pervading confusion. A fast retreat was in his best interest.

A cacophony of gulls wheeled around the *Seahawk* as she glided from the quay. René glanced over at James who stood near the center mast, inspecting each crewman while issuing a steady stream of familiar orders. As boatswain, John Abel seconded those orders, increasing the volume of each with the aid of a powerful voice pitched to pull the cleats out of the gunnels.

"Show 'em how we belay those lines," he bawled to a crewman standing near Khalid and his men.

The man muttered. "I ain't showin' no land lubbin' Musselman how to tie a knot."

Apparently, Khalid had overheard the boatswain's command because he walked over to the seaman. "My men and I would appreciate your assistance."

"Do you see any camels?" the man said.

"No."

"Then stay out of the way, Musselman." The sailor pushed past Khalid and swaggered toward the sheets.

René's curiosity peaked. He remained behind the capstan and watched. Khalid followed the man to once again stand before him. Reaching over and pulling one of the belaying pins from the pin rail, he casually held it in front of the seaman. "I believe you were ordered to show us how to tie the lines off to these."

"Well, I will tell ya what to do with that pin. Stick it..."

Before the sailor said another word, Khalid turned his back on him and, using his body to shield his actions, he rammed the belaying pin into the sailor's solar plexus. He turned back to face the sailor and swung the pin again its movement so swift that naught but a blur was visible until it connected with the man's skull behind his ear. The sailor dropped, unconscious, to the deck. Khalid casually placed the belaying pin back into its slot and walked over to the boatswain. "Mister Abel, the seaman tasked with assisting us appears to be indisposed. Would it be possible to assign someone else? We are eager to be of service to the ship."

"What happened?"

"I think the man had perhaps too much to drink before leaving port. He was saying something about camels when he struck his head. I do not believe he is permanently injured." Khalid kept his gaze on the boatswain.

Abel glanced in René's direction, fighting a grin. "That has been known to happen, but I will make sure it don't happen from here on. Abbot," he called to a seaman in the rigging. "Get down here. I got a job for you."

Abbot climbed down the rigging and then presented himself before the boatswain.

"This is Khalid Ghassan and those are his men." The boatswain nodded toward the group. "You will stay with these men until their nautical skills meet those of the rest of the crew. These are fighting men, and if we get into it, you will be very glad to have them aboard. The lieutenant has requested we make these men part of the crew. It would make Mister Bailey very unhappy if that were not to happen. Am I making myself perfectly clear?"

"Yes, sir."

"Mister Ghassan, I have every confidence in you and your men. I do not believe we should experience any more difficulties."

"Thank you Mister Abel." Khalid bowed to the seaman. "Mister Abbot, we were ordered to belay some lines, and welcome your assistance."

Abbot put his knuckle to his forehead, saluting the boatswain, and then followed Khalid.

John Abel looked back at René and caught his nod.

Akeefa paced the small cabin like a caged tigress. Unable to remain cooped up, she dressed appropriately putting on a hijab and went above deck for some air. Once on deck, her eyes widened in disbelief. Khalid was on his knees helping the sailors wash the deck. He noticed her watching him and grinned. After saying a couple of words to the others he joined her.

"Good afternoon, Akeefa."

"Whatever are you doing?"

"Washing the gun carriage."

"I saw that, but why are you performing such menial work?"

"The efficiency of the cannon is dependent on the ease with which the carriage moves, so it behooves us to keep them clean," he said with a smirk.

At the respective ages of eight and seven, shortly after a drubbing Akeefa had given him, the two had become best friends. That particular dispute had involved a pastry.

"I am so glad you have finally taken an interest in cleaning. Sabah was saying to me she needed someone to help her clean the cabins. I am certain she will be honored to have your assistance."

"I have no doubt that if you decide on it, I will find myself doing such work. But in truth that will not benefit us nearly as much as the integration of our retainers into this crew. The easiest way for me to affect this is to show the men that even I am not above doing what needs to be done. Man's work. I cannot expect you to understand." He jerked away as he said it, and her hand missed his nose. "A jest, dear sister, only a jest."

"Is it working?" Her interest was piqued and her tone became serious as her thoughts ran to another.

"Of course. They are good men, and they realize our safety lies in unity of purpose and action. Mister Bailey knows his ship, and he is consistent and fair. Until we see action—and I hope we never do—we will not be brothers, but we will be able to function as a crew. How is the situation below? Seems to me I heard some raised voices." Khalid leaned on the rail, avoiding her eyes.

"It surprised me, is all. This is a smaller ship than we are accustomed to. I will manage. What do you think of our captain?"

"Well, I hope to never cross swords with him. Never seen anyone move so fast, except maybe you." Khalid gazed into his sister's eyes. She involuntarily glanced toward the deck. "You have feelings for this man."

"Me? Well, I..." Akeefa fell silent. She was unwilling to lie to her beloved little brother. "Some."

He shook his head. "Some? I have never known anyone else to so consistently choose the more difficult path. Does father know?"

"Is there *anything* father does not know?"

"Probably not," laughed Khalid. His smile faded and his gaze captured hers. "Beloved sister, you know I will support you always, but forgive me if I voice my reservations. Others often misunderstand the meaning of our actions."

"You mean like washing the gun carriages?" She forced her smile back in place.

"Yes." The resignation in his voice and his habitual sardonic expression betrayed his awareness that he had lost again. "Like washing the gun carriages. Speaking of which, I have wasted enough time and need to get back to work."

"Wasted..." she said, her voice rising.

"Wrong word." He backed away with a grin. "I needed a rest and am recharged by speaking with you. I will go back to work now and re-double my efforts."

"You had better," she laughed.

The *Seahawk* left Marseilles on the afternoon tide. With a good following wind, she spread her sail and left the coast behind. They marked her doing eight knots, and fully rigged, she was capable of nine or even ten. With a reasonable wind, few would be able to catch her. René had been serious with Akeefa about his teaching the men to fence. With only sixteen cannon, they were at a distinct disadvantage when it came to naval warfare. They had a slight speed advantage, but even that might be lost when fully loaded with Spanish steel.

René stood on the afterdeck and addressed the crew. "I will make this short. I am René Dalembert, and I am the master of this ship." There were grumbles from some of the men. Young captains were far from popular, and James had led the men to believe he was the one in charge.

"I ain't shippin' under no boy," yelled one of the seamen in the back.

"*S'il vous plait,* come forward and voice your opinions, sir," René said in a pleasant tone.

A large, gruff man walked up to René. "I ain't takin' orders from no boy."

The men who had seen René aboard the *Vrijheid* took a step back in unison.

"I see I must convince you otherwise."

The sailor outweighed René by at least sixty pounds, and from the scars on his face and arms, he was no stranger to fighting.

"You gonna stab an unarmed fellow?" the man jeered. "I heard you were good with that pot-sticker, but you will sail this ship without a crew if you kill me. We ain't that far from port."

"I own this vessel, and as captain you know I have the authority to kill you where you stand for your insubordination. You are, however, correct. I cannot run this ship alone. I need your willing help, or we might as well put back into port." René eased his sword from its sheath and handed it to John Abel. "Mister Abel, I believe you held this for me once before. Would you be so kind as to take care of it for me again? I will reclaim it shortly."

"Yes, Captain." The boatswain flashed a knowing smile.

"Is that better, Monsieur...? Forgive me, I do not have all the names down yet," said René.

"Wade, Gavin Wade is the name you will soon regret addressing." He took off his shirt. There were stripes on his back, and his muscles rippled across his shoulders.

"Mister Abel, would you be so kind as to clear a space for our exercise?"

"Move out of the way there," John bellowed, and the men backed up, allowing a circle of space on the deck. The late afternoon sun painted long shadows across the deck. René centered himself. The men moved farther back, sensing the danger.

"Do I need to insult you, sir, or can we begin?" René asked.

Wade rushed René with both arms outstretched to grab him in a wrestling hold. René swiveled left and allowed him to rush by. Red in the face, the sailor bellowed and charged in again. René slid sideways, and again the man clutched air.

"Stand still, ya coward. Do ya bloody mean to fight or don't ya?" he yelled.

René remained silent. *Never allow your opponent to choose your tactics.*

Wade rushed him once more. This time René ducked under

his outstretched arms. He flat-palmed a strike into the man's kidney as he passed. Wade was panting, trying to gain his breath. Though in pain, he reached for René again. Grabbing the man's arm, René used his momentum and pulled him forward and down. Wade crashed into the deck face first. He rose, bleeding and shaking. He growled like an animal and rushed René again. This time he changed direction at the last moment.

As René spun away, Wade grabbed him in a bear hug from behind, his arms constricting with bone-crushing pressure. René stamped on the man's instep. Wade eased up for a second. That was all René needed. Using only his arm strength, René broke the man's grip and faced him. A strike to the other kidney and a flat palm strike upwards into the chin, and Gavin Wade's eyes glazed as he dropped to the deck unconscious. René addressed the men.

"This ship needs Monsieur Wade, and so I have done my best not to disable him. I am the captain of this ship, and I will not hesitate to defend that position. Do not underestimate me because of my youth. If I am truly threatened, I will do what I deem necessary. I do not expect you to simply accept my word, but in truth, you do not have the power to take this ship from me. If you choose not to sail under my colors, our next port is Malaga, and you may get off there.

"Mister Abel, can we find a bucket of water to wake Monsieur Wade? I believe he may want to be in on this discussion."

The boatswain barked out an order, and one of the men fetched a bucket of water, which he emptied onto the sailor.

Sputtering and shaking his head, Gavin Wade gradually returned to consciousness. He blinked rapidly in an attempt to refocus his vision.

"Are you satisfied, sir, or do you still require proof I am in earnest?" René asked.

"You are quicker'n spit. I believe I would rather wrestle a bear, but I like your spirit." Wade tried to stand and failed.

René extended his hand and helped Wade to his feet. "May I have my sword, Mister Abel?"

"Yes, sir," the boatswain replied.

With the sword in René's hand, not a man moved.

"I will not defend my position again in this manner. You know our lives depend on our working together. The sea will not forgive us our disunity." René addressed his crew while he held the sword casually, but in a manner that left no one unsure of its deadly potential. "I will not tolerate dissent. Are there others who have a problem serving under my command?" René paused long enough for the quiet to make its point clear.

"There are nineteen men aboard this ship who have sailed with me as captain. I offered them the opportunity to debark at our first port of call. You will find they are all still aboard. At this point in our venture, I can guarantee you nothing but hard work. You are all men of the sea. When has it been otherwise? If we survive, you will be well rewarded, in both coin and experience. If we fail, perhaps we will meet somewhere warmer and discuss it."

A wave of laughter took the men as René turned to look at the boatswain. "*S'il vous plaît*, Mister Abel, relieve Mister Bailey at the whipstaff."

"Aye, aye, Captain." The boatswain headed aft to relieve James. René nodded to James after he had walked over. "This is Mister Bailey, lieutenant aboard the *Seahawk*. You have made his acquaintance, and you will direct all of your communications to him. I believe you will find me a gentle and forgiving soul compared to Mister Bailey, and I release you into his capable hands."

James nodded in return, "Captain."

René joined Mister Abel at the whipstaff. He smiled to himself as James bellowed orders.

CHAPTER TWENTY-SIX

AFTER TRIMMING the hold, James managed to clear out a practice space barely large enough for René and Akeefa to spar, but it was sufficient. Akeefa had taught René how to access the emotions of others. The next step was how to manipulate those emotions.

"Emotions are a double-edged sword," she said as they moved through the ballet of a new riposte he was teaching her. "It is possible to be swamped in the same emotions you have helped intensify."

"Are they then not controllable?"

"Yes they are, but it takes great effort and a good deal of strength," she said. "That something is possible does not always mean 'tis appropriate to do it. I am certain your master taught you to conserve your strength and expend it with patience and precision."

René laughed. "Often. How do you know when to use this technique?"

"The same way you know when to employ any technique. By trial and error, and when possible, following advice from one who has already experienced the outcome of using it." Akeefa twirled, bringing her sword horizontally above her head to block and then slashed down to the right.

Swords flashed as they moved smoothly from position to position, all the while commenting on the work. They came to a position of rest, going from movement to absolute stillness together, in perfect unison. Not a word spoken.

René grinned, and she flashed back another of her heart stopping smiles. To be able to exercise one's skill matched with another equally skilled was exhilarating. "How did you know I was thinking of the Maestro and that I had only beaten him once?"

"I knew nothing of your past or your fears. Ordinarily I would have found out as much as I could about you before sparring. It was not possible to do that. My next option would have been the emotions most people display all the time and even say aloud. You did neither."

"Then why attempt to manipulate my emotions at all?"

"Because I had never sparred with anyone even close to your skill, and for the first time in my life, I was afraid. Not of being hurt, I knew you were much too good for that, but of being thought less of because I am a woman." A rosy flush crept across her creamy cheeks. "That is my weakness, my Achilles' heel."

Do not rail at the pattern within which you find yourself. You are not there by chance, and if you allow anger to cloud your vision, you may miss the best opportunity for you to learn that which you are here to learn.

"My master said that the thing which claims your attention the most is that which you should look at with the clearest eyes," René studied Akeefa as she wiped down her blade and placed it within the case. "May I ask you what my master often asked me?"

"Of course," she said.

"Where is your power?"

"It resides within my heart."

"In what state is your power at its maximum?"

"In stillness," she said, without batting an eyelash.

"Is anger ever still?"

"No."

"My master rewarded me with pain whenever I would choose the weaker path of anger, toward myself or toward others. 'Anger is for stupid amateurs,' he would say, 'and you are neither.' Akeefa, do not pretend to yourself 'twill be easy; we are no longer children. Children change patterns as easily as they change clothes. The facility wanes as we get older. Still, you can learn and change and have already begun." René smiled.

"Do you have time for a cup of tea?"

"Not at the moment. I have duties above deck. Perhaps you would like to get some air after I have finished?"

"I would love to. It is a little cramped down here."

"'Tis a beautiful day indeed. When I have finished, we will spend time on deck," René said as he escorted her to her cabin. He then made for the newly installed stairs.

"Mister Merchant, stay lively up there." James bellowed up at Andrew. "Keep those young eyes peeled." Andrew was taking his watch in the crow's nest. Young eyes were always best.

"How is he doing up there?" René asked.

"Ah, the lad is a natural—attention and balance. Kinda like someone else I know." James let go a hearty laugh.

"Glad to hear it. *S'il vous plaît*, report," René said.

"Cargo's battened down and in trim. We've a full spread of sail and are making good speed. Found a couple of barrels of salt beef short-weighted, but not enough to make a difference. The gun crews are competent, and I believe we might stand our own in a fight."

René smiled at his lieutenant's use of the word competent. René had been on his father's ships, and he knew the gun crews of the *Seahawk* were a damn sight better than competent. James had put Farraj Haddad, one of the sheikh's men, in charge of the cannon. The man's expertise surpassed that of anyone aboard. Of the sixteen three-man crews, three were from the Moroccan contingent, and the competition had become fierce. "I need to shoot our position and make my log entries. Is there anything I should know?"

"No, sir."

"Have you found quarters for the surgeon Al Zahrawi?"

"I asked him, and he said he was most comfortable with the rest of the Musselmen."

"And are the men comfortable with him as a doctor?"

James paused and cleared his throat. "Well, not so much at the start, but he is their man now. Men can tell a genuine leech from a fake, and Al Zahrawi's a real doctor. Makes no difference that he ain't Christian. We're lucky to have him aboard. I remember old Doc Hopkins from the *Albion*. When he wasn't tight, he was a right good doctor. When he was, you had to hope to all hell you didn't get hurt. He'd as soon take your leg as look at ya. Not Al Zahrawi. He'd rather you kept your limb, and he don't even drink. He's got some crazy notions though. Don't even believe in bleeding a man. We've a good crew, Captain, and a better ship. Is there anything you need, sir?"

"Not at this time, Mister Bailey."

"Then I will be about my duties, sir." James faced left and then made for the main mast.

CHAPTER TWENTY-SEVEN

RENÉ HAD shot the sun's position and was in the sheikh's cabin making his entries into the log.

"We will be in sight of Malaga within ten days." René finished his entries and closed the book with a satisfied sigh.

"The men who attacked us in Marseilles knew nothing that proved to be of any worth," the sheikh said. "Still, I have a theorem. Moulay al-Rashid has a younger brother who at best is impatient and at worst...well, I have heard rumors. He knows it has been my task to gather European support for al-Rashid."

"Will you be in greater danger in Morocco?"

"No more so than here or anywhere else, I expect. After all, I have you and Akeefa. Hard to imagine anyone getting through you two."

"You give me more credit than I deserve, and I am only one man. Even with Akeefa, we are not invincible, and to think so would be folly."

The sheikh smiled.

René sat back in his chair. "You do not indulge in folly, as far as I have seen, so I am certain there are more forces on the board."

The sheikh's smile widened. "Come, my young friend. Did I not hear you promised Akeefa a walk on deck?"

"I did and while we speak of folly, breaking a promise to Akeefa would perhaps add reckless to its definition."

When Akeefa stepped above deck, every eye tracked her movements as though magnetized. She wore a black burqa so only her eyes showed. Sabah, who kept her gaze fixed straight ahead, marched in front of her as if to intercept the thoughts and intentions of the sailors before they reached her charge. Making eight knots, the *Seahawk* glided over the swells, its cream-colored canvas snapping in the wind.

René led the way up the stairs to the forecastle. Peering over the bow, he gestured. "It seems we have company." His guests joined him at the rail.

Akeefa clapped her hands and exclaimed in delight at the dolphins that raced along the bow wave, crossing back and forth in front of it as if the ship was motionless.

"So graceful." She leaned a bit over the rail pointing first at one and then another, fascinated by their play.

"They are supposed to be good luck." While she enjoyed the antics of the dolphins, René was captivated by her grace, the movement of her hands, and the joy in her voice.

"Sail, ho!" Andrew yelled from high above in the crow's nest.

René's gaze followed Andrew's arm to the quadrant from which threat could come. He turned to Akeefa and her father.

"It would be best if you went below decks."

She took a deep breath and, with her hand on her hip, stared at him.

"For now. Just for now. I am sorry, but you do not know what to do and will only be in the way. If your sword is needed, I promise I will not be shy in inviting you to join the party." René squinted in the direction indicated by Andrew. He could not see the ship yet. Thankfully, Andrew had keen eyes.

"Come, Akeefa, We will do as René suggests." The sheikh took her arm.

"We will be called if we are needed?"

"If it comes to that, you will know." René kicked off his shoes and made for the mainmast. The crow's nest was not a customary perch for a captain, but he needed to see the flags the ship was flying. The men gawked as he scampered up the rigging and in a blink he had joined Andrew. "Which direction, Mister

Merchant?"

"That way, sir." Andrew pointed.

René focused on a ship visible against the horizon. Fortunately, the setting sun gave a clear outline of the vessel. The flags... there was something about the flags.

"Damn. 'Tis the *Belle Poulé*. Run up the Gilbert flag," he called down to James. "Bring down the main sail, but keep her trim. Let her come alongside."

The ship he knew so well turned toward them. As it grew larger on the horizon, a feeling deep within expanded. Something was wrong. He asked Andrew for the ship's glass to gain a better look. Squinting and closing one eye, he saw that the *Belle Poulé* wallowed. Something had happened to the sprightly vessel he remembered. He studied her. One-half of her yardarm was missing, and there were holes in the rigging. The *Belle Poulé* had been in a fight. Had she won or lost? He would not know until he spoke with her master. He prayed it would be Jacques, but his growing sense of dread argued against the hope for that outcome.

"Andrew, keep your eye on that ship. Sing out if you see the gun ports opened or anything else that looks out of the ordinary. If we get into a fight, you stay up here. Do you understand?"

"You don't think I will be any help in a fight." Andrew's shoulders dropped and his gaze lowered to the planks of the crow's nest. "I understand, sir."

"*Non*, you do not. I need you where your eyes and voice can help me the most. You know how to fire a weapon. Go down now and claim one with enough powder and shot. You will be able to see me clearly when I go across to the *Belle Poulé*. If you see me draw my sword, fire a signal shot so the crew will know we are in a fight. Can you do that?"

"Yes, sir, I surely can," Andrew called, already out of the crow's nest and on his way down the mast.

René looked at the *Belle Poulé* and a jolt of premonition surged through him. His awareness deepened fractionally. He climbed out of the lookout and went down the rigging only a hair slower than Andrew had.

"James," René called.

James ran up to René "Yes, sir."

"Call the men to quarters, but quietly. Do not open the gun ports."

"I thought this ship was one of your father's?"

"'Tis, but something is wrong." René continued to stare at the oncoming ship.

"Do you know what it is?"

"*Non*, and we may not until the last moment." René paused, deep in thought. "Have John prepare to put twenty men into the longboats on the port side of the ship. We will keep starboard to them when they tie up. Tell him to take the boats around to their starboard and be ready to board her. If we need him, he will know it. Arm the rest of the men, but tell them to keep the arms under cover. I do not want to provoke a fight, but I will not have us caught with our powder wet, either."

"Aye, aye, Captain. And the Musselmen, sir?"

"If we are joined in battle, it will not be with cannon, so have Khalid gather his men and remain aboard ship to protect his father and sister. I want you beside me. Remember, keep the arms out of sight until we know."

"Yes, sir." James hurried aft to find John Abel.

René made for the hatch to inform the sheikh and Akeefa of the ship's contact. Before descending, he took one more look at the *Belle Poulé*. His expression changed from one of concern to one that entertained much darker thoughts. He fought against the grim truth his intuition brought him, against the pain and death he would visit on those responsible. He breathed evenly, initiating certain physiological responses that would prepare him for battle, and then went below deck.

"I prefer you remain here until I can ascertain the situation with the *Belle Poulé*," said René to the sheikh and Akeefa.

"You sense something is amiss?" asked the sheikh.

"*Oui*, I do."

"Then you will need our help." Akeefa took a step forward.

"If I do, you will know. I have detailed Khalid and his men to guard the hatch. Should it become necessary, you will be able to come above deck. *S'il vous plaît*, Akeefa, understand I am not posturing. Strategically it is our best course of action to keep you in reserve. Besides, I am not yet convinced there is a problem."

"Oh, yes, you are. You refuse to accept what you know, because you do not want it to be true. You had friends aboard that vessel?" she asked.

"*Oui*, now will you do as I ask?"

"Yes," answered the sheikh for himself and his daughter.

"*Merci*." Like striding against an ebb tide, René went up on deck to meet his old ship.

The *Belle Poulé* was much closer now, and it was obvious she had been in a serious battle. The damage was apparent, but more concerning was the way she moved. She wallowed through her tack. He had served aboard the *Belle Poulé* twice, and the crew he had trained with were not sailing this ship. The *Seahawk* could easily have shown the *Belle Poulé* her wake. Any other ship and he might have done just that, but not the *Poulé*. This was *his* ship. When it was finally within hailing distance, a voice he recognized called out. It belonged to Emile Lamert, first mate of the *Belle Poulé,* and he relaxed—a little.

"Ahoy, the ship. We be the *Belle Poulé* out of Bordeaux,"

Although Emile stood at the rail, hand to his mouth, none of the sailors that slouched around him were familiar.

"Ahoy, the ship. We are the *Seahawk* out of Marseilles," James bellowed. "Heave to and tie up."

The *Belle Poulé* was a galleon of the low-charged design. She had a relatively high aftcastle and a low forecastle, making her maneuverable but with plenty of space for cargo. With half of her yard gone and the sails and shrouds in distress, she was not going anywhere fast. The *Belle Poulé* slowly came alongside the *Seahawk* and presented her port side. The two ships came within boarding distance of each other, and coils of rope came across.

"James, make fast the ropes, but tie 'em so we can get loose in a hurry if need be. I do not recognize anyone aboard that ship except Emile Lamert," René said under his breath.

The customary practice was for the captain of the smaller vessel to cross to the larger vessel in the absence of known rank aboard either.

"Permission to come aboard, sir," René called to Emile. Emile's eyes widened in recognition, but the man gave no other sign. Another sailor moved closer to Emile and said something to him.

"Permission granted, sir," Emile replied, as if René was a stranger.

The rope ladders thrown over the side of each ship made it easy for either crew to cross over to the other vessel. René jumped across with James right behind him. Both men were armed.

"I am René Dalembert, and this is my lieutenant, James Bailey, of the ship *Seahawk,* recently out of Marseilles," said René, as if meeting Emile for the first time.

"Emile Lamert, acting captain of the *Belle Poulé*," Emile's voice was a growl, and he accented the word "acting." Before he said anything more, the other sailor, a large man with broken teeth, cut in. "P'rhaps the captain would like to take tea in his cabin with this young gentleman captain." He had a cutlass through the sash around his waist, as did all of the men except Emile, who was not armed.

Emile's left arm hung limp at his side. René sensed the battle raging within him.

"We ran into some bad weather, and I have spent enough time below decks. Do you think we could have tea here out in the sunshine?" René asked Emile.

Emile stood silent.

"Of course. Let's have tea out here in the sunshine." The man with the broken teeth turned to a pirate standing behind René. "George, we will be taking a spot of tea out here on deck. P'rhaps you can find some crumpets to go with it." He nodded to the man.

René had been ready from the moment he stepped aboard. The man behind him was reaching forward with his cutlass to stab him through the back. René had already turned, however, and with one swipe took the man's hand off at the wrist. The man screamed and clutched his stump. René plucked his cutlass out of the air and threw it to Emile.

"Good afternoon, Emile. 'Tis nice to see you, sir," he said, as he ran the screaming man through.

"We thought you was dead, Master René." Emile swiveled to face the large man with the bad teeth.

There was an immediate report from the crow's nest aboard the *Seahawk* as Andrew fired his weapon. The battle started. The pirate captain turned and fled aft, screaming at his men as he went.

"Where is Jacques? Is he still alive?" asked René as he waded through the pirates.

"He is locked up in the hold, along with the rest of the *Poulé's* crew. Those Anton there has not killed," Emile said through gritted teeth, as he cut through the throat of the man in front of him.

René sensed the rage and frustration radiating from the big man in waves. "Can we get to him?"

"We can try to free the crew, but Jacques has been wounded bad. We will not be moving him." Emile engaged the next man.

Men from the *Seahawk* poured over the sides, but they were badly outnumbered, and the pirates were also crossing to the *Seahawk*. A rude surprise awaited them when they reached the *Seahawk's* hatchway.

The *Belle Poulé* was a large ship, and if it was fully crewed, the advantage would be almost two to one. René was glad of his crew's fencing drills, for without them, two to one odds were fearsome, especially at sea where reinforcement was impossible and retreat improbable. He planned to reduce the odds a bit more.

With that thought, René centered himself and began a deadly march through the pirate crew, disabling when he could, killing when there was no alternative. He intuitively swayed aside as a musket ball flew through the space he had occupied. He completed the movement by turning and throwing his knife. One of the pirates fell from the rigging, a blade jutting from his throat.

"There," Emile pointed to the hatch cover. He wheezed and bent over to get his breath. The pirates had worked him hard and treated him worse. Jacques Coudray's life and the lives of his shipmates had been hostage to his good behavior.

René released the pins holding down the hatch and then clutched the metal rings. "Emile, will you watch my back up here?"

"Better than I did in Bordeaux," Emile said with a determination that sounded like death.

"It was not your fault, my friend. It was an idiot young man's prank that was responsible, and if you think you could have watched me every minute of every day, you are wrong," René rested his hand on Emile's shoulder. "Just young stupidity. You cannot protect against that. Let us get through this, and we will sort it all out."

René threw back the hatch and started down the ladder. He jumped the last few rungs, making certain there were no surprises waiting for him. He knew this ship. The only place large enough to hold Jacques and the crew was in the forward hold. He moved quietly, his senses alert to anyone in his way.

Four men guarded the hold door. René stood silent, collecting information. The guards were hardened sailors armed with cutlasses, and within this cramped space, the shorter sword gave them a small advantage. There would be no quarter given. With that thought, he threw his last knife into the eye of the man on the right and advanced toward the remaining three. He switched the sword into his left hand and struck down the man nearest him before he stepped back out of sword range. Now there were only two, their faces frozen in disbelief at the speed with which this boy had reduced their number by half. They rallied and attacked as one.

René spun around the first pirate to reach him, stabbing him through the kidney as he went by. That left one pirate who, by the fear written across his face, knew he was dead. There would be no escape. René blocked the only exit. He aimed a wild slicing cut at René that would have taken his head clean off if it had connected. René was no longer in that space, though. And with a flick of his blade, the man fell to his knees, his life bubbling out through the hole in his throat.

René pulled the pin from the latch and opened the hold door, stepping back as he did so. He yelled into the dark space. "I am

René Gilbert, of Gilbert Ltd. I would speak with Jacques Coudray, captain of this vessel."

A raspy voice came out of the darkness. "What name did you go by when you worked in my hold?"

René smiled at the memory. "You enjoyed calling me Worm, and I had the pleasure of serving aboard the best ship on the seven seas."

"Strike me a light, boys," Jacques wheezed. "I believe this ship has reverted to her original owners. 'Tis about time, too."

René stood aside as the men came out, carrying Jacques. He was in a bad way. They all were. Jacques's right arm ended in a blood-stained bandage at his wrist, and the rest of him looked like death. He had been a giant of a man, in spirit as well as physique. The man before René was shrunken and appeared much older, with watery eyes sunk deep into their sockets. If René had not recognized his voice, he would have doubted this was Jacques Coudray.

"Will you be all right, Jacques? I have more work to do top side. I need a couple of you men to stay with the captain and the rest to come with me." René took Jacques hand. "We will talk later, old friend. I am certain you have enough stories to keep me up all night."

"'Tis good to see you, son. We thought you were dead. 'Tis good to see you," he said again, his breathing ragged.

"I will be back as soon as I can." René leaned down to retrieve the knife he had thrown. Then he was gone, up the ladder and back into the fight, followed by the original crew of the *Belle Poulé*.

The fight still raged aboard the *Poulé*, but some of the pirates, including their captain, had crossed to the Seahawk. They wanted an undamaged ship, *his*. He spotted James.

"James, finish cleaning up this ship and then come find me aboard the *Seahawk*. Did John and his men come aboard all right?"

"Broke the back of the fight. I sent 'em back to the *Seahawk*. I will be following you when I have finished here. Go ahead, you still have work to do." James turned to parry a sword thrust from one of the remaining pirates.

René crossed to the *Seahawk* and then paused to take in the situation. He looked critically at the obvious difference in sword skill between the two crews. The grin on his face would never be taken for humor, but he was more than satisfied with his men's skills.

A large man pressed a group of pirates to attack the Musselmen who guarded the hatch. Dead bodies surrounded Khalid and his men. They, in return, had not suffered any casualties. He fought his way toward them, keeping his eye on them as he waded through the melee. A musket boomed. He turned in time to see one of the pirates at his back fall, clutching his chest. Up in the crow's nest, Andrew was reloading his firearm as fast as possible.

René's grin returned.

Perhaps this alone was responsible for the rapid clatter of weapons striking the deck. René knew full well it did not look like someone taking pleasure in an activity. It was more reminiscent of a mountain lion spreading its mouth to bare its fangs. Combined with implacable eyes and the elegant carnage behind him, his expression had made more than one man lose heart and surrender.

René's attention was now on Khalid, his group of men, and the pirates facing them. The hatch cover was open, and he was quite certain who waited on the other side of that hatch. The pirate captain loaded and primed his pistol and then brought it to bear on Khalid when a long knife, thrown from within the hatch, sprouted from the man's right eye. René waded into the fray, joining Khalid and his men. This last group of pirates, exhorted on by their remaining leaders, refused to lay down their weapons.

Blocking a vicious cut, Khalid deflected an attacker's sword down and to the right. His own weapon was a blur coming back up across the man's arm. It completed its lightning-swift arc by passing across the pirate's neck. Blood exploded from the opened artery. The man's eyes widened in surprise. Khalid completed the turn in time to see a pirate jab a six foot pike toward René's back. Instinctively, he threw his scimitar. Glittering through the air, the sword competed with the pike's trajectory and won. The weapon slammed into the man's side with the smacking sound of a cleaver meeting a side of beef. Released from dead fingers, the iron pike clattered to the deck, followed by the pirate's body.

René faced Khalid, and for a moment out of time, the battle ceased. Both men nodded. True brotherhood is often exchanged without fanfare or words.

"*Merci*," René said.

"My pleasure." Khalid leaned down to retrieve a sword dropped by one of the fallen pirates.

The awareness that the battle had been lost washed across the faces of the remaining pirates aboard the *Seahawk*. Clenched hands released weapons that clattered to the deck.

"Khalid, will you inform your father and sister the battle is over." said René.

"Perhaps you might care to accompany me?"

René laughed. "Do you anticipate a greater danger below than experienced up here?"

"I do not see *you* moving toward the hatch," said Khalid.

"I do not have to. I am the captain. Take some of your men with you."

Khalid's face wore its usual sardonic smile. "The risk will be the same. I do not have enough men."

René laughed and called out as he crossed the deck to John Abel, "I will see you later."

"Hopefully," Khalid murmured and turned toward the hatch.

"Are you wounded, Mister Abel?" asked René.

"No, sir."

"Secure the pirate survivors in the hold and take the badly wounded among them to Doctor Zahrawi."

"Yes, sir."

René surveyed the *Seahawk*. His men had done well. There would be a butcher's bill to pay, there always was, but the *Seahawk* had proved itself a fighting ship.

As René entered the captain's cabin aboard the *Seahawk*, he found Emile drinking a brandy while he inspected the colorful carpets and silks that now decorated the floor and walls. The doctor had reset Emile's broken arm, which was bound and immobilized.

Emile met his gaze. René knew the man well enough to hear the unspoken question and smiled at the thought of all the stories they would share. "In time, Emile. We will sort it out in good time. For now, are you up to taking command of the *Belle Poulé*? Jacques will not be fit for a while, if ever. Al Zahrawi is working on him, but the possibility exists he will lose the rest of the arm. Was he injured in the fight?"

"No. We torched their ship, and they had nowhere to go. Like rats, there were too many of them. Jacques surrendered before they could slaughter us all. That damned pirate had his hand tied to the rail. He made us watch, with our hands tied and a dozen muskets trained on us. Said Jacques needed to be punished for destroying his ship. He lopped his hand off with a cutlass. Had to chop twice. Told me every time I said no he would take someone else's hand. I been sayin' yes ever since. I cannot tell you how much I appreciated bein' able to say no today. To answer your first question, I am able to command the *Poulé*, but I do not deserve the post." Emile studied the floor as if unable to meet René's eye.

"And why is that?"

"I been lickin' spit for the last two months. Always thought I had at least as much courage as the next man. Seems not."

"You must not mistake courage for stupidity. How many of your men still have two hands? You protected this crew in the only way open to you. We will have justice, and I believe you have the right to decide on it. For now, however, I need someone to take command of the *Belle Poulé* and see to her repairs. Will you take command, Mister Lamert?"

"Aye, sir," Emile said and stood to leave.

"Emile, you are not at fault here."

"Will that be all, sir?"

"*Oui.*"

Emile closed the door behind him. The cabin's lantern rocked easily on its gimbals throwing the flickering light against the scenic carpets on the walls.

Four months. A mere blink of time. Four months ago René had ridden with Martin and Clarisse. And now he was the captain of the *Seahawk* and responsible for the wellbeing of every soul aboard the *Poulé*. Lives rested in his hands and his history of protecting others was filled with failure. He now understood the weight Emile labored beneath, but their roles had changed.

Command by its nature is solitary. Fear must never be shared. Not by word, look, or deed. To do so is to release a contagion that can never be cured. Transfer its fire into anger against your enemies, but do not ask for solace from your allies.

And Clarisse. He tried to avoid thoughts of her but that was impossible. He had sent disguised letters from Marseilles, but had no way of knowing if they had been received. She must think him dead by now.

René opened the ship's rutter and dipped the sharpened quill into the small bottle of ink. Thoughts of Clarisse and his father would bear inedible fruit whose only use would be to siphon his energy from the task at hand. He began to write.

CHAPTER TWENTY-EIGHT

"*MAMAN*, I allowed you to badger me into coming, but I refuse to participate in this ridiculous charade." Although Clarisse forced herself to remain in her chair, she barely managed to keep her voice at a reasonable volume.

"Clarisse, dear, it will not hurt you to meet some of these *very* eligible young men." Her mother tapped the closed fan against her palm.

Her mother's lips were pinched tight as she too maintained an outward air of decorum in contrast to the raucous frivolities of the Twelfth Night festivities that filled the room. "The decorations are magnificent, are they not?"

"*Oui, Maman.*"

"You do realize how fortunate we are to have been invited to this particular *soirée.*" Her mother turned to face Clarisse. "The young men here are—"

"Children."

"Clarisse! They are young scions who will mature. One day they will assume their fathers' rank and wealth. The young man you pine for has been gone for almost four months. I am sorry, dear. I know you loved René."

"Love, *Maman.*"

"If he were alive, would he not have gotten word to you?"

Her words created an abyss filled with silence. And intense pain.

Clarisse stood, every muscle taut with repressed anger. "René is alive. I cannot tell you how I know this to be true, but as I stand before you, he is alive and he will return to me."

Her father chose that moment to carry over three small plates of cake.

"'Twas my good fortune to have been close by when they cut the Twelfth Night Cake. I forget they do so early in the evening so the children may partake. Perhaps one of us will find the bean inside and become the king or queen of this evening's gaiety."

The smile dropped from his face as he handed Clarisse and his wife each a small gilded plate. Clarisse remained silent and so did her mother. The silence lengthened.

"The decorations are magnificent, are they not?" her father said around a mouthful of frosting.

"*Oui*, Edmond," and "*Oui, Papa*," were voiced simultaneously and with equal enthusiasm.

Clarisse set her untouched cake on a small table.

"*Papa*, I have a headache. May I retire from this evening's merriment?" Casting a glance at her mother. "I fear the pain will only increase as the evening progresses."

"Of course, dear. I will notify Alfred to bring the carriage around."

"*Merci*."

He raised his hand to signal a passing servant when he caught sight of an old friend. "Arnaud," he called out. "Clarisse, you remember Doctor Cloutier."

A distinguished looking middle-aged gentleman approached them, accompanied by a strikingly handsome younger man.

Clarisse looked on the two with resignation and barely managed to relax the frustration on her wrinkled brow to an expression of social correctness. Regardless of its setting, this was to be a negotiation and Clarisse had learned from the best, her father. She sighed once, and then settled into the role of the dutiful daughter.

Her father gripped his friend's hand. "Ah, Arnaud, 'tis so good to see you. I did not know you were in Bordeaux."

"At the last minute, I was asked to replace Doctor Patin at a symposium here in Bordeaux. His health kept him in Paris. Unfortunately, the topic was Wren's transfusion experiments, and although of dubious utility, I did my best to give a credible report.

"But enough of that. I am pleased to see you under more auspicious circumstances. I am still saddened by the loss of those young men. Such a waste."

Involuntarily Clarisse's facial muscles hardened and then relaxed as she fought to remain calm.

Conversation paused.

The doctor turned to Clarisse, his expression contrite. "I am so sorry, my dear. How rude of me to bring up recent sorrows, especially at a pleasant occasion such as this one. *S'il vous plaît,* forgive me."

"Not at all, doctor. I am grateful you accompanied my father to the duel."

"I am only sorry there was nothing I could do."

Clarisse remained still, willing the tears to remain unshed. "*Merci.*"

Her father coughed and then said, "Arnaud, you remember my wife, Anne."

"How could I forget such a lovely woman?" The doctor bowed and then brushed her hand with his lips. "'Tis nice to see you again, Anne."

"The pleasure is mutual, Arnaud. But who have we here." To Clarisse's chagrin, her mother pointedly nodded at the young man standing beside the doctor. She then grasped Clarisse's arm and artfully turned her to face him.

"May I present my son, Nathan, a recently graduated physician who I am pleased to have join me at the symposium. Nathan, allow me to present my good friends *Monsieur* and *Madame* du Bourg and their daughter Clarisse."

"*Monsieur, madam, mademoiselle,*" Nathan bowed. "'Tis a pleasure to make your acquaintance.

"*S'il vous plaît, Papa,* my headache," Clarisse said under her breath.

"Perhaps I might help. I suffer from occasional headaches and always carry some tincture of feverfew with me. I find it to be most efficacious."

Clarisse hesitated.

Nathan held out his arm to Clarisse. "Moving away from stressful situations is also helpful."

She studied the tall physician. Dressed impeccably, he was clean shaven with brown hair tied in a queue at his nape. Clear brown eyes twinkled back at her.

"*Merci, monsieur.*" Clarisse took his arm. "I believe a glass of wine might help as well."

"*Madam, monsieur, Papa.*" Nathan nodded to each and then guided Clarisse across the edge of the dance floor. He signaled a servant who brought them both a glass of wine.

"I really do carry some tincture of feverfew." Nathan reached into his coat.

"*Merci,* but there is no need. You were correct. My headache has receded with the distance from its source."

"Powerful thing, distance. My father told me of the sorrow you recently experienced. I am sorry and will understand if you prefer to be alone."

"*Merci,* Doctor Cloutier, but I am fine."

"Nathan, *s'il vous plaît.*"

Clarisse eyed the young man standing before her and saw only honest intent. "Nathan, tell me what excites you most about your profession."

"We live in a violent world. Healing others, or at least attempting to heal others, gives me satisfaction that I cannot seem to find in any other endeavor."

"I know someone who felt—feels the same. You are fortunate to be able to exercise your satisfaction. Will you return to Paris after the symposium?"

"*Non,* actually. I have been offered a position at *La Maison Charité* here in Bordeaux."

"Is that not the poor house? Of what use can you be there?" Clarisse regretted the insensitive challenge the moment she voiced it.

"The poor get ill with the same pains and symptoms as those in this room." Nathan dropped his gaze to the floor. "I apologize. Your statement was nearly identical to one I have been arguing with my father over these last few days. I think it touched a foul humor within."

"The apology is mine for such a thoughtless comment. I too must have echoed some left over anger from a previous conversation with my mother."

They both laughed.

Clarisse's laughter died. "The irony is that my statement is similar in its thoughtless assumption to a dear friend's recent comment about war's usefulness."

Nathan's face was wrinkled as if he had just bitten into a lemon. "I fear I will be apologizing to you all night. My command of social speech rivals that of the unmitigated boor. I lack the patience to craft gentle speech. What I think just seems to come out. I am better with patients."

Clarisse cast a glance toward her mother only to find the two of them closely inspected. She sighed and then took his arm and guided him toward the far end of the salon. "Our conversation will go even better from across the room. Tell me more about *La Maison Charité*. Do they accept volunteers?"

CHAPTER TWENTY-NINE

FORTUNATELY, THE *Poulé*'s carpenter had survived. With both ship's carpenters at work, the *Belle Poulé*'s yardarm, shrouds, and braces went up quickly. They put the *Seahawk*'s old sail to good use so the *Belle Poulé* could enjoy a full spread of canvas. The remaining pirates were locked in the forward hold. René had crossed to the *Belle Poulé,* awaiting word from Al Zahrawi about Jacques.

"What is your cargo, Emile?" René's gaze held fast on the hatch.

"Well, 'twas mostly alcohol, wine and brandy."

"Was?"

"There has been a continuous party goin' on, and a good portion's been drunk up or destroyed. I guess they had no need to be tradin' it."

"What else have you got? I know my father, and he would not have filled this ship with just wine and brandy."

"No, sir, your father is a wise man. We got the usual: iron, trinkets, textiles, and some odds and ends. You never know what you will need in the way of trade goods. 'Tis always something small that seals the transaction."

"Emile, would you inventory what is left aboard? We need to work the *Belle Poulé* into our plans. How is your arm?"

"'Twas not pleasant getting it set right. That damn Musselman had to break it again, but he assures me 'twill heal straight, and I will have almost full use of it. Good thing 'twas not my fighting arm. Still and all, I am glad it remains attached." Emile's voice softened. "Well, work's not being done while I stand here. Will that be all, sir?"

"*Oui.*" As Emile began to walk away, René called to him. "You see that someone else moves the cargo. You are the acting captain, and I want you healthy."

"Aye, sir," he called back.

René paced a few feet and then stopped. Ordinarily he was calm in a stressful situation, but he had never felt more helpless. He could do nothing but wait, and he had never been good at that. Finally, Al Zahrawi came up the ladder. The look on his face was one that doctors had learned to wear from the beginnings of their profession. The news was not good.

"I am sorry, Captain, but there is nothing I can do for this man. The sickness in his arm has already gone too far. Taking the arm would not be enough. Perhaps the great Galen in ancient Rome would have known how to save this man's life, but I do not."

Everything stopped. René had known, but he refused to accept a world without Jacques. "I am certain you have done everything possible, and there is no fault attached to you. *Merci,* sir." He paused, trying to reorganize his chaotic thoughts. "Can you tell me how long he has left?"

"Not long, sir."

René stared at the hatch as a flood of memories assaulted him.

"With your permission, sir, I will continue tending to the rest of the men," Al Zahrawi finally said.

"*S'il vous plaît,* and *merci* for all your good work." René addressed the doctor without seeing him. What he saw was a young boy who worshiped the captain of the *Belle Poulé* and who had to face him and admit to some misconduct or mistake he had made.

There will be times when all your skill, all your training, and even all your love will not be enough for you to face what a moment has brought to you. There is a nameless force beyond this small world. To name it is to circumscribe it, and it has no boundaries. Still, it exists as you exist. I believe it is benevolent. Others do not. It matters not, but that it exists. Center yourself, and ask for support. Ask without expectation, without condition, and you may receive what you ask for.

René put his hand on the hatch and paused. In that moment, he reached out and sensed a pattern of loving thoughts surround him. Akeefa. She could not help but respond to his need. Then a far greater energy enfolded them both. It was indescribable, as far above love as love was above the small emotions of anger and fear. The energy surrounded them both for an interminable moment and then released them with a gentle breeze of assurance.

He had been about to sink into the abyss of guilt. In his heart he knew had he been aboard her, the *Belle Poulé* would have defeated the pirates. Without that one night of rebellious freedom, he would have been on this ship when the pirates attacked. He had not had a choice that night. The Maestro believed one's destiny was not fixed, however, there must be moments within one's story that were necessary to the integrity of a life's plan. René knew in his heart that night was one of those moments.

James had been overseeing the reconstruction of the *Belle Poulé*. He walked over to René. "Is there something I can do for you, sir?"

René drew in a deep, calming breath. "There is. Would you locate Mister Lamert and ask him to join me in the captain's cabin?"

"Yes, sir."

René climbed down the ladder into the passageway and walked toward the captain's cabin. His steward stood in front of the door as if guarding it.

"May I see the captain?"

"Yes, sir. He said to send you right in." The steward opened the door.

Jacques lay on the bed with his eyes closed, but René knew he was awake. Before the steward closed the door, René said, "When Mister Lamert gets here, send him right in."

"Yes, sir, straight away, sir."

The captain's cabin was well appointed with fine mahogany furniture, including a large table and dresser. A gentle sea breeze came through the open window. The room was quiet with only the occasional thuds and shouts as the repair work continued. René sat on a chair next to the bed. Jacques would open his eyes when he was ready. René peered closely at his previous captain. He seemed so much smaller than the force of nature that memory served.

René's initiation into the crew of the *Belle Poulé* flickered though his mind. He had been eleven. The crew had tied him to the figurehead at the front of the ship. There had been a chop that day, and about every fourth swell, a wave had risen, drenching him with salt water. They left him there for a good part of the afternoon. In the early evening, Jacques had come forward to squint at René.

"Hey, Worm, how you gonna serve my dinner—you bein' otherwise occupied?"

"I do not know, sir," René said.

"You agreed to take the job, and I am hungry."

"Perhaps we might get someone to take my place while I serve your dinner and then I could return," René offered.

Jacques laughed. "Perhaps we could, Worm, or I bein' the captain could cut you down and call it a day."

"I would not want to get special treatment, sir."

"Not to worry son, you're gettin' plenty of treatment and ain't none of it special," Jacques said in that deep bass voice of his. Turning to the nearest sailor, he yelled, "Cut 'im down. If my dinner ain't served on time, I will have you out there instead."

"Hello, Worm." Jacques opened his eyes.

"Hello, Jacques."

"Kind of casual, ain't we, Worm?" Jacques tugged a smile onto his weathered face.

"Sorry, Captain," René was unable to think of a single thing to say.

"Cat got your tongue, boy?" Jacques tried to sit.

"Here, let me help you, sir." René adjusted the pillows behind the captain's back. "Are you in much pain?"

"Nah, the Musselman gave me some laudanum. That stuff's better'n brandy. Don't hardly feel nothin' at all." He paused and studied René face. "I ain't gonna make port this time, am I, son?"

"*Non*, sir," Rene said quietly.

"Well, in all my days, my only real regret was my failure to protect a young man given into my charge, and now here he is sittin' in front of me, full of life. 'Tis much better to leave out here on the ocean than rottin' away in some tavern tellin' lies. I will miss watching you, son, and that is a fact. I got more pure pleasure out of seeing you make your way than I can say. I used to tell your father I appreciated the loan of his son. He answered back that he expected interest on the loan. Does your father know you're alive?"

"I could not take a chance on writing him directly, but I wrote to Henri and to Clarisse, and if either one got through, then he will know. You are aware of my situation. I cannot return until I have the power to defeat the elder Gaspard." Frustration filled René's voice.

"Looks to me you made a pretty good start. You got two good ships. Men have begun with a lot less. When you see your father, give 'im my regards, and apologize for me."

"Apologize for what?"

"Well, I ain't never lost a cargo before," Jacques muttered.

"Far as I can tell, you have not lost this one either. I know they drank some of the wine and brandy, but we still have plenty to trade with, and a ship to trade in. You did not lose anything, and I will tell my father so when I see him." René reached for Jacques' shoulder.

The steward knocked on the door. "Enter," said Jacques.

The door opened, and Emile stepped inside, cap in his hand. "How you doin', Cap'n?"

"I have been better, Emile." Jacques inspected his first mate. "René, would you mind stepping outside for a moment. I believe Monsieur Lamert and I need to talk for a bit."

"Not at all, sir." René walked into the passageway and closed the door behind him.

René heard Jacques speaking. He remembered the tone of voice, and it was almost like old times. René allowed the minutes to wash over him and then the door opened and Emile beckoned him inside.

Emile was once again the old, sardonic sailor who had taught him most of what he knew about cargo and its storage. Jacques, however, had shrunk even further, having expended most of his remaining strength.

"I relinquish the captaincy and this ship and request and advise you assign it to Mister Lamert," Jacques said, in a barely understandable voice.

"I reject your resignation, sir. You will remain the captain aboard this ship until either you leave it or it leaves you," René said. "Mister Lamert will have the title and the ship in due course, but not yet."

"Gettin' a bit of your own back, are ya, Worm?" asked Jacques.

René smiled. "Something like that, sir."

Jacques took a deep breath. "'Tis been an honor and a pleasure serving with ya both." He looked at René and his eyes widened, as if he were seeing something other than the man standing before him. Jacques smiled and then the smile faded. He tried to breathe, but only managed a weak cough. A trickle of blood ran from the corner of his mouth. He tried again and then with a certain amount of stubbornness, his eyes closed, and Jacques Coudray relinquished both his captaincy of the *Belle Poulé* and—of lesser importance to him—his sojourn upon this earth.

René and Emile stood for a moment. Even the *Belle Poulé* settled quietly, and the sounds of repair ceased, as if the ship knew. "*Au revoir*, sir. It was an honor and a pleasure serving with you as well." René turned to Emile. "Mister Lamert, are you prepared to captain this ship under my colors?"

Emile straightened. "I am, sir. I accept the commission and the ship."

"Emile, I must ask. Have you dealt with your demons?"

"The captain had a word or two with my demons, and I believe they will be of service to me now, and not the other way round."

He smiled his crooked smile. "Do you have specific orders, sir?"

"Continue making your ship sea-worthy, and let me know when she is. We will have a service for Captain Coudray this afternoon at two bells into the dogwatch. *S'il vous plaît*, advise the crew. That will be all, sir." René sat beside Jacques to spend time with his grief.

"Thank you, sir." Emile nodded toward Jacques and left René alone in the cabin.

At the appointed time, the crews of both vessels assembled aboard the *Belle Poulé*, amidships. The setting sun glinted from a calm swell, the whitecaps sparkling against a background of dark green as the sea paid homage to one of its own. They had wrapped the body in sailcloth, with each of the men who had sailed under Jacques—including René—adding a stitch to seal it. Two six-pound cannon balls were sewn into the bottom of the shroud as well, to help Jacques on his way. The body rested feet first atop a wide oak plank placed through an opening in the starboard gunwale. The sea quieted, and the men followed suit.

The duty and privilege of giving the eulogy belonged to Emile as captain of the *Belle Poulé*. René was content with this; he was not certain he could have spoken at that moment even if he wanted to.

Emile wore his dress uniform, as did the other officers from both ships. The rest of the men wore whatever passed for their best clothes.

"I had the honor..." Emile began, and then paused to take a breath, steadying himself. "I had the honor of sailin' with Jacques Coudray for ten years. I never met a living soul with a clearer sense of integrity. If I were to list the things Captain Coudray accomplished in a single lifetime, we would still be standin' here watching the sun rise tomorrow. I can hear Jacques' voice in me ear though, saying, 'Get on with it.'" Emile walked over and put his hand on the sailcloth shroud. "Jacques, I cannot let you go without saying *merci*. *Merci* for keeping me in the flesh on more than one occasion. *Merci* for teaching us all you could. To transfer everything you knew would have taken more than one lifetime. And *merci* for the good name of this ship in all the ports she has ever touched. You will be missed, Captain." Emile nodded to the boatswain, who gave the command to the starboard gun crew. The even numbered cannon fired. The noise and smoke broke the silence, and time seemed to restart.

René went over to the shroud and placed his hand on it. "I will add my *merci*, sir. May you have a safe journey, with the wind at your back."

Emile nodded to the honor guard standing beside the body. They lifted the board, allowing Jacques Coudray to leave the *Belle Poulé* for the last time. As the body entered the water, the sun began to set in earnest, and the sea turned a darker green.

CHAPTER THIRTY

A FULL week passed and the *Belle Poulé* was as ready as she would ever be. Still, the Seahawk would need to shorten her sail so the *Poulé* could keep up with her. The plan seemed prudent given that both ships were running with minimal crews. René and Emile leaned on the railing of the *Belle Poulé's* aftcastle, watching the late afternoon sun finish its artwork for the day.

"We will be travelin' through the Balearics, and I intend to find an appropriate home for 'em there." Emile smiled, an expression devoid of humor.

There were thirty-eight pirates still alive, housed in the forward hold. In England or France, the authorities would have hung them. In Spain, where slavers ravaged the coast and able bodied seamen were scarce, they would be indentured into service.

"Emile, you have the authority here, and 'tis your ship that demands justice. I will abide by your decision, but are there none among these men that could be put to better use?"

"I would be happy to hang 'em all from the yardarm we replaced, but I will not foul this ship further. This group is as close to animals as makes no difference, and I will not be responsible for their preyin' on anyone else." Emile's voice was a growl. "We will drop 'em off on a likely island. If their god wants 'em off, he will take 'em off, and if not, they will rot there."

They had obviously reached the end of this conversation. "We will take the ships into Malaga. Our intention is to trade for goods, mainly Spanish swords the new Sultan will pay well for.

You do not have to abide by my wishes, of course. My father has not seconded them, and he is the one you work for. You know the situation. I offer you the choice of returning to Bordeaux or accompanying me."

Emile laughed. "I will not likely be desertin' you now. We both know your father, and I have no doubt he'd approve your decision. Oh, he might not be so tickled at your destination, but he'd want you as strong as possible and that means with the *Belle Poulé* alongside. Speakin' of which, you promised me the mysteries would be sorted out soon as we got the *Poulé* repaired."

"*Oui*. Come to the *Seahawk* for dinner tonight, and I will fill in as many blanks as I can. We will get the ships under way after that. How is the arm?"

"Better every day. That Musselman doctor knows his stuff, and you are lucky to have 'im. We lost Doc Flaubert in the fight. He never was much of a fighter. We lost a lot of good men. 'Twill ease their memory a bit to drop off our unwelcome passengers and get this business done with."

"I will return to my ship then." A rope ladder was thrown over the side. The rope ladder went down to where one could easily jump across to the same thrown over the *Seahawk's* side. René climbed down and prepared to cross over to the *Seahawk*. "Until tonight."

When René entered the captain's cabin aboard the *Seahawk*, he was transported to another world. Akeefa had taken responsibility for the evening's dinner, which she would be attending. She had redecorated the cabin to reflect the sheikh's status as well as her own. Not an inch of wall was without a fabulously colorful carpet or silken work of art. Precious metals and stones sparkled from some of the wall hangings. Several of them depicted stories or scenes where fantastic beasts competed for the eye with mundane trappings that could have been from any farm in France. The tablecloth was more muted, a cream-colored work of the finest linen, but it was no less impressive. The eating utensils were silver with intricately carved ivory handles.

René found Emile in animated discussion with Khalid and the sheikh. "Welcome, my young partner." The sheikh smiled broadly. "Come and join us. Monsieur Lamert has been regaling us with your youthful exploits."

"I was afraid of that. How am I to keep any respect if all my youthful mistakes are shared with my partner?" René laughed. "Mister Lamert, I am counting on your discretion."

"And you shall have it, sir, within the bounds of reasonable social discourse."

"Somehow I am not reassured, sir. I—"

Akeefa entered the room and all conversation—and all René's thoughts—stopped. Attired in a European-style gown of the palest blue silk, she glowed. The bodice of the gown was made of fine lace that rose up her neck. Sleeves of the same lace were caught at the wrists with ribbons of matching satin. By the European standards of the day, she was modestly covered, but the form-fitting gown left no doubt that this was a beautiful young woman. Breaking from the spell, René bowed to her and offered her his arm. She nodded and placed her hand on it. He escorted her over to Emile to introduce her, avoiding the sheikh's and Khalid's eyes.

"You look beautiful," he said. The words felt, and sounded, strangled.

Akeefa smiled that smile at him. "Thank you, sir. You look quite dashing yourself."

Clearing his throat to make certain of his voice, he began the introductions. "Monsieur Lamert, may I present Akeefa bint Ammar Faruq Ghassan. *Mademoiselle*, I am pleased to introduce Monsieur Emile Lamert, captain of the *Belle Poulé*."

Emile bowed with his best French manners and held her hand. Having at least a general acquaintance with Moroccan culture, he did not kiss the young woman's hand. That was just as well, for the atmosphere of disapproval in the room was already thick enough to cut with a rapier.

"'Tis a pleasure to meet you, *mademoiselle*."

"The pleasure is mine, sir. I have heard all about your bravery and look forward to hearing about the fight to secure your vessel," she said. Then she turned to the sheikh and bowed low to him. "Father, thank you for allowing me this evening. I understand the distress it must be causing you, and if you require it, I will repair to my room. These few moments have made me so happy that I will be content."

With those few words the tension in the room evaporated, and it was trusted friends enjoying a meal again.

"My beloved daughter, we are among friends. For this once, I am disposed to put aside our customs in honor of the men who have seen us safely through our recent difficulties."

Akeefa turned to Khalid. "Beloved brother, are you also amenable to my being present in this fashion?"

Khalid was nonplussed to be asked. Despite their paternalistic society, he was the youngest of the sheikh's children, and the two were the closest of friends. He recovered quickly, put on a sardonic expression and raised one eyebrow. "My beloved sister, in whom the sun rises and sets, far be it from me to take affront when our esteemed father has not. As always, and however you wish it, I am your servant." He executed a flamboyant bow.

A moment later, Sabah entered the cabin carrying a tray of hot and cold salads. She refused to even so much as glance toward Akeefa. She left the food and returned with warm flat bread, which served Moroccan culture as both staple and utensil.

Mister Downs, the *Seahawk*'s cook, was not in evidence, and René wondered at his absence.

The dinner was lengthy and exquisite. A cuisine experience, each new dish competed with and complemented the previous one. As Sabah brought in the courses, René's amazement increased at the variety of foods aboard that he knew nothing about. In truth, he had not paid that much attention to the mix of victuals.

"Did you bring all of this food aboard with you, or did you somehow convince James to load it on?" asked René.

The sheikh smiled. "Well, there are limits to those comforts which I am prepared to surrender, and decent food is one of them.

You have been too busy to notice, but you have eaten better than would be expected aboard ship, although not with the variety we enjoyed tonight. Given our recent victory, I felt tonight's meal should be a bit more celebratory.

"I agree," said René. "Who prepared the food?"

"Well, I think Mister Downs and Sabah have come to an accommodation," said Akeefa. "Given there is only one galley aboard this ship, they were forced to accept a truce."

"I thought Mister Downs had been injured in the fight," said René.

There was a brief silence.

"Oh, I am certain the man was injured in the line of duty," Emile said, graciously filling the empty space. "He's none the worse for it, and the food is excellent."

"Monsieur Lamert—" Akeefa began.

"Emile, s'il vous plaît, mademoiselle," he interrupted.

"Emile," she corrected herself. "What is to be done with the remaining pirate crew?"

Apparently this was not a question Emile expected from a young woman, and he paused, clearing his throat. Not knowing what to say, he looked to René for assistance.

"You may answer her, Emile. Akeefa is quite able to withstand the knowledge."

"I intend to toss 'em out on the first suitable atoll we come upon once we reach the Balearic Islands." All pretense to polite conversation drained away.

"That seems like a lenient punishment to me," the sheikh said.

"'Tis not my intention the island be life-sustaining," Emile said. "No fresh water."

"Ah," said the sheikh.

"I expect the island to be free of its human garbage within short order," Emile said, without emotion.

"Monsieur Lamert, I am confident you will find no difficulty understanding the culture I come from. Now I believe a cup of coffee would be appreciated." The sheikh leaned back in his chair.

As if by magic, Sabah and Mister Downs entered the cabin. The cook carried a tray of small cakes, and Sabah bore the ever-present pot of strong, sweet coffee. There was also brandy for Mister Lamert. Downs had a large bruise on the side of his face that was strangely similar to the shape of the coffee pot.

"*Merci*, Mister Downs, the meal was excellent," René said, acknowledging him as the cook of the *Seahawk*.

"My pleasure, sir." Mister Downs covertly glanced at Sabah. "*Madame* Sabah and I decided, ah... she would serve, and I would mind the food. I am glad you enjoyed the meal." Sabah could have been cast from stone for all the reaction he received. "I must say I was ably aided by my assistant, *Madame* Sabah." Downs moved so that René's chair was between himself and the woman.

There was a slight rise in temperature at the word 'assistant.' Akeefa made a small head movement and the atmosphere calmed.

In order to prevent another, possibly deadly, encounter between Mister Downs and Sabah, René added, "Sabah, I am certain some of these dishes must have originated with you, and the food was excellent. I appreciate your contribution. We have all thoroughly enjoyed this meal."

Sabah came from a long line of women used to disguising their emotions, but René sensed her satisfaction. He also noted the smile Akeefa sent his way.

"Thank you, sir." Sabah turned to the sheikh and bowed deeply. "Will there be anything else, Abu?"

"No, thank you. The dinner was well prepared."

Her eyes widened as the compliment registered. The sheikh used compliments sparingly with his family. There would be no battles going on within the galley—if only for tonight.

One problem at a time.

"I believe you gentlemen will want to move on to a discussion of trade and other subjects to which I will not be able to add measurably, and so I will thank you again, beloved Baba, and you, my brother, for this memorable evening." Akeefa rose gracefully and walked over to her father, gave him a kiss on the cheek, and then followed Mister Downs and Sabah out of the cabin.

Emile asked permission to light a cigar, and the men got down to the task of planning a coordinated trading venture using both ships instead of the one.

"We should keep whatever alcohol that remains on board the *Belle Poulé* for trade once we reach Morocco," the sheikh said before sipping his coffee.

As the sheikh turned to Emile, the diamonds and rubies set into his tunic reflected the candlelight. René smiled to himself at the lengths a father will go to please a daughter. Sheikh Ghassan's customary dress was more utilitarian.

A truly powerful man has no need for you to be aware of that fact. The Maestro's voice was clear in René's mind.

"I thought your religion did not permit drinkin'," Emile said.

"The fact the Koran forbids the use of alcohol does not cause its use to disappear. Do the injunctions and prohibitions of your religion meet their intentions?"

Emile laughed. "Not by a long shot." He coughed, choking on a sip of brandy.

The sheikh smiled. "We will be smuggling, but in truth even the Sultan al-Rashid has been known to imbibe now and again. Perhaps more 'again' than not. The wine and brandy will lubricate our business dealings, and is it not true that often the success of a large business transaction depends on the smallest details for its completion?"

"I know we are supporting the new sultan, who you say will be more amenable to reason than his predecessor, but I am still uneasy about supplying weapons. What guarantee do we have these weapons will not be used against Europeans?" asked René.

"None," replied the sheikh. "I have never found a guarantee at either end of a sword. By Moroccan standards, however, al-Rashid is a more reasonable and moderate man than either his father or the majority of his siblings. At the moment, I, and others like me, have considerable influence with him. He knows that in order to enlarge his holdings and take his place as a modern ruler, he will have to have alliances with the west. That will mean curbing the Barbary corsairs and the white slave trade. It sounds contrary to reason to bring weapons to your enemy, but if your enemy is willing to accomplish your goals, it behooves you to assist him by helping him to remain in power. Do you believe I am using you for my own ends?"

"*Non*," replied René, who needed to stand and walk. "If the players on the board obey the rules of the game and continue to play, I am confident of our conclusions. That we must protect al-Rashid in order to help create a more moderate state is true. In all selfishness, I need a powerful patron if I am to best François Gaspard and have any hope of returning to France. Still, I am unsettled." He paused. A vague sense of uneasiness wove through him. But nothing more specific than that made itself known.

Once you have decided, put away conflicting thoughts, keeping them against the time when you may have to recalculate your conclusions. Until then they only weaken you. Do not entertain them.

"I cannot find fault with our plan, nor does a better alternative present itself to me. Therefore, we will continue with an enlarged version of our original plan," René said.

They discussed the expanded details of the venture until all were clear with their respective parts.

"I believe I will take a turn on deck to check on those who were injured." René nodded to Emile and then turned to Sheikh Ghassan. "With your leave, sir."

"Please do, sir. I shall remain and listen to a few more of Monsieur Lamert's tales. My credulity has been assaulted, but is not yet overthrown."

Emile raised his eyes in mock surprise. "Are you implying, sir, that I have employed some exaggeration in my accounts?"

"I am certain I never used the word 'some.'"

René laughed and closed the door. He was confident the good-natured banter would continue late into the night. He was glad it was not his cabin, however, as it had been a long day, and he was tired. Still, he needed to check on his men first.

CHAPTER THIRTY-ONE

"LAND HO," Andrew called out from the crow's nest. "Starboard, twenty degrees."

"*S'il vous plaît*, Mister Abel, signal the *Belle Poulé* we are changing course." René raised the spyglass to his eye. "Shorten sail, sir."

"Aye, aye, Captain."

The boatswain turned and yelled orders to the sailors in the rigging.

"James, have the men take soundings as far in front of us as possible. Charts say it gets shallow in these waters, and it shifts."

"Five fathoms," the sailor on the starboard lead line called out.

The *Seahawk* could make do with fewer than two fathoms, but the *Belle Poulé,* being larger, needed more depth or risked grounding.

"Four fathoms five," called the sailor on the port side.

The small bit of land in front of them was about a half-mile in diameter. It was mostly sand, with some sparse vegetation. There was no sign of a fresh water source, and René's charts made no mention of it.

"Drop anchor at three fathoms, sir," René ordered.

Three fathoms was sufficient for the *Belle Poulé*. René had qualms about this, but it was better than having the thirty-eight men hanging from the yardarm like curing pheasant. The *Belle Poulé* came to rest fifty yards from the *Seahawk*.

"Mister Abel, signal Mister Lamert to come aboard," René said.

"Aye, aye, Captain."

"Emile, you know I am not squeamish, but there are thirty-eight men here. Is there no other alternative?" René paced his small cabin.

"These scum'll have a larger chance than all of the innocents they sent to the bottom of the sea. Could be more of the same'll come by and pick 'em up. How appropriate, them bein' made slaves by the Sallee Rovers? That'd be pirates enslavin' pirates. You know what'll happen if we turn 'em over to the Spanish authorities."

"They will be auctioned off to whatever trading company offers the most silver."

"And we will end up facin' 'em again." Emile came to attention and addressed René. "Is that to be your orders, sir?"

"I said you would be responsible for seeing justice meted out to these men, and I hold to what I say. I wanted one last chance to come up with something that does not bloody our hands."

How much blood can my soul withstand?

"We live and die in difficult times. I believe Jacques would've been about followin' the same course of action, and if you think for a second, you will know 'tis but the truth." Emile's voice was quiet.

"He would have tossed 'em all overboard and saved himself the trouble."

"He would have, at that." Emile barked a quick laugh. "Your orders, sir?"

"Drop them off with a jug of water per man, and toss them a half dozen knives once the last man is ashore." René gave the order. Responsibility for his ships was his to accept.

"Aye, aye, Captain," said Emile as he clambered down into the ship's boat tied up to the *Seahawk*. Four sailors took up their oars and rowed him back to the *Belle Poulé*.

Longboats ferried the pirates out to the atoll. The men were dropped in the shallows, their hands tied. Each one had a jug of water about his neck. The last man ashore had an additional gift, a sack holding a half dozen knives. As he reached the shore, the other men converged on him like blow flies on a dead squirrel.

"Get us out of here, Mister Abel," commanded René.

"Make sail, Mister Wade," yelled the boatswain.

"Aye, aye, sir," Gavin Wade replied. He and the other men hoisted the main sail. As if even the ship wanted to be away from this place, the *Seahawk* showed her wake the moment her sails went up. In no time, the atoll had faded from sight, and they were back into the deeper blue waters of the Mediterranean.

René passed the watch to James and retired to his cabin.

René sat at his desk trying to meditate. This night his thoughts would not be tamed. There was a knock on the door.

"Enter."

The door opened, and Akeefa stood there. She was dressed in the loose-fitting garment worn by Arab women including a hijab that covered her hair. Out of deference to her father and brother, she wore traditional garb outside her cabin.

"May I come in?" she asked. "I do not mean to intrude, but I sensed your distress."

René jumped to his feet and pulled the chair out for her. "*S'il vous plaît*, come in. Is Sabah with you?" he asked, looking out into the passageway.

"No." She closed the door and then sat in the proffered chair. "I felt we could speak more easily without her continuous disapproval to muddy the air." Akeefa removed the hijab. "Are you uncomfortable with me being here alone?"

"I would not like to duel your father or brother should you be found in here with me."

"Do not worry, I will protect you." She cast a smile at him.

His heart beat faster. When Akeefa smiled, the world changed. It was as simple as that. "Well, then I will put my worrying aside. What would you like to talk about?"

"Are the pirates no longer aboard?"

"*Non*, and in truth most will be dead by the end of the day." He shook his head. The stronger would have already killed the weaker for their water. There would be fewer alive by tomorrow, and fewer still the day after.

"That is the reason for your sadness?" She held eye contact with him.

He sat on the bed, and then stood. The need to move overpowered him. The cabin was so small there was not enough space to wander around without bumping into her.

"I am merely feeling sorry for myself. I have no doubts these pirates merited such justice, but I am frustrated and saddened the responsibility for their deaths should have to rest with me."

"Are we not responsible for our own lives, within the destiny given to each of us?"

"I believe we are."

"Then where does the responsibility lie?"

"With the decisions made by each man," he responded automatically.

"And what then is *your* responsibility?" she pushed.

"To protect those I love." He dropped down again.

"And have you done that?"

René was silent for a moment, thinking of Martin. When he answered, he spoke as if each word spilled into a still pool. "I have not always succeeded, but in each instance, I believe I have tried to do so to the best of my ability."

The atmosphere in the cabin was thoughtful, but it began to heat. The tension rose a hundredfold. René again stood in an attempt to pace. Blocked, he turned to her.

"Would you like to spar? I could do with some exercise." He cleared his throat.

"I would love to, but I thought the hold was taken up by the injured."

"One has died, but the rest have recovered to the point where they can be taken back above deck. I will meet you in the hold in an hour."

René moved aside to allow her to pass.

Akeefa replaced her hijab. Her eyes sparkled with excitement. "In an hour."

René sucked in a deep breath and then let it out as he dropped onto the bed.

The hold took the better part of that hour to be cleaned of the remaining infirmary waste, used linens, and makeshift cots. Fortunately, Doctor Zahrawi demanded an immaculate workspace and lectured the crew to improve both their hygiene and the cleanliness of the ship. With the men moved, only the pungent smell of lye remained.

René loosened up and awaited Akeefa. She came into the hold wearing her traditional attire. Once she assured herself they were alone, she removed her outerwear to reveal the clothing she wore while sparring— shiny black silk pantaloons with a white silk blouse. She had braided her deep black hair securely atop her head. Without being obvious, he hoped, he looked at her closely. Had she bound her breasts? Having seen her in European garb, he knew she was much more buxom than he had previously thought. He supposed it had something to do with the economy of movement critical to fencing at their level. He allowed her time to warm up, watching as she gracefully moved through her exercises.

"*En garde,*" Akeefa called out to him, and they began their deadly dance.

The rapiers they had chosen came together with a rasp. Akeefa was a master of most edged weapons but she clearly enjoyed practicing with those she rarely used. In their sparring together, they had worked through many different types of swords.

Feint, high block. The swords sang through the air. Despite their adeptness, neither René nor Akeefa had yet managed to disarm the other. As they continued to spar, perspiration made Akeefa's blouse stick to her body. It became more transparent as the moments passed.

"You seem distant," she said as she slid round a thrust and took a wicked swipe at his head. He blocked. "Are you attempting a new type of centering technique?"

René was doing his best to center himself. He had never felt this way before. Rather than serving him, his internal focus was growing more disorganized by the minute. He blocked a cut to his leg and followed through toward her torso. The swords came together with a loud snick. Hers circled his with a familiar rasping, and in the next instant, he found himself standing there empty-handed. Motion stopped. They were both shocked. He looked at his sword lying on the deck and stepped back, shaking his head in disbelief.

Your inner self is a horse that is never broken. Do not ever think it has been; it will surprise you at the most inopportune moment. By the same token, however, do not fear it, for it is this untamed vital flow that powers your sword and your life. The Maestro had delivered this advice whilst taking a vicious cut at René's neck. *It is guaranteed to surprise you when you have the hubris to think nothing can.*

Akeefa leaned down, retrieved his sword, and held it out to him. Her expression changed as if she were preparing a sarcastic comment. Then she looked into his eyes and came to rest, still holding the sword. "René, are you hurt?"

"*Non*, I was remembering. There are things we must speak of, for I have encountered a weakness I do not think we can afford." He took her arm, leading her to a bench on the side of their space. "I am struggling with the remaining shreds of honor I possess, after having run from my home and those I love."

"But René—"

"I know," he interrupted her. "All of the reasons for my continued flight are valid, and 'twould be useless to throw my life away for no gain. I know all of this in my head, but my heart, Akeefa, cannot agree. I left behind a young woman who my soul recognized. I would not for my life betray her, but evidently, my heart is capable of recognizing more than one soul, and I am at a loss."

She shook her head. "I do not understand."

"*Oui*, you do, my dear friend, for you can see my heart as your own. And if I have no control of my heart, it appears my body will join the rebellion as well." René's hot face reflected his embarrassment as he fought the chaos within.

"What would you have me do?"

"Try not to kill me when we spar," he said, with a poor attempt at a laugh.

"As if I could ever do so. That, however, was not what I meant. You once told me that only in complete trust and honesty would we remain alive. I believe you were correct then, and only truth will save us now. I am also attracted to you. I do not know what love is, so I am unable to name what I feel. I know it empowers me at times, and at other times, it completely weakens me. I have yet to be able to control it, or even know which emotion it will bring. And yet, I trust you, and I trust our destiny. Somehow, I know that trying to force our destinies together or apart would be disastrous. For now it will have to be enough that we both know. We could not long hide our emotions from the other anyway. When you become distracted, if I must, I will help you focus your attention. You must do the same. Fortunately, we have a fine doctor aboard."

René glanced at her to see if she was smiling. A momentary jolt shot through him that she was not. They paused and then both smiled at the same time.

"Shall we begin again?" he asked as they stood and returned to their places. "I will do my best to hang on to my sword this time."

"You better," she said, and attacked.

CHAPTER THIRTY-TWO
Château Gaspard, Bordeaux, France

THE HOUR crossed midnight when the horses approached Château Gaspard. The noise caused Horemheb to glance out through the bolt holes that had been enlarged to create windows beside Victor's bed. Although firmly in control of Victor's body, even the slight movement that allowed him to see through the window brought excruciating pain. The torch light from the battlements reflected scarlet from burnished armor. Tied to his saddle, a man weaved back and forth, his struggle to remain upright a last effort to maintain what small hope survived. As they approached the bridge, his armored escorts pulled him from the saddle. One of the men banged his steel gauntlet against the château's massive wooden door. He was answered from above by no fewer than a dozen muskets aimed at his heart.

"Who goes there?"

"Auguste Curie, on the business of the *Comte*," said the armored man.

After a short wait, the door opened. The men entered, dragging their charge with them.

Horemheb summoned his servants. The majordomo was sure to lead the men to the *Comte's* library. And he intended to be present.

The rapid movement through the hallways caused Horemheb a great deal of pain, but his bearers managed to carry him to François Gaspard's library in time to intercept the guards and their prisoner.

The majordomo rapped his knuckles against the thick wood. "*Oui*," said François Gaspard.

"The men you were waiting for, sir, and your son."

"Enter."

Horemheb motioned to his bearers to move him to the corner of the room away from the *Comte's* desk. His gaze met that of Victor's father, but he remained silent.

The fire roared in the huge hearth, its heart beating chaotic patterns on the furnishings and books, bathing the room and its occupants with moving shadows. The guards escorted their prisoner, who was barely able to remain on his feet, into the room. No one spoke.

"It has come to my attention that the boy you were paid to remove a second time is still alive and healthy." Victor's father drummed his fingertips on the desktop.

"I was assured the boy had drowned," rasped the mercenary. He sounded as if he had difficulty breathing. "The captain accepted payment."

"I am aware of that, and the captain will be dealt with appropriately. Still, we are left with the fact you have failed. A second time."

"The boy is unusually skilled," the man pleaded. "I thought that was understood when the first two mercenaries were unable to kill him."

"That is unfortunate for you, is it not?" Gaspard sipped his wine, appearing to savor the moment, and then turned to the larger of the armed men. "Drown him in the moat and then return. I will need you to carry a message to Paris. 'Tis a pity there are no sharks in that ditch."

The prisoner struggled as the two armored men dragged him from the room.

"Father." Horemheb hated that Victor's damaged voice sounded like a stiff bristled brush scraped against a sandy floor, interrupted by higher pitched sounds he could not control. His vocal cords might never recover from the damage sustained from Victor's screams.

The elder Gaspard remained silent, obviously aware that something between him and his son had changed.

"Forgive the interruption, but since we are discussing my adversary, I feel it necessary to speak."

One of the armored men averted his eyes from the bloated abomination on the stretcher.

"Look at me," Horemheb commanded. The temperature dropped as if a door had opened and death had entered. "Your eyes belong to me, and if they are not used for my purposes, I will have them."

The huge man redirected his gaze.

"Forgive me again, Father. I have no right to usurp your authority. I have a certain amount of," he paused, "frustration tied up within this issue. I believe you were about to have this man killed. Am I correct?"

"You are," said the elder Gaspard, the beginnings of a smile appeared on his face. "What would you have me do with him?"

"I would like the opportunity to question him. After all, if not for him, I would at least experience the comfort of knowing my adversary was dead." He turned to the man in chains. "I must now take comfort where I may."

Without the mercenaries holding him on each side, the prisoner would have collapsed to the floor. The light in the room seemed to dim.

"Take him to the dungeon and see that he remains alive until my son can question him."

The *Comte's* retainers dragged the prisoner from the room and closed the door.

"We will have to devise an easier, more comfortable way for you to move about the château," said Gaspard.

"*Merci*, Father."

"I have arranged for the king to sign a *Lettre de Cachet* naming young Gilbert traitor." The elder Gaspard poured himself another glass of wine. "Would you like some wine?"

"*Non*, continue."

A less than subtle role reversal had taken place. The very air snapped with a power and focus of intent that appeared to make François Gaspard uncomfortable. Accustomed to creating discomfort, it was clear he struggled with its effect. "I doubt the king's agents can apprehend him, but it will give us legitimacy should he return. The cost to buy a *Lettre de Cachet* these days is outrageous," he said, with an attempt at humor.

"The crown will never apprehend him." Horemheb paused, deep in thought. "We must take further steps to ensure he returns."

"How can that be accomplished? My resources are seeking word of him, but as of yet, we only know where he has been."

One of the servants holding the stretcher moved slightly, to ease the strain on his arms. Horemheb groaned with the movement. "Remain still." The servant froze, his face blanched white. "He will soon be on the African continent."

"How do you know that?"

"I have certain resources in the area. We need to ensure he returns to Bordeaux."

François swirled his wineglass before the candle. The red liquid lapped against the crystal. "And how may we do that?"

"There have been sporadic outbreaks of plague in the countries around us, most notably in London last year. I suggest we assist its visit to Bordeaux." Victor attempted to smile, but due to the pervasive scar tissue, it served only to highlight the gruesome caricature that was his face.

"The plague!" François exclaimed, naked fear written across his face. "You jest."

"I do not."

"How will we prevent it from striking us?"

"We cannot. You and mother will have to leave for a time."

Unnerved, the elder Gaspard was unprepared for the role reversal and responded as if to a superior. "How long?"

"Until the plague has worked its way through Bordeaux. Perhaps a year."

"You risk much. How can you be certain he will return?"

"Those he loves are here. He will return." Horemheb ended the discussion with a gesture to his servants. "Take me to the dungeon where I may visit with our inadequate assassin."

Even the horrendously damaged body he was forced to wear failed to overshadow the satisfaction Horemheb took in the exercise of power. For the first time in three thousand years, the exhilaration of command surged through his emaciated form. Destiny was now his to control.

CHAPTER THIRTY-THREE
Malaga, Spain

THE SHEIKH and René stood at the rail admiring the fortifications visible from Malaga's harbor. The mighty La Alcazaba's triple walls soared upwards in the distance. Built in the eighth century, the massive fortress looked as if it had grown from the bedrock itself.

"Impressive, is it not?" the sheikh asked.

"They say there is even a Roman amphitheater within, as well as extensive gardens."

"Fortunately, we will not have to storm it." The sheikh stared at the edifice for an instant longer.

"I have sent a letter of introduction to the Gilbert Ltd. factor within the city who will help sell our cargo. On your advice, we will keep the remaining brandy and wine aboard the *Poulé*."

The sheikh nodded his agreement.

"Where will I meet Abdul Karim to facilitate the transfer of the weapons?"

"My friend Miguel Zaportas has a villa up the coast. I have arranged for you to stay with him. He comes from a family of wealthy Jews who were forced to convert to Catholicism."

"Why do you smile?" asked René. "I cannot think being forced to worship someone else's God would be humorous."

"I smile at the memory of my old friend. The Zaportas have never worshiped any God but the Jewish God. They have maintained two faces and have returned to Spain to protect the few remaining Jews here who secretly remain Jews. My family and theirs have been close for many years. I think you will never meet a more honorable man than Miguel Zaportas. He will be a good man for you to know. Abdul Karim will join you there. Ah, here comes the harbormaster. If you will excuse me, I will retire. Do you have the requisite silver he will need to forgo inspecting the ships?"

René glanced at the sheikh and was about to say something, but refrained. He nodded.

The sheikh paused. "I must apologize, sir. I know that having grown up in a trading company, you have some experience in this area. Please do not take my previous comment as an insult. That was not my intention. You must forgive an old man who is unaccustomed to sharing responsibility."

Sheikh Ghassan, like his daughter, was a man of rare empathic power. René did not believe it was possible to lie to this man.

"I am honored to have you as a tutor, sir, and will endeavor not to act the callow youth."

The sheikh laughed. "As if you could."

René watched the man walk toward the hatch. "Destiny," he said quietly.

He brought himself back to the present as the harbormaster's longboat gently bumped against the *Seahawk*. As the man came aboard his ship, René's eyes widened at the greed written on the factor's face. Avarice animated his every gaze as he cataloged and estimated the baksheesh he expected to exact in order to allow the ship to dock. This would be less expensive than he had prepared for. His father had always told him the greedier the man, the less he will be satisfied with.

Later that afternoon, with both ships tied to the quay, René and James disembarked and made their way through the La Puerta de Atarazanas gate into the square at the center of town. They proceeded to the *suburbs*, the interior district of the wall, where the taverns and mercantile stalls were found.

"Do you think we could be about sampling what the locals

drink? Might be we'd find somethin' worth trading." James licked his lips. "Awful hot today."

René laughed. "'Tis winter, James."

"Still, pretty warm in these southern climes, and anyway, I thought we was collecting information like usual."

"Are you certain you would not rather see the inside of La Alcazaba? There is a Roman amphitheater, you know," René said with a straight face.

"Ah, well, is it something to do with our trading?"

"*Non*, just sightseeing. We should head to a tavern and get a feel for what's going on." René fought to keep a straight face.

"You were jokin' with me all the time."

"Well, I would be interested in seeing the place, but I expect it can wait a bit."

They stopped in front of a likely tavern with a stylized woodcarving of a dove out front. The name *La Paloma Blanca* was easily understandable. James spoke no Spanish, but René was confident he could make himself understood. The tavern had tables out front, but in the heat of the afternoon, they were unoccupied. Going through into the cool darkness was as refreshing as the wine promised to be. The Spanish were famous for their fortified wines, especially those that came from the region of Jerez.

René and James found an empty table next to the wall and waited for the tavern maid. She was struggling to extricate herself from a table of rowdy young men. By their dress, they were either nobility or of the wealthy trading class. The serving girl—a shapely young woman—had barely been able to place their drinks on the table before being handled, pinched, and passed among the men. René hated bullying of any kind. Though he knew it to be incredibly stupid, he was about to stand when she managed to get loose and back away from the table. She straightened her clothing and continued, as if what had transpired had been an annoying but expected part of her job.

"*Buenos días, señores*," she said, maintaining a discreet distance from the table. She had clearly had enough pawing for one day. "May I get you something to drink?"

"*Por favor*, I would like a glass of Jerez. The finest available," René said—or at least that was what he hoped he had said.

"The sherry produced in Jerez is indeed the finest. Far better than Cadiz or Sevilla." She smiled, obviously pleased to see some manners in evidence.

"A glass of that would be fine, and perhaps some olives or almonds."

James cleared his throat, claiming her attention. "I will be about drinkin' something as well."

"I speak some *Inglés*, *señor*. What for you to drink?"

"Rum'll be fine." James sounded enthusiastic.

"*Sí*, rum and sherry. *Bien*." she sauntered away.

René had already memorized the layout of the tavern and noted where everyone sat, an unconscious process he had learned long ago. The group of young men were still rowdy, but at least they kept it to their table. The only women in the tavern were the young tavern maid and a large older woman working behind the scarred mahogany bar. The drinks arrived, and the tavern maid was pleased enough with her tip to curtsey to René. In her smile were the beginnings of a network of information similar to that which had proved so valuable in Marseilles. The sherry was good, if perhaps a little too sweet for his taste. Still, it would make an excellent addition to the cargo he planned to bring back. James took a sip and sat back, at peace with the world.

"Is the rum satisfactory?" René asked.

"Is there a rum that is not? This one suits me fine, thank you."

The young dandies tried to stand, some having more difficulty than others. They managed to collect their things and stumble their way toward the door. As they passed René's table, one pushed another, who fell against yet another, which caused the last to spill his drink onto René's table. James and René jumped up and backed away in order to avoid the wine now dripping onto their seats. The young man inspected his empty glass, then the wine on the table, and finally his bloodshot eyes focused on René.

"I believe you owe me a glass of wine, *señor*." The Spaniard used the careful speech of one who'd had too much to drink.

"Why is that?" René replied in French.

"Ah, a Frenchie," murmured one of the others. "Typical."

The offended Spaniard, clearly educated, easily switched into French. "Because you tripped me, which caused me to spill my wine—" He held up the empty glass wistfully. "—which I had my heart set on drinking."

"How could I have tripped you while I was seated here?" asked René pleasantly. "I am sorry, 'twas not me. I believe one of your friends may have accidentally bumped you."

"Raphael, he is calling you a liar," another in their group slurred.

"Definitely calling you a liar," echoed one of the others.

"How dare you call me a liar?" Raphael struggled to draw his sword. "Here, hold this." He handed his wine glass to René so that he could use both hands to remove his sword from its sheath. The young Spaniard was clearly the son of a nobleman. His wine-colored velvet waistcoat, stained and dusty, attested to some vigorous activity earlier. His dress, along with the silver buckles on his shoes shouted wealth. Definitely not the clothes of a peasant. He blinked his clear blue eyes rapidly as he tried to focus on the pommel of the sword, which evidently refused to remain within his field of vision. Although he was dressed as a dandy, the sword he struggled to withdraw was a fine weapon, used and utilitarian.

"Careful there, you will hurt someone with that." René stepped back.

Finally, with a sigh of great satisfaction, Raphael grasped the sword with his right hand and pulled it free. At the sight of naked steel, everyone, including his friends, backed away from him. The act of pulling the sword free had turned him around, and his back was now to René. He waved the sword and called, "Where are you, sir? Have you run like the coward you must be?"

"*Non*, I am still here," René answered. "There is no need to do this. If I somehow caused you to spill your drink, I apologize and will gladly replace it."

Raphael wobbled around and sighted René through glassy

bloodshot eyes.

"There you are. *En garde!*"

René surveyed the group of young men, hoping to find one who might be sober enough to put an end to this. Each one, however, was deeper into his cups than the next. He searched elsewhere, but found only amusement and interest in diversion. Just like the jaded nobility of Bordeaux, these people would be happy for someone to be hurt as long as it was not them. If it happened to some stranger, all the better.

René reluctantly drew his sword. "James, will you keep this one on one?"

"Aye, aye, Captain." James lifted the pistol from his belt, checked that the weapon was primed and cocked it. "If you gentlemen will be so kind as to back up there and not interfere, I will be so kind as to not blow your heads off."

Raphael's inebriated companions backed up as quickly as their drink sodden muscles would carry them.

"Thank you." James leaned back against the wall, his pistol at the ready.

"So then. How will this duel proceed?" asked René. "Will we fight to first blood or to incapacitation?"

"Firsh blood will be fine. I do not need to kill anyone today," Raphael was trying, without complete success, to hold himself in an *en garde* position.

"That is a good thing, because frankly, today is a poor day for me to be killed. *En garde*, then."

The way the man stood, or tried to stand, made it clear that he was a trained swordsman. That was good. Training made him a little less liable to hurt himself by doing stupid novice moves.

Raphael thrust the sword at where René had been standing, only to find he was no longer there. René had moved aside, still in *en garde* position. Raphael thrust at him again. There was a rasping sound, and the young Spaniard stood empty handed.

"You have stolen my sword, sir," he accused René.

René laughed and bent down, picked up the sword, and handed it to Raphael. "*Non, monsieur*, you dropped it. Here you are."

"*En garde*, sir." Raphael thrust forward with a stamp of his foot.

Again, that rasping sound. Again, the sword lay vibrating on the floor.

Raphael stared at his empty hand, a bewildered expression on his face. "We cannot fight if I do not have a sword."

René bit the inside of his cheek to stop from laughing. This was obviously a gentle soul, and René had no interest in humiliating him, let alone hurting him. "I think there must be some defect within the sword itself, sir." He reached down and picked up the sword and then handed it back to Raphael.

"Are you insulting my sword, sir? I will have you know this blade is from Toledo. Finest steel there is." He took a deep breath, swayed, and then began to fall. René reached out to catch him before he crashed into the table.

"I guess I showed you all right," Raphael snorted.

"I guess you did. 'Twas a fine duel. I barely escaped with my life. Do you think you can make it home all right?"

"You know, you need to be careful dueling. You could get hurt," Raphael slurred as he teetered back and forth.

"I will have to keep that in mind." The moment René let go of his shoulders, Raphael started to fall. Turning to his friends, René asked, "Would one of you gentlemen come and see Raphael home?"

"What am I, a child?" Raphael bolted upright and then weaved his way toward the door, followed by his friends.

"What is your name? In case we should meet again," called René.

"Zaportas. Raphael d'Ortega Zaportas, at your servish, sir."

He attempted a bow. Fortunately it was aimed at the entrance, as it carried him through the door to crash outside.

The name caused René to stop. *A relative perhaps?*

Coincidence had long ago lost its meaning for René.

René ran to the door to make certain Raphael had not accidentally stabbed himself. The young nobles were struggling to assist each other onto their saddles. Except for the one who climbed on top of a horse trough. Finally, they were all mounted. If the horses failed to find the way back to their own stables, these men would be riding around until they sobered up. Returning to the tavern, René spotted Raphael's sword on the ground.

"It is an insult to your sword to find itself on the ground. It came from the earth, but it no longer belongs to the earth, having been purified in the fire. You, however, have not been purified in the fire, so do not be insulted if you find yourself in the dirt." The Maestro offered his hand to René to help the boy up.

That had been a long afternoon of open-handed techniques which left René almost continually on his backside. He smiled at the fond memory and retrieved the abandoned sword.

CHAPTER THIRTY-FOUR

JAMES AND Emile were unhappy. René did not care. "Let me repeat myself so as to remove any misunderstanding. Under no circumstances are you to take anyone aboard against his will, and that includes the drunk or unconscious.

"Aye, aye, Captain. But we are gonna have a hell of a time findin' enough bodies to man both ships," James complained.

"Be that as it may, we will not have anyone aboard who did not intend to be aboard. Is that perfectly clear?" René asked, his voice a notch quieter.

The men nodded, realizing the discussion was at an end.

"Yes, sir," Emile answered for both of them. "Understood, sir. And we will find enough men pleased to sail aboard our ships."

"We will?" James asked.

Emile winked at him. "Oh, yes, we definitely will."

René allowed himself an evil smile. "I know the both of you, and if you offer the men more than we pay, I promise you will have the privilege of paying them the difference out of your own wages. Is that understood?"

"Aye, aye, sir," said Emile, deflated.

"We will do our best."

"Of that I am certain. Now if you will excuse me, I would like to speak to Sheikh Ghassan before I leave. I will be at the Villa de Zaportas for a few days until Abdul Karim arrives. We have negotiated a satisfactory price for our cargos, but if the factor encounters any difficulties, you can contact me there."

René rode up to a filigreed wrought iron gate where two young men stood guard. They appeared to be awaiting his arrival. Well dressed, they wore shoes and stockings. Unusual attire for servants in a semi-tropical area such as Malaga. René introduced himself, first in French and then in halting Spanish when it became clear they spoke nothing else. They recognized his name and both bowed.

"*Bienvenido, señor.*"

"*Gracias,*" René replied.

The servant smiled, took the horse's reins, and led him toward the hacienda.

A broad veranda of polished cedar stretched the length of the house. Sleek ceramic vases overflowing with flowers formed nooks along its length coupled with comfortable-looking chairs. Flowering vines ran up the stone pillars that supported the overhanging roof. René dismounted and climbed the broad steps to the porch. The Zaportas family boiled out of the doorway to meet him. The sheikh had told him he would be welcomed. He should have known it would be enthusiastic.

"*Monsieur* Gilbert!" *Señor* Zaportas hugged René. "I cannot tell you how glad I was to hear from my old friend Ammar. Hospitality demands I wait to hear all the details of his recent exploits, but you must assure me he is well."

"He is in good health, sir, and sends you, in his words, 'Every joy an old man can find.'"

"Old man? Bah!" Miguel Zaportas paused, his expression one of remembering.

An image of the sheikh and Miguel as young men, full of intelligence and spirit and bent on molding the world to their ideals, flew into René's mind. The man's pale blue eyes projected a strong intelligence and a powerful awareness. Tall and slim like his son, his balanced stance showed that he too was a trained swordsman.

Señor Zaportas expressive pause happened in the blink of an eye and then, with an almost audible snap, he was fully back in the present and focused on René. Only the Maestro had ever shown the intensity of focus now directed at him. Zaportas smiled and in that smile, somehow, René was welcomed, not only into a family, but also into a larger reality.

"I am so glad he is well." Zaportas looped his arm around René's shoulders. "Allow me to introduce you to my family. My wife, *Señora* Rebeca Zaportas."

"*Señora*." René bowed to her. "Ammar Faruq Ghassan has me say he apologizes for his absence, and that he still feels Miguel is the luckiest of men."

She was a petite woman with warm brown eyes. Standing close to her, René sensed the vital force snapping around her. She reached her arm out and linked it through his, bringing him in closer to her. René had caught the wink she directed toward her husband that was filled with an intense exchange of communication.

"And you may tell that old liar he had his chance long ago. Opportunities rarely come by twice," she said with a laugh.

"I will relay what you say word for word, *señora*," René said, grinning.

"My son, Raphael." She swept her right hand toward him. René met Raphael's eyes, eyes filled with a desperate plea.

"'Tis a pleasure to meet you, *señor*." René extended his hand as if they were meeting for the first time.

"And you, sir." Relief swept across Raphael's face.

"And last, if only in age, my daughter Raquel," said *Señor* Zaportas.

The young woman, who René judged to be about fifteen, was already showing signs of becoming a true beauty, with long auburn hair and flashing dark eyes. She cast an appraising glance in his direction.

He bowed to her. "*Señorita*, I think the sheikh will be surprised to see you. You are most definitely not the little girl he described to me."

"You are too kind, *monsieur*." She dipped in a practiced curtsy.

"I do wish he had come as well. Will we be able to visit him aboard your ship?"

René caught her father's eye and received a nod. "Raquel, I promise you we will have a party aboard the *Seahawk* before we depart. I know Akeefa and Sheikh Ghassan would not want to leave without seeing you."

Raquel's smile grew wider at the mention of a party. "Father, may I show *Monsieur* Gilbert to his rooms?" Her voice rose in excitement as all attempts to emulate adult reserve vanished.

"*Si,* you may, my dear," he said. "*Monsieur* Gilbert, I will have the servants collect your things and bring them to your rooms. Rest. We look forward to dinner."

Raquel took possession of René's arm and led him into the house. He glanced at Raphael and mouthed "I have it," to let him know he had brought the sword. Then he turned his attention to Raquel's rapid-fire questions about life on the high seas.

His room was luxurious in the extreme. Glass inlaid doors opened out onto a private veranda and garden. In the center of the garden, brilliantly colored carp swam in a tiled pool that circled a bubbling fountain. The heady scent of flowers filled the room. One wall was decorated with a huge tapestry on which animals depicted the story of Genesis. The floor was cool tile covered with finely woven carpets, and a large canopied bed made of Lebanese cedar promised a comfortable sleep.

In an adjacent room, René was amazed to find a basin through which a steady stream of water flowed. As he walked to the back of that room, he found a marble seat with a hole in it, underneath which water rushed. He eyed the seat until he finally figured it out, and was even more impressed at the creativity involved. A five foot square empty marble depression with stairs leading into its depth graced the corner of the room. René looked forward to taking his first hot bath in a long time.

A knock sounded on his door. He left off his inspection and returned to the main room.

Raphael stood sheepishly in the doorway. "I wanted to apologize before you rested."

"Come in. I hope you are feeling better." He walked to his bags and then passed the wrapped sword to Raphael. "I am certain you have learned that too much wine and a sharp sword do not mix well."

"My behavior was inexcusable." Raphael lowered his head and accepted the sword. "As you must realize, I am not an accomplished drinker. In fact, I rarely have more than a glass of wine. We had come from a bullfight, and our man was victorious. I was already drunk before we left the arena. I would be grateful if this incident were to remain between the two of us. My father would be less than pleased to hear of my behavior."

"What incident?" asked René with a grin.

"Exactly," Raphael laughed. "*Gracias*. I will leave you to rest, and I do suggest you try to do so, for between my father and my sister you will have none until late this evening. I must admit, I too cannot wait to hear of your adventures as well as your proposals for more to come."

"I assure you, adventures are not nearly as much fun when you are in their midst as when you are relating them over a fine dinner. I will take you up on the offer to rest, but first I must ask how to fill the bathing pool. Is it possible to get hot water? I assume that it is for bathing."

"My father is an inventive man, which is probably why we are still alive and prospering here in Malaga, instead of living in Marrakech or Alexandria. Come, I will show you how to work it." Raphael walked into the next room. "You may have all the hot water you wish."

After perhaps the most luxurious bath he had ever taken, René took Raphael's advice and collapsed into a bed filled with goose down. Too much time had passed since he was this comfortable and relaxed. His eyelids grew heavy as the late afternoon sounds lulled him to sleep.

"*Señor*," a female voice called through René's closed door. "Master Zaportas suggests you awaken and dress. He requests the honor of your presence for a glass of wine, and if I may enter, he sends some cakes to take the edge off your hunger."

"*Por favor*, come in." René tugged the covers over his bare shoulders.

A young woman entered, and keeping her eyes focused on the floor she set a tray with coffee and small cakes on the bedside table. She bowed and backed out of the room.

"*Gracias, señorita*," René called after her.

"*De nada*," she said as his door clicked shut.

He jumped out of bed, pulled on his breeches, and then poured himself a cup of coffee. He had been looking forward to Spanish coffee. For some reason, he was more optimistic than he had been in a long while. Filled with excited anticipation, he sipped the coffee. It was still sweet, but not as thick as that which he had enjoyed as a guest of Sheikh Ghassan. He ate one of the small cakes, savoring the delightful taste of almonds, citrus, and honey. With cup in hand, he walked out to the veranda and then sat on one of the chaises to relax with the early evening sounds and smells of the garden.

He closed his eyes and allowed his senses to expand. The experience filled him with awe. He had never sensed a group of souls in more harmonious cooperation than those here. These people were content and felt safe. They were awake for he sensed a heated discussion between two women baking bread. Rather, it was as though these people knew they belonged, knew what was required of them, and had unquestionable faith that Miguel Zaportas would protect them. It was a wonderful feeling, strange and unusual in his world, but wonderful just the same.

"*Why is it so rare for people to work together to accomplish what appear to be reasonably common desires?*" Thirteen-year-old René asked the Maestro as he walked across the courtyard, arms extended, with a brick in each hand.

"*Your error lies in the word 'reasonably.' You assume our species is, or can be, reasonable—that is, to come to conclusions based on reason alone.*"

"*Even with training?*"

"*It is a function of who we are, and not who we want or choose to*" *be."*

"But you have taught me to control my emotions," René said, carefully placing the bricks down and returning to the pile for two more.

"And have I not also taught you that your emotions are horses that can never be completely tamed?" the Maestro asked before taking a sip of tea.

"Then we are doomed."

"Perhaps."

"Perhaps? What is the answer then?"

After a slight pause, the Maestro replied. "I do not know."

That was the first time René ever heard the Maestro say those words. They stopped him as if he had run into a wall. René looked at the Maestro, who, until that moment, he had thought was in possession of every answer to every question. All of a sudden, the ground seemed to move, and he felt a new fear.

"You do not know?" asked René, hoping he had misheard. "But there may be an answer. Oui?"

"Looking around at the world, I am confident the perfection that is evident extends to us as well. The fact I haven't been able to discern it yet doesn't negate the possibility of its existence. Frightening is it not?"

"Very."

"There is no natural destructive force greater than fear. I have taught you not to fear that which you know, and now it is time to learn not to fear that which you do not know. Please pick up your sword; we will spar while we are talking. Time is also a resource not to be wasted."

René stood, a greater sense of purpose crystallizing within. He would surround those he loved with this sense of peace and safety. If Miguel Zaportas could create this oasis, so could he. He had no illusions he could do it immediately, or without pain, but here finally was something he could build instead of destroy.

CHAPTER THIRTY-FIVE

THE 'GREAT room' in the Zaportas' estate was dominated by an oversized hearth and fireplace. Its polished wooden floors were covered with Arabian carpets. A round table of dark mahogany sat off to one side. Stuffed leather chairs were situated around the room in intimate groupings. Paintings decorated the walls, some undoubtedly of ancestors. One large wall mural depicted a naval battle which René thought must be the Spanish Armada's loss to Sir Francis Drake. There were two deep burgundy leather chairs facing each other in front of the fire, and he only now noticed *Señor* Zaportas seated in one of them.

Miguel rose from his chair and smiled. "I usually give people a moment to take in the room. I am proud of it. *Por favor*, sit." He indicated the chair opposite his. "Will you take a glass of sherry?"

"*Merci,* that would be fine." René accepted the glass and seated himself. Like everything he had seen in this home, the chair was engineered to give maximum human comfort, and it succeeded.

Señor Zaportas refilled his glass and settled back into his own chair. There was a moment of quiet as each man took the measure of the other.

"Ammar has written to me of you. He says you are a most unusual young man. Perhaps the man in this next generation to carry on for us, when we are no longer here." René had the strange sensation that Miguel was looking into his soul. "Are you that man?"

"What am I meant to carry on?"

"Why, the fight to preserve what is decent within man, and to protect those who cannot protect themselves."

"That seems like a Herculean task," said René, struggling to understand.

"It is and requires no less than a hero to accomplish it, for even a moment of time." *Señor* Zaportas sipped his wine.

René was at a loss for words, unable to encompass the scope of the ideas this serious man had just proposed, but evidently, Zaportas had seen what he needed to see. His demeanor switched back to that of the heartily cheerful man from earlier. "Tell me of my old friend Ammar."

René sucked in a deep breath and allowed himself to enter that unique sense of focus where time slowed. Fully invested in *Señor* Zaportas' brief description of his and the sheikh's expectations, he wanted to know more.

They had been sparring and practicing basic thrust-and-block techniques for over two hours, and René was getting bored.

"Patience is a power to be cultivated," said the Maestro.

"Is it more important than balance?" asked ten-year-old René.

"Say rather that it is an integral part of balance," said the Maestro. "The planets are in balance, and their power is limitless. Yet there is a sublime patience to their dance through the ether beyond the earth, for were they to be impatient, they would surely fall into the sun and burn up. The biblical 'To everything there is a season' is truth. We will practice patience until it is second nature to you, and in its mastery you will know when to rest and when to act."

As the Maestro said the last word, he brought down a slashing cut to René's shoulder that René automatically blocked.

"That was the appropriate time to act. Never use more effort than the moment calls for, and you will have all you need." Maestro returned to basic thrust and block techniques.

"The sheikh is in excellent health and condition," he answered, remembering the fight within the tent.

As if he sensed René's thoughts, Miguel turned to glance into the fire. A long moment later he returned his gaze to René. "He always was quite the swordsman. When we were younger, we were both proud of our prowess. He writes that you are perhaps the finest swordsman he has ever seen."

"I am certain he exaggerates."

"I am certain he does not. Of all the men I know, Ammar has always been the most sparing in his praise for his fellow man. Do you not find him that way?"

"*Oui*, I must agree. He is less demonstrative with his praise than he is with his acceptance." There was far more information flowing between them than the spoken words suggested. René found the plane of conversation rarified, but exhilarating.

"Just so. Which brings me to a favor I must ask of you, even before we have dinner. You have met Raphael."

The declaratory statement implied a greater awareness of his son than had the brief meeting at the door. René settled even deeper into his center. While this was not a battle, it was a kind of sparring, and he had given his word to Raphael. Miguel Zaportas would know a lie, and yet René was determined to honor his word.

"I have," René said, giving neither more nor less information than he had received.

Señor Zaportas smiled in genuine pleasure. "We are living in the era of the duel, and while my son has had the advantage of every teacher of the sword I could find, I am still not satisfied as to his safety."

"There is never safety within the controlled chaos that is a duel."

"Raphael is a fine swordsman, and yet there is something lacking which I fear will be his downfall. He can see nothing but good in his fellow man, and I am afraid this empathy will blind him. I believe Raphael used up his allotment of good fortune in meeting you." He shook his head. "I wonder if what I see is true, or merely a doting father's fear."

The father was clearly aware of the 'duel' that had taken place. There was no anger coming from the elder Zaportas though, only relief and worry. Apparently within the confines of Malaga—and perhaps all of Spain—not much transpired that Miguel Zaportas failed to know about. "How may I help you, sir?"

"Ah, Ammar is correct, as usual. I would have you tutor Raphael in the sword while you are here. I realize you may not be at our hacienda for long, but perhaps you could find the time to give him a greater appreciation of the weapon he wears. Would you be willing to teach him?"

"On one condition."

"And that is?"

"That he is willing to learn, and not because you wish it. I can force my men to learn to defend themselves with the threat of my sword, but I cannot do that with your son. If he does not have a deep desire to learn, I will be unable to teach him, and the result will be nothing but frustration for all concerned."

"'Tis his desire to become proficient with the sword. I will let him ask you himself. You are a perceptive judge of men, sir. I leave it to you to judge his intentions and abide by your decision."

René nodded.

"I will not embarrass you with an offer of gold, for I am certain you perceive that my son's safety is beyond any value to me. I will rather offer you the gratitude of a father and hope one day you find my assistance as valuable to you as yours is to me."

Miguel settled deeper into his chair. René also allowed himself to relax now that this particular exercise was completed. The quick burst of euphoria that always came after a particularly strenuous sparring session with someone of equal skill and power wrapped around him. He fancied he saw a hint of it in Miguel's eyes, too. They raised their glasses to one another and sipped their sherry.

"I believe I hear the impatient conversation of my lovely wife and daughter coming from the dining room. It might be unhealthy for us to tarry in here much longer." *Señor* Zaportas stood. "Shall we join them?"

"I would be delighted to, sir." René followed Miguel into the dining room.

An elegant Arabic carpet of deep reds and grays woven in linked floral patterns covered the entire floor. Suspended from the high ceiling, a finely crafted chandelier of wrought iron, gold leaf, and crystals sent a warm glow over a large mahogany dining table. Embroidered red and gold tapestries graced the chairs while a tablecloth of pale linen set with porcelain and intricately fashioned silver completed the table setting. At the end of the room, a fire burned in a magnificent hearth. Eight feet wide and five feet high, topped with a large mahogany mantle, this hearth radiated warmth and welcome. In winter evenings, the temperature along the Spanish coast cooled quickly, and the crackling fire added an even greater sense of comfort. René had seen many a gracious dining room in Bordeaux but none that surpassed this one. René was seated next to Raquel with Raphael across the table and *Señor* and *Señora* Zaportas at its ends.

"I trust you had a nice rest, René?" asked Rebeca. Elegantly coiffed, she seemed a completely different woman from the one who had greeted him earlier. Her dress was of wine-colored silk with complex geometrical patterns in black moving across the material. For jewelry, she wore a black silk ribbon with a large pearl suspended from it, matched by dangling pearl earrings.

René was transported once again to the glittering nobility of Bordeaux. If Rebeca was beautiful, Raquel was stunning. In a green velvet gown with her shining auburn hair piled atop her head, Raquel was a heart-stopping announcement of the beauty she would soon become. Around her neck was an emerald necklace that must be worth a king's ransom. As accustomed as he was to the glitter of the wealthy merchants of Bordeaux, it took a moment for him to reclaim speech. "I have not slept more comfortably or more soundly since I left home. 'Twas wonderful. *Merci* for your gracious hospitality."

In honor of René, the first wine served was from Bordeaux, which he immediately recognized as having come from Cos Gilbert's own vineyards.

"How...where..." he stumbled at a loss for words.

"I have certain resources. Once Ammar had written to me, it was not difficult to locate a wine with a reputation as good as this one's. Have no fear, we are aware of your situation and will not betray your existence." Miguel stood and lifted his glass toward René. "And now, our first—but not last—toast to a gallant young man. May your endeavors bear fruit that will feed many. *Salud*."

Everyone stood and *"Salud"* echoed around the table.

"May I return your good wishes?" Still standing, René held up his glass. "To life."

There was a moment of silence around the table. Heat crawled up René's neck. Had he insulted his hosts? But then the elder Zaportas bowed his head, as did the rest of his family, and they all but whispered, *"L'chiam."*

There was a pause and then Miguel asked everyone to be seated. Seeing René's discomfort, he explained. "You must know from Ammar that we are Maranos, converted Jews. We are Catholic on the outside and Jewish on the inside. The toast you made is one filled with meaning for us. One we do not often say aloud, since it belonged to our homeland in Judea. That we remain Jewish in our hearts is a closely held secret. To treat it otherwise would endanger us all."

"I understand, sir. You may be assured I will not betray your confidence."

"René, no one enters my home I cannot welcome as family. In all the years I have known Ammar Ghassan, I have never heard him say, 'Welcome this one as my son.' From our brief time spent together, I heartily concur with my friend."

"How have you managed to remain in Spain?"

"It has not been easy. Jews have been imprisoned, tortured, and burned here for the last three hundred years."

"There were many different levels of Maranos," Rebeca added. "Some who embraced Christianity whole-heartedly, some who did so for their own protection, and some who were called *Judíos Escondidos,* or hidden Jews. This last group remained Jewish, continuing to follow their traditions when they could, but always at great risk. Our family comes from one such group."

"Nevertheless," continued Miguel, "Spain became too dangerous— even for us. My grandfather Arturo Diego Zaportas moved our family to Morocco where we forged a deep friendship with Ammar Ghassan's family. My father grew up in Morocco, and I brought the family back here with his passing. Unfortunately, the storm has not abated, it merely waxes and wanes. The tide is, I believe, coming back in, and I fear it will soon be too dangerous for us to remain in Malaga. I am preparing to move my family to our estates in Morocco." *Señor* Zaportas shook his head. "But I am embarrassed. How have we descended to this level of hospitality? Surely we can find something more uplifting to discuss."

How about pirates?" Raquel piped in.

Laughter broke out around the table. It was as though they had cleansed the air of fear, and the dinner proceeded with gusto. Course after course rolled by with various wines served to compliment each dish. Red peppers stuffed with tuna, grilled sea prawns, chicken consommé, Segovian style trout, gazpacho, and they still had the meat courses to go. René told them of his earlier difficulties in Bordeaux, and of the *Vrijheid,* now renamed the *Seahawk.* He started to tell of the *Belle Poulé* when Raquel interrupted.

"Is Khalid with you?" she asked.

"As a matter of fact, he is."

"Oh." She suddenly took a great interest in sliding her food around her plate.

"She has quite the infatuation with Khalid," offered Raphael.

"I do not." Dramatically indignant, the flush of her face gave conflicting testimony. "I was only interested in who would be at the party, and anyway—"

"He is much too old for you," Raphael said.

"For now," she said, with a knowing smile.

Miguel shook his head and looked at his wife, who nodded in return, but her expression remained blank.

"What was it like in Morocco?" asked René.

"Much like anywhere else, only poorer. We lived in Marrakech, and there were kasbahs that were hovels alongside some of the most beautiful of palaces. We continued in our profession as merchants and traders, and while there were difficulties, we managed." Miguel took a bite of lamb tagine.

"What of the Salé corsairs?"

He swallowed and then continued, "They were still active, but my father generally managed to come to some accommodation with their leaders, often with the help of the Ghassans. You see, we were all refugees."

"Refugees?"

"Almost sixty years ago, Philip III forcibly expelled one million Spanish Moors. Some, called *Hornacheros,* after their mountain home in Spain, settled in the coastal town of Rabat and named their settlement New Salé. They learned to sail square-riggers, made alliances with various pirates, and the rest is a sad and often bloody history of slave-trading."

"The English call them Sallee Rovers," Raphael said. "To their Islamic brethren they are known as *al-ghuzat,* after the warriors who fought with Mohammed. Since like them, we were outcasts, they tolerated us."

Miguel paused, sadness replaced his usual cheerful expression. "My father did his best to protect and repatriate the Spaniards who were taken into slavery, but it was hard acting on behalf of the people who had persecuted us."

"Jews have always been familiar with slavery," Rebeca said.

"What of Sheikh Ghassan's family?" asked René.

"The sheikh's ancestors were expelled from another part of Spain but fortunately were able to join family already living in Morocco," Miguel said. "My brother David and his family still live in Morocco. They moved from Marrakech to Meknes some time ago. We felt it prudent to maintain a place of retreat should the situation warrant our leaving Spain again."

"Do you believe the situation here has reached that point?"

"Sadly, I do. I have already moved most of my resources and business out of Spain. Perhaps my love for this place has become too deeply rooted, but I find it hard to leave this home. It has been a place of love for a number of years now, but I cannot delude myself into thinking us safe. The last *auto de fe* was nine years ago, and I sense another one building."

Servants cleared away the dishes while others brought in dessert, along with coffee. A young woman placed assorted almond confections on the table, and a large older woman, clearly in charge of the dinner's preparation, placed a pastry with a delicate crust in the shape of a half moon in front of each of the diners.

"What is this? It looks wonderful," said René.

"We call it Floron," answered *Señora* Zaportas. "It is Segovian pastry with a cream custard filling. I think you will like it."

"Will there be anything else, *señor*?" asked a woman whose very presence commanded attention.

"*Gracias*, Carmen, the dinner was excellent as usual. At this point, not even your great skill can induce us to eat another bite."

Carmen failed to hide her grin as she nodded to the servants who followed her out.

The pastry was indeed wonderful and disappeared quickly. Even as full as he was, René considered asking for another piece, and as if someone had read his mind, there materialized in front of him another dish of Floron.

He smiled sheepishly. "*Gracias*."

"Our pleasure," said *Señora* Zaportas.

"Dinner was exquisite, as usual." Miguel patted his stomach. "*Gracias*, my dear."

"May I also add *gracias*, *señora*? Welcoming me into your home has been special, something I will never forget," René said.

"*Por favor*, you may consider yourself a part of this family, and we do not take family lightly. I hope we will enjoy many dinners like this one."

"So do I, *señora*, so do I."

"Well, dear, may we be excused?" Miguel asked his wife. "There is still some business to be discussed and some brandy to be drunk."

"Of course." She stood and beckoned to Raquel. "Gentlemen."

René pushed his chair back and then bowed to the ladies as they left the room.

René followed Raphael and *Señor* Zaportas into the great room.

There were now three of the deeply stuffed leather chairs facing the fireplace, each with a small table beside it. Miguel took his accustomed chair and Raphael sat across from him, leaving the chair in the middle for René. A servant entered and poured brandy snifters for each of the men, then offered each a cigar, beginning with *Señor* Zaportas. For a time, they sat in silence, drinking brandy and occasionally puffing on the cigars.

"Are you in agreement that Sultan al-Rashid should be supported?" asked René.

"To exist anywhere in even minimal safety, one must establish some line of communication and expectation with the existing rulers," Miguel answered. "The reason we managed to flourish in Morocco is because no central government or ruler existed. Morocco was ruled by different clans or tribes, some more powerful, some less. In the last seventy years or so, since the fall of the Saadian dynasty, that chaos has allowed our families to prosper."

"And now that Moulay al-Rashid has declared himself Sultan of all Morocco, it behooves us to establish a connection with him by sending him support in a form that will help him the most," René said.

"Exactly." Miguel stood and walked to the fireplace.

"Weapons have always been a commodity in great demand by the pashas and sheikhs," said Raphael. "Gold and silver, they have. Weapons and those trained to use them, they lack."

"Sheikh Ghassan believes al-Rashid will be more moderate than most," said René. "Do you believe this as well?"

"Moderate? No, that is not the word I would use. I believe, however, he will act in his own interest, and it will be possible to align our interests with his," Miguel said. "There will be risk, but when is there not? With your permission, I would like Raphael to accompany you, to begin preparing for our emigration back to Morocco."

"Of course, he is welcome to join us."

"Raphael is an accomplished pilot and will earn his keep by helping you navigate the waters around Morocco," added Miguel as he turned to look at Raphael.

Raphael's expression of surprise made it clear that he had been unaware of his father's plans. He sat up straighter. "I accept the faith you place in me, Father, and will do my best."

"I know you will, and I ask your forgiveness for not having spoken with you about this before. It was not until tonight's conversation that I knew the time was now. I have seen what I wished to see, rather than what is. I only hope I have not waited too long."

Conversation ceased. René glanced at his hosts. Both men stared into the fire as if contemplating the future and the speed with which it could arrive.

CHAPTER THIRTY-SIX

THE NEXT morning Abdul Karim Ghassan came into the dining room as René poured himself a cup of coffee. The sheikh's eldest son was a big man who exuded confident power with every movement. Dressed in breeches and waistcoat, his coal black hair neatly tied in the back with a leather thong, Abdul Karim looked the part of a wealthy young Spaniard. His mustache and beard were trimmed in the current fashion, and his perfect fluency in the language completed the transformation. His appearance and demeanor, along with his trading experience, was why he had been chosen to travel to Toledo for the swords.

"*Monsieur* Gilbert, 'tis good to see you," boomed Abdul Karim. He glanced at Raphael and said, "And *buenos dias* to you, my old friend."

"'Tis good to see you as well," said René. "Your smile tells me your business was successful and that we are moving ahead with our plans."

"Yes, I have had the weapons unloaded into a warehouse near your ships. We will transfer them aboard tomorrow." Abdul Karim pulled over a chair and then sat.

"'Tis been a while since I have seen you, but you look to be in one piece," said Raphael.

"I think the biggest challenge was the food."

"The food?" Raphael asked.

"Every time I took a bite of dried beef, I could not help but think about Carmen's cooking. I am glad to finally be here."

The two men laughed.

"And we are glad you made it safely," said Miguel, as he walked into the room. "Carmen! These men are starving."

"*Señor.*" She nodded and waved in a line of servants, each carrying a steaming platter. The table soon groaned beneath the weight of all the food. "There will not be any starving going on in this house."

"Not likely," Miguel laughed. "*Gracias*, Carmen."

Abdul Karim faced her and put his hand on his heart. "*Muchas gracias*, dear Carmen, from the bottom of my heart."

She blushed. "Abdul Karim, you have always been a charmer," she said as she ushered the last of the servants out.

"Did you encounter any difficulties in obtaining the weapons?" asked Miguel.

"We ran into some bandits on the way back from Toledo, but the fight was short, and none of my men were badly injured."

"How many were there?" asked Raphael.

"Eight."

"How many men were with you?" asked René. "And what became of the bandits?"

"I had three men with me. Since the bandits were unable to run, being injured or dead, we helped the survivors into the afterlife so they could be with their friends," said Abdul Karim with a cold smile. "Frankly, I am embarrassed it took the four of us. I have neglected my practice and will address that as soon as possible. I may even ask Akeefa to spar with me." He glanced at René and shuddered. "I have seen you in a fight, and I will pass on sparring with you."

"'Tis an eye-opening experience," said Raphael. "René has agreed to work with me and I have experienced one lesson. I welcome your presence."

"I think you might need someone with more medical training, but I will be happy to join you."

Miguel put his coffee down. "Abdul Karim, tell me, what arrangements you have made?"

"Once the factors complete the inventory and exchange papers, we can begin loading the ships. René, I heard you added another ship to your armada. I look forward to hearing that story in detail."

"We missed you. It will be good to have you on board."

"And I am glad to return home. It has been a long time, and I sometimes find it difficult being with you infidels." He laughed.

"Infidels!" said Raphael. "I will ask Carmen to come in here so you can call her an infidel."

"I would prefer a thousand cuts with a dull blade. You must forgive me. There is hardly any blood in my head. It has all been diverted to my stomach." Abdul Karim rubbed his belly.

"Well, I will let it pass this time, since you apparently have managed to fulfill your part of our business. But with the next derogatory word that passes your lips, I tell Carmen." Raphael broke into a broad grin. Turning to René, he said, "That threat always worked when we were children, and 'tis good to see it still holds power."

Miguel smiled at the banter. "René, I see by your expression that some confusion over our families and relationships has emerged. Ammar and I wanted to give our children the widest experience possible, so we fostered our sons with each other's family. Abdul Karim spent some years with us, and Raphael spent time with the Ghassans. Currently, my brother David's eldest is living with the Ghassans."

"*Merci.* That does clarify things," said René.

"May we be excused, Father?" asked Raphael. "We have important matters to discuss."

"I am certain you do." Miguel laughed. "Keep me informed. I would like to have those weapons loaded aboard the *Seahawk* as soon as possible."

"We will." Raphael stood and headed toward the great room. Abdul Karim and René, who were already discussing the transfer of cargo, followed him.

CHAPTER THIRTY-SEVEN

RENÉ LEANED on the rail of the *Belle Poulé* rereading the letter he had received from Henri. The Gilbert Ltd. factor in Marseilles had been instructed to forward any mail for a *Monsieur* Dalembert to the harbormaster in Malaga.

Dear Monsieur Dalembert,

It was so nice to hear from you. I cannot even begin to express our joy in finding you well. We were saddened to hear of your recent difficulties but pleased you have been able to work your way through them.

Chez Gilbert has seen better days but is now on the mend, seeing that the weather has changed. Marie had taken ill at the news of her favorite nephew's demise but has now recovered her spirit and is once again the ruler of our kitchen. I, too, have been suffering from melancholy but am pleased to report I have smiled more in these last days than in my whole life

John has been working with Orion. The strangest thing happened. When you last left us, the horse went off his feed. I have never seen a horse respond like that. Damned horse would have died if not for John, who eventually was able to bring him back to health.

A young woman you met when you were here last has, I believe, also received a letter from you. Be assured she is well, and you may expect to hear from her.

If you notice my handwriting changes from time to time, please excuse me, as I sometimes get the rhumatisme in my hand.

The handwriting changed. Henri had written the first page to help disguise the letter in case of interception. The rest of it was from his father. Every word connected René to the life he had known and at the same time made him acutely aware of the distance between them.

It is difficult to find the words to express my relief and joy that you are safe. I have written to your teacher to apprise him of the situation but have not yet heard back from him. I am certain he would be pleased with the way you have handled this business.

Trade has been good, with one competitor fiercer than ever. This competitor is in Paris meeting with the new finance minister, Colbert, where he is surely helping devise something financially destructive for the wealth and well-being of the merchant class. The new finance minister is cold and driven and appears determined to consolidate all financial power into the hands of the crown. We anxiously await his declarations with our wallets and remaining freedom. This new chain of events, however, fills me with determination, and I am positive Gilbert Ltd. will not only survive the onslaught, but triumph.

As per our discussions, I have deeded the Belle Poulé to you. You will also find letters of credit established with the following factors. (See addendum.) I am confident that together our business will prosper. I have reviewed your business plan, and while the risks seem great, the rewards seem so as well. As you may deduce, I am not overjoyed at the level of risk this venture entails but well know from years of experience that it is often impossible to evaluate a plan from a distance. The captain of the ship must have the authority to change direction

*as he must to accommodate wind and weather. We have
Gilbert Ltd. factors in the ports of Tangier, Casablanca,
and Alexandria who may be of service to you. I have
alerted each to the possibility of your trading there. No
matter what transpires from this moment on, I am proud
of you, and I will always be so.*

*I am sitting here at the dining room table sipping my
tea and working over my reports, and I envision you
coming down the stairs to join me. I am in good health,
and God willing we will meet again to discuss our mutual
concerns and joys.*

*With great affection I remain,
Henri Bouvier*

René stood savoring the gentle rocking of the ship. Two
competing emotions vied for his attention: regret that he was
yet unable to return to Bordeaux, unable to join his father at the
dining room table in the morning, discussing the day's prospects,
while at the same time he experienced deep satisfaction at the
way he had been able to influence events. He now officially owned
two ships, and Jacques was right when he said many had started
with less.

The refit of the *Belle Poulé* was almost finished. René had
promoted James to the captaincy of the *Seahawk*. René would
move over to the larger ship with the Ghassan family and their
retainers. The carpenters had been busy, and the *Belle Poulé* now
boasted six cabins, with one of the additional two housing Raphael
and Abdul Karim. He questioned himself as to why he added the
sixth cabin, since it cut into the cargo capacity of the ship. But he
had long ago learned to accept whatever information his deeper
self offered. He rarely thought long about it now; he acted on it,
and in so doing, strengthened the faculty. They had replaced all of
the sheets and sail on the *Belle Poulé,* as well as the jury-rigged
yardarm, and had repaired the other battle damage.

A powerful wave of energy impinged against his own, and René
turned as Akeefa came on deck. As usual, she was covered head to

toe. He marveled at her grace as she walked toward him.

"Good afternoon," he said.

"And to you as well." She came to stand beside him at the rail. "How does the loading go?"

"Smoothly so far. We will finish this afternoon and set sail in two days."

"When will Raphael come aboard?" Akeefa asked.

"He should be here already. I was waiting for him to show up."

"I am eager to see him," she said with a thoughtful look in her eye. "He is a fine swordsman."

René laughed. "He recalls sparring with you, as well."

He was watching the dock as Raphael raced up the road toward the ships, but something was wrong. No one ever rode that fast unless there was trouble.

"Akeefa, something is wrong. *S'il vous plaît*, alert your family. I will go to meet him." René was already sprinting for the amidships railing. He dashed across the boarding plank to the quay.

He got to the end of the dock as Raphael rode up, his horse lathered and blowing. Raphael jumped from the horse and grabbed René by the arms. "They have taken them. I was on my way here when I heard musket fire from the house. I went back, but hid on the ridge. There were too many. Come, we must go." Raphael wheezed, struggling to regain his breath.

René radiated stillness. As it had all those months ago, everything stopped. "You are not a callow youth. *Oui*, I know 'tis your family, but if we rush forward without a plan or sufficient resources, we will be of no service to anyone."

Raphael breathed deeply. René knew that he was desperately trying to center himself.

"We will free them, I promise you. Do you know who is responsible?"

"I recognized two men," said Raphael, coming aboard the ship beside René. "They were Ignacio Pedro Rodriquez, our local Jesuit priest, and Manuel Hugo Medina, a wealthy landowner, whose property is adjacent to ours. There was another priest with them, unfamiliar to me, along with nine men-at-arms."

By the time they reached the deck, Sheikh Ghassan and his

sons were waiting for them. Emile had caught the urgency of the moment and had signaled for James to come aboard the *Belle Poulé*. "Come, let us go to my cabin." René led the way to the galley hatch. "Emile, have James join us as soon as he arrives." "Yes, sir." Emile turned and shouted to his boatswain.

They all filed into René's cabin and took seats around the large table. Raphael remained standing. Unable to sit, he paced, anger coming from him in waves. His impatience was palpable. James arrived and quietly took a seat.

René poured a glass of brandy and handed it to Raphael. He started to wave it away when René spoke, "I am certain your throat is dry, and I am confident we need not be concerned about inebriation."

Raphael's smile flickered at the inside joke.

"All right, tell us from the beginning," René said.

Before Raphael began, the door opened and Akeefa entered. She wore a hijab. She bowed her head. "Father, I believe I will be needed. May I attend?"

Abdul Karim pushed his chair back. The sheikh laid a hand on his arm. "Your intuition has served us well in the past, even to the point of saving lives." The sheikh looked pointedly at Abdul Karim. "There are beloved lives at stake here, and I would be remiss to leave out any weapons or chances for their safe return. Please be seated."

"Raphael," René prompted.

"I was on my way to the ship when I heard musket shots from the direction of the hacienda. I returned to the ridge overlooking our valley in time to see a group of men leading my family from our home. Their hands were tied behind them. They were dragging my father. He appeared to be unconscious but how badly injured, I could not tell. There were a dozen men, including the Jesuit Priest Ignacio Pedro Rodriquez. I also recognized Manuel Hugo Medina, that son of a—" Raphael stopped and glanced at Akeefa. "They put them on horses and rode from the hacienda heading toward me. I hid in the lemon grove, and then followed them after they passed. They have taken my family to La Alcazaba, to the fortress. From the way the other priest was dressed, I would say he was a higher-ranking Jesuit. They will take them to Cordoba, to stand before the *auto da fé*.

"Medina owns the land adjacent to ours. He has been trying to buy or steal our valley for the last twenty years. I am certain he sent lies to the tribunal in Cordoba, in the hopes of seizing our home afterwards. There is no way Ignacio betrayed us. Our priest is a gentle man who has been to our home many times, and I find it impossible to believe he turned us over to the Inquisition." Raphael paused. "As I live, Medina will never enjoy the fruits of this day."

"When do you think they will be moved from La Alcazaba?" asked René.

"There is no way to know. Nor how many men will accompany them. Medina will know I am still free and that I will try to rescue my family. He is wealthy enough to employ many swords to join with the soldiers." Raphael was clenching and unclenching his right fist as he paced from one side of the cabin to the other. "Your men are sailors. I have no doubt they can fight, but can they fight on horseback? I think not."

"Then we will have to take them while they are still in Malaga," said James.

"They are in La Alcazaba," said Khalid.

"'Tis said to be impregnable," said Emile.

"The impregnable fortress is an illusion, as is everything else our world rests on. The highest mountain will become a plain given enough time and effort. Everything is a function of time and power. With less time, you require more power, and the inverse is true. The proper application of power, however, will also have the effect of accomplishing your ends while shortening the amount of time required," the Maestro said.

"If we cannot break into La Alcazaba by force, then we must use guile." René glanced at the sheikh. "I have an idea which I am loathe to advance, and I ask your forgiveness for even voicing it. Properly dressed, Akeefa can go into the fortress on the pretext of bringing food to one of the prisoners. There she must disable or kill the guards, free the Zaportas, and open the gate to the rest of us."

There was silence in the room. No one spoke, no one moved, no one breathed. A suggestion like that could be interpreted as a vile insult, and there were three men at the table who could respond to that insult. Akeefa stood straighter. Wisely, she chose to be silent.

The sheikh glanced at René with tears in his eyes. "Miguel Zaportas is my brother, and I could not sacrifice him for all the honor in this world or the next." He clasped Akeefa's hands in his. "Are you willing to risk this, my beloved daughter? You will not be able to take a weapon in with you."

"Beloved Father, have you not taught me that the weapon is not the sword or even the hand that wields it? My life is yours, as it has always been, but I could not live with myself were the Zaportas to be imprisoned, or worse." She squeezed his hands and turned to Abdul Karim and Khalid. "Beloved brothers, will you also allow me this service? I promise you no man who sees me will live to tell of it." Not a man seated there had the slightest doubt of her statement.

"Is there no other way?" asked Khalid.

"Not without an army," said René.

All eyes turned to Abdul Karim. "Forgive me, dear sister, but I can see no other way."

Akeefa's eyes widened in surprise.

"I know I am considered a hidebound traditionalist," Abdul Karim continued, "determined to hold to every custom, but in truth, my over-protection of you has always stemmed less from any loss of honor than from my love for you and my need to keep you safe." He failed to meet her eyes.

"I am always safe when you are around, elder brother, and I will come through this safely as well." A gentle smile curved her lips. "I think I know what will be required of me, and we will have a surprise for the men in La Alcazaba."

"All right, then," René said. "Let us plan this out. James, invite Mister Wade to join our number, and gather the arms we will need. Eight will be enough. Any more than that will arouse suspicion. Emile, prepare both ships for a quick departure and then join us. We will time this so we leave on the afternoon tide."

CHAPTER THIRTY-EIGHT

THEY ENTERED the square through the La Puerta de Atarazanas gate in ones and twos. Akeefa and Khalid headed toward La Alcazaba. She wore a burqa, but was dressed differently underneath. After a loud argument, she and Sabah had taken her only European dress and ripped off all the lace, leaving a pale blue silk sleeveless gown cut very low in the front. She had shortened the gown and then crushed it in her fists so it appeared more worn. Even then, cut and torn, the quality of the cloth would never have been worn by a servant. They dirtied the cloth and cut several rents in it. She tried it on. For a woman raised in the Arab tradition, appearing naked or near-naked in front of anyone other than her husband was punishable by death. She felt naked in the dress. Sabah kept her eyes directed at the floor and finally left the room in tears.

Akeefa held out her hand mirror. She had let her hair fall in waves about her shoulders. The revised neckline barely covered her breasts. They had decided she was to pose as a servant bringing food to the Zaportas. She was certain she could convince the guard to take her into the dungeon. The delivery was simple fare, so the guards at the gate were not tempted by it. Khalid escorted her behind a stall close to the La Alcazaba gate and squeezed her hand. In the square, René leaned casually against a pillar thirty feet from the La Alcazaba gate. He smiled reassurance, and his unique mental field surrounded her. Nothing in heaven or hell would prevent him from reaching her, should she encounter difficulty.

Taking a deep breath, Akeefa let the burqa drop. With an appearance of confidence she barely felt, Akeefa stepped away from her security and into the sunlit square. She was barefoot, as none of her shoes, or even Sabah's, would have been reasonable for a servant. Akeefa took the tray of food from Khalid and walked toward the fortress gate.

She had seen how European women walked, and given her training and control, she had no trouble mimicking the swaying gait of the prostitutes in the plaza. In the fifty feet she walked toward the fortress every man in the square, and there were many, turned to stare at her. She caught a glimpse of René from the corner of her eye and almost laughed. He had slipped from the pillar he was leaning against and seemed to struggle to remain standing. Then she was at the gate and facing two sour-looking guards who stood complaining in the hot sun.

"I have food for the Zaportas who have recently been brought here," she said, her eyes downcast. The men never looked at the food. She probably could have carried a blunderbuss on the tray. Ordinarily, the guards would have taken the food, and depending on the amount of the bribe offered, considered giving it to the prisoner. In this case, the bribe was carrying the food.

"I will take you inside," said the short fat guard. "I know a nice quiet spot where we can rest along the way."

"I am senior here, and I will be the one to take her inside," said the taller of the two.

For a moment it looked as if they would fight for the privilege, but then the junior guard grumbled and returned to his post.

"*Señorita*." The senior guard offered his arm. He smiled. His mouth was filled with stained, broken teeth.

They walked beneath the portcullis, a huge rusted iron grate that was raised and lowered by winch. From there, they went through a long, narrow tunnel with another portcullis at its end. Murder holes, like evil eyes, were spaced evenly along the tunnel ceiling. Even if René and her brothers got through the portcullis, they would be easy marks for the musketmen above, who would decimate their ranks before they could get to the next gate. If that were lowered, it would trap them within the tunnel. As they walked into the darkness, the portcullis guard put his arm around her, grasping at her breast with his right hand.

"Perhaps we might make a little stop before you deliver the food." His face was close to hers. Her eyes watered as his vile breath swept across her face.

Akeefa nimbly danced away from him, maintaining her hold on the tray. She smiled at him and added him to the list of men who would fail to see the sunset. "I can see you are a strong man. I would not mind a detour with you, but I must deliver this food while 'tis hot, or I will be punished and then I will never be able to come back here." She smiled what she hoped was a seductive smile and leaned forward a little to show more of her breasts. "Perhaps after I come out we can dance a bit."

The guard smirked. "Hurry back, my dove. I will wait for you right here."

She breathed a sigh of relief and continued walking. Soon they passed beneath the second portcullis. If the guards lowered either of the two, she would be trapped within one of the strongest fortresses in Spain. Too late to worry about that now. Before her was a large courtyard surrounded by battlements and a door directly ahead that led into the inner keep. Memorizing the courtyard, she saw another door at the opposite end. Did it lead to the barracks? If so, she did not want to see that door open.

"Do not forget, I will be waiting beyond that portcullis." The guard winked.

She counted five men walking along the battlements above. The situation was graver than she thought. They needed a signal for René and the men to begin their assault. All had agreed Akeefa would have to come by a musket or pistol and fire a shot. That would alert the guards above, but there was no helping it. She hoped to have the Zaportas beyond the second portcullis by then.

The senior guard banged on the door, and a huge man wearing a dented armor breastplate opened it. "Servant sent with food," the portcullis guard said gruffly.

The giant armored guard stared at her while she focused on the floor. "Who you comin' for?"

"I was sent to bring food for the Zaportas," she replied meekly, working hard to restrain her anger.

"Go back to your post," the armored guard said.

The portcullis guard turned without a word and shuffled back toward the tunnel.

Time came to a standstill while the giant surveyed her. He finally nodded for her to follow him. This one seemed unaffected by her attitude and clothes, and that concerned her. He led her through the inner courtyard and keep to an anteroom occupied by three officers, by the cut of their garments. As she entered, she stood straight, smiled, and took a deep breath. They stared at her, speechless.

"Servant with food for a guest," the armored guard said with an evil grin. "Certain you lads can handle it?"

The best-dressed man spoke, "Go back to your post."

"*Si, Capitán*. Are you certain you will not need any help, sir?" His voice was filled with sarcasm.

"Vargas, if you do not return to your post immediately, you will find yourself walking the battlements at noon for a week," the captain barked.

Vargas saluted and left the room, closing the door and leaving Akeefa alone with the captain and his men. The hottest part of the day, siesta time, was on them and the head-count was light.

The stairs leading down from one end of the room were just ahead. She hoped this was the entrance to the dungeons.

"What have we here, *señorita*?" The captain peeled back the cover over the food. "Nothing special. But this," he said, leering at Akeefa, "is special."

"May I take the food to the Zaportas, sir?" She smiled coyly at him. "I am a little afraid of the dark, and perhaps you might consider taking me to them yourself."

"Rule is we do not go down into the dungeon with fewer than two men." The captain drew his fingers along his waxed goatee.

"I would feel so much safer with two strong men than with just one," Akeefa said.

"Castillo and I will escort the young lady," the captain said. As the third guard started to protest, he continued, "And you, Lopez, will escort her out."

Lopez grumbled but accepted that between the anteroom and the front gate he would have his turn.

Castillo puffed out his chest and crossed the small space to stand beside her. His face was cratered and pitted, a gift of the pox. His smell was overpowering, and this caused her involuntarily to move closer to the captain. Bathing was clearly not an important part of Castillo's routine.

The captain, on the other hand, was a dandy, with his custom uniform and silver buckles. Affecting a rakish smile, he smoothed his long mustachios in anticipation. Akeefa smiled back and brushed against him, checking to see what weapons he carried other than the visible sword and pistol.

"This way, *señorita*." The captain waved his hand indicating the stairs she had noted earlier.

Akeefa paused. "'Tis so dark down there. I fear I might drop the food."

The captain took the tray from her and handed it to Castillo.

"Carry this." He put his arm around her, pulling her closer.

"How strong you are." She linked her arm around his waist. The granite stairs were wide, and the air was dank and wet.

Their footsteps echoed from the walls. The captain had taken a torch from the anteroom, and the light from the fire reflected spots of algae growing on the wall. Akeefa counted the steps. *Twelve, thirteen, fourteen...* At twenty-five steps the ground leveled out, becoming a narrow tunnel that opened into a huge cavern, dimly lit by torches. Iron cages were aligned in rows as well as tunnel openings in the walls that apparently led to other dungeons.

"They are not expected to stay long, which is why they remain on this level," said the captain.

This level!

How deep into the earth did the dungeons go? Most of the cells were empty, but some held what had once been men. Those that could move came to the cell bars and extended their hands.

"Water, *por favor*."

Castillo banged the tray against one man's hands. "Shut up."

"Where are the Zaportas?" she asked.

"Over that way." The captain nodded to his left.

"Then why are we going this way?"

"I thought we might get to know each other better," he said laughing.

"I would *love* to get to know you better, but this food is cooling by the minute, and it will make me so sad if I cannot give it to them at least warm. I am not much fun when I am sad."

"Me either," laughed Castillo.

"The last thing we want is for you to be sad, right Castillo?"

"The very last thing," said Castillo.

The captain turned around, and they headed in the opposite direction. Soon they were in front of the cell that held the Zaportas. The captain took the torch and held it close to the cell. *Señor* Zaportas was lying on the ground. Rebeca tended him while Raquel hovered over him.

"'Tis me, Maria. Carmen sent me to you with something to eat." Akeefa hoped they understood and did not call her by her real name. "These kind men have brought me here."

Castillo opened the cell with a key from a large chain. Akeefa went in and placed the tray on the ground, then embraced Rebeca and Raquel. "The *Señor*?" she asked. "Will he live?"

"I do not know. They have not allowed us a doctor, Maria," she said loud enough to be heard by the guards. Then softer, "You should not have come here, dear. There is nothing to be done for us, and you have put yourself in great danger."

"We shall see." Akeefa hugged Rebeca again. "Be of good cheer. I will return." Then speaking louder, "I will return with more food as often as I am able, my lady. Take heart, as I am certain this awful situation will be resolved soon."

"*Gracias*, Maria," said Rebeca as the man closed and locked the cell.

"This way, *señorita*." The captain took her arm. "We hope you are not too sad. Right, Castillo?"

"We surely do," Castillo said, his smirk illuminated in the flames.

They led her over to a deserted corner and put the torch into a holder on the wall. Castillo was already loosening his breeches.

"Let me see what you have." The captain spun her around to

face him.

He raised his hand to pull the gown off her shoulder. She reached down, pulled his sword from his scabbard, danced away two paces, and stepped forward again. As she did so, she extended the tip of the sword. It slid a precise three inches into his chest, through his ribs, and killed him instantly. Withdrawing the sword, she turned to Castillo and smiled.

He stood frozen, staring at the captain crumpled on the ground. The sword made a swishing sound as it cut through the air, and then Castillo was dying. Blood poured from his open throat.

"I am not sad at all now." Akeefa leaned over and took the key ring from the man's hand. She pulled the pistol from the captain's belt, and checked to make certain it was loaded. That was everything she needed. There was no way for her to know whether a new or larger shift of men waited above, but she had no time to worry about that now.

Akeefa returned to the Zaportas's cell and opened the gate. She hugged Rebeca and a sobbing Raquel. "It will be more difficult having to carry *Señor* Zaportas, but we will do this."

"*Si*," said Rebeca. "Raquel, I need you to be stronger than you think you are. Your father needs your help, as do I."

"I will do what is necessary." The young woman took a deep breath and stilled her tears.

"We must carry *Señor* Zaportas out." Akeefa tucked the pistol and sword through the sash around her waist. She picked him up, holding him under the arms, while the other two women lifted his legs. Fortunately, Miguel Zaportas was not a large man, but it still took all three to carry him.

They managed to carry him to the stairs, only resting twice briefly along the way. They gently lowered him to the ground.

"There is no way we will be able to lift him up those stairs," said Rebeca, gasping for breath.

"I agree," Akeefa thought hard and came to an unhappy decision. "There is nothing for it. We must leave *Señor* Zaportas here for the men to carry."

"Akeefa, I will not leave my husband. Take Raquel and whatever happens, happens." Rebeca hugged Akeefa again. "Know I love you for what you tried to do."

"Mother, I will stay as well." Raquel said quietly. "There is nothing I can do to aid Akeefa. I will only be in her way. We will live together or not, as God wills."

Before Rebeca could protest, Akeefa spoke. "Beloved second mother, I am afraid she is right. Having to protect her will diminish my options when I get above. As she says, we will all live together or not, as Allah wills."

Rebeca bowed her head in acquiescence.

"Come, let us move him over there, out of the way of the opening," Akeefa said.

They shifted Miguel once more. Rebeca brushed her hand along Akeefa's cheek and then Akeefa was moving toward the stairs. She paused in the middle of the stairway to center herself, bringing her body and all of her faculties under control. She hoped there was only one man in the room above, but she would accept whatever fate had written. She came up silently into the shadow of the opening, her sword in front of her. Lopez was the room's only occupant. He died before he knew she was there.

Now comes the hard part, crossing the courtyard.

She had a plan. Further ripping open her bodice, she revealed more of her breasts, then tore cloth from her right shoulder, and prayed Allah was looking the other way. As much as she wanted the sword, she forced herself to leave it behind. If she was to convince the soldiers she was a frightened girl, she could take only the pistol. But she did take the eating knife from the dead man's hand. Then she drew the pistol from her sash, and checked that it was primed. Pulling the hammer back to its cocked position, she paused and collected herself. With a deep breath, Akeefa opened the door, and rushed through the deserted inner keep into the courtyard. She slowed and came to a stop in the center. As she hoped, Vargas, the armored man who had escorted her earlier, strode to meet her, a vicious sneer on his face. She glanced up at the men on the battlements who turned to watch. They saw her and raced for the courtyard stairs. Obviously her rape was not something to watch from a distance.

You wanted a chance to signal René and your brothers. Now

would be a good time.

Akeefa aimed the pistol at Vargas, doing her best to imitate a frightened, helpless young woman, including waving her arm around. The pistol did not concern him in the slightest. She fired, taking care to miss wildly. She glanced up at the battlements and was relieved to see all of the men had come down into the courtyard. Now it was all down to René arriving before she got into trouble.

In the next instant, Vargas had reached her. She turned aside, but he managed to grab her shoulder, pulling the bodice completely off. For his size, he was much faster than she expected. Akeefa danced away from him, barely avoiding his grasp. The leering faces of the other guards surrounded her. The huge man lunged for her again, and once again, she eluded him to the shouts and jeers of the other soldiers.

He paused, breathing heavily. "You might as well stop running. There is nowhere for you to run. So relax, little minx."

One of the men yelled, "Vargas, what the hell do you care about the woman? You do not even like women."

"No, but you do, and once I get a hold of her, it will cost you." Vargas smiled as he circled Akeefa. "Come on, little lady, I am not going to hurt you—much."

René burst through the portcullis at a dead run, followed by Raphael, her father and brothers. Emile, James, and Gavin Wade were not to be seen. Hopefully they had dispatched the two soldiers stationed at the entrance by luring them into the tunnel and now guarded the outer portcullis gate. René moved toward the armored man, but Akeefa yelled at him, "No, he is mine."

She faced Vargas and dropped her impersonation of a helpless girl. Discarding the useless pistol, she pulled the small knife from her sash and waited.

Vargas stopped. Something had changed. His expression shouted imminent threat, but it was obvious by the growing confusion on his face that he had failed to locate its source. The courtyard continued to fill with soldiers jeering at him and then at the half-dressed girl. Like a maddened bull, he shook his head, drew his sword, and charged Akeefa. As he rushed her, she swayed aside to avoid his thrust and smoothly drew the sharp knife under his ear, slicing the artery cleanly. He dropped to the ground choking, disbelief written across his face.

"That did not hurt much, did it?" she asked. When she looked up from the dead man, her father, brothers, René, and Raphael had surrounded her. She tried to pull her dress around her, and realized the futility of it. "The Zaportas are through the anteroom, at the foot of the dungeon stairs. *Señor* Zaportas is unconscious."

René pulled his shirt off and put it around her. "Khalid, Akeefa, stay here with your father and guard our retreat. Raphael, Abdul Karim, come with me."

The three men headed for the dungeons.

Akeefa pulled René's shirt over herself and then retrieved Vargas's sword. The guards that had come down from the battlements milled around in confusion after witnessing Vargas' death at the hands of this slip of a girl. Such a thing was patently impossible. Perhaps it was the timing, or the sound of the pistol, but her attention was drawn to the creak of the barracks door as it opened. The sleepy soldier returning to duty paused for a few seconds while his mind made sense of the scene. He turned and yelled, and soldiers began to erupt from the doorway.

"We need to move closer to the barracks to maintain a line of retreat for René and the Zaportas," said her father. The three of them raced forward to engage the new arrivals.

What the soldiers saw was an old man, a young man, and a girl. There was no way they could be prepared for the ferocity that met them in the middle of the courtyard. The three formed a circle with a deadly barrier of steel around its circumference. In reality, it was only minutes before René, Abdul Karim, and the Zaportas were out of the door and heading toward the second portcullis, but it felt like hours. Abdul Karim had Miguel over his left shoulder. He moved easily, as if the dead weight of a man was nothing. He stopped. His intense expression shouted his desire to join the fight.

"Get the Zaportas family back to the ship," yelled René as he joined Akeefa. "We are right behind you."

With the addition of René, the tide changed, even though there were at least twenty men in the courtyard with more coming through the doorway. Within minutes, the soldiers struggled to fight their way back through that door. Akeefa turned to watch René, fascinated. In that instant, she knew and accepted she would never equal him in this lifetime, let alone surpass him. The thought, which would previously have angered her so, now gave her a warm feeling of pride in his attainment.

"Fall back!" René yelled over the din. "'Tis time to leave."

As the soldiers continued their retreat, the four of them dashed through the gate and into the tunnel. Akeefa hoped they got through it before the soldiers regained the battlements.

"Keep going," René yelled as he stopped in front of the inner portcullis. The rope that held it up was inside the courtyard. Taking out a razor-sharp throwing knife, he sliced through most of its width. Their panic already subsiding, the soldiers gathered to rush the gate again. A musket discharged, blowing a piece of mortar from the wall beside René. He moved just inside the portcullis and threw his knife. It flew true, severing the remaining strands of rope. The iron grate crashed to the ground with an explosive thud. René turned and ran to catch up with the others. Fortunately, none of the soldiers had remained on the battlements above. Unscathed, René rejoined Akeefa at the first portcullis where they met Emile, James, and Gavin, who were on their way back into the fortress to retrieve them.

"Good afternoon, Mister Wade." René grinned.

"Top of the afternoon to you, Cap'n."

"I think I have done all the sightseeing I care to. What say we return to the ship? 'Tis a fine day for a sail."

The group headed for the La Puerta de Atarazanas gate and the open sea. As they approached the boarding plank to the *Belle Poulé*, René turned to James. "I am sorry we never managed to see the gardens. I know how much you were looking forward to it."

"Maybe next time," James said, trying to catch his breath and laugh at the same time.

Once on board the ships, Emile and James gave their commands to cast off. The ships raised sail and moved out smartly on the afternoon tide. From the rail of the *Belle Poulé*, René saw the soldiers boiling out of La Alcazaba like red and yellow hornets from a disturbed nest. One threat remained. The fortress would turn its great cannon on them. Their escape depended on how quickly the soldiers readied the cannon to fire—and how accurate they were.

"Mister Lamert, signal Mister Bailey to take an evasive course and then settle on south by southwest," René said. "If we become separated, we will rendezvous off Mijas before making the run through Gibraltar."

"Aye, aye, sir." Emile went to the rail to shout René's orders to the *Seahawk*, the ships still being close enough for communication.

Raphael walked up to René. "May I have a moment of your time?"

"Of course. Things have changed a bit now that your family is aboard. You may choose to be a passenger or crew. Either way, we can remain informal in private. How is your family?"

"My father has not yet regained consciousness, but Doctor Al Zahrawi assures me the signs are good he will. My mother and sister are shaken but in good health. You have saved my family from certain death. While I may never be able to repay you, I will spend this lifetime trying."

The Raphael who stood before René was a different man. "We did what was necessary. All of us. Akeefa is the one who saved your family."

"Akeefa is already my sister, and she knows I would gladly give my life for her. I find I must ask yet another favor of you."

"You have but to ask, you know that."

"Put me ashore near our hacienda. I have business to conduct, and I will not leave Spain without completing it."

"I will go with you," René answered, knowing exactly what business Raphael proposed.

"No, René, this must be done by me alone. I will not take long, or I will not return. Twelve hours is what I ask. Take me in by longboat, and return in twelve hours to pick me up. If I am not there, you are to leave. Do not look for me." Raphael met René's eyes. "I want your word you will not seek me out if I fail. The rendezvous will occur in twelve hours, or not at all."

"Think, Raphael. You are allowing your emotions to govern your actions. Allow me to accompany you. I promise I will not act unless the situation requires it. Your family has been attacked. Your objective is to remove the threat and the possibility of any future threat, not satisfy your inability to protect your family from a dozen men."

"What would you have done in the same situation?"

René paused in thought. "In truth, if the incident had occurred before my sojourn in a slave hold, I might have charged ahead and paid with my life for my stupidity. Even with training, our emotions can carry us to our disadvantage. Let me act as a reserve force. No general with an ounce of strategic intelligence commits his whole force without knowledge of the enemy. Act with power but not in thrall to ignorance."

"You will not interfere unless I ask."

"Raphael—"

"Your word, sir."

There was silence for a beat before René spoke, "You have it. I will not act unless you request it."

"Nevertheless," Raphael said with a fleeting smile, "If we both have underestimated the enemy, you will leave me and take my family to safety."

"I will, and you have my word on that as well."

"*Gracias.*" Raphael extended his right hand, and the two men clasped hands.

"Mister Lamert," René called out to the big seaman. "Change course to west by southwest up the coast three leagues. Be on the lookout for the Zaportas dock."

"Aye, aye, sir," Emile called back.

CHAPTER THIRTY-NINE

THE *BELLE Poulé* dropped anchor a mile above the Zaportas plantation later that afternoon. The grounds extended to the sea, and while there was a protected quay and dock, René had directed the crew to bypass it for the less conspicuous anchorage. A cool wind blew across the deck, and the sun melted the horizon crimson with the promise of good weather. Raphael said his goodbyes to a tearful mother and sister and asked them to remain with their father in the cabin.

René, Emile, and Gavin Wade accompanied Raphael in the longboat to shore. "Are you certain you will not consider a couple more companions?" asked Emile.

Raphael met the big captain's gaze. "I am certain, *Monsieur* Lamert. René will accompany me and that will have to be sufficient. *Gracias* for your offer."

The boat touched the sandy beach, and they jumped out to pull it to shore.

"*Bon chance*," Emile said.

René clasped his hand. "We will return. There is much left to do in this lifetime." With that, he and Raphael disappeared into the forest that skirted the beach.

Raphael and René avoided the road from the dock to the sorting house and went through the citrus groves instead.

"Medina will not wait even one day to install himself as the new owner of the hacienda." Raphael trampled the tall grass between the rows of trees as if it were his enemy.

"Control your anger." René ducked under a low branch. "You are better trained than that."

Raphael nodded and held up his right hand. They silently approached the hacienda and counted five horses in front of the veranda.

Raphael led René to an unremarkable copse of buckthorn bushes. "My ancestors survived many narrow escapes over the centuries. My father engineered an underground tunnel connected with the hacienda in three locations. This one will come out in the root cellar, an unlikely place to meet intruders." Raphael pushed aside the bushes planted around the doorway, then he brushed away the earth and pulled open the wooden door into the tunnel. Once within, he lit the torch placed there for such contingencies.

René stooped and then followed along until they were standing on the other side of the root cellar door. A long moment of listening revealed only silence. Raphael released a hidden latch and soundlessly pulled the door open. He then slipped into the cellar, followed by René, who closed the door behind them.

"I have a good idea where Manuel Medina can be found," whispered Raphael. "I only hope that Carmen has remained in the kitchen and that he has not hurt her." When they got to the kitchen the room was empty and cold.

Raphael leaned into René. "Medina will have brought men to ransack the house for valuables. No matter what, Medina must not escape."

René nodded. Raphael's plan was exactly what René would have done had it been his home being looted.

They entered the great room through the dining room. Raphael pointed to Medina seated in his father's chair. That magnificent room, and that chair, embodied the power and respect accorded *Señor* Zaportas. Earlier, Raphael had explained how Medina had spent years without success trying to purchase or cajole acceptance into the small circle of intimates who found welcome at the Zaportas' hacienda.

Raphael moved up behind the chair. He aimed his pistol at the back of Medina's neck. "Get the hell out of my father's chair."

Medina jumped as though branded with a cattle iron. He swiveled around and reached for the pistol in his belt.

"Do not prove your stupidity," said Raphael.

René moved into the room to stand a distance behind Raphael and to his right. His sword was drawn.

Medina lowered his hand to his side. His gaze touched on René and then focused on Raphael.

"Drop the pistol to the floor, butt-first," Raphael ordered.

"It was not me," Medina whined. "It was the priest, I had no choice. He came to me and threatened my eternal soul."

"Move away from my father's chair."

"I tried to protect Miguel."

"Move, or I will kill you where you stand." Raphael waved his pistol toward the center of the room. "Draw your sword. My mother will be furious if I stain her carpet, but every breath you take is offensive to me."

Medina's demeanor changed when he realized that Raphael was not going to just kill him out of hand, and he added a swagger to his movement. "You Jews thought you could get away with it. I own this land now."

"No, you do not." Raphael drew his sword and put the pistol down on a side table. "You never could best my father, and you have failed once more. He had prepared for our move and sold the land, and the hacienda, six months ago. We leased it. No matter what happens, our home is beyond your grasp."

"The *bastard*." Medina charged Raphael.

"Life is so unfair sometimes," Raphael said as the swords clanged together. The man's guard was sloppy, and Raphael slashed his blade through Medina's cheek.

Medina shrieked and disengaged as he stumbled backwards. "*Por favor,* I will give you money, much money. And I will talk with the Jesuit on your behalf. He is a reasonable man. I will tell him it was all a big mistake."

"Yours." Raphael advanced.

"Is there a problem, *Señor* Medina?" a man's voice asked from behind them. "You want me to shoot him?"

Time stopped for what seemed an eternity.

"Drop the sword, son, and I will not hurt you." Medina's lips curled into a cruel smile. "I have an inquisitor you need to meet. But do not count on *him* not hurting you."

Raphael leaned forward for a last lunge toward Medina as René prepared to charge the man behind them.

A loud musical thud rang out. René turned in time to see the man behind him crumple to the floor.

"Take care of that other weasel." Carmen had one hand braced on her hip and the other wrapped around the handle of a cast iron frying pan.

René glanced back at Medina. The man tried to claim the advantage of the distraction with a quick thrust at Raphael. Raphael, however, refused to be distracted twice. Manuel Medina died an instant later, his heart skewered by Raphael's sword. Raphael wiped the blade on the dead man's shirt and then sheathed his sword. In quick strides he was at Carmen's side hugging her.

"Enough of that." Tears spilled onto her wrinkled cheeks. "There are others in the house." As Raphael made for the doorway she said, "Wait. Your mother and father and sister—"

Raphael interrupted her. "Safe aboard the *Belle Poulé*, which is where you will be shortly. Now we must greet the rest of our visitors."

"What are you going to do?" she asked.

"Since they are not invited guests, I see no reason to be polite," he said with an evil grin.

René helped Raphael drag the last corpse out of the house and push it off the veranda into the dirt. He and Raphael made a pile of them with Medina on the bottom. It was a shame the new owner, Juan Alvarez Ramos, would have to clean this up, but every hour the Zaportas family remained within the Inquisition's reach, the danger of apprehension increased. René followed Raphael back into the hacienda to help him gather the household's portable wealth, and any items of historical value to the family.

Raphael summoned the servants into the courtyard. He gave each one more than enough money to relocate if they wished, advised them to leave the area for a time, and to contact *Señor* Ramos if major problems arose. Raphael began to hitch horses to a produce wagon when the retainers rushed over and grabbed the harness.

"*Por favor*, stop." Raphael held up his right hand palm out. "When they ask if you helped me, I want you to be able to say no and have it be the truth. You can say you saw me, but I was armed and there was nothing you could do.

Raphael reached for the horse collar the man held. "Francisco, *por favor*. I do not want you implicated any more than you already are."

From his previous visit, René recognized the man as the foreman of the Zaportas hacienda, Francisco Barba. The others stopped.

Francisco refused to relinquish the horse collar. "Carmen told us that *Señor* Zaportas, your mother, and your sister are safe. That is all we need to know. When they question us, they will not believe us whatever we say, and so we will say nothing. We know you cannot take us with you, so we will wait for your return, or perhaps the return of your children. All we ask, *señor*, is that you allow us this last service."

A lone tear inched along Raphael's cheek. These people were his family. He was running away, but he had no choice. Death waited for him, for them all, if they stayed.

Raphael glanced at Francisco and the others. "On my life, we will return as soon as we are able. Francisco, Pedro, will you hitch up the wagon?" Raphael's voice was rough. He cleared his throat and took a deep breath. "Carlos, Daniel, help René and me load the wagon. The rest of you can help Carmen pack whatever she wants to take. I hope we will not need another wagon." The servants laughed. He paused, and gazed at the foreman. "*Gracias, mi amigo.*"

Francisco nodded and placed the collar he held on one of the horses.

With the aid of the retainers, Raphael and René were able to pack most of the things the Zaportas needed. They had to add a second wagon, which was soon filled. Apparently Carmen was determined to dismantle her entire kitchen and move it aboard ship. After some heated discussion, with René's support, they were finally able to convince Carmen that more would be impossible to transport. The spices alone would tax the longboat.

The time had come to leave. Raphael shook hands with the men and hugged the women goodbye. From where he sat at the head of one of the wagons, René followed Raphael's gaze back to the servants. Their tear streaked faces were reflected in the light of the torches they held. The beginnings of a gray dawn appeared on the horizon. Raphael breathed in deeply, as if to commit to memory the smell of the citrus groves in the early morning. He climbed up to sit beside Carmen and gathered the reins. He nodded to René and then snapped the reins out over the horse's backs. *"Arre!"*

CHAPTER FORTY

Château Gaspard, Bordeaux, France

WOOD STRUCK stone, and a man cursed.

"If I am jarred again, you will take up residence here," growled Horemheb, through the guttural remains of Victor's vocal cords.

His chair was carried by four brawny men. Like the royal chair of a pharaoh, stout poles on each side supported it. An ungainly way to descend stairs, but it was possible if the bearers turned sideways. The men carried him to the occupied cell while a fifth man opened the locked grate. In the center of the cell, a raised pedestal of stone was outfitted with various sizes of iron rings. The men lowered the chair beside the pedestal.

The château's dungeon reminded Horemheb of the cells filled during his early days as Pharaoh. The walls, twelve feet thick, allowed no sound to escape the space, but from within, each of the large iron-barred cells permitted its inhabitants to see and hear what awaited them in the fullness of time. There were six cells, three on each side, separated by paths which allowed no physical contact between prisoners.

Torches could be placed around the circumference of the room when light was required. The work done within sometimes required the same levels of light a surgeon might ask for, but ordinarily a lone torch provided adequate illumination for the ministrations performed. Today, there was but a single occupant chained to the wall of one of the cells. His expression was a wash of terror.

"Strip the prisoner and secure him here beside me," Horemheb said.

"*Oui, monsieur*," said the fifth man. They unlocked the metal collar around the prisoner's neck from the wall, stripped his ragged clothing from him, and then dragged him to the center of the cell. Two men secured his collar to a ring set into the granite pedestal while the others secured his arms and legs.

The prisoner pleaded. "I can kill the boy. 'Twas not my fault. I can still be of use."

"In that you are correct." Horemheb faced the terrified servants. "Leave us. I will call when I am ready for you."

The men needed no urging to hurry from the oubliette.

"It has been a long time since I have done this, and I apologize if my skills are rusty." Horemheb grasped the metal collar and then pulled the prisoner's head toward him. The man rattled the cuffs securing his limbs to the pedestal and gibbered in fear.

"You see, I need your life force. I intend to remain in this pathetic boy's husk, and in this, yes, you can be of use. You will find this unpleasant. In fact, it will be the most painful thing you can imagine." He stroked the man's head, and a pale violet glow became visible. Horemheb leaned over, closed his eyes, and began to absorb the glowing energy. The man's scalp blackened and crisped as if in a fire, darkening with each draw of his life force. Well-versed in the application of pain though they were, the fools waiting at the top of the stairs had never before heard a human make sounds as terrible as these.

CHAPTER FORTY-ONE

Off the coast of Spain

AFTER MEETING the *Seahawk* off Mijas, the *Belle Poulé* and her companion made their way toward the Strait of Gibraltar. The weather was even, and the winds fair. The most dangerous part would come when the width of the strait narrowed to fewer than three leagues. At present, the ships were about a thousand yards apart and had managed, with the assistance of lamps, to remain within visual distance through the nights as well.

It was early evening, and René had finished supervising fencing practice. He was wiping his face when Dr. Zahrawi came up from below. He walked over to him. "How is *Señor* Zaportas, doctor? Any change?"

"He remains unconscious." The doctor took in a deep breath of fresh sea air.

"Is there nothing more that can be done for him?"

"In my experience, no. He will either awaken or not. I have instructed *Señora* Zaportas and the family to remain with him, to talk to him, and to remind him his work here is not done."

"Would I be intruding if I visited?"

"Not at all. I am certain they would welcome a diversion. To sit a vigil with someone you love is hard work."

"*Merci*, doctor." René nodded and then headed toward the galley hatch. He stopped by his cabin first. A few minutes later he continued on to the Zaportas' cabin. René stood outside the cabin door and listened for conversation. The last thing he wanted to do was to wake someone. Hearing voices, he knocked.

"Enter," said Rebeca.

René opened the door and stepped across the threshold.

"Oh, 'tis you, René," Rebeca said with a tired smile. "I never did get to properly thank you. Come here."

René crossed the cabin to stand before the *señora*. She wrapped her arms around him and hugged him then kissed him on the cheek. "*Gracias*, my dear man, for saving my family."

"As I told Raphael," he said, looking at Raphael, who smiled and shrugged. "Akeefa is the one who took all the risk. I just came along."

"I know what Akeefa did, and I know what it cost Ammar, Abdul Karim, and Khalid for her to do it. You, however, were instrumental in bringing together the means of our survival, and I am grateful." She stepped back. "What is that you have in your hand?"

"A lute I bought in Malaga. I thought perhaps *Señor* Zaportas might enjoy some music." René grinned. "Be assured I use that term loosely."

"We would love some music. Mother?" Raquel perked up for the first time since they boarded the ship.

"That would be lovely, René." Rebeca changed seats to sit closer to Raphael. "Raquel, give René your chair and sit on the bed beside your father."

René sat in the offered chair and tuned the lute. He was a little self-conscious, as he had not practiced, let alone played, for quite a while. He hoped it was something that stayed with you. All he knew were French folk songs. Marie, their cook, used to sing them to him until he echoed them back to her. Most were bawdy and inappropriate for the time and place, but there were a few that sang of beautiful things such as the ocean, wine, and children playing. He would begin with "Glory of the Sea," one of Marie's favorites. The old Irish sea chantey had been translated into French. It told the story of a selkie, a magical being who changed form from a woman to a seal and back again until she met her true love. Then she would remain in the form of that love, be it seal or human, never returning to the joys of the other.

He began to play quietly and then to sing along. He had a clear baritone that was pleasing to the ear. People always seemed surprised by that, and he had no idea why. Akeefa and Khalid entered the cabin and stood just inside the doorway. The music of the song was repetitive and lyrical, and René always found it had a soothing effect on him. He sensed it had the same effect on the others as well.

The song took him back to his summers aboard the *Belle Poulé*, when Jacques would call to him to sing. The men would clear a space for him, and then crowd around, hungry for something to break the monotony, or perhaps something to remind them of the distant land. Singing had gotten him out of many a dreary task aboard ship. He smiled at the memory. He was just getting to his favorite verse when Raquel cried out.

"He gripped my hand," she said. "I was holding his hand, and I felt him squeeze mine."

Rebeca rushed to her husband's side and took his hand from Raquel. "My beloved, *por favor,* come back to us."

Slowly, Miguel blinked his eyes open and breathed more deeply. Consciousness dawned. "Rebeca?" he said, struggling to speak.

"Miguel." Tears streamed from her eyes. She fell forward to embrace him. "Oh, Miguel."

Señor Zaportas caught René's eye.

"You are aboard the *Belle Poulé,* and all of your family is safe," René said, and then turned to Akeefa and Khalid. "We should give them some privacy. I will notify Doctor Zahrawi that *Señor* Zaportas is awake."

They left the cabin and closed the door behind them. As they climbed the stairway to the upper deck, René could not help but stare. Akeefa was not wearing her customary hijab. Her hair shimmered in black waves on her shoulders. He pushed open the hatch, and they exited into a calm, starry evening.

The doctor was forward checking a sailor with a bandage on his wrist. René turned to Akeefa and Khalid. "You two go over to the aft rail. I will join you after I speak with Dr. Zahrawi."

"See, he did not even notice," Akeefa said to Khalid.

"Oh, he noticed, all right. He is too polite to speak of it."

"I will not remain covered while other women aboard—whom

we love and respect—breathe the air freely without a burqa in front of their noses," she said, her frustration long-earned.

"I know, I know." As they arrived at the rail, the moon-glazed ocean stretched out in front of them. "I was there during the conversation with father and Abdul Karim, remember? Your arguments were persuasive and forceful, and both bowed to your courage in the fortress and to your will. I will do my best, beloved sister. There is logic and there is heart, and the heart does not give up its learning easily. Our society teaches the male his purpose is to protect the female so she may continue and increase the family. And I know it gives us a puffed up self-image, which we tend to magnify at times—"

"At times?" huffed Akeefa.

"All right, most of the time." Khalid inspected the deck. "And though the thought of needing to protect you is ludicrous, the question remains. If protecting the female is not the primary role of the male, what is? Do we have a purpose at all? And how are we to face the world without a purpose?"

"I see your point, and I will not even pretend I am powerful enough to exist alone, so your purpose remains. Still, there are times, like now, when the chances of my beauty driving one of the sailors to accost me are slim, even were I not able to defend myself. You should try walking around on a hot day with your face and head covered."

"I expect it is uncomfortable."

"That is an understatement. I have promised to tailor my wardrobe to meet the demands of the society I am within. When we reach home, you may rest assured I will once again be properly covered."

René walked up to them and paused as though he sensed their discord.

"I have notified Dr. Zahrawi, so we will wait to hear what he says. He has told me before that if a man wakes, there is a good chance he will recover."

The contentious atmosphere cleared, and there was a pleasant silence.

"Well, I will bid both of you good night as I have reading to do.

Father believes an ocean voyage is the perfect time to study."
Khalid nodded to René and flashed a smile at his sister.

"He is a good man," said René as Khalid walked toward the
galley hatch.

"One of the best," she agreed. "There are a number of good men
aboard this vessel."

She glanced out over the moonlit sea.

"I noticed you changed your wardrobe."

"Do you approve?"

"Very much. I cannot think 'tis comfortable wearing a mask all
the time. Ah, I am sorry, I did not mean that the way it sounded. I
think you look fine however you dress," he added lamely.

Akeefa laughed at his discomfort. "René, you do not have to
mince words with me. There is always a risk of offending someone,
and in my case, it might be more dangerous than most, but I
appreciate your honesty."

"I never liked the thought of being a courtier, fawning over
people with power, but your father has taught me that words can
be either a weapon or a tool, and like a sword, they need to be
properly utilized."

"Father has always been rather insistent on our studying," she
laughed. "I have my own course of study, but over the years I
have been able to adjust it now and then toward those subjects that
interest me." The ship's wake bubbled up white and silver, leaving
an iridescent streak on the ocean. "'Tis so beautiful out here.
Peaceful."

"It is now, but the sea has many faces. Probably why 'tis so
fascinating. Look how smartly the *Seahawk* moves." He pointed
toward the other ship. "She is only using three quarters the sail we
are, so she can keep her distance."

A smile tweaked Akeefa's lips as René unwittingly changed the
subject.

CHAPTER FORTY-TWO

THERE WAS a knock on the cabin door. "Enter," said Miguel, seated at the desk.

Sheikh Ghassan came in carrying a small cloth bag and closed the door behind him. "I thought you were supposed to stay in bed and recuperate," he said and then nodded to René who had been visiting Miguel.

"I am fine. 'Twill take more than a gun-butt to the head to take me from the board." Miguel pushed his chair back.

"Stay seated." The sheikh walked over to shake hands.

René rose from his chair and then sat on the bunk. The sheikh pulled the chair up across from the desk. He placed the cloth bag he carried on the desktop.

"'Tis good to see you, Ammar." Miguel smiled. "And good to see you still boss people around."

"Only when they are too stubborn for their own good," said the sheikh.

"Rebeca fusses about me like an old hen, and Raquel is worse. 'Tis galling to be an invalid." Miguel did not attempt to hide his frustration. "I know I came close to leaving and that frightened them, but damn it, I am still here so be done already. What have you in the bag?"

"Well, if things have followed true to form, the only thing you have had to drink has been goat's milk and water, correct?" The sheikh slipped a bottle of brandy out of the sack.

"I have so missed getting into trouble with you, old friend.

There are glasses in the cupboard over there. René will you get them? Let us not waste time talking. Let me see what you brought." Miguel took the bottle. "This will do nicely."

René brought over three glasses and placed them on the desk. The sheikh poured brandy into each. He handed one to Miguel, a second to René, and took the last glass for himself. He raised his glass. *"L'Chaim!"*

Miguel clinked his glass against the sheikh's and, meeting his eye, echoed the toast. "To life!"

Miguel glanced at René, then back to Sheikh Ghassan. Neither spoke. René sensed his presence was an intrusion. He set his empty glass on the desk and walked to the door. "Gentlemen, I must return to my duties."

"Sit, René," said the sheikh who looked at Miguel and received a nod in return.

"You are an integral part of our plans and I would not exclude you from any discussions of the future. Aboard ship, however, is not the place or the time to answer the myriad of questions which must arise from entering into our current discussion. If we sound cryptic in our deliberations, it is as it must be, for you are yet to be initiated. Are you willing to sit quietly and restrain any questions until we judge the time to be proper to answer them?"

"If you feel it wise for me to remain, I am willing. When you desire, I will be happy to leave you to your considerations and will find the patience to await answers in their own time." René met the gaze of each man.

"May we dispense with the recognition ritual and consider ourselves to have recognized each other in proper fashion?" said Miguel.

"We may," answered the sheikh. "I would recognize the signature of your vital energy anywhere, my friend. There are not many of us. Your near-departure is, and should be, a matter for grave consideration. I believe you misjudged the climate within your country, and it was only by good fortune you and your family are still with us."

"As much as I am embarrassed to admit it, I believe you are correct. I allowed the land to enter my heart to such an extent that

I was unable to consider leaving it, even though I knew it was time to go. I am angry at my blindness."

"Our mission has not been compromised." The sheikh stood and paced, apparently too filled with excitement to remain seated. "We will proceed with the initiation once we reach Meknes. You concur?"

"I agree. Are there any of our brothers or sisters in Morocco or reasonably nearby?" Miguel asked.

"At least one, but we will know when we reach land."

"We will have our work cut out for us, I am afraid. Moulay Ismail's patience for his brother's throne has limits." Miguel sipped his brandy.

"Battle plans never survive the first strike. We are at once stronger and weaker than we anticipated. But enough of this for now. If I overtax you, Rebeca will turn her attentions to me." The sheikh stood. "René, let us take our leave."

"But René was sharing his plans for our proposed trading venture. Surely I can continue with that conversation."

"There will be plenty of time tomorrow for business. Rest well my old friend."

"I will check in on you tomorrow," said René who made his way toward the door.

"Make sure you bring the manifest."

"I will." René left the cabin, but heard the two old friends last comments.

"He is the one in this generation," said Miguel.

"I am sure of it," said the sheikh.

CHAPTER FORTY-THREE

'TWAS A fine afternoon for a party. The sea was calm, and even though it was winter, the trade winds off the coast of Africa kept the temperature reasonable. The *Seahawk* rested alongside the *Belle Poulé*, and James and the first group of sailors had come aboard.

There was plenty to eat, and while there was drink, René had limited the strength of the punch. They were still in enemy waters, after all. The men had drawn lots, the losers taking the first watch and then exchanging after two hours. They still had three days' sail before reaching safe harbor in Larache where they would offload the weapons.

Mister Downs and Sabah had worked with Carmen to create a truly memorable feast. The savory food filled a long trencher table set up on the *Poulé*'s deck. René played and sang until he exhausted his repertoire of songs. One of the men from the *Seahawk* took over, playing a squeezebox that set the crew dancing aboard both ships.

As the afternoon wound down, René sat talking with *Señora* Zaportas. When she turned to answer a question from the sheikh, he leaned back, pleasantly full, contented. A gust of wind came across the deck, ruffling Akeefa's shawl, which she had left draped over the back of a chair. The temperature on the ocean often changed precipitously, as now, with a chill on the breeze. René picked up the shawl, then took it over to where she stood at the rail, gazing toward the sunset. She had been pensive during the afternoon. René sensed an unusual level of worry radiating from her. He placed the shawl around her shoulders.

"Thank you, René." She continued to stare at the sun reflecting off the waves.

"You are quiet tonight."

"I am happy Raquel got the party you promised her."

"I have seen you happy, and this is nothing like my recollections." He put one hand on his chest and the other before him like an actor might and grimaced.

She laughed and then became serious again. "I am truly happy at *Señor* Zaportas's recovery, but there is a stronger foreboding I cannot seem to shake. I am afraid, René."

"Afraid?" He had difficulty understanding the word, especially when referring to Akeefa. He had never met anyone less afraid in his life. "Of what or whom?"

"That is what disturbs me. I do not know." She turned and watched Raquel dancing with Khalid. She wanted him to dance with her as an adult, but Khalid would only hold her hands, as if they were children playing. "She has grown."

René followed her line of sight. "I think she has an infatuation with your brother."

"She could do worse."

"She is still young."

"Women mature quickly in this part of the world. She will not be a child much longer," she said, her voice full of sadness.

René had no response to Akeefa. They stood quietly, enjoying the gentle wind and the music in the background. After a time, he sensed her levels of discomfort increase and tried to quiet her unease. "We may run into the Salé pirates, but with the two ships, I do not think they will risk attacking us. I know they are reputed to be fanatical and crazy, but there is crazy and then there is suicidal. Are they the cause of your worry?"

She linked her arm through his and shrugged. "'Tis just a feeling, but one so strong I can feel my body preparing for battle. I know you can sense my concern. Be still for a moment and see if you can sense what I am receiving. Maybe you will understand it better than I."

René stilled his mind and allowed her emotions to penetrate his. With them came a wave of unease. His inner senses shouted threat, and he had learned not to discount his intuition. He couldn't tell from what quarter trouble would come, but soon something would challenge them. A strong gust of cold wind blew across his face, as if to punctuate his awareness of impending attack.

"*Oui*, there is something. 'Tis time to end this party and prepare."

"Do you know what to prepare for?"

"*Non*. We must be ready for everything. Emile," René called to the big captain. "End the party and separate the ships."

"Aye, aye, sir," said Emile. "Do we have trouble, sir?"

"I do not know," René said. "*S'il vous plaît*, Akeefa, apologize to Raquel and the Zaportas for my stopping the festivities so abruptly, and if you would ask them and your father to go below, I would appreciate it." He turned to go.

Akeefa put her hand on his arm. "Thank you, René."

"Thank me when we are safely docked in port."

Black clouds collided above the ships. Darkness was falling fast. A storm had exploded out of nowhere. James crossed over to the *Seahawk*, and gave the order to cut the ships loose from each other. René found it difficult to refrain from issuing commands in a situation like this. All he could do was watch while Emile battened down the ship for a blow. Raphael reported to the helm. They had found that among his other talents, Raphael had a sure hand on the whipstaff.

"Release all lines," yelled Emile. He ordered enough sail to take the *Belle Poulé* away from the *Seahawk*. The wind was now whipping through the sheets, and Emile called to Raphael to turn her into the wind. The *Seahawk* dropped away quickly. René hoped to rendezvous with the *Seahawk* before they reached Larache. While he was confident the *Belle Poulé* could defend herself in an attack, with two ships there would be no attack. He winced as the wind blew first from the port quarter and then from the starboard. Crosswinds made for a nasty sea. He was glad Raphael was at the helm. Even though the sun was not yet down, it was fully dark now. The darkness of a storm was different from the dark of night. It was a cloying, clinging type of darkness, more an absence of sight than of light.

Promoted to first mate and transferred aboard the *Poulé*, Mister Wade audibly took charge of the men in the sheets. This was dangerous work, up in the rigging in an angry sea. René fought his way through the wind and crossed the deck to Emile.

"Is there anything I can do?" he asked.

"Are you taking command?" asked Emile, waiting.

"*Non,* you are in command. I will retire below decks, but if you need an extra hand, do not hesitate to call me."

"Yes, sir. We can handle this. The *Poulé* has ridden many a blow, and she will ride out this one," Emile said with a confidence born of long experience.

"I have no doubt," called René, as he made his way toward the hatch below. After checking on the Zaportas, he moved on to visit Akeefa before he retired. As he expected, she was reading, and her cabin had been properly battened down.

"Do you feel any different now that the storm is upon us?" He hoped their premonition had been about the storm.

"No. I cannot see clear what it is, but 'twas not the storm, or at least, not only the storm. The worst part is the feeling of inevitability that hangs over me, as if nothing I do will change the outcome. René, I have never felt this way before."

"We are as prepared as we can be, and to second guess ourselves is a waste of time and effort," he said. "Rest easy. This is a sturdy ship with an experienced crew. We should be fine."

She nodded and returned to her reading.

René closed the door, sensing again that empty inevitability of which she spoke.

"Is a man's destiny written?" Fourteen-year-old René asked the Maestro, taking a vicious swipe at his leg.

The Maestro easily blocked the thrust, and sent a counter stroke singing toward René's shoulder. Anticipating the strike, René turned enough so it slipped past him with a whisper of clearance.

"I do not believe a man's destiny is written in whole, but it

appears there may be parts, which are inked in to give a general direction to the soul's objective." The Maestro circled to René's left.

"Is the day of our death fixed?" René quickly switched the sword from his right hand to his left.

"I do not know," replied the Maestro. "I do not think so. I think rather it is in response to the choices we make or have made, in addition to those choices made before we're born."

"So if the choice to die is made by us, for some reason before we are born, then is that not still destiny?"

The Maestro feinted and then brought his sword lightly across René's chest, cutting the boy's shirt and leaving a thin red line. "You mean like choosing not to pay close enough attention, so you get cut? I suppose you might call that destiny, but I call it stupidity."

After two hours, René could no longer remain in his cabin. He put on a woolen overcoat and went above deck, opening the hatch into a sailor's vision of hell. The wind that had howled through the ship was now shrieking. There was little canvas showing, only a storm jib for some maneuverability. René had been in bad storms but never one like this. Thirty-foot waves crashed over the bow and then over the side. Visibility was limited. The men tied themselves to their posts to keep from being swept overboard. He made his way aft to spell Raphael for a while on the whipstaff. Only his long-honed sense of balance allowed him to navigate the pitching deck. He passed Emile, who was tied to the main mast, where he could see and direct those men remaining above. They nodded to each other. There could be no speech unless you were right beside the man.

The *Belle Poulé* plunged like a wounded beast.

Crack.

A six inch spar had snapped with a retort like a musket shot. Freed, it swung unhindered, its arc speeding it straight toward a sailor in the rigging striking his head a glancing blow. Robert Fortin jerked once and then went limp. The only thing that kept him from plunging fifty feet to the deck was the rope that secured him to the yard. Fortin had taught René knots when the eleven-year-old first sailed aboard the *Poulé*. René kicked his shoes off and tossed his heavy coat to the deck. He raced to the main mast where Emile worked to untie the line that held him fast. When René came up beside him, he laid his hand on Emile's.

"Stop." René yelled in his ear, "I am better than you are in the rigging, and you know it."

"You may be, but I am the captain, and that's my man up there."

"You are the captain of this vessel, and you are not stupid. I am commanding you to stay put. At this point in our venture, I am expendable. You, however, are not. Remain where you are, Captain!" René held Emile's eye until he reluctantly nodded and moved aside as far as his tether allowed. René began to climb the swaying rigging. He needed every ounce of strength in his hands and arms to hang on to the rain-slicked ropes. One minute the mast was vertical and the next nearly horizontal, as the ship heeled way over, low enough for water to come pouring over the gunwale.

René loved this ship. She had taken him through his adolescence, and he could count on her. He silently thanked the Maestro for every brick as he climbed up to the yard. One of the other men was beginning to untie himself to aid his shipmate.

"*Non*," René yelled. "I will get him." He was accustomed to walking this yard, but that was impossible in weather such as this. He clasped the yardarm with his arms and legs and inched along toward the man hanging in the rigging. When he reached Fortin, René checked that he was still alive. He was breathing, but unconscious. There was no way to lower him to the deck. The swaying ship would dash him to death against the mast. The only option was to fashion a harness and carry him down, tied to René's back.

René secured himself to the yard and cut enough rope to make a harness. He tied it securely around the sailor, encircling his legs and arms. He left loops of rope to put his arms through, got into the harness, and looped another coil around Fortin's waist and his own. René tested that the lines were tight and released the man's secure rope. He kept his own loosely around the yard, only releasing and reattaching it when he came to another piece of rigging on the yard. Robert Fortin was of medium build, but unconscious, he was nothing but dead weight. René sucked in a deep breath and maneuvered along the yard toward the main mast.

He only had thirty feet to scale, but it felt like ten leagues. René was drenched with sweat despite the bitter, freezing wind. He finally reached the main mast and secured both of them. He needed to rest and gather his resources. René had never pushed himself this hard before, and he still had to get them both down to the deck. Although the shrieking wind filled his ears, he heard someone yelling. A sailor was on the opposite side of the yard, holding a large coil of rope.

"I will belay you down," he yelled.

"Do you have enough line?" René shouted back.

"*Non*, but what I have is better than nothing. I think I can get you most of the way down." The sailor tied the rope to the yard and was preparing to toss it to René.

"Throw it," René called.

The sailor flung the coiled rope toward René. The wind and swell chose that moment to heel the ship over until the mast pointed at the horizon, and it was all the men could do to remain on the yard. The man pulled back the line and prepared to throw it again.

"Now," yelled René.

The rope sailed over the yard, and this time René caught it. He tied it securely to the center part of the harness at shoulder level.

"You ready?" yelled René.

The sailor braced himself. René threw a short line around the mast and used it to rappel himself and the unconscious man down to the deck. Even with the belaying line and the sailor's aid, it was a fight. The wind and waves were determined to tear René from the mast. An eternity later, René's foot touched the deck. The rope had given out twenty feet ago, and René had done the last twenty feet on determination alone, for even his great strength had been exhausted. "I will take him from here," said Emile, making certain first that René had secured himself to the mast. He and another seaman managed to get Robert below decks to Doctor Zahrawi. René nodded to the sailor in the rigging, who laughed and waved and then grabbed for the yard as the ship heeled over again. René heard him curse and then laugh again. This storm was not going to take the *Belle Poulé*, but it was going to be a long night.

René collapsed into his bunk. The storm had taken its time leaving and only abated in the early morning. René, Raphael, and Gavin had taken turns at the whipstaff, two of them on at every moment. Steering a ship within a storm like that was an exhausting task. Not only did the sheer power of the water and wind have to be continuously wrestled to maintain the ship's heading, but the task also demanded a level of finesse that was, perhaps, even more exhausting. The biggest danger for a ship in a storm was to lose its rudder. Without it, the ship would turn her side into the wind and scuttle. As strong as the rudder was, the power of the storm could snap it like a matchstick in the blink of an eye. Only an experienced hand—or, in this case, two—could gauge the pressures that kept the rudder in one piece. They maintained their rotation throughout the night, René and Gavin fell to the deck when Emile sent sailors to relieve them once the storm had lessened.

When the clouds cleared, Emile would call him to shoot the sun. Until then, it was a blessed relief to rest. After a time the cabin door opened and closed as Raphael staggered into the room, but it could have been a dream. René was too tired to move a muscle.

There was a knock on the door. "Cap'n says the sun's up, sir," said a sailor from the other side of the door.

'Twas not possible. He had just gone to sleep. "What is the hour?" René called.

"Mid-morning, sir."

"Tell him I will be out directly." Had five hours really passed? René assessed his condition. Everything seemed to be in working order, but he hurt. The pain brought back memories of exercises with the Maestro. He had often experienced the edge of total muscle fatigue. He stood, noting that Raphael had not even awakened. He went through a brief series of stretching exercises, grabbed his astrolabe and logbook, and left the cabin. He came through the hatch to a beautiful day with not a cloud in the sky. A brisk wind filled the sails and the water sparkled. René walked to Emile.

"I relieve you, sir."

"I can stay up for a while longer." René waited patiently.

"All right, I will go below and get some sleep. I have rotated the crew, and most of the men have rested. We did all right on canvas, since we had little on when the storm hit. Still, what was on is in pretty bad shape. The men are replacing it now. We have been maintaining an easy west by southwest course since the storm slacked off. Either we have run the strait, or the storm's pushed us back."

"What about mast damage?" asked René.

"Not too much. Some minor spars and some of the rigging were lost, but we have plenty of lumber and hemp and will make all of that good before the day's out."

"Casualties?" asked René.

"Just Mister Fortin, and the doc says it was only a slight concussion thanks to you. I always said that man's got a hard skull. Saw him butt heads in a fight once; I thought both of 'em would hit the deck. Didn't even faze Robert. Good thing."

"Make certain all the men get something to eat and are allowed to rest. Watch on, watch off. Then get some rest yourself."

"Aye, aye, sir." Emile turned to leave.

"Oh, and Emile," René called to his back.

Emile glanced over his shoulder. "Yes, sir?"

"Will you send up someone with food and coffee for me as well?"

"Right away, sir. By the way, that was a fancy bit of mast work last night, Worm," Emile said with a laugh as he made his way toward the hatch.

Hearing his old nickname again brought a smile to René's face as he set up the astrolabe to learn their location.

As near as he could tell, the storm had blown the *Belle Poulé* through the Strait of Gibraltar and into the Atlantic ten leagues or so from the French port of Tangiers. They could have made for it, but since the ship was in good shape, René elected to continue for their destination of Larache. The plan was to off-load there and then ship the weapons overland to Fez, where Moulay al-Rashid had set up his sultanate. René called to the first mate, "Change course to east by southeast, Mister Wade."

"Aye, aye, sir," Gavin said, calling in turn the same instructions down to the sailor on the whipstaff.

The *Seahawk* was nowhere in sight. René hoped she had survived the storm. He was confident James and her crew had the skill to bring the ship through safely, but nothing on the sea was certain. Nevertheless, there was a problem. Two ships were most likely safe from attack. One ship was fair game.

"*S'il vous plaît*, Mister Wade, double the lookouts and bring the ship to standby quarters," René said.

"Aye, aye, sir." Gavin searched the calm sea.

"We are in enemy waters, and this ship is a tasty bit of loot coming into port. Make certain the falconets are manned and armed. Arrange for a system to wake the men who are down if we sight a ship," René added. "And tell the lookouts to stay sharp."

René imagined Andrew up in the crow's nest aboard the *Seahawk*. That boy had a keener eye than anyone René had met. Right now, he wished the lad was aboard the *Belle Poulé*.

René finished his log entries and went below deck to stow the astrolabe and log. He left the room without disturbing Raphael and returned to the deck. Walking forward to the forecastle, René stood at the rail and scanned the empty horizon. The *Belle Poulé* was making good speed toward the coast of Morocco with a strong tail wind. He sensed Akeefa coming up the stairs. She emerged through the hatch dressed in a traditional satin long sleeved Arabic dress, but without her hijab, her hair and face were uncovered. Her expression became more animated as she approached.

"Are you all right?" he asked.

"I am fine, as are all of our other passengers. There is, however, nothing worse than a bad storm after a large meal," she said with a rueful smile.

René laughed. "The next time I know a bad storm is coming, I will suggest we eat lightly."

"Please. How far are we from Larache?"

"About seven or eight hours if the wind holds. That storm cut a whole two days from our schedule." He offered her his arm as she stepped onto the forecastle. "Are you still feeling the same?"

Akeefa nodded and glanced at the hatch as the sheikh and Miguel came above deck. Both men were armed.

"René, please prepare the ship for battle," said the sheikh.

René scanned the sea around the ship. Nothing. "Have you seen something, sir?"

"Not with our eyes," said Miguel. "But we will soon be in a fight for our lives."

René maintained eye contact with Miguel, and then called to Gavin. "*S'il vous plaît*, Mister Wade, call the men to quarters. Get Mister Lamert up here and have someone awaken the rest of the crew."

"Aye, aye, sir," On a calm day like this one, Gavin Wade's stentorian voice rang out, heard from one end of the ship to the other. Men began to move.

The sheikh turned to Akeefa. "My dear, please change into your sparring clothes. We will need your help, and your current attire is not conducive to free movement."

"Yes, Father." She turned to go below, but not before catching René's eye.

Well, at least the wait is over.

The lookout in the crow's nest called, "ship aft starboard," and then again, "ship aft port. Make that three ships."

At the same time, Emile burst through the hatch. He turned to yell at René, "I relieve you, sir!"

"I stand relieved, sir."

Emile sized up the situation and called out new orders. "Mister

Wade, get on every scrap of canvas we have. They're xebecs and I believe we can outrun 'em with this wind."

Mister Wade relayed the commands. Men scurried up the rigging, pulling out all of the sail the *Belle Poulé* could show. The ship charged ahead as if released from restraints.

Raphael came up through the hatch, still a little groggy. He shook his head as if to clear it.

Emile yelled to him, "On the whipstaff, son. Hold the wind abeam. Squeeze every knot out of her you can. Once we get in sight of land, get us into a port."

"Aye, aye, Captain." Raphael ran for his post.

The enemy ships were visible now along the horizon. They were indeed xebecs, a cross between a galley—with oars or sweeps—and a lateen-rigged sailing vessel. The lateen sail was triangular and allowed the xebec to sail closer to the wind, adding points on the tack and making the ship more maneuverable than the larger galleon. The sweeps allowed them to maneuver closer in to land, where the wind dropped off. While the smaller ship boasted a narrow hull for speed, it also had a wide beam, which meant upwards of a hundred and fifty men. Still, the *Belle Poulé* could outrun the smaller ships if the wind held. If it held.

Fortunately, Mister Haddad was still aboard, training the *Poulé's* crew. Emile sent him to man the stern chaser. The man was a crack shot with the long nine, and should the Salé pirates get close enough, they were in for a surprise. The wind had lessened, and the corsairs were closing the distance using the sweeps to add speed.

"Mister Wade, arm the men!" bellowed Emile.

While both the sheikh and *Señor* Zaportas were armed, René was not. He had a flash of the Maestro shaking his head as he headed for his cabin to retrieve his weapons. Moving down the stairs and into the narrow galleyway, he almost ran into Akeefa, She was dressed in her sparring clothes, heading above deck. They stopped short, facing each other. She hugged him and then skirted around him and flew up the stairs.

René returned above deck armed with his sword and pistol. The corsairs were much closer, almost within the cannon's range. At least they were with the nine-pounder in the hands of a gunner like Mister Haddad. Emile had strategically placed musketeers in the rigging. The hatch had been closed and pegged, and its defense would be a last ditch effort by the *Belle Poulé*. René hoped it never came to that.

He walked over to Emile. "Your orders, sir?" he said.

"René, captain the men on the port side. On the sheikh's recommendation, the young woman will captain the men on the starboard side." Emile sounded doubtful. Even though he had heard of her actions in La Alcazaba, he had not seen her fight. Given the customary exaggeration of most seaman's tales, his hesitation was understandable.

"Emile, she disarmed me whilst sparring," René said. "Do not spare a thought for the starboard side. If the corsairs come to her, they will have little time to entertain their regret."

Emile nodded. "I have assigned Khalid to captain the men in the forecastle, and Abdul Karim to take charge of the men in the aftcastle. The sheikh and *Señor* Zaportas will reinforce as they think necessary."

The wind had been falling off steadily, and one of the xebecs was coming into range. Mister Haddad fired the first shot. It was eight hundred yards if it was a foot. The men swiftly reloaded the cannon, their hours of practice having brought the reload time down below three minutes. Still, those minutes were like hours as the slow match on the longer barrelled weapon gave off a sizzling sound. Then the world was rent again. The cannon fired its deadly gift—grape shot, small balls and scraps of iron strung together like evil pearls reaching out to grace the throat of the enemy mast and bring it crashing to the deck.

Mister Haddad reloaded and fired again, this time taking out the triangular lateen sail aboard the closer of the three ships. The storm of grape shot swept through the slaver's foredeck, causing a wave of small explosions as wood and flesh disintegrated in its wake. The men aboard the *Belle Poulé* cheered. The Salé pirates returned fire, but their aim was random and fell short. Mister Haddad, a short, intense man, had changed to ball shot and fired again, getting the range but missing the ship. On his next shot, however, the nine-pound iron ball went through the slaver's hull on the port side, at the water line. There was a rumbling sound, as if the xebec was trying to digest the iron. Then a huge explosion sent splinters and bits of the pirate ship out over the sea. A lucky shot had hit the ship's armory. As what remained of the slaver ship moved through the smoke, she began to go down. They could hear the pirates screaming. This far out, going overboard was a death sentence.

For a short while, it looked as if the *Belle Poulé* might outrun the remaining two ships, until one after the next her sails began to luff, going slack in a dying wind. The two xebecs, like wolves, moved closer as the *Belle Poulé* slowed. The slavers were now close enough that those aboard the *Poulé* could see the mass of pirates, packed to the gunnels of both ships, waiting to board. Mister Haddad targeted the remaining ships, but they were better conned, and under oar they managed to avoid the cannon's fire by taking random zigzag courses. He changed back to grape shot. Perhaps the scattered shot would catch one of the remaining slavers on its tack.

The *Belle Poulé* floated motionless in the dead calm of a windless ocean. The approaching slavers moved swiftly toward her stern, keeping away from the firing lines of the *Poulé's* broadside cannon. A black rain of grappling hooks descended over the gunwale, and the first group of slavers poured over the side of the ship. The second enemy ship continued around, crossing the bow of the *Poulé* to her starboard side. As it came past, the forward falconet crew fired a round of grape shot directly down into it, cutting a swath of destruction through the men waiting on its deck. The shot had little long-term effect other than to further enrage the screaming pirates. As a return gesture, a volley of musket fire sleeted through the gun crew frantically reloading their weapon.

A grappling hook materialized in the bow gunwale. Then there were two, ten, and then twenty as the ship's bow dipped with the weight of men coming over the side. Within moments, all parts of the ship were engaged. The *Belle Poulé's* complement of one hundred and twelve men was outnumbered nearly three-to-one as the deck took on the appearance of an apple core covered with hungry black ants.

René allowed his training to take over. He settled into that cold killing place as he faced the screaming men that clawed their way over the side. Swarthy men with shaved heads and tattooed faces, these pirates haunted the shipping lanes. Their prizes fed the slave markets of Algiers and Morocco. The slaver's weapon of choice was the scimitar, though some musket barrels were visible in the mass of men.

The first slaver to die aboard the *Belle Poulé* came at René, shouting in Arabic, and spraying spittle while waving his scimitar in a circle over his head. René moved aside, allowing the man's momentum to carry him past. A swift tip cut to the man's raised wrist severed the tendons, and his weapon fell from a lifeless hand. René spun around and reached out with his rapier, backhanding the man's neck. The corsair's continued forward motion caused the weapon to slice through his jugular. Shock and surprise animated his features as his mouth gaped open and then he was gone. René leaned down and retrieved his scimitar.

With two weapons, the dead quickly piled up before him. The odd sensation was like gracefully wading through quicksand— a macabre ballet whose set was the deck of a ship painted in shades of red, perfumed with the smell of blood and fear, and accompanied by the orchestral screams of the dying. At times like this, René hated and appreciated his skill with equal intensity. Every time he killed a slaver, another took his place. Akeefa was on the other side of the ship. René's connection with her gave him confidence that she held her own. Sheikh Ghassan and Miguel were fighting alongside Raphael and Abdul Karim on the aftcastle.

René turned forward and a chill crept down his spine. Because of the newer design of the *Belle Poulé*, the forecastle was lower than the aftcastle, increasing the ship's speed and maneuverability. The drawback was that boarders had lower gunwales to overcome in the bow—a disadvantage that would require payment.

Khalid had taken up position on the forecastle, along with eight of the Musselmen. Within minutes, enemy musket fire had killed three of his men, and the six remaining were now facing at least twenty corsairs with more coming over the bow. Akeefa tried to fight her way in the direction of her brother, but there were too many pirates. The same held true for René. He could not kill them fast enough.

"Focus your fire on the forecastle," he yelled to the men in the rigging.

The crew redirected their fire toward the mass of pirates confronting Khalid, but it had a negligible effect. Two more men died protecting him, and now they were four. At last, Akeefa edged toward her brother as the men facing her struggled, frantic to get out of her way. Still, there were too many. Time had always been subservient to René's perceptions, but on this occasion, the sound of the fighting faded to silence as time stopped altogether. Frozen, his consciousness expanded until it encompassed the entire ship. He felt every heartbeat and knew Khalid was about to die. He would fail again to protect one close to him. The wrenching sadness and guilt that descended upon him jerked him out of his expanded consciousness, and the world began again.

René was closer to Khalid than Akeefa, but not close enough. He glanced to his left. Khalid was alone, the last of his men dead at his feet. Akeefa screamed as the slavers repeatedly stabbed her brother. An emotional explosion ripped through René, and for a split second the battle aboard the ship stopped.

Then it began anew.

René reached out to Akeefa with the deepest level of his being. Together they drew on a power hundreds of times greater than he had ever experienced. They closed on the pirates at the forecastle. René, a sword in each hand, flicked out death with both. The pirates near Akeefa were in full flight now, doing their best to escape her blade and failing. They were both covered with blood. Not one pirate would live to tell of this day. Not one. Those emotions came more from Akeefa than from himself, but for now, he allowed her the control. He settled into his role as the killing machine he was.

Both slave ships had cut their ropes in an attempt to escape the tide of death aboard the *Belle Poulé*, which gave the French ship's starboard cannon a chance to open up. Grape shot blew a storm of lead through the starboard slaver, destroying her rigging and decimating those on her deck. The *Poulé* turned on the swell, her port cannon firing another broadside, and the second xebec began to sink. On the *Poulé*, pirates jumped over the side, preferring their chances in the sea rather than face Akeefa.

René and Akeefa made it to the forecastle at the same time and dispatched the remaining boarders. She reached for her brother and took him in her arms. He was bleeding from multiple wounds but still clung to life. René stood behind her, his hand on her shoulder.

"Beloved older sister, do not grieve for me. I believe I have lived a life of honor and am satisfied in the manner of my death." Khalid's breathing was labored, and blood trickled from his mouth.

"Beloved brother, I beg you not to leave me," said Akeefa, sobbing.

Khalid spoke to René. "Watch over her for me."

"I will guard her with my life."

Khalid smiled at Akeefa. "I will wait for you, but take your time. There is no rush. I love you."

"Please, Khalid," she begged, but he had already gone. She eased him to the deck then stood and turned, facing the ship and those pirates still alive. She walked slowly toward the fight and then charged the remaining enemy, as if she might miss killing one last slaver. René followed at her heels, frightened by her pain and the emotional price this day would demand. He forced that line of thought closed. There was still a fight to be finished. He hated this part. The outcome was not in doubt. Only the killing was left.

The remaining battle was short and bloody. Not one pirate survived. Of the *Belle Poulé*'s crew, thirty-six were dead, and most of the rest carried wounds of some kind. Fortunately, Doctor Zahrawi had escaped unscathed. He moved methodically now, applying aid to those he could help and quietly blessing those he could not.

René and Abdul Karim carried Khalid below, followed by the sheikh, Akeefa, and Miguel. Carmen and Rebeca took charge of

Akeefa and led her away to her cabin. The men took Khalid's body to the sheikh's cabin to clean and prepare for burial. The wind resumed without apology. The *Belle Poulé* got under way as they gently laid Khalid on the bunk.

CHAPTER FORTY-FOUR
Château Gaspard, Bordeaux, France

THE CHAIR was ugly and utilitarian. An improved version of the invalid's chair originally made for Philip II, it had wooden wheels and a crank on the right side. Its direction could be changed by using the lever.

"Move me into the study and have the sorcerer brought to me," said Horemheb. Long, stringy black hair hung over the sides of his head, partially covering the pathetic stumps of what had once been ears. His continuous battle with death drained every pretense of youth and vitality. His left arm, which lay useless in his lap, was a source of continuous pain.

He had many agents out searching for a sorcerer advanced enough to be able to travel the spirit pathways. Victor's body was slow in healing, and he could not risk leaving it himself. Fortunately, there were always men and women—both good and evil—who had accomplished the separation of the physical body from its finer non-physical versions.

The man who now approached was dressed flamboyantly and his face wore a bored expression, tinged with contempt. Horemheb had known him for a charlatan the moment he stepped inside the château.

"I am told you are a sorcerer with miraculous powers." His voice was a painful grate.

"I have abilities beyond those of mortal men," declared the sorcerer. "Are you in need of a potion or curse to remove a competitor? Perhaps one to attract a young woman..." The sorcerer peered closely at him and closed his eyes, moving his head as if he was receiving something from other realms. "*Non*, you have called on me to heal the disfigurations that cover your face."

Horemheb felt the servant holding the back of his chair tremble. His face assumed the caricature of a smile. The charlatan nattered on unaware that he faced death incarnate. Horemheb refocused his attention on the sorcerer and the amusement he might offer.

"What disfigurations do you speak of, sir?" he asked.

"*S'il vous plaît*, I have the power to see the past as well as the future. You have come off poorly in a fight, most likely a duel over a woman. Tell me, is that not the truth?"

"How could you know?" Horemheb's face moved slowly toward the expression that served him as a smile.

The sorcerer pulled back. Reaching into the folds of his voluminous black robe, the man pulled out a vial. "I have here an elixir, the ingredients of which come all the way from India. This powerful mixture will restore your face to its previous youthful glow."

Horemheb pulled a handful of gold Louis d'or coins from his pocket. "Will this cover your expense?"

The sorcerer's eyes widened. Surprise and greed were written across his face as he struggled to regain the power of speech. "Uh, well, the ingredients in this special elixir are only found atop the tallest peak of the mighty Himal-yuan mountains." The man paused for effect. "Very difficult to acquire."

His mispronunciation of the mountain chain was so dreadful—and so amusing—that Horemheb almost decided to let the idiot live. Almost. "Would double this amount be sufficient?" he asked.

"*Oui*, I believe it would," managed the man. Horemheb gestured to the servant.

"We will repair to the treasure room down below, so we may pay this gentleman properly, and in full." He turned back to the sorcerer. "As a man of dark mysteries, I think you will find the room intriguing. I may even have some small magic to show you myself."

His thoughts were already a continent away.

CHAPTER FORTY-FIVE

ONCE RENÉ had dealt with the physical destruction endured by the men and the ship, he had to face Akeefa. Her pain pervaded the ship in waves. Even the men standing beside René appeared restless, as if they felt something outside of their normal awareness.

"Emile, get sail up as quickly as you can with the men you have. The sooner we make port, the easier I will rest. Another attack would be disastrous," said René.

"Aye, aye, sir."

"Raphael, can you remain at the whipstaff?"

"Of course."

All three men remained silent; there was nothing to be said. René cast around for something that needed his attention, all the while aware that Emile had the ship in hand. He had been trained to befriend pain, to redirect it and manage it properly. No one could train to withstand the pain of a loved one. He turned slowly toward the hatch.

"I will be below if you need me,"

The deck was still sticky with drying blood and caused his boots to make an obscene sucking sound as he crossed to the hatchway. The hatch opened easily on well-greased hinges. He went down the stairs and paused before Akeefa's cabin. He had no words of comfort and yet, he could not leave her to her grief alone. Taking a deep breath, he knocked on the door.

"Enter," said *Señora* Zaportas.

He entered the cabin. *Señora* Zaportas and Sabah flanked Akeefa, all three were seated on the bed. The two older women had been crying, and their faces were drawn. Akeefa sat staring straight ahead. She did not acknowledge his entry.

"*Señora* Zaportas, Sabah, I know 'tis against tradition, but I would like to speak with Akeefa alone, if I may."

Sabah began to protest, but the *señora* took her arm and led her toward the door.

"Sabah, he will not harm her, and we don't have the skill to reach her. Come, dear." She led a tearful Sabah from the cabin.

René sat beside Akeefa. This close it was all he could do not to vibrate in sympathy with the incredible anger that animated her vital field. Enormous guilt clamored within his own psyche over his inability to protect Khalid. He closed his eyes and sank down into battle calm. He continued down past the point of physical reality following the psychic trail that connects all life.

He found her standing on a desert plain. Not the glowing, living desert of Morocco, but instead a gray desolate landscape, unfinished and draining. She held a scimitar.

René walked toward her. "Akeefa," he said in a quiet, calm voice.

She turned tortured eyes toward him, eyes that held no recognition.

He sensed she would kill anything that entered her space, and still he approached her. When he got close enough, she attacked, and he was forced to materialize a sword to meet hers. The dissolution of consciousness was a very real prospect on this plane of existence. What the soul believed became reality.

Her will to defeat Khalid's death empowered her. All of René's training and skill would not be sufficient to block her lust for death. In this place, at this time, he could not withstand her. He said the only thing, perhaps, that could reach her. "He would have been disappointed in you."

She stopped cold, her arm suspended in mid-strike. The scimitar shattered and disappeared. Akeefa fell to her knees. He joined her and then wrapped his arms around her. She began to cry, and in that instant, they were back in her cabin aboard the *Poulé*, his arms still tight around her. Both opened fully, allowing their auras to blend. All of his grief combined with hers and for an instant, both were plunged into a dark hopelessness more than either could bear, and they sobbed. Then that calm, loving energy René had experienced after Jacques's death surrounded and filled them. It didn't extinguish the pain, but it placed it into a perspective that could be borne. They could do nothing but hold each other.

CHAPTER FORTY-SIX

THE *BELLE Poulé* limped into port. Its tattered sail and rigging gave mute evidence of its recent encounters. Three more sailors had succumbed to their wounds, bringing the final count to thirty-nine. They were buried at sea in a somber ceremony, the bodies sewn into their own clothing and anchored with lead shot. As they were a half-day from port, the sheikh decided that Khalid would rest in the soil of his home.

Larache was primarily a trading port on the banks of the river Loukos, currently under Spanish control. A forbidding fortress commanded the northern bank of the river. It brooded over the entry to the port, its decaying towers silent.

The sight of the *Seahawk* resting easily at the quay brought René a fierce moment of relief. If the storm had sent the *Belle Poulé* scudding at great speed, the lighter, faster *Seahawk* must have traveled even farther. He went below to let the others know.

René knocked on Akeefa's cabin door.

"Enter."

In that one word, René heard Rebeca's love and grief along with an underlying iron determination to protect her family. He found both her and Raquel sitting with Akeefa. The atmosphere in the room was better. Rebeca had lived all her life with the fear her loved ones would be taken from her, and it had given her a strength and compassion that was healing to be around. They were working on repairing a damaged but salvageable sail.

"We are coming into port, and the *Seahawk* is safely docked ahead of us." René studied Akeefa's face for the spark he hoped the news would bring.

"That is good news." She smiled, but with steel in her expression. "I will be all right, René. 'Tis time for you to get some rest. Emile will be able to organize the offloading and the refitting of the *Belle Poulé*."

"I am fine—"

"No. You are not, and neither am I, nor is anyone else aboard this vessel, but we will be. For now, however, we need you at full strength. This is a time for clear heads and a show of strength, if we are to establish ourselves here. We will leave for the burial ground late this afternoon in order to get there before the setting sun. You have a few hours. Will you use them to sleep?"

"*Oui.* I will inform your father and Miguel regarding the *Seahawk* and then speak with Emile and James."

"Emile and James..." Akeefa's voice had an edge to it.

"Briefly. I will have a couple of words with them and then go directly to my cabin. Good day, *señora,* Raquel." With that, he left the cabin.

After giving his news to the sheikh and Miguel, he went topside and found Emile. "We have been given an honor guard by the Sultan. Wait until the sheikh makes contact with al-Rashid's retainers before we begin off-loading. I would like the *Poulé* repaired and reprovisioned as soon as possible."

"Aye, aye, sir." Emile kept an eye on the repairs in progress. "Do you want me to purchase new tack here?"

"If 'tis of a quality you consider sufficient, then *oui.* If not, buy only what you need right now, and we will wait to get better from Casablanca. Make certain of the water first and the dry goods. We will meet tonight after the burial, but make the ship as seaworthy as possible in case we need to leave in a hurry. Please relay all that to James, too, along with my apologies for not immediately meeting with him."

"We're going to need to recruit more men," Emile said, frowning. "A lot more men."

"Begin now." René glanced toward Larache. "You know who we

want. Do not take a man because he is wearing two arms and two legs. Have Abdul Karim help you. I would rather run light on both ships than take on a load of misfits."

"Aye, sir." Emile nodded in agreement. His expression filled with the discomfort of a man struggling to hold larger truths than fit into his accepted version of reality. "Do you think we could ask the sheikh to vet the men we find? I have spoken to him a little, and I don't know what 'tis about him, but I don't think it possible to lie to him."

René laughed. "I know what you mean. And you are right, the last thing we need is to have spies or corsairs aboard. An excellent idea, Emile, and I am certain he would be happy to assist. Oh, one last thing. Gilbert Ltd. has a factor here in Larache. *S'il vous plaît*, send someone to see if we received any letters or instructions." René paused. "Emile, I am going to catch a few hours rest. Send someone to wake me. I usually have no problem awakening by myself, but I am not so certain this time. I cannot remember ever having been this tired before."

"I will make certain you're awake in time, sir." Emile's concerned frown relaxed and a smile made its way to his face. He was obviously delighted someone had finally persuaded René to lie down.

"*Merci*," René called, already moving toward the hatch. He reached his cabin, and took out the ship's rutter. *I'll just make a couple of notes.* He put the pen to paper, but his mind refused his request for words. Resigned, he sat on the edge of his bunk and kicked off his boots. *An hour. I just need an hour.* He was asleep before his head touched the pillow.

René dreamt about holding wolves at bay armed only with his bamboo training sword when someone pounded on the door, awakening him. He sat up, his senses dull. He felt lethargic and disconnected. His vision was blurry as though he saw the world through murky water.

The door banged open and then the sheikh was in the room. René had never seen the man like this. A nimbus of blue light crackled with power around him. Holding a glowing dagger, he was saying something René could not hear and gesturing to the four corners of the cabin. When he brought the dagger down in a diagonal slicing gesture, it was like the hot sun burning through a dense fog. René's mind cleared, and he found he could move and think. He did not wait for an explanation but jumped from his bunk and armed himself.

"We are being attacked by forces loyal to the Sultan's brother, Moulay Ismail. This time, however, they are attempting to attack us on other planes of existence as well. I have warded this ship, and Miguel is aboard the *Seahawk* doing the same. I will explain later, but for now, detail two men to protect the gunpowder stores. Meet me on the wharf. I would prefer to fight this one on the land." They headed above deck with the sheikh in the lead.

René called to Gavin, "Mister Wade, call the men to quarters and put a guard on the gunpowder stores. Have them do the same on the *Seahawk*. Where is Emile?"

"The captain is aboard the *Seahawk*, working over some last minute plans with Mister Bailey." The boatswain turned to bawl out commands to the crew.

Just then, Emile climbed back aboard the *Poulé* and headed toward René.

"Emile, move the ships out. Get them out of the port and into the open ocean. I do not care if you have to tow them. Get them free!"

The *Poulé's* captain looked up at the top gallants blowing in the ever-present warm wind coming off the land. "We'll be out of here in two shakes. I will signal the *Seahawk*."

René headed toward the gangway. "Hey, Worm!" Emile yelled.

René stopped and glanced toward him. "You be careful out there, you hear."

René grinned. "You get this ship out. *Bonne chance.*"

"To you as well," said Emile before he strode toward the rail that faced the *Seahawk*.

René ran across the boarding plank to the group waiting on the quay. He joined Miguel and Raphael, Abdul Karim, Akeefa, the sheikh, and the fifteen guards sent by the Sultan. They waited.

Rebeca, Raquel, and Carmen were already aboard the *Seahawk* for safety. There was a moment's pause before black-robed men poured from the medina into the square.

The ships remained in port.

Damn that Emile.

More and more turbaned men in black charged into the square. With a sword in each hand, René moved forward to meet his attackers. He sensed Akeefa's presence, thirty paces behind him and to his left as she advanced toward the assassins.

One of the men, standing at the rear of the attacking force, wore a silver breastplate inlaid with the gems of a shaman. He appeared to be otherwise unarmed and had positioned himself to one side of the now berserk mob of sword wielding attackers. The sheikh had also not drawn his sword, and he now faced the sorcerer. Almost as if the two existed in another time, the forty paces between them remained empty. Both were speaking and making figures in the air with their hands. René frowned and then was forced to focus on the battle that surrounded him. He settled into that place where his sense of time slowed, raised his sword, and then waded into the fray. These attackers were better-trained than the assassins in Marseilles. The Sultan's guards fell like wheat before a scythe. Raphael was wounded but he managed to kill his assailant. Nevertheless, the press of men attacking them were too many. Their rapidly diminishing group did not have the means to win this battle. He channeled his anger and frustration into his sword.

There will come a time when you realize you cannot win. This will make you angry at all the time and effort spent, only to die without completing your goal. It will be at this moment that all of my teaching will be for naught if you cannot maintain control. Anger is only fear disguised, and it will drain your focus if not properly channeled. You will claim victory from defeat only if you can manage to remain true to your inner self to the end, no matter what that end might be. You may fail to survive and yet still be victorious. Use everything in the service of your will.

René and Akeefa paused within that timeless space called now. Their communication required no time or words or even sight.

The moment passed, and they both settled back into the fight.

Turn. Allow the blade to slip by. Move within the attacker's guard. Thrust through the heart, blocking with the other hand. Disengage to tip-cut wrist tendons. Step forward. Snap a kick to break the kneecap. Cut his throat as he goes down.

The world became a point of pressure and counter-pressure, and then the pressure lessened.

With an explosive retort, the sorcerer in the breastplate erupted into a fountain of flames. The sheikh drew his sword and joined the fight. With their shaman dead, the assassins edged backwards in disarray.

The momentum changed completely when the men of the *Belle Poulé* and the *Seahawk* charged onto the quay. René intended to have private words with Mister Lamert about following orders. But for now, he was grateful to have been disobeyed. He moved toward Raphael to help him disengage from the fight. Apparently Akeefa had the same thought for she stood in front of him. Even hardened assassins thought twice about facing that demoness when she smiled. What began as a trickle turned into a rout as the remaining attackers fled back through the stone arch into the medina. The sounds of steel on steel dropped away, leaving only the moans and cries of the injured.

Of the fifteen guards the Sultan had provided, only two remained, and of the two, only one still stood.

René and the sheikh walked over to where Doctor Zahrawi was treating Raphael. Akeefa and Miguel were already there. "How is he?" asked the sheikh.

"He may lose some of the mobility of that arm. Although painful, 'tis not life threatening."

"I will be fine." Raphael turned to Akeefa. "*Gracias.*"

"I did nothing."

"No, but you were prepared to."

Emile and James approached the small group. "Are you all right, sir?"

René's stare would have melted wax.

"You see, the wind fell off, and we couldn't get the long boats unloaded fast enough to tow us out. So as long as we were still here, we figured we might as well get some exercise. Didn't we, Mister Bailey?"

"That we did, Mister Lamert. That we did. And right good exercise it was," said James with a smile.

Back on the ship, René sat at the chart table and slid the letter from his pocket. The guilt over his failure to return to Bordeaux and protect his family and Clarisse gripped him. He stood and paced. How much more harm had befallen them because of him. He forced himself to return to his seat and then opened the letter.

Dear Monsieur Dalembert,

I have sent this letter to all of the Gilbert Ltd. factors in hope it will reach you via one of them. The political climate of France is changing. With the passing of the Queen Mother, all pretenses to moderation concerning relations between the crown and the people have vanished. Your instructions, therefore, are to explore the possibilities of trade in the area where you find yourself, remaining there until conditions here have changed.

As a matter of common interest, the crown has issued a spurious Lettre de Cachet against my son René. We have grieved for him these last months, thinking him surely dead, and have still had no word of him. Influence from Bordeaux, however, has evidently come to other conclusions and has arranged to have the Lettre issued. The king will sign whatever is placed in front of him if it will increase the treasury. The Lettre names René traitor, with various penalties awaiting him, the least of which would be long imprisonment. I have not been privy to its contents, and with our power and connections at ebb tide, have been unable to secure its repeal. I should rejoice to know that my son is indeed alive, however, and I will work tirelessly to have this false accusation rescinded.

Climates change, and for ships to sail into weather prejudicial to the safety of crew and cargo should, in every case, be deemed ill-advised. That said, with faith in the Lord, the ill winds may abate, followed by calm seas and conditions better suited to the continued strength and health of our common interests.

A business associate in the cheese trade has asked me to convey her deepest appreciation for your last communication. She assures me you will understand the reference. I am certain she has herself written, but it seems prudent, in these days of uncertainty and business competition, to add word of her should the mail packets be misdirected or delayed. Your associate has spent many a day with us and is as outraged at the business climate that prevails as I am, more so perhaps, as she would prefer to take direct and more vigorous action. It is clear to me her affections have not changed, although her frustration has certainly increased. She has taken to helping at the La Maison Charité and seems to find some comfort in her work. Henri has been spending time with her and wants you to know he will watch over her until you return.

I will continue to send copies of my communications to each of our Gilbert Ltd. factors in the hope of reaching you.

With continued respect and appreciation, I remain,

Armand Gilbert

René read the letter again. He gazed through the open window at the rear of the cabin deep in thought.

CHAPTER FORTY-SEVEN

THREE WAGONS waited on the quay to take Khalid and the small group up to the cliffs above Larache. Before leaving, Sheikh Ghassan had poured a cup of water onto the ground, a tradition asking for a safe trip and return for his youngest son. They gently laid the white shrouded body onto the wagon bed.

Akeefa took her seat beside Abdul Karim and her father. She was dressed in a black burqa. Only her dark eyes were visible.

In the wagon that followed, Raquel sat between her mother and father. Her face was drawn, her tears exhausted as she leaned against her mother. James drove the third wagon with Sabah and Raphael seated beside him. René and Emile completed the burial party on horseback.

The afternoon was clear, with cool winds wafting from the heights. The sun's sparkling reflection off the ocean added a turquoise beauty to the poignancy of the moment. Khalid would rest in the Christian cemetery up on the cliffs. The well-kept burial ground overlooked the ocean to the west, the medina of Larache to the south, and the whole of Morocco to the east. A Musselman cemetery would have been preferable, but given the hot Moroccan climate, burial in a Christian cemetery was permissible by both custom and the Spanish authorities. More important, Khalid was home.

The ride up to the cliffs was silent, reflective. René thought of the friend and brother who would no longer accompany them. Khalid had been irrepressible, a buoyant, courageous young man whose wit and intelligence had enhanced their fellowship. Even though he was but slightly younger, Khalid had been to René the younger brother he had never had.

They stopped with the cemetery a hundred yards in the distance, as women were not permitted at the actual burial. The burial party climbed down from the wagons, and Emile and René dismounted. All then faced the sheikh. His back was toward the ocean, his hands, palms touching, were pointed forward. The sun painted the entire landscape with the warm golds of approaching sunset. The wind had died down, almost as if the landscape was waiting for Sheikh Ghassan. An unusual surge of vital force circled René. The sheikh spoke a prayer for the dead, and finished by proclaiming *Allahu Akbar*—God is Great—three times. The group remained silent.

Abdul Karim climbed onto the driver's bench to drive the wagon that carried Khalid's body the few remaining yards. Akeefa stood beside the wagon, her hand on the rail. Abdul Karim was silent. No one spoke or moved until the sheikh wrapped her in his arms. She lowered her head to his chest as he spoke quietly. When he finished, she stood straighter. She released her hand from the wagon and stepped back into Rebeca's welcoming arms. Sabah stood beside them and clasped Akeefa's hand.

The men walked beside the wagon as Abdul Karim slowly drove toward the burial site. The grave had been dug. René and Emile lifted Khalid from the wagon. With his left arm bound up, Raphael was unable to help them. They lowered Khalid into the grave, arranging his body so that he lay on his right side, facing Mecca. The sheikh asked that they give him a moment alone with his son. Everyone backed away from the gravesite, leaving only Sheikh Ghassan, his form backlit against the setting sun.

A soft white light surrounded the sheikh growing in size and brilliance. As René focused on the light, it increased tenfold. Within it, Sheikh Ghassan was speaking to someone. The figure of Khalid stood before his father. Khalid's image was at first blurry and unfocused, as if uncertain where it began and the light around it ended. Then the figure solidified. René blinked, certain he was hallucinating. When he opened his eyes, Khalid still stood there wearing the same sardonic smile as the day they had met.

The light grew even brighter. René began to discern others standing around the father and son. He could not make out faces or details, but others were present. The vision lasted a moment longer and then the light and the figures faded as a wave of acceptance flowed out to surround René and the men awaiting the sheikh. The wave of love expanded to encompass all who stood upon the hilltop before finally dissipating into the ether, much like the sound of the muezzin's last call to prayer. Sheikh Ghassan motioned for them to join him. Each man put a symbolic shovel full of soil into the grave and then René and Miguel filled it in.

They returned to where the women waited. After handing the women up to the wagons, the men regained their seats while René and Emile mounted their horses. The trip back to the ships was peaceful, the Moroccan landscape warm and welcoming in the last gleam of the afternoon sun. Fragile in its timelessness and yet powerful beyond conception, for that short space of time, pain and fear disappeared, and the heart rested. The peace would be temporary but for now, René gave himself over to it.

CHAPTER FORTY-EIGHT

Château Gaspard, Bordeaux, France

THE SOUND of the peasant's last scream died, and his breath ceased. The vibrations of terror remained, like waves upon a shore, echoing against the dim rock walls of the dungeon. Tendrils of smoke rose from the shrunken body on the granite slab. Burned charcoal outlines of the energy centers decorated the centerline of the body like evil flowers. Beside it, Horemheb rose from the invalid chair. He was wracked with pain, but still he stood. The pain was something he had learned to appreciate, if not love, for it served to remind him of his great enemy. The beloved brother initiate, now turned focus of an all-consuming hatred. Filled with energy for the moment, Horemheb allowed Victor's soul to gaze out at the world.

"You promised that I will be present at his death." Victor's thought echoed within the matrix that formed their current incarnation.

"I will honor that promise," said Horemheb.

"How will you maintain my body? 'Tis dying," said Victor.

"A supply of peasants will provide enough vital energy."

"You can barely stand."

"Unfortunately, the peasants lack the stronger energies I need to heal. Fear not. Soon this body will regain its full vitality and remain young and powerful forever. I will not leave this earth again. There is a soul whose power will be more than sufficient. He remains ignorant of the extent of that power, but it exists nonetheless."

"Will there be pain?" asked Victor.

"How can there be vengeance without its flavor? Physical pain pales beside that of having one's soul extinguished. In that instant before the soul's final destruction, immeasurable sadness pervades the spirit that knows its unique part will never be played."

Horemheb pushed Victor back into the matrices of potentiality and once again looked out from sunken eyes—terrible eyes, focused to a point of black fire—seeing only the extreme suffering of one soul and then a wave of darkness.

END

EXPLORE THE WORLD OF THE SUN GOD'S HEIR TRILOGY

Can't wait to find out what happens to René, Akeefa, and Clarisse after *Return*? Look for the thrilling sequel, *The Sun God's Heir: Rebirth*, in April 2017. Available at Amazon, Barnes & Noble, Kobo, Apple, and other retailers.

REBIRTH

Rebirth continues the stunning saga of René, a young French swordmaster, who must remember and reclaim powers earned in an ancient Egyptian incarnation if he is to return to Bordeaux to protect those he loves. Matched against an unknown adversary, a powerful dark pharoah who has returned to embodiment bent on his destruction, René must first evade the Sultan's Bukhari who are intent on bringing his head back to their master. René continues his quest in a tale of soul destroying vengeance and ultimate loyalty.

READ MORE...

René stood at the bow of the *Belle Poulé*. Blood no longer puddled on the deck, but the images were not scrubbed away so easily. In his mind's eye, scimitars rose and fell, wielded by dark tattooed men as they repeatedly stabbed Khalid, followed by the explosion of rage from Akeefa as her younger brother was murdered. René experienced again that moment of expanded awareness, of foreknowledge, and the helpless feeling and guilt that he would not reach Khalid in time. And with that failure, a flood of memory washed over him. The sounds of sporadic musket fire, the screams, the rust smell of blood...

The Poulé's crew was outnumbered almost three to one. If not for the level of swordsmanship René had demanded, they would all be dead or chained, chattel awaiting shipment to the slave markets of Africa. Khalid and ten men were assigned to defend the forecastle. Screaming slavers came over the gunwale in dark waves.

René and Akeefa struggled to reach Khalid, but movement through the forest of waving scimitars was a swamp contesting every step, even when the pirates began to fight each other in desperate attempts to escape René and Akeefa's blades. They failed. Akeefa was unable to reach her brother in time, and Khalid died in her arms.

Another pointless death.

Was this to be his life? The death of everyone he loved.

Only six months had passed from that day beneath the sun of Bordeaux with his best friend and the woman he had come to love. The images sped past to Martin's death and René's duel with his murderer.

Rene raised his eyes to the lone gull hovering overhead.

So many dead.

Do not waste time reliving events past. That energy is better served in the present.

His old fencing master's voice echoed in his head and pulled him back to the moment at hand. The Maestro never tolerated waste, neither time nor energy.

René looked out over the *Belle Poulé*'s forecastle at the stern of his other ship, the *Seahawk*. The horizon and sky were an unremitting gray, a dull sameness that closed in around him. The northwest coast of Africa crept along their port side. The faster brigantine had taken the lead as they cut through the darker brown water at the delta of the river Bou Regreg, home to the very corsairs who had attacked the *Poulé* a fortnight earlier. An unnatural quiet belied the tension on the faces of his crew. Both ships ran easily over a dead calm sea, tacking west by southwest, on a steady southerly wind.

Making four knots, the *Poulé* glided by the northern shore of the river. The *Seahawk* ahead of them reduced sail and tightened the separation between the ships to three hundred yards. A forest of masts came into view off the port side. The full might of the Moroccan slave trade stretched in an endless line across the harbor. Bristling with weapons and swarthy tattooed men, the corsair's ships remained motionless as the *Poulé* and the *Seahawk* sailed before them. Fifty ships of all sizes, from the large Xebecs carrying upwards of a hundred and fifty men, to small swift sloops with twenty men, bobbed silent on the tide. Waiting. The silence was oppressive. The wave of hatred and frustration coming from the pirates was so great that the air itself seemed thicker, harder to breathe.

Even standing off a thousand yards, the fortress on their port side brooded dark and menacing as they approached the slavers' homeports. Within these two towns, one on each side of the river's mouth, lived the fathers, brothers, and sons of the recently deceased pirates who had attacked René's ship. The same pirates who had killed thirty-nine good men from the *Belle Poulé* in an attempt to enslave them all.

Of the three hundred slavers who had attacked the *Poulé*, not one survived. Not one. The sheik's daughter, Akeefa, had assisted every corsair within the reach of her sword in finding their final resting place at the bottom of the Mediterranean. As lethal with a blade as anyone René had ever met, with the possible exception of the Maestro, Akeefa had raged through the remaining pirates, her face rigid with vengeful zeal that even one might escape her blade.

"Emile, keep the gun ports closed. Signal the *Seahawk* to do the same." Seconds would be lost having the gun ports closed, but there was no advantage in provoking a battle.

"Aye, Sir." The big captain of the *Poulé* yelled orders to his first mate. Signal flags passed the order to the *Seahawk,* producing an immediate and ordered activity aboard her.

A fortnight had passed since the *Belle Poulé* limped into the Moroccan port of Larache damaged and bloodied.

René sensed, rather than heard, Akeefa come above deck followed by the sheikh, Miguel Zaportas, and her brother Abdul-Karim. René turned toward them, never quite losing his focus on the emerging ports of Salé and Rabat. Akeefa was robed in a dark blue burqa, but as evidenced by the scimitar she held, she was dressed differently beneath to allow her greater movement should her sword be required.

The men nodded. There was no way to reach Casablanca without passing the homeports of the Barbary pirates. Given the number of pirate vessels based here, only death or slavery awaited them if the corsairs chose to ignore the sultan's command to allow them safe passage.

Tension increased as the two ships made way past the silent northern fortress, the only sound, that of the waves crashing against the dark pockmarked volcanic rock that robed its lower walls. Although they were beyond the range of its fixed cannon, moving farther from shore would avail them of nothing. The number of men and ships sent on the wings of vengeance would surround and overwhelm René's two ships, no matter how fast or well armed.

Akeefa came to stand next to René. "At least you have not asked me to remain below."

"If we are attacked, there will be no need for a reserve force," said René.

"Coming up on Salé, Sir," Emile called out.

"*Merci,* Captain." René stood at the port gunwale and peered through his spyglass.

The English called them Sallee Rovers. Slavers by trade, they had decimated villages along the southern coast of Europe, stripping away whole towns, men, women, and children. The old, the infirm, and those children too young or unable to survive the mattamore, the infamous slave pens, were killed. Their ships, like hungry sharks, lurked along the Mediterranean sea lanes often sinking the ships with their cargo, taking only the men.

The *Seahawk* and the *Belle Poulé* continued to make way before the pirate fleet. René felt the *Poulé* shudder. A fluttering sound accompanied the ship's change and he looked up at her expanse of sail dreading what he knew he would see. One by one the sails luffed in the dying wind. Both ships settled as their headway bled off. Motionless in the center of the channel. Nothing moved, no flags in the wind, no birds. Nothing. Almost as if the port held its breath. Minutes passed in tortured silence until finally, the wind picked up, mere gentle gusts at first teasing the waiting canvas and then exhaling its power as one sail after the next filled and his ships began to move.

As the town of Rabat on Bou Regreg's southern shore receded astern, René exhaled, and willed his muscles to relax.

ACKNOWLEDGMENTS

I'd like to thank Mrs. Lillian Walker, who lifted an ADD child by introducing him to the author Walter Farley, who introduced him to Robert Heinlein, who introduced him to the universe.

To my children Jason, Stacy, and Eric, and my son and daughter-in-law, Keith and Natalie, who have humored me in my creative aberrations and surrounded me with love anyway. Thank you.

I'd like to thank Cheryl Julien for turning me on to NaNoWriMo, Tim Dedopulos and Salome Jones at Flourish Editing, Tom Colgan, Amy Paulshock, Amy Sue Nathan, Karyn Cumberland, Kerry Doherty, Mary Ellen Humphrey and everyone else who shared their time with me.

To BNI for showing me the power of networking.

To Kelly Shorten for a most excellent cover. Your talent on my behalf is greatly appreciated.

To Sloane Taylor, my editor whose support and creative vision has been most instrumental in graciously showing me the errors of my ways. Notice I used the plural. Thank you.

To Sally Ann for every single read through.

ABOUT THE AUTHOR

©Chura's Photography Fine Portraits

Elliott Baker is an award-winning novelist and international playwright
with four musicals and one play published and performed throughout the
United States, as well as productions in New Zealand, Portugal, England,
and Canada. Elliott is pleased to release his first novel, *Return*, book one
of The Sun God's Heir trilogy. A member of the Authors Guild and the
Dramatists Guild, Elliott lives in New Hampshire with his wife Sally Ann

www.ElliottBaker.com

BOOKS

The Sun God's Heir is a swashbuckling series, set at the end of the seventeenth century in France, Spain, and northern Africa. Slavery is a common plague along the European coast, and into this wild time an ancient Egyptian general, armed with dark arts, has managed to return and re-embody, intent on recreating the reign of terror he began as Pharoah. René must remember his own former lifetime at the feet of Akhenaten to have a chance to defeat Horemheb. A secret sect has waited in Morocco three thousand years for his arrival.

THE SUN GOD'S HEIR

The Adventures of René, Akeefa, and Horemheb continue in *Rebirth* and the rest of the The Sun God's Heir series.

Book I: Return

Book II: Rebirth

Book III: Redemption

CPSIA information can be obtained
at www.ICGtesting.com
Printed in the USA
LVHW030451010423
743125LV00001B/25